AGAINST THE TIDE

Books by Elizabeth Camden

The Lady of Bolton Hill

The Rose of Winslow Street

Against the Tide

AGAINST THE TIDE

A NOVEL

ELIZABETH CAMDEN

BETHANYHOUSE
a division of Baker Publishing Group
Minneapolis, Minnesota

Published by Bethany House Publishers
11400 Hampshire Avenue South
Bloomington, Minnesota 55438
www.bethanyhouse.com

Bethany House Publishers is a division of
Baker Publishing Group, Grand Rapids, Michigan

Printed in the United States of America

Library of Congress Cataloging-in-Publication Data
Camden, Elizabeth.
Against the tide / Elizabeth Camden.
p. cm.
ISBN 978-0-7642-1023-5 (pbk. : alk. paper)
1. Women translators—Fiction. 2. Bostom (Mass.)—History—19th century—Fiction. I. Title.
PS3553.A429A73 2012
813'.54—dc23 2012028727

Scripture quotations are from the King James Version of the Bible.

This is a work of fiction. Names, characters, incidents, and dialogues are products of the author's imagination and are not to be construed as real. Any resemblance to actual persons, living or dead, is entirely coincidental.

Cover design by Jennifer Parker
Cover photography by Yolande De Kort / Trevillion Images

12 13 14 15 16 17 18 7 6 5 4 3 2 1

For my husband, Bill . . . the inspiration
behind every hero I've ever written.

For my husband Elliot, the inspiration
behind every hero I've ever written.

Prologue

Boston, 1876

Lydia was embarrassed to wear a damp dress on the first day of school, but it rained last night while her clothes were strung across the boat's rigging to dry. She was lucky to be going to school at all, and tried not to think about her clammy dress as she walked to the schoolhouse, her hand clasped in her father's work-roughened palm. He seemed more nervous than she was as they walked to the school, almost a mile from the pier where their boat was docked. The school was a fancy brick building with real glass in the windows. There were no windows on the boat where Lydia lived, just oiled parchment that let a little light into the cabin where the whole family slept.

Papa did not want her to go to school at all. Last night he and Mama had a big fight about it, and Lydia had heard every word. They made her and Baby Michael go beneath the hatch, but living on a boat as tiny as the *Ugly Kate* meant she could hear everything.

"That girl doesn't speak a word of English!" her father roared.

"What is the point of sending her to school if she can't understand what they are saying?"

"She will learn," Mama said. "Look how quickly she learned to speak Italian when she was just a small child. She already knows Greek and Turkish and even Croatian from the year we lived there. She is good with languages, and she will learn English. Lydia is nine years old, and it is time for her to be in school." They never stayed in one place long enough for her to go to school in the past, but that was supposed to change now that they were in America.

Lydia had been a baby when they left their tiny Greek island. Papa said they had to leave because people did not like that he married a Turkish woman. They sailed away in a fishing boat Papa had built with his own hands, hugging the coastline of the rocky Adriatic shores until they got to the islands of Italy. That didn't last very long either. From there they spent time on the coasts of Albania and Croatia.

They lived on Papa's boat, casting nets into the crystalline sea and hauling aboard prawns, bluefish, and bass. Lydia's earliest memories were of sunbaked days sorting the fish into baskets on the deck of their boat. In the evenings they pushed the nets and tackle to the side and laid their bedding beneath the stars. Lydia's entire life was on that boat, from cooking meals over the gas burner, sitting on Mama's lap to learn her letters, and twice a week washing her hair in the salty water of the Mediterranean Sea. Mama said it was the salt and sun that put coppery glints into Lydia's dark hair. "Just like a brand-new penny," Mama would say as she combed Lydia's hair to dry in the sun. Her brother, Michael, was born in Sicily. He was four years old now, and she was supposed to stop calling him "Baby Michael," but it was still how she thought of him.

Lydia wasn't sure why they had to leave Sicily, but over the summer they got on a huge ship and sailed all the way across the

Atlantic Ocean until they reached Boston. Papa said things would be better here, but Lydia was not so sure. Their fishing boat wasn't nearly as nice as the one Papa had built in Greece. He tried to fix the *Ugly Kate,* but water kept seeping through the hull, and it was Lydia's job to fill cans and throw the water overboard. Five times a day she emptied the bilge, but there was always at least an inch of water on the floor of the cabin where they slept. Papa said the sloshing water meant their cabin was always clean, so they should be grateful they had such a special, self-cleaning boat. It was all part of his plan, he had laughed.

Lydia didn't care if they lived on a lousy boat. For the past three years, the only thing she had asked for every Christmas was to go to school. She had seen glimpses of other children walking to school in the village in Sicily and daydreamed about all the wonderful things they must be learning behind those closed doors.

Papa still did not want to let her go to school. He had pointed to Lydia's thin cotton smock that was six inches too short. "You want to send our princess to school looking like that?" he roared at Mama, gesturing to Lydia's ankles showing beneath the bottom of her dress. Two weeks ago her hem caught fire when she brushed too close to the cooking burner, and Mama had to cut it off. The scorch marks no longer showed, but Papa was still upset about her only dress.

"I won't have it," he said with resolution. "I won't have my princess being ridiculed by the hoodlums of Boston." His face crumpled up, and Lydia thought he might be about to cry.

She scampered across the deck and threw her arms around his waist. "Don't be sad, Papa. I'll learn English right away, and then I'll be able to teach you and Mama and Baby Michael too. We'll all be able to speak it."

Papa, whose calloused fingers stroked the hair from her forehead, cradled her as he rocked her from side to side. "My poor little water sprite, you don't know how cruel children can be."

"I don't care if they make fun of me," she said. "And Mama can wash my dress so it won't smell, and I'll look just as nice as any of the other children."

"We will wash your dress tonight so it will be fresh and pretty for school tomorrow," Mama said. "Lydia *must* go to school. It is time." Lydia smiled when she recognized that tone. Papa usually got his way, but when Mama's voice grew firm like that, he always obeyed.

It rained overnight. When fat raindrops began spattering on the top of the cabin, she raced aboveboard to yank the dress off the rigging. She fell flat on her face when she tripped over the crab traps that slid to the middle of the deck, and by the time she pulled the dress from the rigging it was soaked. It was still damp as she walked to the schoolhouse the next morning.

Lydia sat in the hall while her father talked to a lady in an office near the front of the school. Rather, he was speaking words in Greek and gesturing with his hands, which the woman did not understand. When Papa turned around and pointed to Lydia sitting on a bench in the hallway, comprehension dawned on the woman's face. Lydia slid off the bench as the frazzled lady came to stand in front of her. The lady spoke very quickly to Lydia, then waited as if she expected Lydia to say something. The lady seemed very stern as she scrutinized Lydia's dress, especially when she reached out to feel the still-wet cloth. Now the lady was muttering beneath her breath and glaring at Papa, even though it had been Lydia's idea to wash the dress.

Lydia stared at the lady's mouth as she said the same phrases over and over and then waited, as if she expected Lydia to respond. Lydia knew only one word in English, and perhaps this was the right time to say it.

She looked straight into the lady's eyes, smiled, and said, "Okay."

That seemed to satisfy the lady, who turned and gestured to Lydia to follow. Lydia knew she had been accepted into the school and felt like the sun was bursting inside her. She whirled around to wave goodbye to Papa, who twisted his cap between his hands, anxiety written all over his face as he waved goodbye to her.

Lydia darted to follow the lady down the hall. She was going to school! The hallways were wide and straight, and the floors were polished to a high shine. The air smelled so fresh it made her feel good just to breathe it.

It was obvious she was late for class, because the other students were already in their desks and a man at the front of the room was writing on one of those fancy black pieces of slate. The door creaked open and all eyes in the room swiveled to stare at her. The angry lady talked to the teacher while Lydia turned to look at the students lined up in their neat, orderly rows.

They looked so *clean*. All of them had their hair combed and wore socks under their shoes. Did they always look so tidy, or only today because it was the first day of school? The teacher pulled Lydia's hand to lead her to a desk at the back of the room. Her very own desk. It had a matching seat and she wouldn't even have to share it with anybody! The man started speaking to her, but she didn't understand. His face was kind as he knelt down beside her desk and repeated himself more slowly this time. It didn't make any difference. She didn't have any idea what he was saying, but she knew he was friendly and was waiting for some kind of answer from her.

She smiled broadly. "Okay," she said, and once again it seemed to be the answer he wanted to hear.

The teacher returned to the front of the room, and the class began.

Lydia ran as fast as her skinny legs could carry her. She hurtled through the air as she rushed to the pier to meet Papa after school. It didn't take long to spot him pacing along the pier, his face still drawn and worried. Lydia could tell the moment he saw her because he whipped the cap from his head and came striding across the pier in those giant steps of his. She thought her lungs would burst as she raced even faster to fling herself into his arms. "Oh, Papa, it was *perfect*!"

The word seemed so puny to describe the joy that bloomed inside her. She should tell him how wonderful the school was, how kind the teacher had been to her. There was so much more she wanted to say, but her throat clogged up when she tried to speak. Why was she crying when she was happy? But a fat tear rolled down each side of her face, and it was impossible to talk through the lump in her throat.

"The teacher's name was Mr. Bennett," Lydia told her parents once they were back on their boat. "I saw the letters of his name written on the blackboard, and at lunch he sat with me and repeated it over and over until I understood. He was very nice, and he even gave me part of his sandwich for lunch."

Mama had not realized that children were supposed to bring something to eat for lunch, and she said that tomorrow Lydia should bring Mr. Bennett a nice piece of fresh cod to thank him for being so nice.

"And what about the children? They were nice to you?" Papa asked, guarded worry in his eyes.

Lydia wasn't stupid; she had seen some of the girls laughing at her short dress and whispering behind their hands. Not that she cared. Why should such a little thing bother her when she had a sturdy desk all to herself and when there were so many fascinating things in the classroom to look at? Maps on the walls showed the outline of all the countries in the whole world, and in one corner there was a stuffed eagle with its wings stretched outright. But her father was worried, and he was waiting for her answer.

"No one said a single bad thing to me," she said truthfully.

And it didn't really matter that she didn't speak English, because the next day Lydia learned that two of the children in the class spoke Italian, and there was another little girl who spoke only Russian. She made friends with them and sat beside them at lunch every day, easily picking up a number of Russian words to add to her repertoire of languages.

And as the weeks rolled by, Lydia learned more and more words in English. Mr. Bennett seemed particularly pleased with how quickly she was learning. "Clever girl," he said as he patted her on the top of her head. Lydia wasn't certain what "clever" meant, but she knew it was good and she loved it when Mr. Bennett called her a clever girl, which he did a lot.

But on this particular chilly day in October, Lydia did not feel so clever as she stood at the pier to wait for Papa. Normally, Papa and the *Ugly Kate* were already waiting for her after school. It was a windy day, so getting sail power back to the harbor should not have been a problem. Lydia sat on a bench, swinging her legs and kicking at a discarded pile of rope to pass the time until the *Ugly Kate* got there.

By the time the sun started to set, hunger gnawed at her tummy and it was starting to get cold. Papa would not forget to come get her after school, so that meant something bad must have happened to the *Ugly Kate*.

She didn't know what to do. As the sun sank lower, boat after boat pulled up to the dock. The sailors unloaded their tackle, secured the rigging, then slung their haul over their shoulders and left the pier for their homes. By now Lydia was shaking so badly she didn't really know whether it was from the cold or from the fear. Maybe she would have to spend the entire night here on the dock.

It wouldn't be the first time she slept outside. When they first came to Boston they spent two weeks living in a public park while Papa looked for a boat to buy. He told them it was a grand adventure. "Think how lucky we are not to live in a smelly old tenement when we can sleep under a cathedral of the stars," he had said. At the time, Lydia would have preferred the smelly old tenement, but her father assured her that sleeping under the stars was all part of his plan. "Breathe in that clean American air!" he had said. "Sleeping outside is the only way to experience it, and we would not want to miss out on it!"

Lydia tried to savor the clean American air as she sat huddled on the dockside bench, but it was too cold to draw a deep breath. There was a big difference between sleeping outside in August and sleeping outside in October. She found a piece of discarded sailcloth near the end of the wharf and wrapped it around her shoulders.

It was stupid to be worrying about Papa. He was the best sailor in the world. He had built the boat they lived on in Sicily with his own two hands, and he had fixed up the *Ugly Kate* to make her sail again, even though Mama called it a "floating heap."

Once or twice she started to doze, but she always jerked awake as soon as she relaxed the grip on the sailcloth and the cold air pierced her thin dress. As the weak light of dawn illuminated the bay, Lydia scanned the dozens of boats lashed to the docks, praying the *Ugly Kate* had sailed into port overnight and she had missed it. Her father would laugh and tell her how foolish she had been for thinking, even for an instant, he would not come for her.

She stood on the bench and scanned the pier, filled with dozens of boats coming in and out of the harbor. As far as her eye could see, none of the boats resembled the *Ugly Kate*.

Lydia fought to understand the words that were being spoken around her, but all the grown-ups were speaking so quickly and no one took the time to help her understand. Mr. Bennett, her teacher, was there, and so were two men wearing police uniforms. Another man had a funny shirt with a white notch cut into the collar, and Lydia thought he must be some kind of minister.

Certain words she heard over and over. *Orphanage* was one of them. *Deportation* and *Greece* were the other words they kept saying. She had no idea what *orphanage* meant, but she thought it must be a good thing, because Mr. Bennett seemed to be in favor of the orphanage. He got red in the face and shook his head when the others spoke of "deportation."

It had been five days since that awful night she spent outside, and her family had not returned for her. She knew Papa would never abandon her, and that meant the *Ugly Kate* had probably sunk at sea. Which meant Papa and Mama and Baby Michael were all dead, and Lydia refused to believe that. They must have lost their way, and they would come back soon.

She had been staying at a place called a convent, where a lot of women wore all black, but there were no children and the ladies in black did not know what to do with her. Yesterday they brought a Greek fisherman to the convent to translate for her. He had massive gray eyebrows and the skin on his face was like leather, and he asked all kinds of questions about her family back in Greece.

"I don't have any family in Greece," she said.

The man scoffed. "Everyone in Greece has family," he said.

"Big families. Huge families. You will like it in Greece. Now tell me about your family in Greece and where they live."

Lydia tried to remember any family names she heard her father mention, but she could think of none. "Papa said he had to leave Greece in a big hurry."

The man quirked one of those thick brows. "A big hurry, eh? Why was that?"

"Papa said it was because Mama is a Turk."

"Oh," the fisherman said with sad understanding. "That would do it." He turned to the policeman standing behind him and spoke in English. The words were simple enough even for Lydia to understand.

"This child has no family," he said.

Mr. Bennett seemed pleased that she was going to an orphanage. It was on the other side of Boston, and the policeman was going to take her there and she would never be coming back to this wonderful school with its nice sturdy desks and clear glass windows. Mr. Bennett hunkered down so he could be at eye level, but she could not bear to look at him when she knew he was saying goodbye to her forever. Mr. Bennett was the only person left in the world who cared about what happened to her, and now she was losing him as well. He took her hand in his and gave it a little tug.

"You will do well," he said slowly. "You are such a clever girl."

Her eyes clouded up when he called her a clever girl. She didn't feel clever right now; she felt weak and scared and alone. But maybe Mr. Bennett was right. Maybe the orphanage would be a wonderful place where she would be able to learn and find a new family.

It did not take long for Lydia to learn there was nothing wonderful about the Crakken Orphanage.

1

Fifteen years later, 1891
The Boston Navy Yard

"It looks like the Russian navy has just launched a new gunship," Lydia said.

It was hard to tell from the grainy photograph, but the ship looked different from the others reported in the Russian newspapers. Lydia rose from her desk and walked across the office to show the newspaper to Willis, whose encyclopedic memory of warships was astounding. She only hoped he would be willing to help her. She had been working at the research wing of the United States Navy for more than four years, but it still irked Willis that a woman had been hired for this sort of work.

Lydia handed Willis a magnifying glass to better scrutinize the photograph. "I don't remember the Russians ever having a rotating gun turret," she said, "but it looks like they have one, don't you think?"

Willis Colburn was so thin it looked possible to shred cheese off the blades of his cheekbones. He pushed his spectacles higher as he studied the picture. "You know, Lydia, you are supposed to be the expert on Russian," he said pointedly.

Actually, Lydia was the expert on Russian, Greek, Turkish, Italian, Albanian, and Croatian. Her job was to scan journals, technical reports, and anything else sent from southern Europe in search of innovations in ship design. When she first saw the job advertisement looking for someone with multiple language skills and an intimate knowledge of ships, she nearly levitated with excitement. Her first two years after leaving the orphanage were difficult, laboring at the fish canneries and packing tins with salted mackerel until she couldn't see straight. It was monotonous, smelly work, and at the end of the week she was barely able to pay the rent on a room in a boardinghouse, which was why she was so eager to land the job at the Navy Yard. The position called for someone who could read foreign documents and make sense of developments in ship design.

Lydia remembered everything about the sails, tack, and rigging of fishing boats, but when she first saw the imposing battle frigates in the Navy Yard, she wondered if she had overestimated her knowledge of ships.

Admiral Fontaine did not seem to care. A ruggedly attractive man who seemed far too young to have attained the status of admiral, he merely shrugged. "I can teach you the particulars of warships easier than I can train someone in half a dozen languages," he had said. "You are hired."

Who could have believed it? The little girl from Greece who grew up on rickety fishing boats and never had a decent pair of shoes was now a trusted assistant to an admiral in the United States Navy. Each day she walked past acres of towering ships docked in the Navy Yard before reporting to work. The office had a view over the dry docks where navy cruisers and battleships were overhauled and refitted for service.

And Lydia knew her job was vitally important. At the end of the Civil War in 1865, funding for the U.S. Navy had been slashed to the bone as resources were funneled to the army for a massive westward expansion. Other than providing basic coverage of domestic ports, the government lost interest in maintaining a navy. In the midst of one of the greatest technological booms in history, the U.S. Navy became stagnant while the maritime nations of Europe poured funding into ironclads, steamers, torpedoes, and long-range artillery.

It was only after an embarrassing incident when the United States was forced to back down from the Chilean navy that Congress was driven to act. A bureau to collect intelligence on foreign naval technology was created. Naval attachés were sent all across Europe to research shipbuilding technology. Most of the research was aboveboard, but some of it was clandestinely gathered. Whenever those officers found printed material of interest, they sent it home to Admiral Fontaine for a complete translation into English. Each week Lydia received stacks of newspaper clippings, product manuals, and technical journals. She translated, cross-referenced, and indexed every scrap of it.

Watching and trying to play catch-up with the great maritime powers was hardly the way to achieve naval superiority, but at least it provided funding for the team of translators sitting directly outside Admiral Fontaine's office.

"This Russian turret looks a bit like what the British use, don't you think?" Lydia asked Willis, turning the page of the pamphlet to show him the rest of the article, but he cringed and clasped both hands to his forehead.

"Lydia, please. The noise of that paper crackling is like knives across my skin." Yesterday the scent of the juice she had been drinking made him dizzy, and last week he complained that the weight of the air was making him suffer a rash. Yet when Admiral Fontaine was in the room, Willis always seemed to be as hardy as a mountain goat.

Lydia lowered the tone of her voice, which often placated Willis, and tried again. "Is this turret the same as what the British have, or is it something entirely new?"

"It is not new," Karl Olavstad said from his desk on the opposite side of the office. "The Norwegians have had such a turret for at least three years."

Karl handled the translation work from northern Europe and Scandinavia, while a young man named Jacob Frankenberg tracked western European developments. Willis was a naval historian from London, and his command of shipbuilding throughout the world was unparalleled. He kept track of developments in the British navy and provided insight for everything the team of translators brought to him.

"The Norwegians copied it from the British," Willis said in a tired voice. "The Norwegian navy would sink to the bottom of the sea if they could not emulate the British."

Lydia propped her hip against the side of Willis's desk, eager to see how Karl would respond to the salvo. When she first started work at the Navy Yard, the jousting between her officemates had confused and alarmed her. At the Crakken Orphanage when disagreements broke out among the children, Lydia ran for cover in the broom closet, but she soon learned Karl and Willis enjoyed matching wits.

"Let us hope the Norwegians don't start emulating British cuisine," Karl said. "They would perish from the sheer monotony of boiled cabbage, boiled peas, and boiled beef."

From his desk beside the window overlooking the dry docks, Jacob set down his German newspaper and joined the fray. "Don't forget boiled tongue," he said with a shudder. "The only time Willis invited me to his home, his wife served boiled tongue and pickled onions. I had only been in this country two weeks, and it almost sent me rushing back home to Salzburg."

Lydia knew it would never happen. Every person in this office was an immigrant, and yet each of them had already planted roots as tenacious as those of a mighty oak tree into the rich Boston soil. Was it because she had never had a place to call home that Lydia was so fiercely loyal to Boston and her employment at the Navy Yard? Her respect for Admiral Fontaine certainly had something to do with her pride in working here, but it was more than that. After years of anxiety and loneliness, first at the orphanage and then at the canneries, she had at last found a sense of belonging within the bustling harbor of the Navy Yard. Jacob, Karl, and even the maddening Willis were like a family to her, and she thrived amidst their unconventional friendship.

"What is the proper name of this gun turret?" she asked Willis. "And can you tell me if the gun is smooth-bore or rifled?"

Willis pinched the skin at the top of his nose. "Just tell the admiral it is a Hotchkiss quick-firing gun, modified for shipboard use. That will be adequate for his purposes."

Lydia fidgeted. She didn't want her reports to be merely adequate; she wanted them flawless. The report was due by the end of the day, and she needed Willis to cooperate. His teacup was empty, and she knew how much the man adored his Earl Grey blend.

"How about I brew you another cup of tea?" she asked Willis. "By the time I have the water heated, perhaps you can have a list for me of every British and Norwegian ship with the same type of Hotchkiss gun?"

"Deal," Willis agreed, as she knew he would. The office had a coal-heated burner in the corner of the room, which helped satisfy Willis's roaring dependency on Earl Grey tea. Lydia opened the trapdoor of the heater and added a few more coals.

"You could afford to ease up a bit, Lydia," Jacob said. "Not every report needs to be footnoted, cross-referenced, and triple-checked. You'll make the rest of us look bad. Besides, maybe the admiral fancies a girl who can relax for once."

Heat flooded her cheeks. That was the second time this month Jacob teased her about liking Admiral Fontaine a little too much. Which was ridiculous. "Jacob, your adolescent imagination is running away again."

"Come on, Lydia. Plenty of girls are carrying a torch for Admiral Fontaine," Jacob said. "The lonely widower. Powerful. Rich as sin. Half the girls in Boston are crying into their pillows over him."

She closed the door of the burner with a clang. Okay, maybe she had a tiny case of hero-worship for the admiral, but never once had she toyed with any ridiculous fantasies. Besides, the admiral's office was directly behind her, and for all she knew, he could be listening to every word. "First of all," she said tightly, "I never cry. Ever. And I haven't prepared my reports for the admiral with any more care than the rest of you."

Karl did not even lift his nose from where it was buried in the open pages of a Norwegian newspaper, but his voice was pointed. "You learned Albanian for him."

Jacob pounced on the opening. "Yeah, Lydia, you learned Albanian for him!"

She gritted her teeth. She hadn't learned Albanian for the admiral; she did it because they had a language deficit in the office and she was the one most likely to quickly master the language. It didn't mean she carried a torch for the admiral, and she couldn't afford to let this sort of talk get out of hand. She set the water in the kettle to heat, then moved to stand beside Jacob's desk. "Please, *please* don't tease me about this," she said, her voice uncharacteristically serious. "You don't know how hard it is for a woman to find professional employment, and any whiff of gossip could cost me my job. Can you understand that?"

Jacob blanched. He didn't have a mean bone in his scrawny body and never considered what his teasing could do to her. "Okay, sorry, Lydia," he quickly agreed, pushing his round spectacles higher up on his nose. "I'm sorry if I said anything—you know—stupid."

Now Lydia felt guilty for scolding. "No man who reads six languages is stupid." She gave him a cuff on the arm. "You idiot."

She returned to tend to the teakettle and added more water. "Make a whole pot, please," Karl said. "The Adonis is coming this afternoon, and you know how surly the admiral is after those meetings."

Her hands froze on the kettle. It was never a good thing when *that man* came to see the admiral.

His name was Lieutenant Alexander Banebridge, but Karl had dubbed him "The Adonis" because of the man's ridiculous beauty. None of them understood his mysterious business at the Navy Yard, but after each visit, the admiral was always grim and pensive. Moody, even. Anyone who caused the famously even-tempered Admiral Fontaine to become surly was someone Lydia instinctively mistrusted.

Lydia suspected Lieutenant Banebridge might be one of the foreign attachés funneling them reports about overseas ships, but there was no way for her to know. The man never said a single word to her. He merely breezed into the admiral's office and left a pall behind him with each meeting.

She couldn't afford to worry about the admiral's mysterious

visitor. After setting the kettle over the burner, she opened the canister of tea and let the scent soothe her. If she lived to be one hundred, she would always love the mild scent of Earl Grey tea. Was it because it reminded her of the office? For the first time in her life, she had a job she loved and earned a respectable salary that allowed her to afford a safe apartment of her very own. That apartment had a solid floor, a ceiling that did not leak, and allowed her to fall asleep without fear of vicious children stealing her shoes if she took them off before going to bed.

The door of the office flew open, banging against the wall with a crash. Lydia was stunned to see Big John, the man who owned the coffeehouse on the ground floor of the building where she lived. His face was flushed, and he was barely able to get enough air into his lungs.

"Lydia, you are being evicted," he said on a ragged breath.

Lydia dropped the canister, scattering loose tea leaves across the floor. "*What?*" The word escaped from her throat in an ungainly screech.

"Workmen just arrived," he said. "They started putting your furniture on the street outside the building. I told them they can't evict you yet, but they started anyway."

"They can't do this! I have papers saying I can stay. Admiral Fontaine drew them up himself." Panic flooded her at the thought of losing her home. It was more than mere sentimentality tying her to her modest fourth-floor apartment in a building improbably named the Laughing Dragon. That apartment was her *sanctuary,* the first home in her entire life where Lydia felt completely safe.

She needed to get home right away. "Tell the admiral what is happening," she called to Jacob as she raced out the door, then clattered down the office staircase and into the street. She hauled up her skirts and ran as if her life depended on it . . . which it rather did. Since the morning she left the orphanage, she had devoted every hour of her day to earning enough money to create a stable home for herself. Now that she finally had it, she would battle all the plagues of Egypt to keep it.

2

Lydia shouldered through dense foot traffic as she ran across the Charlestown Bridge, then cut through the lawn of the Old North Church. A stitch in her side pinched harder as she ran down crooked alleys and twisty cobblestone streets toward home. It was a mile before she reached the Laughing Dragon, where her armoire was on the street alongside wadded-up piles of her bedding. Two workmen were navigating her mattress out the front door. Mrs. Brandenberg stood on the curb with a notebook, making notations as she scanned Lydia's belongings.

"What are you doing?" Lydia managed to gasp as she skidded to a stop. She was panting so hard she could barely stand upright. "You can't throw me out; we have an agreement."

Mrs. Brandenberg tightened her lips. "Miss Pallas, you have not lived up to the terms of our agreement and are therefore a trespasser. You are being evicted."

Last month the Laughing Dragon had been sold to the Brandenbergs, and they had no interest in leasing either the apartments or the coffeehouse on the ground floor. The tenants needed to purchase their unit or leave immediately. Since Admiral Fontaine had a law degree from Harvard, she had instinctively run to him for help the moment she saw that awful notice. He scrutinized the eviction notice and found a loophole the new owners had failed to close. The admiral helped Lydia negotiate for additional time to come up with the funds to purchase her apartment, and in exchange she was to provide minor clerical services for the new owners. She still had four months to come up with an additional six hundred dollars to purchase her apartment, or else she would lose the only decent home she had ever known.

Her desk had not been brought down yet. The papers proving she had until December to buy the apartment were in the top desk drawer. "I've done everything outlined in the agreement. I'm going upstairs to get the contract."

Mrs. Brandenberg's beefy arm shot out to block her path. "Not if it requires entering the building. This is private property and you have no right to enter the premises. Mr. Brandenberg paid a visit to your bank this morning, and there is no evidence you are anywhere near securing the necessary funds to purchase this apartment."

It was true, her odds of earning six hundred dollars in the next four months were slim. She earned thirty dollars per week at the Navy Yard, but after expenses, she could save no more than five dollars each week. She had been taking in extra translating work wherever she could find it, but it was unlikely she could earn enough money before the end of the year, and the Brandenbergs knew it.

"Now step aside, Miss Pallas," Mrs. Brandenberg said. "It will be easier on all parties for you to leave the apartment today."

"Easier?" Lydia asked. "I think you will *sleep* easier if you abide by the document you signed last month." But as another workman tossed a heap of drapery beside her mattress, a wave of anguish swelled inside. She had sewn those drapes with her own two hands, and her cherished possessions, the symbols of all she had managed to achieve in the years since leaving the Crakken Orphanage, were dumped on the dusty street like mounds of abandoned trash. Perhaps in a few months she really would be forced out of her home, but she wasn't going to surrender yet.

And then she saw him coming. Pedestrians moved to the side of the street and children stopped to stare as a fine black stallion moved toward them at a brisk trot. Admiral Eric Fontaine, dressed in full military uniform with epaulets and a high starched collar, was riding to her rescue. With those fierce eyes and his crisp military bearing, the admiral was the sort of commander who could glare down legions of invading Persians at the pass of Thermopylae. He was a bit too rugged to be considered classically handsome, with dark hair and a weather-beaten face so deeply tanned it made his pale gray eyes gleam like chips of ice.

Lydia watched as Mrs. Brandenberg's confidence shriveled like autumn leaves in a gale-force wind. The supercilious look fled, replaced by fawning deference as the admiral drew near.

"Mrs. Brandenberg, perhaps there was a misunderstanding as to the terms of the agreement I drew up for Miss Pallas," the admiral said as he swung down from his horse. His tone was faultlessly polite, but there was iron beneath the words.

Mrs. Brandenberg smoothed a lock of hair that had slipped from its moorings and cleared her throat. She gave a fawning little curtsey. "Good morning, Admiral. Commandant. Sir."

As Commandant of the Boston Navy Yard, civilians were often unsure exactly what to call Admiral Fontaine, but he preferred to be known by his rank. With over two thousand sailors and civilians employed at the Navy Yard, the fact that Lydia was even personally acquainted with Admiral Fontaine was unusual, but the office of foreign translators had been his idea, and with office space in the

Navy Yard scarce, they had been tucked into the reception room immediately outside his office.

The expression on her employer's face did not waver as he surveyed the sorry heap of her belongings piled in the street. "It would be a shame if you suffered the consequences of an unlawful eviction. Miss Pallas has full legal right to maintain her current place of residence for . . ."

The admiral struggled to remember the details of the contract he had worked out for her, so Lydia stood on tiptoe to whisper in his ear. "For another four months," she supplied.

"Four months," the admiral said. "And at the end of four months, she is entitled to . . ."

"Another two weeks to clear the premises," Lydia whispered.

Admiral Fontaine nodded. "She is allowed another two weeks to clear out. She must be served official notice as well, so don't neglect that, or we can reopen the case. Are we clear on that, Mrs. Brandenberg?"

Mrs. Brandenberg struggled to maintain a serene expression on her face. "Of course!" she said brightly. "You and I are in agreement as to the dates of the contract. *Complete agreement!* The problem is Miss Pallas's lack of cooperation with the rest of the agreement. In exchange for additional time to purchase her unit, she was to provide clerical services to Mr. Brandenberg. She has not done so, and we are *forced* to take this action."

The admiral's gaze swiveled to Lydia. "Miss Pallas? Is this true?"

Lydia worked hard to keep the anger from her voice. "I have done every bit of clerical work requested of me. I have also walked their dog, gone to the market, baby-sat the children, and ironed Mr. Brandenberg's shirts. Last night I declined Mrs. Brandenberg's invitation to bathe her children. I believe this might be the cause of the trouble."

The admiral said nothing, just turned his piercing gray eyes to Mrs. Brandenberg for her response. When it did not immediately come, he arrived at his own conclusion. "Your husband agreed to provide an extension on Miss Pallas's lease because his original eviction was illegal and he knew it. The agreement was for Miss Pallas to provide *minor* clerical services. You cannot break the contract by making unreasonable demands of Miss Pallas. Is that clear?" Up until then, the admiral's voice had been calm and methodical. When Mrs. Brandenberg failed to answer, his voice lashed out like a whip. *"Is that clear, ma'am?"*

Mrs. Brandenberg nearly jumped from her skin. "Yes, of course!"

"Excellent. Have your men return Miss Pallas's furnishings to their proper place. I'm sure I do not need to state the legal remedies she will be entitled to should any damage to her belongings occur between here and her apartment, do I."

It was a statement, not a question.

"No, sir." After a brief, heated glare at Lydia, Mrs. Brandenberg ordered the workers to carry Lydia's belongings back up to her fourth-floor apartment.

Admiral Fontaine was already mounting his horse when Lydia walked up to thank him. This was the second time he had come through for her. When she had first seen that awful legal notice tacked to her front door, she had panicked and instinctively rushed to him to interpret it for her. Not only had he explained the mass of legal intricacies, he had offered to represent her for free in negotiating additional time to purchase her apartment. How many employers would have performed such an act of sheer human decency? Lydia shaded her eyes as she looked up at him.

"I hope it is not becoming tedious, saving me at the last moment like this," she said. "You must be getting awfully tired of riding to my rescue."

"Indeed. Next time I shall shriek and flee in the opposite direction."

Lydia bit her lip, never quite certain when he was joking. Lydia was about to respond, but her gaze was snagged when a workman hoisted her bedside table over one shoulder while scooping up a pile of her bedding under a thick arm. She tried not to wince, but it was painful to see her belongings treated so carelessly.

"Take a few hours to put things to right," Admiral Fontaine said. One corner of his mouth tilted in an almost infinitesimal smile. "I know your quirks will render you completely useless in discerning the finer points of naval armaments until your belongings have been restored to meticulous order. Good day, Miss Pallas." With a flick of his heels, the horse sprang into a trot as he turned the stallion back toward the Navy Yard.

Lydia noticed that every female eye on the street was trained on the admiral. There was no doubt he was the most eligible bachelor in all of Boston. Or all of New England, for that matter. Maybe even the United States, if one wanted to be very precise. The admiral was attractive, but he was also the most formal, rigidly proper man in all of Boston. Karl once said the navy must have used so much starch in his uniforms that it seeped into the admiral's skin. And even though everyone in the office teased her about her hopeless case of hero-worship, Lydia never truly had any designs on the admiral. Frankly, she was too in awe to ever feel comfortable around him.

Nevertheless, she was grateful for the time he had given her to restore her possessions to their proper place, for the admiral had read her correctly. Order was important to Lydia, and she drew a steadying breath before opening the door of her apartment. She cringed at the sight of her clothing piled in an ungainly heap on the sofa, but at least her furniture was back where it belonged.

She clutched a volume about the travels of Lewis and Clark to her chest before setting it back on her bookshelf. In her two years working at the canneries, books had been her only luxury. The noise and stench and monotony of packing salted mackerel was bearable only because at the end of the day she could escape into the wilds of the Dakota Territories with intrepid explorers. Or gaze at her book of great architecture of the world, with countless etchings of castles, cathedrals, and mighty fortresses. These books had been her salvation during those bleak years, and she handled them gently as she set them back in their proper place.

On her windowsill she arranged her bottles. Two bottles of perfume in squat little flacons in the center, then the jar of skin cream for cold New England winters. And then a dark blue bottle of her headache medicine. She uncapped the bottle and took a sip of the syrupy liquid, hoping it would ease the pounding headache caused by the prospect of losing her home.

She clutched the bottle in her hand as she looked out the window to the street below. The three flights of stairs she walked up each day were no bother, for where else would she have such a spectacular view of the harbor? She loved every weather-beaten flowerbox lining the tidy shops, the lobster boats bobbing in the harbor, and the sound of herring gulls on the morning air. From this window she could see the ships sailing in and out of the harbor. They came from Antwerp, Rotterdam, Cuba, and Quebec. Some came from the sparkling waters of the Adriatic, which Lydia once called home. It had been years since she had longed for the warm waters of the Mediterranean islands. Boston was her home now. She had no sense of wanderlust nor any desire to venture outside of this neighborhood. This was her *home* and she would do whatever was necessary to preserve it.

It was after lunch by the time Lydia returned to work. The walk was over a mile, and she was tired after making the journey for the third time in one day.

Willis weighed in immediately. "I should have thought Admiral Fontaine would have provided you with transportation back to the shipyard." Which showed Willis was not the best judge of human character, as Admiral Fontaine would never do anything to cast a shadow on his sterling reputation. Riding a horse with an unmarried woman clinging behind him would definitely qualify as improper.

"He thoughtfully allowed me a bit of time to restore my apartment to order," Lydia said as she lowered herself into her desk chair. She went through the ritual of straightening her dictionaries, ink bottles, and pictures, and was prepared to get back to work, but both Karl and Jacob gathered beside her desk.

"Is everything all right, Lydia?" Karl asked gently, just a trace of a Norwegian accent lingering in his voice.

"Perfectly fine," she said with more confidence than she felt. Everything was perfectly fine *today,* but she would be in this same situation in December if she could not earn an additional six hundred dollars.

"Is there anything I can do to help?" Karl asked. Everyone in the office knew her situation, and Karl had offered to loan her fifty dollars if it would help, but Lydia would never accept it. Karl had a wife and four children, and that fifty dollars was probably the only buffer he had. Jacob had offered a few dollars as well, but he was saving every dime so he could bring his parents and sisters over from Salzburg.

"Thank you for the offer, Karl, but I'll be fine," she said. Karl nodded and returned to his desk, but Jacob lingered. He had always been like a brother to her, and she could not truly hide her feelings from Jacob.

He squatted on his haunches beside her chair. "You'll tell me if things get really bad, won't you?" he asked quietly. "There is a rooming house near the canneries that accepts women, and maybe I could help you find a place there."

"I'll find the money somehow," she said with more confidence than she felt. She knew the tenement of which Jacob was speaking, and the specter of sliding back into a life of squalor was too wretched to contemplate. She pulled the Russian pamphlet toward her and was relieved to see that Willis had provided the list of British and Norwegian warships as she had asked. In the corner, someone had cleaned up the tea leaves she had scattered. Everything was back to normal, and if she moved quickly, she still had a chance of completing this report before the end of the day. She would probably need to stay late, but she did not mind. A cup of tea would help keep her energy alive through the long afternoon. She walked to the corner table and was about to pour a cup when the door banged open.

The most oddly annoying man Lydia had ever encountered strolled into the office. The Adonis. She knew his name was Alexander Banebridge, although Lydia thought she had heard the admiral call him Alexander Christian once.

He was in full dress uniform. Blond hair framed a perfectly molded face that looked like it belonged to a warrior angel. Most arresting were the lieutenant's icy blue eyes, set above impossibly high cheekbones.

"Good afternoon, everyone," the lieutenant said as he weaved through the desks of the office, flashed a brief smile to Lydia, then rapped a quick knock on the admiral's door. Without waiting for an answer, he slipped inside and closed the door behind him.

Willis suppressed a delicate shudder. "I find the sight of that man's posture aggravating. It makes my spine ache just to look at him."

Lydia tried not to laugh as she returned to her desk with her tea. She was about to sit down when she noticed something wrong. Her Russian pamphlets were where she left them and the foreign dictionaries were in precise order, tilted at a perfect forty-five-degree angle . . . but the ink bottles were wrong. She always kept them with blue first, then black, then red, but they were entirely out of order from the way they had been only moments ago.

"Did you touch my ink bottles?" she asked Jacob, who looked at her as if she had lost her mind.

"I would not dare disturb the fastidious order of anything on your desk," Jacob said.

Lydia glared at the closed door of the office where Lieutenant Banebridge had entered. Every time that man was in the office, something turned up askew at her desk. A picture was upside down or her dictionaries were no longer in alphabetical order. She had been staring straight at the man as he crossed through their office, but he still managed to tamper with her belongings and escape her notice. Lydia's mouth narrowed to a thin line as she rearranged the ink bottles, knowing it would be impossible to concentrate until they were in proper order.

"I *really* don't like that man," she muttered under her breath.

Karl looked up from the document he was translating on the far side of the room. "I have heard some strange things about him," he said. "My sister lives near the Canadian border in Vermont. She said the governor of Vermont wanted to build a bridge that would link up to Canada, but that Banebridge fellow showed up and objected. When the governor refused to stop the bridge, the crew who was building the bridge walked off the job. The governor brought in another crew, but Banebridge showed up a week later, and then they quit too. After that, no workers in the entire state were willing to do the job."

Lydia stared at Karl's grave face. What kind of power would it take to intimidate an entire team of workers to walk off their job? Lieutenant Banebridge did not seem physically big enough to threaten anyone. He was not that much taller than she, but he still seemed dangerous. A panther was not terribly large, but none of the other animals in the forest wanted to tangle with it.

"Why would the Adonis object to a bridge to Canada?" Jacob asked.

Karl shrugged. "Who knows? The following year the governor lost his bid for reelection and that bridge was never built."

Lydia stared at her ink bottles, the sun from the window casting a little glint along their shiny glass surface. She was almost embarrassed to ask, but the question came out before she could stifle it. "Has Lieutenant Banebridge ever tampered with anything on your desk?" she asked Jacob.

"I don't have anything on my desk worth stealing."

Lydia shook her head. "He has never stolen anything," she said. "He just disturbs things. Moves my pencil cup where it does not belong, turns a dictionary upside down. That sort of thing." She looked at Karl and Willis to see if they had experienced anything similar and got the same blank looks. She threw up her hands in frustration. "I have never exchanged a single word with that man, so why does he pick on me like this?"

"You are prettier than Willis?" Jacob offered. "Perhaps the Adonis is carrying a torch for you."

Lydia rolled her eyes. She supposed she was attractive enough, with red glints in her dark hair and cinnamon-colored eyes that people often complimented, but she was nowhere near the splendor of Lieutenant Banebridge's perfection. "Men like him have no interest in mere mortals," she said. "Besides, any man with feelings for me ought to go paint the cabinets in my apartment. *That* would get much better results." She glowered at the closed door leading to Admiral Fontaine's private office. How was it possible the man sent her off-kilter merely by striding through her office? Other than his bizarre quirk of tampering with her desk each time he came to see the admiral, they had no communication whatsoever.

Then again, even Admiral Fontaine seemed to be in a foul mood each time the man darkened their office. Perhaps Lieutenant Banebridge simply had a talent for sowing discord wherever he went.

3

The numbers did not add up. No matter how many times Lydia tallied the figures or trimmed her budget, she simply could not make the numbers work. Which meant that she needed to start earning twice as much money as she currently made or face eviction from the only decent home she had ever known.

"Let me top off that chowder for you." A gnarled hand reached across the surface of the mahogany counter as Big John took her empty bowl to the cooking pot for a refill. "It's on the house," he said as he slid it back to her.

Lydia tried not to smile. "I'm not *that* poor."

"The new owner will never know," Big John said as he flashed her a wink. Last week Big John's purchase of the Laughing Dragon Coffeehouse had been finalized, but he had taken on a hefty debt to make the deal go through. As he pushed the bowl of steaming clam chowder across the counter toward her, Lydia knew it would be rude not to accept the gesture of kindness, even though she cringed at the implication.

She and Big John shared the same dilemma. Both of them had

lived in this waterfront building for years. John operated the popular coffeehouse on the first floor, and Lydia lived in one of the many apartments on the top floor of the building.

Big John had been sweating bullets for weeks, but he had at last succeeded in getting a loan to buy the coffeehouse. The Laughing Dragon was more than a place for a mug of coffee or a quick dinner. It was a place where merchants sold cargo, politicians planned strategy, and off-duty sailors played chess and traded stories. The century-old coffeehouse was lined with dark mahogany and old brass fittings. The walls of the public room were covered with schedules displaying the arrival and departure of ships. The Laughing Dragon also served the best New England clam chowder in town, with just the right amount of hickory-smoked bacon to season the thick broth of cream and potatoes. Lydia's apartment had no kitchen and she took all her meals at the battered mahogany countertop of the Laughing Dragon.

She turned her attention back to the figures. She was used to working amidst the steady din of background noise of the coffeehouse, so it seemed strange when the noise dwindled away. The drone of laughter and conversation tapered off, a busy waitress stopped her order in midsentence, and even the fiddlers in the corner stopped playing. Lydia looked up to see what had caused the drop in conversation.

Oh my, my.

What was Lieutenant Banebridge doing at the Laughing Dragon? His crystalline blue gaze sliced through the dwindling twilight that illuminated the coffeehouse as he scanned the occupants. The man was not particularly tall. Indeed, compared to the oversized longshoremen who filled the room, he seemed almost slight, but he radiated a calm sense of power as he navigated through the cluster of tables and barrels, and headed toward the serving counter.

Lydia's eyes widened as his gaze riveted on her. A hint of a smile lifted the corner of his perfectly shaped mouth, and Lydia's breath froze as he strode directly to her.

"Lydia Pallas?" he asked as he slid onto the vacant stool next to her. How did he know her name? It was the first time he had ever spoken directly to her, and she wondered how he knew where she lived. All she could do was nod.

"I hear you read Turkish," he said as though that were an entirely natural opening line. "Eric recommended you as someone who was willing to pick up a little translation work on the side."

It took her a moment to process what he had said. "Eric? Do you mean Admiral Fontaine?"

"Yes, Admiral Fontaine. He said you have a remarkable ability with languages."

"I've never heard anyone refer to him as 'Eric' before," she said. "It would be like calling Queen Victoria 'Vickie.'" She glanced at the insignia on his uniform. "And I certainly did not think that lieutenants ever called admirals by their first name."

That lazy smile could probably slay damsels at a thousand yards. "I don't report to Eric. He is a friend, not someone in my chain of command. I am Alex Banebridge, but everyone just calls me Bane. Eric said you might be able to help me with these."

The lieutenant reached inside a satchel and pulled forth a foul-looking heap of papers that seemed to have been pulled from a pile of garbage. They smelled that way too, but the lieutenant was quite charming as he apologized for the state of the papers—his housekeeper had accidentally tossed them out before he could rescue them—and said he needed a translator and was willing to pay her extra, given the shoddy condition of the papers.

Ever since that awful eviction notice had been tacked to her front door, Lydia had been taking in extra translating work wherever she could find it. The work usually came from a local newspaper that wanted to reprint stories about the Italian opera or the never-ending conflicts between Greece and Turkey. It was odd for a complete stranger to approach her with work. Especially a man so attractive and who stared at her as if she was an object of immense fascination. Men that stunningly handsome simply did not pay attention to girls like her.

Then she caught herself. Was she actually considering turning down a job merely because the man was *attractive*? She straightened her shoulders and pulled the ratty stack of papers toward her. A glance at the top sheet revealed a tidy row of Turkish script.

"Certainly I can translate these. When do you require them back?"

"Tomorrow. I'm leaving for Philadelphia tomorrow night and I'll need these before then."

Her heart plummeted. "Impossible. The very soonest I can have them for you is sometime this weekend."

And that was because she was committed to be at the Brandenbergs' doing clerical work until ten o'clock tonight, leaving precious little time to work on translation. Thumbing through the stack of Turkish documents, Lydia figured the job would require around six hours. But if this man needed them in a hurry . . .

"How much will you pay me?"

"Five dollars. Plus an extra two on account of the shabby condition."

Lydia shook her head. "Not possible. I'll need at least twenty dollars if I am to forgo a night of sleep over this."

"Twenty dollars would pay your salary for an entire week!"

"It will also pay for an overnight translation." She needed that money and was determined to fight for it. With a casual glance she scanned the other customers in the coffeehouse. "Perhaps someone else could do it? Let's see. Paddy O'Malley, playing chess in the corner, is always looking for work. Perhaps you can ask him. Or better yet, there is a school of architecture just down the street. Perhaps they've got some Turkish translators with a bit of time on their hands."

The way the lieutenant lounged against the side of the counter and kept his blue gaze riveted on her reminded her of a cat watching a canary. "Careful, Miss Pallas," he said. "I'm starting to get the impression you might be a bit on the miserly side. And such a fetching young lady. What a shame."

"I prefer to call it thrifty."

"*Mingy* is what they call it in the navy. You've got it written all over you." She really ought to take offense, but he was so charming as he said it she was tempted to laugh. She forced herself to remain calm.

"Twenty dollars will persuade this mingy young lady to forgo the comforts of sleep tonight. Nineteen dollars will not." She pretended to savor a spoonful of chowder, silently praying she had not pushed too hard. She was demanding a shocking fee, but modesty was not going to accumulate six hundred dollars before the end of the year.

"Come now," he said in a coaxing manner. "I've seen ten-year-olds forgo a night of sleep in order to see Santa Claus. Surely you are up to the task."

"Did any of those ten-year-olds read Turkish?"

She had him there, and the lieutenant's eyes narrowed in amused frustration. What a shocking shade of crystal blue, with the tiniest bit of light gray around the irises. There was no doubt this man could charm the birds out of the trees, but she still didn't quite trust him. She was certain he sometimes used another surname, and what sort of honest man needed more than one name?

"Why does the admiral sometimes call you Alexander Banebridge and sometimes call you Alexander Christian?" The question popped from her mouth before she could call it back. She needed the twenty dollars more than she cared about his use of an alias, yet the lieutenant did not seem to mind her impertinence; he just sent her a lazy smile and leaned in a little closer to her.

"Now, Miss Pallas, we were discussing the flaws in your character, not the trivial inconsistencies in my life story. Tragic, the way young people today are so obsessed with money. I am surprised you are able to sleep at night. Fifteen dollars for an overnight translation." He nudged the stack of papers a few inches closer to her.

Lydia would have taken the job for five dollars, but she could not afford timidity if she wished to save her home. She pushed them back. "I'm trying to eat, and those pages smell like they were used to collect cat droppings." She feigned an air of nonchalance, knowing he would never meet her price if she appeared too desperate for the cash.

She took her time to polish off the chowder, then rose to her feet. "It's been a pleasure finally meeting you, Lieutenant Banebridge. Or Bane, if you prefer. I'm sure you will be flattered to know that my co-workers call you 'The Adonis,' so you can add that to your string of names if you choose." She held her breath as she began walking toward the door, hoping she had not driven too steep a bargain.

She walked only three steps when he slid in front of her, pushed the stack of papers into her hands, and reached for his billfold. Lydia tried to suppress the surge of triumph from showing as he extracted a ten-dollar bill. "Ten now, ten tomorrow evening," he said. "I'll meet you here to pick up the work."

He leaned a little closer and his voice was as warm and smooth as chocolate. "I'll be praying about your mingy ways," he whispered into her ear.

A completely irrational shiver raced through her, but before she could respond, the lieutenant straightened and Lydia stared at his ramrod straight posture as he strode from the room.

4

It was nearing midnight and the Professor was tired, but he carried his treasure as carefully as if it were an injured butterfly, stepping down the carriage steps gently so as not to stress the delicate pages of his latest acquisition.

"You have sanded the walkways properly?" he asked the servant who held the carriage door open for him.

"Certainly, Professor."

"Good lad." It had been raining all day, and these slate paths could be slick. The thought of slipping while he carried this poor, damaged masterpiece was too hideous to contemplate. Warm light glowed behind the windows of his granite mansion, and soon he could transfer these delicate pages into a proper resting place. Never again would the book be neglected in a room too warm, or fingered by stupid people who did not understand the priceless nature of John Milton's *Areopagitica*. Printed in 1644, this volume had survived civil wars, the burning of London, and the slow decay of years. He had traveled all the way to Philadelphia to attend the auction, but it was worth it.

It was a relief to step inside, where he kept the house perpetually cool, mindful of preserving his delicate books. It wasn't comfortable for the people who lived here, but these sacrifices must be made. His eyes dilated with pleasure as he passed through the mansion's great room, the walls filled to capacity with bookshelves towering to the ceiling. More books rested atop the vestibule table, stacked along the hallways, and stashed beneath end tables.

He pulled on a pair of soft cotton gloves, opened the box, and let his eyes feast on the beauty of *Areopagitica*. He winced a bit at the stain that darkened the lower-left corner of the book. Probably some careless reader from centuries ago who did not know how to properly care for a masterpiece such as this. No matter. He would overlook the flaws, no different from a father who would love a child despite a scar.

A whimper disturbed the silence of the night. He lifted his head and cocked his ear. Most definitely, it was the crying of a child. The Professor carefully wrapped *Areopagitica* back in its protective covers and set it within the mahogany case before following the sounds of weeping to the music room.

Just as he suspected. There, curled beside the harpsichord and holding his stomach, was little Dennis Webster.

He closed the door. The weeping immediately stopped and Dennis froze when he saw him standing inside the music room.

"Come now, child," the Professor said. "What is the cause for all those tears? Isn't Mrs. Garfield feeding you well?"

The boy's eyes were huge as he clung to the side of the harpsichord, too upset to speak, and that would never do. "Shall I have her fetch you a bowl of warm soup? Or perhaps some apple pie? She usually has pie at this time of year."

The barest shake of his head was the boy's only answer.

"Well then, if you are not hungry, I insist you tell me what is wrong. We can't have a boy of your age crying like this. It is unseemly. What are you, nine years old?"

The boy sniffled. "Ten."

"Ten years old. Too old to be crying all alone in the middle of the night. Now, tell me what has you down in the dumps, lad."

The boy wrapped his hands around his knees and stared at the hardwood floor. "I miss Tony," he said quietly.

"Ah . . . the Vallins boy. I see," the Professor said with sympathy. He walked across the room and sat in a chair opposite the still quivering child. "What happened to Tony was tragic, but you know that has nothing to do with you. Come now, there are plenty of things here for you to do, even though your playmate is gone. There is fishing and horseback riding. And I hear there is a brand-new batch of puppies out in the barn. You may pick one out for your very own, if you like."

Dennis shook his head and refused to lift his gaze. This was getting frustrating, but perhaps it was only natural for a boy in Dennis's position to be frightened. Natural, but it was time he grew out of it. The boy had been here for three years, and the Professor had never said a cross word to the child. Never harmed him in any way.

"Dennis, you must learn to be a man and grow out of these childish fears. I know you are in a . . . well, a tricky position, but I don't intend to punish you so long as your father continues to be helpful. Which he has been ever since you came to live with me. That was not the case with Tony's father, so I was simply left with no choice. You can understand that, can't you?"

After a long pause, there was the barest nodding of the boy's head. "That's a fine lad," he said soothingly. "And you are in good company. Why, holding the children of important people has been quite common throughout all of history. The first king of Scotland was a guest of the English king for most of his childhood. It wasn't until he was sixteen that James was sent back to his family in Scotland, and by then he had made lots of friends in England and he was a much better king because of it. So it worked out well for all parties," he said warmly.

Confusion and anxiety was still stamped all over Dennis's face. The boy tried several times to say something, but he seemed reluctant to actually get the words out. "Don't be afraid. Ask me whatever you wish," the Professor said kindly.

"What . . . what exactly happened to Tony?"

He breathed a heavy sigh. There was no purpose in telling the boy such things. After all, Tony did not suffer, as the Professor would never countenance unnecessary violence, but Tony's father needed to be sent a clear message. The delivery of a trunk containing the body of eleven-year-old Tony Vallins did the trick. Mr. Vallins had three other children to be concerned with, and the Professor did not expect to have any additional trouble from the harbormaster of New Orleans ever again.

"All you need to know is that Tony did not suffer. His father simply did not love him enough, but that was hardly the boy's fault, now was it? Come, why don't you write another letter to your father and put it in tomorrow's post, if it will make you feel better. I can even help you with some of the harder words. Tell your father what a brave young boy you are, just like the Scottish king."

He smiled at the child. How nice it was to help a boy with his letters. He never had children of his own, but over the years there had been other children just like Dennis and Tony he had welcomed into his home. Very few ended up like poor Tony, as the Professor's reputation tended to be very effective in getting what he wanted.

Only once had he been truly, deeply disappointed in one of the children who came to live with him. Alexander Banebridge had the keenest brain of any man, woman, or child the Professor had ever met. Cunning too. Over time, the Professor decided to raise Bane as his own son. He gave that boy everything. An education. Access to power. He taught Bane the manners of a gentleman, the cultures of the world, and how to operate an international shipping operation. And Bane devoured everything, that lightning fast mind of his locking away the information and always searching out more.

Of course, Bane had ultimately proven to be a terrible disappointment. Who would have predicted that the Professor's most splendid creation would fall victim to a passel of Bible-thumpers?

But the other young hostages had proven quite profitable. Some even went into business with him when they became grown men. Perhaps young Dennis would be just such a lad.

Bane walked into the florist on Cranston Street and was enveloped by the heady fragrance of rose and jasmine. He waited while a young man dictated an insipid love note to be attached to a delivery of roses. "As I would live for your smile, I would die for your love. Sweet Margaret, you make me soar like a dove on the wings of love."

Despite the onslaught of atrocious poetry, Bane kept his face carefully neutral. There were very few things in this world of which Bane could be certain, but one was that he would never gush over a woman in such a pitiable manner.

At last the young man completed his poem, paid for his delivery, and left the store. Bane approached the florist. "Have you any poppies in stock?"

The florist gave a reluctant shake of his head. "It's a bit tough to get them in at this time of year. Perhaps some dahlias?"

In the five years that Bane had been coming to this shop, the only type of flower he ever purchased had been poppies, but he pretended to consider the option. It would hardly do to let the florist think he suffered from some sort of maniacal obsession that motivated every action of his life.

"Let's have a look at the dahlias," he said casually. Bane wouldn't know a dahlia from a turnip, so he followed the florist around the counter and looked at the flower. The wide, sloppy petals were reminiscent of a poppy, but really, only a poppy would do.

"Charming, but I'm willing to wait for the poppies. When can you have a shipment delivered?"

Bane knew it was a tall order. Poppies bloomed in June, and although a few strains could be manipulated to last later into the season, those would require a greenhouse far to the south. The man hesitated. "I'll have to telegraph an order to a supplier in Georgia. Perhaps a week?"

Bane nodded. He slipped the man the hefty fee such a delivery would entail. "I want them delivered to the Rare Book Room at the Harvard library. No note is necessary."

A surge of satisfaction pumped through Bane. Odd, that he could still get a charge out of taunting the Professor. He risked his life each time he lobbed one of these grenades at Professor Van Bracken, but it was worth it. For decades that man had polluted the world with tons of smuggled opium, the lethally seductive by-product of the poppy plant.

For a few years, Bane had been the Professor's willing henchman. He had helped the Professor smuggle, distribute, and sell opium to anyone who was willing to pay the price. When Bane was seventeen, he found God and broke free of the Professor's iron grip, but the shame still lingered on Bane's soul. He would carry that stain for the rest of his life, but at least now he was unraveling the horror he had brought upon the world. He spent most of his time in the bare-knuckle world of political brawling, pushing legislation that would choke off the sale of opium throughout the country, but taunting the Professor was one of the few indulgences he permitted himself.

Ten years ago, shortly after he escaped the Professor's influence, Bane bought a case of poppy bulbs and waited until the Professor left his remote mansion in the Vermont wilderness where he operated his criminal empire. For three nights Bane sneaked onto the property and planted those bulbs everywhere, filling the Professor's lawn, the gardens, even the pasture where he kept livestock. He broke into the Professor's mansion and slipped bulbs inside the potted plants that graced every room. Bane wished he could have been there as those poppies started blooming, but he had been too busy covering his tracks, knowing the Professor's henchmen were still on the hunt for Bane's head.

After that summer, Bane started sending the Professor poppies everywhere. He knew who in the Professor's network could be turned, and Bane turned them. When the Professor hobnobbed with high society, Bane made sure the hostess had lavish bouquets of poppies to fill her parlor. When the Professor met with his bankers, there was a glorious oil painting of poppies on the office wall. All of it was designed to set the Professor on edge, to let him know that Alexander Banebridge was still alive and knew where he banked, with whom he socialized. He wanted to ensure the Professor would never enjoy a single peaceful night of sleep in his life. How ironic that a lovely bouquet of poppies could help make that happen.

Bane stepped outside the shop and noticed the first crisp hint of autumn as someone burned leaves on a distant corner. Strolling down the twisty street, he spotted the besotted young Romeo who had just ordered flowers staring into the window of a jeweler's shop at a case of rings.

Bane's footsteps slowed. "Going to take the plunge, are you?"

Romeo startled, but then a dazzling smile spread over his face. "Yes. It's time."

How could a man reach adulthood and still have that wide-open, innocent expression of adoration?

An unfamiliar feeling niggled at the corner of Bane's mind. Envy? If Bane had not spent his entire childhood under the influence of Professor Van Bracken, perhaps he would be innocent enough to hanker after a woman with that dumbstruck expression. Then again, if the serpent had never offered Eve the apple, they would all be living in Eden.

Bane gave Romeo a brusque nod. "Good luck with it," he said, turning to hike up the hill curving toward Chapman Square, where he needed to meet with the head of the local police union. There were a million things he needed to accomplish during these few short weeks in Boston, but it was hard to drag his mind back to business.

What would it be like to be in love? Bane wouldn't waste time with flowers or jewels to impress a woman. He would sweep her away to see the pyramids of Egypt or sail down the Rhine River to discover the great cities of Europe. When they were exhausted from exploring the palaces and grand museums, he would take her to a secluded villa, somewhere overlooking the rocky shores of the Adriatic and sheltered from the world behind a thick layer of wisteria vines.

He straightened and quickened his step. Pure rubbish, of course. From the moment he escaped the Professor's grasp he had known a normal life was out of his reach, but every now and then these pathetic longings plagued him.

He was good at killing them.

5

Lydia had the Turkish translations in a burlap sack on the floor of the coffeehouse as she waited for Lieutenant Banebridge. This translation job had been as interesting as a cold cup of coffee, a twenty-page discussion of the shipment and distribution of wool from Morocco in mind-numbing detail.

Lydia was tired from only two hours of sleep, but nothing was quite so comforting as a piping hot bowl of chowder and a mug of Big Jim's coffee.

"Clam chowder again?" She looked up to see Lieutenant Banebridge standing beside her. Without asking, he pulled a stool out and sat beside her.

"When I find something I like, I stick with it. Why aren't you in uniform?" Lydia asked.

If possible, he looked even more attractive in the open-collared white shirt and dark wool frock coat. "I'm not in the navy anymore," he said casually. "I turned in my resignation papers a while back. Now I'm just plain Alexander Banebridge."

Something was not quite right. Not that she was an expert, but she would have thought quitting the military was a little more complicated than he made it sound. She narrowed her eyes and scrutinized his perfectly sculpted face, looking in vain for the tiniest hint of embarrassment. "You know, *Bane,*" she said pointedly, "I suppose it is common for people to switch jobs, but they rarely switch *names.*"

Lydia forced her misgivings aside when Bane slid a crisp ten-dollar bill across the table toward her, and, as if in answer to her prayers, he had another set of documents for her to translate. This time the documents were from Greece and Albania.

"I have to charge more for translating Albanian," she said as she flipped through the pages. "It is not one of my better languages and it will take a while."

"Slacked off during Albanian lessons, did you?" Bane asked with a casual air. "Slothful as well as greedy, what a combination. Twenty-five dollars for the lot."

She raised her eyebrows. "No haggling?"

"Nope. I knew Albanian would be a stretch for you. You're half-Greek, half-Turkish, so it is only fair to pay extra for the Albanian."

She folded the ten-dollar bill and tucked it into her reticule, amazed at her good fortune. "How did you know that? About my ancestry?"

"Eric told me."

It was disconcerting to know she had been discussed like that, but at least she was earning additional income. And the admiral did plenty of business with Bane, so that meant she could trust him, right?

Except that the admiral seemed moody and remote every time Bane set foot in his office.

"Are you really friends with Admiral Fontaine?" she asked impulsively. "He seems so glum every time you darken our door."

The lazy smile he sent her made her heart skip a beat. "Nonsense.

I bring sunshine and delight wherever I go. You should have seen how your eyes lit up when you saw me just now. I feared the place might catch fire."

"That was because I wanted the ten dollars you owed me," Lydia said. "Those documents were so boring you ought to have paid me double." She gestured to the Greek and Albanian documents he had brought her. A cursory glance at the top page showed it to be about taxes on Greek plaster. Another thrilling read. "When do you need these?" she asked. "Please don't say tomorrow."

"No, I'll be out of town for a few days. How about Friday? I can swing by your office at the Navy Yard."

Lydia eyed the stack, knowing the work would be quite a slog. But with three evenings to work on them, she ought to be able to complete the task. "Done," she agreed.

It wasn't until after he left that Lydia realized Bane had neatly evaded her attempts to gain some insight into the sobering business he had with the admiral. As she spent the next few days translating Albanian tax reports, her mind kept straying to Bane and his mysterious business with the admiral. He was paying her a shocking amount to translate documents, and accepting such payments from a virtual stranger made her mildly uncomfortable. How easily he deflected the conversation whenever she even attempted to learn anything personal about him.

On Thursday she entered the admiral's private office to ask if Bane was trustworthy. Unlike the front office where the walls were whitewashed, the admiral's office was lined with oak paneling, and a rich oriental rug covered the floor. Outside the window she could see the hull of a battleship in the dry dock.

The admiral appeared surprised by her question. "Naturally," he said. "Banebridge is an extraordinary man, and I never would have put him in touch with you were it otherwise."

"Oh." She stood awkwardly, wishing he would elaborate and give her some tiny glimpse into why Bane's visits always perturbed the admiral. But she could think of no elegant way to pose such a question without being shockingly forward. "Is that his name, then? Banebridge? I have heard him called Alexander Christian."

"Just call him Bane. Everybody else does."

Lydia still felt ill at ease doing such highly paid translation work for a man she knew nothing about. "But who *is* he? He has never told me why he needs these strange translations. I'm not sure if he is in the navy or not. Is he one of the foreign attachés scooping up naval intelligence?"

The admiral did not blink as he scrutinized her, but he took a long time before he formulated an answer. "Bane has done some work for me in the past," he said. "Occasionally I call him back into service for a . . . special project . . . but he hasn't officially been in the navy for years. He is a good man to know in a pinch."

It was an evasive answer, but she knew it was all she was likely to get.

Then the admiral surprised her. "As highly as I regard Bane, you should keep him at arm's length. The man is dangerous. He likes to hide it beneath a veneer of charm, but don't let that fool you. Bane is as lethal as a scorpion. Take his translating work, but stay away from him otherwise." A look of concern was carved into the admiral's rugged face and his voice was earnest. "Is that understood, Miss Pallas?"

"Yes, sir," Lydia murmured as she left his office.

On Friday, Bane came by the Navy Yard to retrieve the translations. She still needed to earn over five hundred dollars if she was to save her apartment, and she had been hoping Bane would have another batch of translation work for her. He came breezing into the Navy Yard office, looking flushed and windblown from an early autumn chill. It was maddening that even with his blond hair tousled by the wind he still looked gorgeous, but Lydia gladly pocketed another twenty-five dollars toward her slowly growing account. Better yet, Bane brought her more documents to translate. Before he gave her the pages, he braced one hip along the edge of her desk and teased her about everything from her hairstyle to her handwriting.

"Rigid, cramped letters," Bane said as he flipped through her translated pages. "There is a Frenchman publishing on the psychology of handwriting analysis and what it reveals about the human psyche. He would have a field day with you, Lydia."

"I have perfect handwriting," she said. Penmanship was one of the few things that had been drilled into her at the Crakken Orphanage. She sat a little straighter and noticed him fiddling with her framed pictures while he paged through her translation. "Quit touching that," she said. "I'm tired of having to put my desk to rights every time you pass through."

Bane set the translated pages down and picked up the picture. "Why an ocean scene?" he asked. "I should think you see it every day and would have no need of a picture."

"It is a Mediterranean island in the Adriatic Sea," she said. "Where I grew up." When Lydia first saw the small watercolor in a shop, the crystalline sky reminded her so vividly of the sun-filled years of her childhood that she saved up her coins to buy the painting. She had no pictures of her parents or Baby Michael, but when she looked at this image, she could almost hear their voices carrying on the warm breeze that whipped across those choppy blue waves.

She snatched the picture from his hand and returned it to its proper place. "Quit fiddling with things on my desk. And what is wrong with my handwriting?" she asked to switch the topic. "I took great care in preparing that translation."

Bane shook his head in mock disapproval. "Look at the uniformity of these letters, the perfect spacing between words. Such control, such order. Charming, but I have an urge to mess them up. I think the Frenchman would say you are afraid of risk. Perhaps even a little repressed, Lydia."

Karl shot to his feet. "That is enough!" he said. "If you have translating work for Lydia, give it to her and be done with it."

Bane didn't budge an inch from the corner of her desk, just kept swinging his leg and looking at her as though she was an object of endless fascination. "What of it, Lydia? Are you up for a little reading about Turkish timber exports?"

Lydia grabbed the pages from him. "I'll have them translated by Monday," she said.

6

Thank goodness for Bane's translation work. Over the coming weeks the steady stream of translation jobs allowed her to amass almost two hundred dollars for her apartment fund. Bane came by her office at the Navy Yard every few days to bring more work. He would drop off a stack of documents on her desk, flirt outrageously with her, and succeed in sending every rational thought in her head whirling away like a butterfly caught in a windstorm.

There was never any consistency in the documents he asked her to translate. He brought her legal documents from Russian courts and scientific research on currents in the Atlantic Ocean. Shipping logs, tax records, census reports, agricultural records, stock market offerings. Most of the work was mind-numbingly dull, but it made use of the full range of Lydia's linguistic abilities. Sometimes the documents were crisp and new, others were crumpled and stained. She was certain one set of ledgers had the juice from a spittoon smeared across it.

The only consistent thing was that Bane never brought any

documents for Jacob or Karl to translate. Only Lydia. Was it possible . . . was it conceivable Bane harbored some sort of romantic interest in her?

It might explain the never-ending stream of pure nonsense he brought her to translate. If he had a logical explanation for the bizarre assortment of claptrap he brought her, she might feel better about his regular visits to the Navy Yard, but he refused to provide truthful answers. Whenever she asked what he needed the information for, he shot her one of those damsel-slaying smiles and told her a bold-faced lie. "I've always been intensely curious about Albanian municipal tax structure," he said in response to her question. "It has been difficult for me to sleep knowing you were about to present me with this new tax schedule. I simply live for such gems," he said as he took the freshly translated tax schedule from her hands.

She forced her misgivings aside because the income from translating was too important to pass up. Lydia knew what it meant to be bone-grindingly poor, and she would never let that happen to her again, but she was growing increasingly uncomfortable whenever Bane was near.

Frankly, she was growing suspicious of Bane. Two weeks ago she had unexpectedly come upon him outside the Massachusetts State House. She sometimes did minor translation work for the government and had been asked to translate business letters written to the Italian foreign minister. She had dropped them off with the clerk, pocketed her five dollars, and been about to leave when she had seen a man she was almost certain was Bane standing with the admiral, the governor of Massachusetts, and some of the state's chief justices.

Lydia had slid behind one of the tall, fluted columns rimming the lobby of the State House. At first she was only able to see the back of the man, but he had a slender build like Bane and the same pale blond hair barely brushing his collar. Even the casual, negligent stance was the same. But she was not quite able to believe what she was seeing. The man was dressed much finer than she had ever seen Bane, almost like an aristocrat. When he turned to greet another justice, she saw the side of Bane's sculpted face, as beautiful and perfect as an archangel.

There was no mistaking Bane's smooth voice. "Justice Stevens, have you met Admiral Fontaine? He has been in charge of the Navy Yard these past nine years."

Lydia leaned closer. She tried not to be obvious as she clung to the side of the pillar, but it was vital she hear what he was saying. Why on earth was Bane mingling with such exalted people? He never presented himself as anything other than an unemployed sailor to her.

"Lethal as a scorpion," the admiral had said about Bane. And yet, there he stood, glad-handing with some of the most powerful men in the state.

She tried to listen through the din of footsteps and voices echoing off the marble floors and vaulted ceiling. They seemed to be speaking about an election. She heard one of the justices say that someone was not likely to "play ball." There was a burst of laughter and some backslapping. "Get Bane to bring him into line! He has already got Senator Wilkinson shaking in his boots," one of the men said. More laughter and then Bane spoke, but his voice was too low for her to hear. As the group broke up, Lydia leaned around the column to get a better look as Bane and the admiral were leaving. Just then Bane swiveled around and locked his eyes on her.

Lydia was frozen to the spot, but Bane did not seem particularly surprised to see her there. He had just dipped his head and flashed her a wink before leaving.

It was the first time she had seen Bane since that day in the State House two weeks earlier. He strode into the office with the catlike grace he seemed to possess effortlessly. Logical thought abandoned Lydia, as it did every time Bane stepped into her view. Her heart started to thud, a flush warmed her face, and she felt like she was floundering without any moorings. It was intensely annoying that he always caused this reaction in her. How could a woman who craved stability and order as much as she did allow a man like Bane to get under her skin? For the sake of her sanity, she needed to keep her distance.

"Are you here to see the admiral?" she asked.

"Yes, but I'd rather chat with you," he said. Did he just flash her a wink? It was impossible to tell because he had turned to retrieve a stack of documents from a leather case at his side. "I've got a bit more translating work for you," he said as he set a short stack of documents on the corner of her desk.

"What were you doing at the State House last week?" she asked. "Those were awfully powerful men you were with. How is it you are acquainted with the governor?"

"Is that a new blouse?" Bane asked. "I don't think I've ever seen you wear lace before."

Lydia glanced down. The Irish lace collar was an extravagance from before she started saving every penny to buy her apartment, but she still took care to press and starch her treasured collar. "Don't try to change the subject. Besides, you looked awfully dashing yourself, conducting business with the governor at the State House. I'm surprised you didn't have a trail of women following you."

Bane flashed her one of those negligent smiles. "Well, it is true I'm terribly sought after. I can hardly walk down the street without women pestering me. I am a victim, really. You should be much kinder to me."

She tried to stop herself from laughing because it would only encourage him, and this was exactly the sort of amiable sidestepping he so skillfully practiced. "What I ought to do is stop translating the nonsense you bring me."

Bane reached into his pocket and held a shiny gold coin before her eyes. "Ah, my little mingy wench. The problem is I know how dazzled you are by the almighty dollar."

And it was such easy money he was offering. The memory of her belongings piled in the center of the street was painful motivation, and Lydia snatched the coin from his hand. "I've done the potato diet," she said as she leaned over to tuck the coin into her satchel. "I've done the roach-infested tenements. Don't think I am insulted by the term 'mingy,' because I see it as insurance against a backslide into grinding poverty."

It wasn't until Bane left that Lydia noticed the paper dust jacket on her Albanian dictionary had been swapped with the Turkish cover.

And she still hadn't gleaned a bit of insight into what business Bane had in Boston.

Traffic was heavy at the Long Wharf, as Bane knew it would be. Stretching two thousand feet into the Boston harbor, it could accommodate dozens of ships from all over the world. The air was filled with the call of peddlers hawking oranges and ribbons, flags snapping in the breeze, and the slosh of waves against the massive boulders that supported the wharf. Warehouses lined the north side of the wharf, but the south side was open to the water. As he walked down the wharf, Bane scanned the crowds of peddlers, sailors, and longshoremen until he spotted Admiral Fontaine with his two young children.

Could that possibly be Lucy Fontaine? Bane remembered the first time he had seen the child. She had been trying to catch butterflies. Too young to walk and swing a net at the same time, she had constantly toppled over as she scampered after butterflies in the admiral's front garden. That was three years ago, but how quickly children grew at this age.

And nine-year-old Jack Fontaine was unmistakable. Bane had never seen the boy without a smattering of army paraphernalia pinned to his clothes. Sometimes it was an army buckle, sometimes a whole set of regulation buttons. He suppressed a grin as he approached the family from behind to eavesdrop on what Eric was telling his children in such passionate tones.

"You see the cruiser pulling in behind that clipper ship? It is homeward bound after more than a year at sea." He pointed to a narrow pennant on the mast, the signal all ships were entitled to fly as they pulled into port after long voyages. "After they lower the pennant, the top portion goes to the captain. The rest will be cut up and divided among the crew." Jack did not look impressed. Poor Admiral Fontaine, doing everything possible to sell the glories of the sea to his boy, but it was hopeless. Bane knew the key to this boy's heart was clear for all to see, sitting right on the lad's shoulder.

"Is that a regulation braid for the U.S. Cavalry I see?" Bane asked.

All three heads swiveled to look at him. Jack straightened the braid, and his grin threatened to split his face in half. "I bought it with my own money," the boy said proudly.

No surprise there. After four generations of men who made money from the sea, young Jack Fontaine was itching to buck the trend and join the army, but Admiral Fontaine had not yet conceded the battle. Even as Jack collected army hats, army regulation buckles, and books about the army's exploits out west, Admiral Fontaine was determined to sell the sea to his only son.

"Look what I found for sale at the Quincy Market," Bane said, bringing forth the slouch hat from where he'd been hiding it behind his back. Jack's eyes widened in delight, and he reached with both hands toward the hat.

"This is what soldiers in the army wear out west," Bane said. "The brim will keep the rain off your face, but the soldiers pin up the right side so it won't interfere with carrying a rifle."

"Couldn't you at least find him a navy hat?" Eric asked wryly, but Bane was having too much fun watching Jack inspect his new treasure. He was already trying to twist one side of the brim up into the classic rakish style.

Bane squatted down so he could see Lucy better. "Do you suppose I found anything a little girl might like at the Quincy Market?"

Lucy was shy and clung so hard to Eric's leg she was probably cutting off circulation, but her pretty blue eyes were tracking Bane's hands as he rummaged through his coat and pant pockets. "I must have something here, somewhere. . . ." With a flourish he pulled out a handful of velvet ribbons. Lucy reached out to grab the soft ribbons and rubbed them against her face.

Bane stood to shake Eric's hand in greeting. "Next time I'll bring them the drum and whistle noisemakers I saw for sale."

Eric's face remained impassive. "One might think you'd show a smidge more gratitude to the man who saved your sorry hide."

Bane shrugged. Actually, it was the admiral's wife who had saved Bane from the thrashing he deserved when he had tried to lie his way into the navy at the tender age of seventeen.

Sick, desperate, and out of options, Bane had showed up at the Boston Navy Yard in hopes of getting on a ship that would take him out of the country. Bane had always looked much younger than his age. At seventeen, he looked no older than fourteen, so trying to pretend he was of age to join the navy was proving difficult.

Navy regulations required boys under the age of eighteen to have the consent of a parent. Bane had no parents, only a huge price on his head and a healing bullet wound in his side when he tried to persuade the sergeant he was eighteen years old and of good moral character. As a newly converted Christian, Bane's moral character *was* pretty good; it was his rich criminal history that was the problem.

Bane was hauled out of the master chief's office and tossed at the feet of Admiral Fontaine's pretty wife as she stepped from a buggy. It was the stroke of luck that altered the course of Bane's life.

Mistaking Bane for a youngster, Rachel Fontaine took pity and offered Bane the lunch she was bringing to her husband. He might have looked like a hungry fourteen-year-old waif, but Bane was clever enough to spot a woman with power, and set to work immediately. During that lunch he told Mrs. Fontaine how tidal currents in the West Indies influenced the spice trade during the Renaissance and catapulted the Dutch to the premier position in world shipping. He described the brilliant designs of medieval Chinese ships that still influenced naval technology. He spoke about the German development of new torpedo boats that were the fastest thing on the water.

By the end of the day, he had persuaded Mrs. Fontaine to help him find a position in the navy. Eric was no fool, and Bane confessed to being on the run from "a spot of trouble." Eric even consented to Bane's use of a false name to better hide his tracks from the Professor. Bane was on a ship heading for Brussels the next day.

All that was ancient history, and Bane was no longer running for his life. For the past five years, he had been doggedly pursuing a new great, unquenchable thirst. And he needed Eric's cooperation to make that happen. It wasn't as if Eric would emerge empty-handed from the plan. If Bane played his cards right, this time next year Eric would be a United States senator, with more power than any Navy Yard could ever provide, but getting Eric's cooperation was proving surprisingly difficult. Still, Bane never flinched from a challenge.

His gaze narrowed on the steam-powered *Protector* as it cruised into view. It was one of three ships used by the harbor police to patrol the waters, and Bane had invested a considerable amount of time garnering the harbor police's support. He nodded toward the ship. "The harbor police would be naturally inclined to support your candidacy for the senate. And where they go, the firemen go. You would do well to start cultivating your ties there."

Eric kept his eyes on the ship as he picked up Lucy, bouncing her casually against his hip. He wasn't quite as disinterested as he pretended. "What about the Boston police? Do they share the same political interests as the harbor police?"

Bane shrugged. "Generally, but they don't move in lockstep, so you'll need to work on them both. I've been trying to meet with the chief of police, but he had a burning need to go to Cape Ann with his wife to celebrate their twelfth anniversary. Apparently, there is a lighthouse on the cape that holds fond memories for them. Idiots."

A hint of humor lurked in Eric's face. "I see you are still the romantic."

Bane rolled his eyes. "Why does the fool need to leave town for a twelfth anniversary? He's already had eleven other occasions to celebrate with his wife."

Eric let a rare laugh slip out as he watched the *Protector* cruise past the wharf. "Someday a woman is going to thaw that block of ice you store your heart in, and then you'll jump to do silly things like rushing off to Cape Ann to please her."

Bane flashed him a patient smile. "I anticipate floodwaters rising in the Sahara desert before that happy event."

Eric bounced his daughter as his gaze scanned the horizon.

"Rachel and I were married sixteen years ago. Each year on our anniversary I remember our wedding day. She wanted the ceremony in her father's garden and spent months making sure all the flowers would be blooming and perfectly groomed. On the day of the wedding it poured sheets of rain, and I thought she would be heartsick, but when I saw her standing in the parlor, she was radiant, and laughing so hard. That is what I'll always remember about Rachel. That wonderful, endless laugh of hers."

Bane knew the appalling circumstances of Rachel's death. Indeed, it was one of the reasons Eric had been so supportive of Bane's cause over the years. The only political candidates Bane groomed for office were those whose commitment to battling opium would not falter amidst the firestorm of pressure in Washington, and that made Eric Fontaine an ideal candidate. It was maddening that Eric still wrestled with loyalty to the navy. The man was dispirited about the pathetic condition of the navy and had been hoping to save it from inside. After more than a year of aggressive lobbying, Bane had finally convinced the admiral he would have more power to salvage the decaying navy with a seat in the U.S. Senate. That meant Eric would need to resign from the navy, which was tearing his loyalties in half.

Bane was not going to give up. Getting Eric elected to the senate meant Bane would have another weapon to use against the hydra-headed beast that killed Rachel.

Lydia usually loved walking home from work, but today she was too consumed with the numbers in her head to enjoy the view of the Charles River slowly flowing beneath the bridge.

She still needed two hundred dollars if she was going to save her home. Even if she kept up a steady stream of translations for Bane, she was not going to reach the magic number by December.

And she was growing increasingly certain she should stop working for Bane. Something wasn't right about that translation work. No matter how hard she pushed, he refused to give her a straight answer about why he wanted these bizarre translations. And he was such a flirt every time he stepped into their office. Completely ignoring Willis, Karl, and Jacob, he arrowed straight toward her like a self-propelled torpedo. The translation work he gave her was pointless, and it seemed like he was making excuses to come in and see her. Very *expensive* excuses that made her feel guilty for taking his money.

Perhaps he had heard of her need of funds and was merely doing her a favor? Accepting six hundred dollars from a stranger was unthinkable, but she would be happy to work for it. If Bane was developing a fondness for her, might this stream of translation work be an attempt to sustain contact with her? Cause her to develop feelings of gratitude and obligation to him? It was hard to turn away from such lucrative employment, but there was something very strange about the work he was asking her to do.

She pulled her cloak tighter and forced her chin up a notch. It was too beautiful a day to let these gloomy thoughts weigh her down. She quickened her pace as she turned the corner and embarked on her favorite part of the walk home. The narrow, twisty streets that led to the Laughing Dragon provided a new vista around each bend. There was a stretch of tidy bow-fronted shops, followed by a series of townhouses with iron railings and glossy front doors. She loved the slant of the late afternoon light that warmed the dusky red bricks and flashed against the tidy brass doorplates.

Each day Lydia engraved these sights into her memory. What if she failed to come up with the necessary funds to purchase her apartment? She could find another place to live, but no place would ever hold the beloved memories of the Laughing Dragon.

Needing some soap and a bottle of headache medicine, she headed toward her favorite apothecary shop. A little silver bell rang as she stepped inside and, as always, she went straight for the basket of scented soaps at the front. It was a treat to sample the various fragrances before settling on the bar with the scent and packaging most appealing to her. There was lavender soap from France, and a pale green bar scented with lemon verbena. Lydia held it to her nose and breathed deeply. Was it just her imagination, or did simply smelling these wonderfully scented cakes of soap make her feel a little better?

Maggie, the store clerk who had been there for years, pressed a bar into her hands. "You'll want to try this new soap we just got in from Kentucky," she said. "It's got roses and jasmine, and smells ever so nice."

The temptation was too great. Lydia took the exquisite package with the lovely illustrations and breathed deeply. "Oh, this is heaven."

"Isn't it just? One dollar will buy a whole case of it."

It was far too dear. Lydia passed the cake of soap back to Maggie. She loved her apartment more than she would like a whole factory of fancy soap. "Just plain old white soap today."

Maggie's brows lifted in surprise. In all the years since Lydia had been coming here, the simple treat of scented soap was one of the few luxuries in which she always indulged. "You sure?" Maggie asked. "It's just hog fat and lye."

Lydia strolled over to a shelf and helped herself to the smallest bottle of headache medicine. "I'm sure," she said as she laid a coin down for her purchases.

She didn't know if she would be able to scavenge another two hundred dollars before December, but, if not, it would not be because she had squandered her savings on fancy soap.

7

How can a planet have two moons?" Jacob's voice dripped with skepticism, but Lydia and Karl both gazed in wonder at the brochure on Willis's desk.

"The astronomers are certain of it," Willis said. "Three independent observatories have verified that Mars has two moons, and they would not have printed it otherwise." Lydia stared at the pen-and-ink drawing of the two moons, and inanely thought of her father. How he would have loved this! He used to look up at the star-spattered sky and spin such wild tales with no basis beyond what he would like to believe. But the brochure on Willis's desk came from the Naval Observatory in Washington, D.C., so she supposed those men knew what they were talking about.

"I wonder if someone standing on the ground of Mars would be able to see both moons at once?" Lydia asked. "Or are they on opposite sides of the planet?"

Admiral Fontaine leaned down to study the article. "If the moons are in close proximity to each other, it would wreak havoc on the tidal patterns."

"Do you suppose Mars has oceans too?" Karl asked.

The admiral looked taken aback. "It never occurred to me that a planet would not have oceans. I suppose when they make a better telescope, we will know for sure."

Jacob sniffed. "I still don't believe it. I think they are making it all up."

Karl proceeded to try to convince Jacob of the brilliance of modern science, and the admiral returned to his office, but Lydia took a moment to gaze out the window overlooking the massive dry docks and hulking ships. It was a blessing to share an office with people who took an interest in science and the world around them. She felt completely at home with them. She was *safe* with them.

Not like Bane.

She couldn't fool herself any longer. The drivel he brought her to translate was pure nonsense. He must be looking for whatever scrap of paper had a language on it she could read. Where he was pulling it from, she did not know. This last batch had a distinctive whiff of rubbish pile.

If he would just give something to Karl or Jacob to translate, she wouldn't feel so insecure, but Bane's entire focus was on her when he came to the office, and she simply could not tolerate it anymore. It was embarrassing to even think a man of such angelic beauty might be interested in her, but what other reason could there be? Even worse, she was fighting a growing attraction to the man. She found herself thinking about him at the oddest times, remembering his quips, his irreverent smile. Even the way he teased her was becoming something she looked forward to.

But this last set of documents had finally pushed her over the edge. She would find some other way to earn the remaining two hundred dollars she needed to purchase her apartment.

When Bane came striding in at lunchtime, looking gloriously

windblown, he was as relentlessly charming as ever. "What bits of Turkish delight have you for me today?" he asked with a disarming smile.

He snatched the document from the air as she tossed it to him and said, "That is a menu from a Turkish restaurant! It stinks like it was used to wrap fish. I'm finished wasting my time translating nonsense." She spoke loudly enough for the whole office to hear. Now she couldn't back down.

Bane pulled a chair up next to her desk and sat. "What exactly do you mean by 'finished'?"

"I mean you ought to find someone else to do your translating. I would prefer not to work for you anymore. I quit."

"You can't be that angry over having to translate a menu, can you?"

Her eyes drifted closed. It wasn't the menu, it was that she did not feel right taking money from a man who seemed to have developed some sort of fondness for her, but how could she tell him that? "Correct. I do not enjoy translating menus. Or grain registers. Or tax rolls. Frankly, I'm tired of all the ridiculous documents you've brought me to translate, and I'm finished. I won't do it anymore."

Bane held up the menu. "How was I to know it was a menu?" he asked. "Come along, tell me what it says."

"Bane, I am quitting."

"You can't quit, or I'll want my ten dollars back." He opened the menu and pointed to an item. "What is this here? This looks interesting." When she didn't respond, he nudged her with his elbow. "Come now, I'm dying of curiosity and I can't leave until you tell me what this says."

Lydia glanced at the menu. "It is *karisik izgara tabagi*. It is a meat dish. Grilled meat, served on a platter."

"Ah. Say it again."

"Karisik izgara tabagi?"

"Yes, I like the way you say that," he said in a soft, velvety voice. "It sounds so exotic. Keep reading to me. It is enchanting."

Willis's eyes were about to pop out of his head. Jacob was pretending not to listen, but she could see him trying to hold back laughter. Karl rose to his feet.

"That's enough now," Karl said sternly. "Lydia, you don't have to read to this man. It is unseemly."

The smile on Bane's face grew larger. "It is a bit, isn't it?" He sprang to his feet. "Not to worry. I'm here to see the admiral. I'm ten minutes late for our appointment." He paused and leaned over to whisper in Lydia's ear. "But how could I resist when a beautiful woman stops and forces me to listen to her read in Turkish. Enthralling."

Shivers still raced down Lydia's spine after Bane was safely behind the door of the admiral's office. It was then she noticed that every one of her ink bottles was out of order again. She had been *watching* for Bane to tamper with her desk, and still she had not been able to catch him in the act.

She put her desk back in order, opened up a Greek shipping manual, and tried to concentrate. She would be insane to continue associating with Bane. He had not even acknowledged that she had quit, and she was pretty certain he intended to bring her another stack of documents soon.

Her concentration was interrupted by angry voices coming from behind the admiral's closed door. Everyone in the office stilled. The sounds were unmistakable. Two angry men, their voices becoming louder and more passionate by the second. Both the admiral and Bane were shouting now, competing for dominance. The admiral accused Bane of being an insane pest. She couldn't make out what Bane was saying because the admiral kept trying to shout him down.

"Willis, how long have you worked here?" Karl asked.

Willis did some mental calculations. "It must be almost nine years now."

"And in all that time, have you ever heard the admiral raise his voice?"

Willis paused, just long enough for another angry burst to be heard coming from the office. "Can't say that I have."

Karl shrugged. "Neither have I."

There was a heavy mahogany door separating the admiral's office from their desks, and the voices were too muffled to be clearly understood, but both the men inside were clearly having at it. Then a silence. Lydia looked at Karl, who looked at Willis.

"You don't suppose they have come to blows, have they?"

The shouting stopped, but somehow the silence was even more ominous. Karl took a few steps forward, fiddling with the buttons on his vest as he looked skeptically at the closed door. "Do you suppose I should go check on them?"

Lydia stood up as well. It seemed ridiculous, but she remembered what the admiral had said about Bane. *"Lethal as a scorpion."* Bane certainly looked glorious, but Lydia always sensed a barely leashed power radiating behind his cool demeanor. But the admiral was a physically strong man who still coached the boxing team of the local Marine Corps, so Lydia was fairly certain he could look after himself. Unless Bane resorted to trickery. The admiral was too honorable to be prepared for that. Karl looked about as anxious to enter the room as he would be to attend his own execution, but as he moved toward the closed mahogany door, a burst of raucous laughter from the admiral made him jump.

Karl looked relieved, and Willis simply looked surprised. "Can't say I've heard much laughter out of the admiral either."

Yet clearly they were laughing . . . that is until she heard the admiral roar with anger again. Something about Bane being underhanded and manipulative.

Karl's face was riddled with confusion, but he tentatively returned to his desk. Lydia sank back into her chair, but her gaze was still riveted on the closed door. There was more arguing, and more laughter too, and ten minutes later Bane emerged from the office looking delightfully smug and composed. All eyes were riveted on him as he ambled out of the office, flashing Lydia a wink that made her heart skip a beat as he walked past her desk.

This time he flipped her island picture upside down without her ever noticing it.

8

Lydia rested her elbows on the rope fence that kept spectators a safe distance from the dry dock. She loved coming to watch the laborers renovate old ships. Winches hauled the ship into the berth, keel blocks were set into position to keep it upright, and lines stretched to hold the vessel in place as workers set about repairing the hull. Something about watching dozens of men scrambling over the ship and securing the mighty vessel into the dry dock was an oddly comforting sight to Lydia. It was as though a tired and exhausted old warhorse was brought home to be cared for by people whose sole purpose was to make it hale and hardy once again.

She only wished there were a crew of healthy workmen who could fix her problems as easily. She had a little over a month to come up with the money to purchase her apartment and was running out of options. Even if she continued to take the piecemeal work from Bane, she would be more than two hundred dollars short.

"If your face looks any more grim, you will start frightening the children."

She recognized the voice. Bane came up alongside her, mimicking her stance by leaning his elbows against the rope fence as he gazed out at the dry dock. She should have known he would not easily be dissuaded from pestering her, but she refused to look away from the ship before her. Perhaps if she ignored him he would leave her alone.

"Please don't operate under the assumption that ignoring me will work," Bane said. "It just makes me more determined to get under your skin."

It annoyed her how easily he read her. She kept her gaze fastened on the ships and asked the question that had plagued her all afternoon. "What were you and the admiral arguing about?"

"You."

She must not have heard him correctly and whirled to look at him. "What?"

"You heard right. We were arguing because I suggested Admiral Fontaine ought to marry you."

Lydia choked on her own breath. She opened her mouth but found she was struck speechless.

"He declined, by the way. When I insisted, he became quite heated about the whole affair."

Bane turned and sat on the sagging rope fence to face her. Everything about his tone and expression was as bland as if he were talking about the price of tea. The early evening breeze ruffled his hair, giving him a decidedly boyish look. There was a youthful, almost angelic look on his stunningly handsome face, but Lydia knew the innocent expression was merely a façade.

She narrowed her eyes as anger took root. Working at the Navy Yard was the best job she had ever had, and Bane had no business toying with it. The ideas Bane was planting in the admiral's head threatened her continued employment.

"Why on earth would you suggest such a thing? The admiral has no romantic interest in me."

Bane leaned forward. "I think you should start calling him Eric."

"Why should I do that?"

"It might help humanize him. Make him seem less off-limits in your mind."

Her eyes narrowed. "He *is* off-limits. He is my employer."

"Wouldn't you rather be his wife? He is in his forties, so not too old for you to consider. And women tell me they consider him a smashing catch. Give me a month or two, and I'm sure I can make this happen, Lydia."

The suggestion was so outrageous, so inappropriate, that Lydia whirled and stormed down the pathway toward the north end of the Navy Yard. Bane always, *always* had the ability to throw her off-kilter. She had half convinced herself his bogus need for a translator was some sort of bizarre form of courtship, when in truth he was lining her up for marriage to another man! He had a lot of gall to meddle in her life that way. It was insulting too. She had been thinking of ways to let Bane down gently when he never had the least bit of interest in her. She ought to be relieved, but somehow . . . Not that it mattered. She would not trust Bane if he told her the sun rose in the east.

Bane strode to catch up with her. "Will you at least think about the idea? It has a lot of merit."

Lydia stopped, and Bane almost bumped into her. She would rather die than reveal the foolish, fledgling fantasies that had begun to take root in her mind regarding Bane, but she had to know the truth and would not settle for any more of his annoying, evasive answers.

"Everyone in the office thinks you are carrying a torch for me." There. She said it. It was much easier to lay the blame on Willis and the others than hint at the fascination she was beginning to feel for Bane. "For months you have been making up excuses to bring me nonsensical translation work," she said. "I want to know if the translation work was completely pointless and if you had another reason for wanting to see me."

He grasped her elbows, and for the first time since she had known him, he seemed to be serious. "It wasn't pointless. I can't tell you why, but I really do need those translations. And I like you, Lydia. I wouldn't try to arrange a marriage between you and Eric if I didn't."

Those words hurt. She was hesitant to look him in the eye, but she needed the truth, and she needed to be looking him square in the face when she asked him. "So . . . you have no interest in me. As a woman, I mean."

A slow, curling smile tilted up one side of Bane's mouth, making him look so deliciously wicked. "I have plenty of interest, but you are off-limits for me."

She raised her chin. "Why?"

"A long time ago I made a vow never to marry. Delightful as I find you, I'm afraid you are a temptation I am simply not allowed to pursue." Bane glanced around at the dense assortment of workmen and laborers competing for space on the narrow walkway surrounding the harbor.

"Let's go get a mug of coffee and I'll tell you what I'm planning," Bane said.

The interior of the Old Galley Coffeehouse was not as crowded as the Laughing Dragon, and they were able to find a booth facing the window overlooking the bay. They slid onto the benches, and as soon as a waiter placed two steaming mugs of coffee before them, Bane wasted no time explaining his plan.

"I want Eric Fontaine to be the next senator from the state of Massachusetts," he said bluntly. "He is wasting himself in the navy, and he knows it. All Eric cares about is overhauling the decaying navy and turning it into the world-class fleet it once was. He has been fighting that battle for a decade, and he has been losing. He will make more progress toward reaching his goal if he quits the navy and sits in the U.S. Senate. I can help him get there."

The moorings of Lydia's world tilted. "The admiral wants to leave the navy?" she gasped. Fear clenched her belly. If Admiral Fontaine left the navy, it would have implications for her job. Not many men would consent to having a woman working in a professional position, but the admiral made it plain he valued her language abilities more than her gender. Another man might not be so pragmatic.

"Yes, he is ready to launch a campaign. He will be a more competitive candidate if he is married."

Lydia drew a quick breath, stunned that she would even be considered in such a capacity. The admiral had never once, in all the years she worked for him, indicated the slightest romantic interest in her. She couldn't quite say the same for herself. Admiral Fontaine was an attractive man, and half the unmarried women in Boston had secretly harbored hopes of helping him get over the grief of having lost his wife. Lydia fingered the sturdy muslin of her skirt. "Surely he would do better with a lady from a more distinguished family."

Bane snorted. "Eric's family has been making a fortune from shipping ever since they stepped off the *Mayflower*. The Fontaine family is the closest thing America has to aristocracy, so he doesn't need a wife to prop up his pedigree. He needs a wife who will appeal to the immigrant voting blocks that make up almost thirty percent of the Massachusetts electorate." The odd half-smile was on Bane's face again. "And that is where a half-Greek, half-Turkish orphan becomes highly attractive."

She had heard stories of how manipulative Bane could be, and now she was seeing, with blinding clarity, how true the stories were. "That seems rather cold and calculating."

"I prefer to think of it as highly effective."

She swiveled in the bench to pin him with a stare. "Why do you care? What do you gain if Eric Fontaine becomes a politician?"

"I gain influence over another U.S. senator," Bane said blandly.

She blinked. "*Another* senator?"

"I helped the senators from Rhode Island and New Jersey into their current positions as well."

Lydia remembered the story Karl had told . . . something about Bane being responsible for a governor losing an election in Vermont. Then there was the time she saw him in the State House, when she overheard the governor of Massachusetts joking about a senator who was indebted to Bane. Frankly, she didn't care about Bane's motives; all she could think of was her cold, stark fear of what would happen if she lost her job.

"If the admiral resigns from the service, who would take his position at the Navy Yard?"

Bane shrugged. "They would transfer some other admiral into the position."

"And would that person be required to keep the same staff?"

"Why should you care? You can be Eric's wife by then. He is obscenely wealthy, so you certainly won't have to work."

Lydia rolled her eyes. "You said he wasn't interested in me."

"Sadly, no."

It was one thing for the admiral to decline to pursue a relationship, another to be so obstinate that his denials shook the rafters.

It was a bit off-putting, actually. "It sounded like he put up quite a fight about it."

Bane bit back a grin. "Indeed he did. I tried to sing your praises, point out your finer qualities as a woman, as a wife. He was having none of it."

Her battered pride needed a bit of propping up. "So what did you say? About my finer qualities, that is."

"I told him you have an iron jaw. That you can take a punch and keep on fighting."

Lydia's eyes widened. "And this was supposed to be complimentary to me?"

"I certainly find it attractive." He said it casually, but the way his eyes gleamed in the twilight made her believe him. She felt a curious little tug in her midsection at the way Bane was practically beaming at her.

"Well, we both know that I'm off-limits for you," she said cautiously.

"Utterly and completely."

"No matter what I do, no matter how fine my qualities, you have no interest in me."

He continued regarding her with warm approval in his eyes. "Correct. Your virtue is safe with me."

How strange that she found Bane even more appealing now she was certain he had no romantic interest in her. Yet Lydia was too practical to overlook the benefits of this new revelation. "Now that I don't need to fear your predatory interest in me, do you have any more translation work? I could use the income."

"Ah, how foolish of me to have forgotten your pecuniary tendencies. Eric alluded to your troubles in purchasing your apartment. Why don't you just find another place to live?"

How could she explain to a person like Bane the difference

between a "place to live" and a sanctuary, especially when she didn't fully understand it herself? "That apartment is my home," she said. "I love it there and I've spent years making it exactly the way I want. I feel safe at the Laughing Dragon. I don't expect you to understand."

"Let me get this straight," he said. Bane sat a little straighter, and a piercing look of concentration came over his face. "As far back as you can remember, your life has been full of chaos and instability. After you lost your parents, you were sent to an orphanage. It was hard, but everyone who came into contact with you was impressed at how well you adjusted, despite the terrible circumstances. You never complained, never cried, because you didn't even know how to express what you needed. How can one complain of not feeling secure when you had never experienced such a sensation to begin with? You grew up on a boat where the dangers for a child were appalling. Heavy anchors strewn about that could slice up bare feet, open water that could swallow a child before her parents even knew she had fallen overboard. At the orphanage you never slept soundly, because if you did there were children who would steal your blanket or rob your pockets. You felt rootless because an orphanage cannot provide the structure of a family, only a never-ending rotation of employees who come and go."

Lydia's eyes grew round as he spoke, for it was as if he were writing her biography. Bane gestured to the waiter, and their coffee mugs were refilled. "And then finally you grew up," he said as the waiter moved away. "When you earned enough money to buy a decent home for yourself, security was the only thing you truly cared about. At last you had the power to build a life *exactly* as you wanted. And you want your ink bottles arranged in a precise manner. You order the same clam chowder at the same restaurant because predictability is important to you. You savor the sensation of order and reliability because these things make you feel absolutely safe and in control of your world."

Bane drew a long sip of coffee and winced at the bitter taste. He popped a cube of sugar into the black brew and casually stirred it with a little pewter teaspoon. He looked up at her and winked. "But you are right. Someone like me probably can't understand."

Lydia stared at him, mesmerized by what she had just learned about Bane. He understood her so perfectly. Only someone who had actually experienced such a life could articulate the bone-deep exhaustion that came from years of childhood insecurity. "Did you ever live in an orphanage?" she asked quietly.

The stirring of the teaspoon stopped. Bane was motionless for the span of several seconds as he stared at a spot on the table. Lydia thought perhaps he was going to refuse to answer, but when he finally spoke, it was with his usual easy casualness.

"Just a single night," he said. "I found it was not for me." He set the teaspoon aside and took a sip of coffee.

"Then where did you go?"

"I found a wonderful family who adopted me, and I lived happily ever after."

She leaned back in her seat and folded her arms across her chest. "Liar."

He winked at her. "Well, you ought to know that about me by now."

She did. She also knew that Bane had no intention of telling her anything more about his mysterious childhood or what circumstances caused him to understand what it felt like to be alone and rootless. He opened the door a tiny sliver and just as quickly slammed it shut again.

That was okay with Lydia. Just as Bane understood her, she was learning how to read Bane. And what she discovered made him all the more fascinating in her eyes. Oh, she was certain he was as dangerous and manipulative as they came. He was a predator accustomed to operating beneath a thin veneer of civilization as he ruthlessly pursued his own agenda. But they both knew what it was to be alone in a storm-tossed world and still maintain a sense of optimism and resilience.

"You still haven't told me if you have any more translation work for me."

A look of fierce concentration came over Bane. She could almost see the wheels turning behind those crystalline blue eyes. A pang of uneasiness crept inside her at the crafty, calculating look seeping onto his face.

"On the off chance I can't persuade Eric to marry you and solve all our troubles, perhaps I can find a better use for your talents. One that will pay enough for you to buy your apartment. How much longer do you have to come up with the cash?"

"Three weeks."

Bane nodded. "This is going to take me a bit of time to work out. I need to head out of town on business, but I'll have a proposition for you when I get back." Bane stood and put a few coins on the table to pay for their coffee. "Meet me at the dry docks next Monday at the close of business. I'll have something worked out by then."

As Lydia walked home, she pulled her cloak tighter, unable to forget the fleeting look on Bane's face as he set those coins on the table. Just for a moment, he gazed at her with such yearning it nearly robbed her of breath. Then he buried it behind the glib façade he wore so well.

She knew he cared for her. No matter how cool he pretended to be, during that fleeting moment, the heat in Bane's eyes could have turned a forest to cinders.

9

As he walked through the forest, Bane heard the echo of steam drills cutting into the stone of the colossal boulders jutting up through the mossy soil of the land around Fall River. Even though granite quarries already pockmarked the terrain, the quarry workers employed by granite baron R. Ross Telenbaugh were still devouring the land, drilling holes at regular intervals, then setting off charges of dynamite to shear off walls of granite. Telenbaugh was a self-made millionaire who fought hard for every dollar he earned, which accounted for the rudimentary shack built at the crest overlooking the quarries. He never spent money where it would not earn a return, and it was from this primitive shack in the forest that Telenbaugh oversaw his granite empire. So miserly was he with his coins that he limited himself to one cigar a day, chewing on the unlit roll of tobacco leaves until after dinner, when he finally lit the tip and savored it down to the last nub.

Telenbaugh was not pleased to see Bane. "I know what you are here for," Telenbaugh said, a film of perspiration gleaming on his balding head. "I have already committed to supporting Senator Wilkinson in his reelection, so you are wasting your time here."

Bane strolled into the overseer's shack and helped himself to a chair, casually stretching his booted feet before him. "I was disappointed by Senator Wilkinson's vote on the opium measure last spring," Bane said. "I was hoping you would reconsider your financial support of the man."

Telenbaugh grabbed the unlit cigar from his mouth and fixed Bane with a stare. "Opium is a perfectly legal substance," he growled. "The government has no business interfering with what pharmacists sell in their shops, and I appreciate a man like Senator Wilkinson, who understands that point."

Opium may have been perfectly legal, but it was also a seductive poison used as an ingredient in innocent-looking preparations all across the country. Pharmacists had been resisting any attempt to rein in the sale of potions containing opium to anyone who walked into their shops, and so far, they had been winning. It was Bane's plan to put an end to it.

Bane settled a little more comfortably in his chair and smiled at Telenbaugh. "Let me repeat," he said calmly. "I was disappointed with Senator Wilkinson's vote on the opium measure and was hoping you would reconsider your support for the man."

Telenbaugh glared as he leaned across his desk and pointed a stubby finger at Bane. "I heard about what you did with that bridge to Canada last year. Don't think you can intimidate me the way you did the bridge-building crew up in Vermont. I am made of tougher stuff."

Bane knew who had been behind the proposed bridge, and it had been a delight to scuttle the Professor's plan to build a bridge that would have made smuggling opium in and out of Canada easier.

Still, he feigned a look of casual surprise for Telenbaugh's benefit. "Who said I intimidated anyone? All I did was inform the team of the governor's proposal requiring immigrants to pay additional taxes if they wished their children to attend school. Almost all of those workers came from Italy, so imagine their dismay when I told them." Bane began picking at a nonexistent speck beneath his nails. "Actually, I was quite pleased I was able to persuade the mayor of the village to work with the local unions to set up rules against that sort of thing. I was even happier when that mayor was elected to the governorship the following month."

Bane straightened to look out the tiny office window. "Are your workers members of the union? I hear rumors the Knights of Labor are thinking of organizing miners up this way." The only sign of Telenbaugh's anxiety was the tightening of his fists, and Bane's gaze went back to his nails. If Telenbaugh's workers joined a union, it could spell disaster for his operations. "It's just a rumor, though."

"What do you want?" Telenbaugh bit out.

Bane leaned forward, focusing his full attention on Telenbaugh. Admiral Fontaine couldn't publicly announce his candidacy for the seat until he resigned from the navy, but Bane wanted the path cleared to ensure an easy election.

"I want you to quit lining Senator Wilkinson's pockets," Bane said. "Tell me what *you* want from a senator, and I'll try to see that you get it. You've got two hundred men out there doing good, honest work. I won't interfere with that, so long as you quit funding the reelection of a man who is allowing thousands of pounds of opium to pump through the bodies of people too ignorant to understand what they are consuming."

Bane could tell he was getting close, because Telenbaugh picked up his cigar, reached into a drawer for a match, and lit the tip. Getting the man to light his cigar at two o'clock in the afternoon was a victory. "I could squeeze you between my two hands and mash you to a pulp," Telenbaugh said, remnants of anger starting to fade as he drew on the cigar.

Bane knew he had won. "You'd have to get in line behind the others who want the same thing. Now, tell me what you want, and I'll see how I can get it for you."

The Professor had been waiting outside the postal station for almost an hour, but the delivery expected on today's mail wagon was too important for him to lollygag at home. Not when a sixteenth-century psalter was about to be delivered into his hands.

His eyes dilated in pleasure as he accepted the package from the postmaster, and he carried his new treasure gently down the steps, across the dusty street, and into his carriage. "Move over," he instructed Boris, the hefty guard who was working a toothpick between his teeth. The Professor averted his eyes. Boris was an ungainly boor, but he had his uses.

Besides, nothing would diminish his pleasure on a day such as today. He slit the brown paper wrapping, opened the box, and extracted his treasure. The psalter was unexpectedly heavy on his lap, and he traced his fingers across the exquisite leather covering the vellum pages within. The artistry lavished on the cover indicated a love and respect for the world of books, and across the centuries, the Professor felt a link with the Renaissance nobleman who had commissioned this volume. With the care of a surgeon, the Professor opened the cover and was greeted by a revolting sight.

A postcard of a field of poppies blooming in the French countryside.

How dare he. How *dare* Bane pollute a priceless book with his petty games. Bane must have a connection with the auction house in Philadelphia, and the Professor would never do business with them again. His lips tightened and his hands curled into fists as he glared at that postcard. Was there nothing sacred? Was there no place in this world Bane's contamination did not reach?

For years his men had been trying to track down Bane, but the man never stayed in one place long enough to be caught. Clearly, that approach had failed. Perhaps he could not find and punish Bane, but he could start attacking him in a more effective manner.

The Professor's eyes narrowed and he hardened his resolve. It was going to be a costly battle, but he was willing to undergo a few losses in order to wipe the earth clean of Alexander Banebridge.

He turned to Boris. "I've had enough of that guttersnipe," he said. "I want you to find something Bane loves. And then bring it to me."

10

Lydia stood before the dry docks, huddled in her thin cloak, waiting for Bane. The cry of gulls carried on the air as the birds scavenged along the marshy banks of the Charles River. Lydia wondered if they were as cold as she. Bleak November evenings like these made those sunbaked days on Papa's fishing boat in the Mediterranean seem like another lifetime.

If Bane didn't have any more translating work, she didn't know what she would do. The idea of marrying the admiral was absurd. It was like a peasant girl aspiring to become a princess, and Lydia had no such illusions about herself. Despite the tremendous ruckus with Bane, over the past week the admiral had not changed his demeanor toward her whatsoever. He was polite, gentlemanly, and businesslike. He greeted her precisely the same way he had greeted her for the past four years, touching the corner of his eyebrow in an almost salute. "Miss Pallas," he would say with a quick nod of his head, and then walk straight into his private office.

The thought of losing her apartment was bad, but after last week's conversation with Bane, her situation was more precarious than ever. If the admiral left his position to go to Washington, she could lose her job as well.

Ever since learning the admiral might leave, Lydia battled with her nerves. A daily sip of Mrs. Winslow's Soothing Syrup eased the headache that throbbed whenever her nerves got the better of her. It was the same medicine the staff at the Crakken Orphanage used to help the children sleep. The label showed a lovely mother spooning a bit of medicine to her delightful baby. Lydia was embarrassed to rely on baby medicine, and whenever she purchased a bottle, she immediately poured the contents into one of her pretty blue bottles so she would not need to see that disturbing picture on the label. Still, Mrs. Winslow's Soothing Syrup was the only thing that had kept her headache at bay this week.

"You look frozen. What on earth possessed you to stand out in the cold with only a scrap of fabric for protection?"

She turned to see Bane looking as dashing as ever, his blond hair in sharp contrast to the rich black wool of his overcoat. Just once she longed to mess up that exquisite blond perfection. "I've been waiting for you," she said through chattering teeth.

Without a word he shrugged out of his coat and dropped it over her shoulders. The heavy wool was deliciously warm from his body's heat and carried a trace of pine-scented soap. For a moment she allowed herself to bask in the comfort it provided. It was more than just the coat's warmth . . . it was the casual way he tossed it to her without a second thought. Lydia was unaccustomed to someone looking out for her, and it was oddly comforting.

"Let's go get something hot inside you," Bane said as he headed toward the Old Galley Coffeehouse. It took a few minutes for the warmth inside the coffeehouse to thaw her out, but the clam chowder was delicious. "Your trip went well?" she asked. It would be bad-mannered to demand translation work right away.

"More or less," he said. "Go ahead and ask me if I have any translation work for you."

Lydia grinned as she spooned another mouthful of chowder down. "And spoil your fun of making me wait for the answer? I'm too considerate for that."

He flashed her his scoundrel's smile. "Fine, I'll make you wait, then." He leaned back in his seat and contemplated her, his calculating blue eyes assessing her for some unknown reason. "Do you know where most of the poppies in the world are grown?" he finally asked.

Lydia had spent her entire life on either a boat or living along a busy city's harbor, so she knew virtually nothing about plants. "I have no idea."

"Turkey. India. North Africa. The opium's sent to Turkey for processing, then shipped throughout the rest of the world for consumption."

Lydia broke off a piece of her bread and used it to scrape the remaining bit of soup in her bowl. "Oh," she said, since Bane seemed to be waiting for some sort of response. "Do you suppose there is any more chowder?" she asked. Normally she would never want to appear so vulgar by shoveling down a second bowl of soup, but she felt perfectly at ease with Bane. Besides, he could practically read her mind anyway, so there was no point in feigning ladylike refinement.

Bane snagged the barkeep's attention and signaled for another bowl of chowder. "I disapprove of the opium trade," he said casually. "Every city in this country has disgusting illegal opium dens where people smoke themselves into a mindless stupor. They become useless to their families or themselves. What is even worse is the legal trade, where pharmacies sell syrups that have opium blended into them to unsuspecting customers who spoon it down their children's throats, even their pets'."

Lydia was only half listening as she watched the barkeep slide a second delicious bowl of steaming chowder in front of her. The fragrance of freshly ground pepper and smoked bacon rose from the bowl, and she closed her eyes in delight as she savored a spoonful.

"Mm-hum . . ." she said, wondering precisely when he was going to bring the subject around to translating work.

"I want a certain set of laws enacted, and the best way to do that is to put people in office who are friendly to my cause." Bane turned, and the cold, ruthless expression on his face almost stopped her heart. "I will work toward that goal for the rest of my life, but I'm not willing to wait for the laws to be changed. That could take decades. I know who controls the illegal opium routes in this country, but I need to find out who his suppliers are. I want to choke the problem off at its source."

Bane went on to explain that opium was cheap to produce, but the American government stamped a ten-dollar tax on every pound shipped into the country, almost quadrupling the price. That meant greedy men were eager to smuggle the drug to avoid those taxes. Smugglers sold the cheap opium to be blended into medicines sold in pharmacies all across the nation. It was because of the illegal opium trade that the medicines sold in pharmacists' shops were so inexpensive.

She wrapped her suddenly cold fingers around her bowl of soup, seeking the warmth of the hot pottery, unaccustomed to seeing this earnest, serious side of Bane. "And where does my translating fit into this?"

"For over a year, I've known that Boston is now the major port on the East Coast through which opium is being smuggled, and I want it stopped. The ships carrying the smuggled opium use code words in their shipping records. Those shipping records would point me to the American smugglers who are transporting the opium. I need someone who can read those documents. Someone who reads Greek, Turkish, and Albanian. I have a contact inside the Custom House who has been collecting those documents for me, and I've been funneling them to you as I get them. I need to move faster. I want you to come with me into the Custom House down by the central wharves, and we will go office by office looking for the person who is smuggling the opium. So this won't be a conventional translation job. The hours are terrible, the work is unpleasant, and it might be a tiny bit dangerous. But it pays well."

If he had suggested he wanted her to join the navy, she could not have been more surprised. It sounded risky and frightening and completely outside her comfort zone. "You want us to *break in* to the Custom House?"

"Please, credit me with a little more sophistication than that," Bane said. "I am friendly with someone on the evening cleaning staff. He will let us in."

Lydia's jaw dropped. "Is this kind of thing legal?"

"Cleaning offices? Of course it is."

"But you are suggesting looking at records on people's desks, in their files."

He pierced her with that blue gaze, assessing her. "Lydia, sometimes there is a difference between things that are legal and things that are moral. I'm looking for smugglers, that's all. Most of the opium in the market is being brought in by a smuggler working in the Boston Custom House. Trying to find him is a worthy goal."

He continued to outline how the operation would work. All ships arriving from overseas had a cargo list in their native language. As soon as a ship pulled in to port, an American cargo inspector created an English-language inventory of everything as it was offloaded. Copies of both documents were supplied to Custom House officials for the proper collection of taxes. Any discrepancies between the original foreign cargo list and the English inventory would likely reflect smuggled goods.

Usually Bane was a relentless flirt. He teased her mercilessly and swaggered about with a confidence that was oddly endearing. But tonight he was different. His face was tightly earnest as he leaned across the table toward her, and it was hard not to get swept up in his enthusiasm. Although Lydia admired adventurers and risk takers, she had always walked a very safe path in life.

The question she wanted to ask Bane was so intrusive, so terribly personal, and entirely none of her business . . . and yet, given what Bane was asking her to do, she had a right to know. "Were you addicted to opium?" she asked. "Is that why it is so important to you?"

A bleak smile tilted the corner of his mouth, but his eyes were infinitely sad. "No. I wish my involvement was that innocent." He drew a heavy breath and kept his gaze locked on hers. "I care because for years I was one of the worst opium smugglers in the country."

Lydia's eyes widened. She was shocked by his confession, but Bane was not finished speaking. "The illegal opium trade in this country is controlled by a man named Professor Van Bracken. I became associated with him when I was very young, and he taught me everything he knew."

Lydia felt like a steel vise was wrapped around her chest, and she found it hard to breathe. Bane had suddenly become a stranger, and it frightened her. "Why are you telling me this?"

As if he sensed her fear, he leaned across the table and met her gaze. "I'm not that person anymore," he said urgently. "I learned that salvation is possible, even for a nasty sinner like me. I learned I had the freedom to make a choice about what sort of person I wanted to be." He gave an ironic smile that was more of a grimace than a smile. "Since the hour I became a Christian, the sun has not set on a single day in which I have not schemed or worked or fought to unravel the damage I have done in this country."

Lydia had always thought Bane seemed a little more devilish than angelic, but he was unabashed and sincere as he spoke. "I was as foul and as rotten as they come," he continued. "I was one of those vicious children who would have stolen your blanket while you slept in the orphanage. I was still an adolescent when I learned how to smuggle opium, and I latched on to it like a dog clamps down on a piece of meat. I was *proud* of my association with the Professor and how fast I rose in the world. By the time I was sixteen, I was making more money than the mayor of Boston. I had more power too. I controlled an army of henchmen to intimidate people and make them obey me. Sometimes I preferred to carry out the dirty work myself. People tended to underestimate me because of my size, but I unfurled a reign of terror on whatever city I had business in, and I loved every moment of it."

Bane's beautiful face suddenly looked older, haggard even. "I'm telling you this so you can understand why destroying the opium trade is so important to me," he said. "When I look in the slum houses and see drooling opium addicts, I blame myself. I was the one who distributed that poison. I was the one who terrorized innocent people so I could smooth the way for my own business."

"Surely you can't blame yourself for all the vices of opium."

His smile was bleak. "I'm not sure you appreciate just how very effective I was in my life of crime." His voice lowered, and that aching sadness was back in his eyes. His voice was soft and full of pain. "Lydia, because of the horror I caused as a young man, I will be doing penance for the rest of my life."

The flirtatious, irreverent scoundrel was gone, and Lydia's heart squeezed at the sorrow in Bane's voice. Now she understood the motivation behind Bane's relentless drive, but what could a single individual do to stamp out such a massive trade? It would be like fighting against the incoming tide each morning.

Suddenly, she was envious of Bane. What must it feel like to be so wholly committed to a cause? To have a purpose that meant her life made a difference in the world? If she joined forces with Bane, she would be working toward a goal larger than herself. Something meaningful and lasting and good.

And yet, a niggling sense of insecurity still plagued her. "Bane, I have a contract with the landlord of my apartment. If I don't live up to it, I will be evicted."

"How much do you need to buy your apartment?"

"I need another two hundred dollars within the month."

"You'll have it. Work with me each night this week, and by the end of it, I'll see you have enough to buy your home."

It was a gamble, and Lydia had never been a big fan of gambling. If it was within her power, she would spend her days in the safety of her Navy Yard job, and the rest of her time in the familiar, cozy little box of her apartment. But the only way she could hang on to her home at the Laughing Dragon was by taking a risk, and she was going to do it.

11

The Custom House was a splendid neoclassical building sitting at the base of the Long Wharf. Fluted columns stretched across the front of a building capped by an immense dome, and Lydia was in awe as she stepped inside the rotunda. The marble floors, magnificent dome, arching Palladian windows . . . all around her was evidence of the fortune Boston earned from its maritime history as the premier port in America. "It's splendid," she whispered, her voice echoing in the darkened interior.

"You don't need to whisper," Bane said as he walked beside her. "We are just here to help the evening cleaners dispose of some trash."

She still felt like a thief in the night. It helped that the real cleaner, whom Bane introduced as Joe Durning, opened the door for them and was now busily pushing a mop across the marble floors.

"We'll take care of the trash collection in the east wing, Joe," Bane said as he flashed a wink at the man.

She followed Bane across the rotunda and into the eastern wing that housed the offices for the cargo inspectors. Bane headed into the first office and took a seat behind the desk. "Pull up a chair and let me show you how this works."

The first thing he did was poke through the wastebasket. "I'm looking for letters or anything that might suggest blackmail or bribery. Someone in this building is being paid to look the other way while the opium is shipped in."

But this particular wastebasket contained nothing but two apple cores and a copy of the *Boston Post*. Lydia understood that looking at the contents of a wastebasket was not illegal, but she grew less comfortable when Bane started riffling through the unknown custom official's desk.

Bane showed her the difference between a bill of lading, cargo insurance forms, and a ship's manifest documents. He showed her the various stamps used on each of the forms. When she had agreed to this job, Lydia did not realize she would be getting an education on maritime recordkeeping, but Bane told her this would expedite their work. "I need you to start going through these stacks for anything that resembles a bill of lading. Set aside anything in a language you can read."

They worked by the light of two lanterns. After several hours, all they had found were three bills of lading, one from Turkey and two from Italy. None of them contained the sort of information Bane was interested in. As dreary as the work was, the hours flew by. They pulled open drawers of filing cabinets, and now that Lydia knew what sort of forms she should be looking for, she was able to start on her own drawer.

Lydia grasped the work quickly, which didn't surprise Bane, since she had one of the sharpest minds he'd ever encountered. She fascinated him . . . a woman whose life had been as chaotic and rootless as his own, yet she had remained pure. Her relentless sense of buoyancy was magnetic. He liked simply being near her, soaking up some of her clean, radiant optimism.

"How was it your family ended up in Sicily?" he asked.

Lydia shrugged. "Papa said it was because Mama was a Turk. He always said it with a huge smile, like he was trying to get a rise out of her. She, of course, said it was because Papa's singing was so bad no one could tolerate us."

Lydia replaced a file and withdrew another. "Looking back on things, I think it had a lot to do with money. Sometimes we left in the middle of the night, usually on days when Papa had a big argument with men on the pier. I knew we were poor, but we never went hungry. Most of my birthdays and Christmases came and went without gifts, but Papa could always make me feel so special on those days. He would pick out a constellation in the stars and make up a story in which I was always the heroine. He would talk about how I slew a dragon or rescued a kingdom. For weeks I would gaze at that constellation and think about the story he made up for me. Other kids might have had toys and fancy clothes, but who else had stories written about them in the stars?"

Her eyes, illuminated by the dim light of the lamp, were haunting in their loveliness. Lydia was remembering something magical, while Bane thought the story rather sad.

"What about you?" she asked suddenly. "I am an open book, but you never tell me anything about yourself."

"What do you want to know?" he asked cautiously.

"Where were you born? Let's start there."

That seemed harmless enough. "San Francisco. I don't remember much about it. I was . . . taken away . . . when I was only six."

"What do you mean, 'taken away'?"

The memory of his mother's screams still haunted him, but he kept his face impassive. "My stepfather was mixed up in the opium trade from China," he said. "I never knew anything about that at the time; to me, he was just a hard, angry man my mother feared. One day a bigger drug lord tried to buy him out, and my stepfather refused. A week later I was snatched out from my mother's arms as she was shopping for fish at the market. Two men walked up to us and grabbed me. One of them threw me over his shoulder and took off running. I remember turning my head up to look back at my mother. One of the men shoved her to the ground. She staggered to her feet and kept running after us, but she had blood on her face and on the palms of her hands. She was reaching out and screaming my name."

Lydia's eyes were round with horror, but he felt compelled to finish. "That was the last time I ever saw my mother. I was put on a train and sent to Vermont, where the Professor kept me holed up in his mansion. He sent notes to my stepfather, threatening to send me back in a coffin if my stepfather didn't comply. That is the way the Professor works. He kidnaps someone of value to force compliance among his enemies. It tends to be very effective."

Bane's early months at the mansion in Vermont had been horrible because he couldn't stop thinking of his mother's terror-stricken face. He had been desperate to get home so he could make sure her hands were bandaged, the blood wiped from her face. She had always tended to him when he was hurt, and he needed to do the same for her. He had begged, pleaded, thrown tantrums. When his rages had grown so loud they disturbed the Professor, the cook fed him opium-laced tea until he was pacified. He had hated that tea. It was sickeningly sweet, and he knew there was something wrong with it. So he had taught himself to control his rages. On the inside he had been screaming, but on the outside he had projected an entirely calm appearance. The ability to mask his emotions had served him well ever since.

"How long were you kept there?"

"Eleven years."

Lydia gasped and dropped the file. "How is such a thing possible? Didn't your parents comply with the demands?"

Bane shrugged. "For a while, but eventually I began ingratiating myself with the Professor. I found him fascinating. My stepfather was a bully who raged and gave his temper free rein. The Professor never did. He always treated me kindly, or it least it appeared so to me. I noticed how all the servants seemed to fear him, and I wanted to earn his approval. Over time, the Professor decided to keep me and dump my father. He raised me as his own son."

Lydia's eyes were huge pools of sadness. "So that was how you got mixed up in living a life of crime?"

Bane hated, absolutely *hated* talking about those years, but she needed to hear about it. He had noticed the way Lydia looked at him with a blend of amusement and fascination in her eyes. Were he ever free to pursue a woman, Lydia Pallas would be the first, last, and only woman he would be interested in, but it was pointless to even dream about it. Lydia was too priceless to entangle in his dangerous world.

"Over time, the Professor's trust in me grew. He wanted me in the room while he planned his strategy. He educated me in the ways of banking, trade routes, political networks. He encouraged me to study history and literature so I could pass myself off as a gentleman. From the time I was twelve years old he paid me a salary, just like his other chief lieutenants. By the time I was a teenager I was carrying out tasks for him in Boston and New York."

Bane had made only one halfhearted bid to escape. When he was fourteen he toyed with the idea of making it on his own. He dodged away into the streets of Philadelphia and tried to go honest. It was the first time he had known what it meant to go hungry, and he had sought shelter in an orphanage simply to get a hot meal. Lining up with a passel of bratty children for a bowl of soup taught Bane to appreciate what he had with the Professor. The Professor treated him like a man and gave him a sense of purpose. Bane had been too young to begin making it on his own, so he had returned to the Professor, who welcomed him back into his corrupt fold.

"The Professor taught me how to build alliances, play one group off the other," Bane continued. "What he never saw coming was that I would find salvation. From that day forward, my whole world turned on its axis. When I began to live for a purpose beyond my own vicious ambition, I saw a glimpse of pure joy and I wanted more." He told Lydia of a woman named Clara who, even though he sinned against her time and again, refused to give up on him.

He dragged a hand through his hair, remembering those first, panic-filled months as he tried to make a getaway. "The Professor didn't just let me walk away. I knew how his operations worked, the names of all his connections. He put a price on my head, and for years I was the most sought-after man in the country. It was an uncomfortable life at first. I never stayed more than a single night in any location. I changed my name a dozen times. I was always on the move, always looking over my shoulder."

What Bane did not add was that in those first few weeks he had succeeded in liquidating two of the Professor's largest bank accounts, one in Atlanta, and the other in Richmond. Bane had had no idea what he would do with the money. Spending it on himself was not an option. The money was tainted with opium and the blood of innocents. Bane had moved the money to several secure accounts and let it accumulate until the day when he would be powerful enough to begin using it to fund his crusade. It was a beautiful irony that the Professor's own money was now being used to fuel the political candidacy of men Bane wanted to see in office.

He continued by telling Lydia how he landed at the feet of Rachel Fontaine and that her kindness had made it possible for Bane to make a clean escape from the country by joining the navy. He became Admiral Fontaine's most trusted associate as he worked overseas, gathering information on foreign naval technology and sending it back to Boston. All the while he had been plotting to someday take down the Professor.

"What was she like?" Lydia asked. "The admiral's wife?"

How could he possibly describe Rachel Fontaine? So many people underestimated Rachel because of her kindness, but Bane never did. The woman had a backbone and a moral compass that were awe-inspiring. "She gave me the chance to prove I was more than a vicious criminal," Bane said. "After I met Rachel, I was put in a uniform and given a chance to earn an honest dollar. Can you imagine what that felt like?"

He told her how he sought out the naval chaplain onboard ship and learned more about his new faith. At each of the dozens of ports where his ship docked, he looked for churches and saw how fellow believers practiced their faith in France, India, and Egypt. The architecture was different, and the music sounded odd, but the timeless thread of the sacred that echoed through the millennia was present everywhere he went. Each church was like an oasis in the desert, transporting him to a place that was pure and holy.

Bane looked over at Lydia. Suddenly, it became very important for him to know if she had the same sort of blessing that Clara had shared with him. "What about you, Lydia? You never mention religion."

She fidgeted a little. "No. It has never been a part of my life."

"Why is that?"

He had asked the question softly, but she still seemed a bit flustered as she went back to sorting through the stack of papers in her lap. "The closest thing I ever got to real training in religion was my father's superstitions." A hint of a blush tinged Lydia's cheeks. "Papa used to say that if you made a wish under the light of a full moon, it was bound to come true."

"Tell me you didn't really . . ."

She shrugged a little hopelessly. "Some of my best memories of Papa are standing on the deck of our boat when the moon was at its very brightest. He would wake me up so we could each make a wish. We were supposed to face the north while we appealed to Artemis, goddess of the moon. He always wished for wild, fabulous things—to pull up a mermaid in our nets or find some long-abandoned pirate loot. I was more practical. I wished for a new pair of shoes or the chance to go to school. I know it sounds foolish, but nights with a full moon still feel very special to me."

He slanted her a glance. "Lydia, do you still go out and pray to a full moon?"

"Are you going to make fun of me if I do?"

His smile grew wider. "Count on it."

"Then have at it." She went back to flipping through the papers in her file, unable to meet his eyes but grinning broadly. "Yes, I go out on each full moon. Always. I still face the north and simply pray a little bit. Not to Artemis or to Jesus or anyone specific. . . . It just feels good to believe *someone* is out there listening."

She pulled out a document. "This looks like a bill of lading, yes?" By the way Lydia had gone back to sorting the stack on her lap, it was obvious to Bane that she was not open to any more talk of religion.

He looked at the paper she held and saw it was in Greek. "Yes. What does it say?"

He watched as her intelligent eyes made quick work of the document. "It's about some sort of cheese," she said.

Bane straightened. Any mention of an agricultural product could be code for cakes of opium. "What kind of cheese?" he asked. "I need to know precisely."

"It says they are shipping *ladotyri*, and it is to be stored in caskets filled with olive oil to preserve it during the crossing," she said.

Opium would never be stored in olive oil. "It's useless," he said. "Let's keep looking."

Lydia looked at him curiously. "The bill of lading says *ladotyri* is a cheese made from sheep and goat's milk. I didn't know they could get milk from sheep. I thought all milk came from cows."

"What do you think lambs suckle from their mothers?"

Lydia shrugged. "I have no idea. I've never seen a lamb. Or a cow, for that matter. I assume they live on farms, but I've never seen a farm."

Bane was aghast. "You live in one of the richest agricultural countries in the world, and you are telling me you have never seen a farm?"

"Where would I have seen a farm, Bane? I lived on a fishing boat until I was nine, and then in an orphanage in the middle of Boston. No farms there."

He covered his mouth to stifle the laughter. "You realize how pathetic that sounds, don't you?"

She tried to look affronted, but she was laughing too hard. And then the look in her eyes changed. It was like watching a playful kitten turn into a hunting panther. "Why don't you take me out to the countryside?" she said. "It would be an act of charity to show a poor city lass the splendor of wild America."

He knew she was scheming something in that clever half-Turkish, half-Greek brain of hers, but it was hard to resist. "Why would I want to do that?"

"Why, to correct this shocking void in my education," she said.

"Now that you have pointed out my howling ignorance, it would be cruel to leave me in this educational deficit."

He watched the way her eyes fairly glittered and her foot tapped out a steady rhythm as she awaited his answer. Truly, if he wanted to correct her ignorance, he would train her not to reveal her thoughts so easily as she planned her little scheme. Her foot tapping was a dead giveaway she was up to something. But really, he was too enchanted and curious to see what she had up her sleeve.

"Never seen a cow . . ." he murmured in warm disapproval. "I'll pick you up on Saturday morning, then. Wear something sturdy."

12

It was a glorious Indian summer day, one of those rare days in early November when the cold lifted and the sky was so intensely blue it reminded Lydia of the Mediterranean Sea. As Bane drove the carriage, she devoured the sight of trees swathed in their autumn shades of crimson and bright, shocking yellow. Every now and then a gust of wind sent leaves swirling through the air. Since arriving at the docks at the age of nine, Lydia had never set foot outside the city limits of Boston, and the countryside was beautiful. She would be dazzled if she weren't so nervous.

For what she intended to do today was the riskiest, most foolhardy and shocking thing she had ever contemplated. Lydia had decided she wanted Alexander Banebridge, and she intended to get him.

Sometime during that long night in the Custom House she had grown sure of it. Who else understood her so completely? Bane discerned each of her idiosyncrasies, and still he seemed to admire her. And she was so tired of being alone. When she was with Bane, she could be utterly and totally herself. Despite the easy camaraderie they shared, he was still breathtakingly exciting to her. He was like a meteor, blazing across her world, leaving everything cold and dark when he left.

So today she intended to tell him how she felt. She could hardly do that at the Navy Yard with Willis and the others looking on. Nor did she want to do it when she had a lap full of translation work piled between them. This was the perfect opportunity to get away from her job and let him see her as a woman.

The first thing she needed to do was banish his ridiculous notion of her marrying Admiral Fontaine. As the open carriage bounced along a rutted country lane, she turned to look at him. "Have you found a suitable fiancée for Admiral Fontaine?" she asked him casually, though her hand was tightly fisted around the rail of the carriage bench.

He slanted her a look. "I presume that means you are no longer interested?"

"I never was, Bane."

He pretended a heavy sigh. "I thought as much. Which is a shame, because it would have been the perfect political alliance, but both of you appear to be shockingly resistant to the idea. Not very logical of you, but I tried my best."

The carriage rounded the corner, a view of rolling countryside displayed before her eyes. A white fence enclosed a huge expanse of land, most of which was an apple orchard. Bane leaned over and whispered in her ear. "Your first sight of a farm, love."

It was a pretty scene, and her gaze devoured the sight of apple trees lined up over the rolling hills. The breeze picked up, carrying the scent of autumn leaves and newly cut grass. The bucolic landscape was probably commonplace to someone as well-traveled as Bane, but to her it was a picture of such loveliness that she felt an odd lump in her throat. A sense of well-being flooded her, and the moment seemed infinitely precious, even more so because she was seeing it with Bane at her side. As always, he seemed to sense her mood.

"Don't go getting all mushy on me yet," he said. "If an apple orchard can do this to you, just imagine what is going to happen when you catch your first real sight of a cow." They continued to lazily make their way down the rutted country lane, the carriage gently rocking them from side to side. Wasn't this what normal people did? People who had families and someone to love them? They went out into the country for a pleasant drive, and if she closed her eyes, she could almost imagine that she and Bane were a pair of young lovers. They would be free to laugh and tease one another. Her fears and insecurities would not seem so overwhelming if she had someone like Bane to help her laugh them away.

She smelled the dairy farm before she saw it. As Bane pulled the carriage to the side of the country lane she could see the cows grazing in the field. From a distance they looked nice enough. Tranquil, even. But she had no desire to get any closer until Bane sprang down from the carriage and held his hand out to her.

"Hop on down, love."

Goodness, she was putty in his hands when he was gentlemanly to her. Usually he was such a wretch, so she got all soft and malleable at the least little kindness. He helped her out of the carriage, then held her hand as she stepped over the low fence to walk across the field toward the cows.

"Watch where you place your feet," he warned after a few steps into the field.

Lydia hoisted her skirt as she walked. "I think this is close enough," she said after going only a few yards. The cows were huge. The size, the smell . . . everything was a little more overwhelming than she anticipated. But Bane strode ahead of her, and not for a treasure chest of rubies would she let on that she found the huge beasts intimidating. There were no fangs or claws on the cows, so what damage could they do?

One of them swung its large head toward her, causing her to feel momentary shock. But when she looked into those huge, liquid eyes, she saw no ferocity, no sense of invasion, so she took another cautious step forward. Really, the beast must be five times her size, simply massive. Then it made an awful bullhorn noise and lumbered toward her.

She yelped. She picked up her skirts and ran, springing over cow pies and around stacks of hay before she reached the low fence and scrambled over. Bane howled with laughter behind her. "Lydia, you can't . . . you can't be afraid of a cow." He could barely get the words out, he was laughing so hard.

"Never underestimate me," she said. "That thing is terrifying."

"Almost as horrifying as the bunnies in the hutch over there." He faked a little shudder.

"You know, Bane, for a moment there I actually thought this was going to be a nice afternoon. That you had undergone a miraculous transformation and were prepared to behave like a gentleman."

"Sorry, Lydia. You handed me the perfect opportunity to tease you, and it would be wrong to do anything other than grasp it with both hands."

He sat on the fence and swung one leg over, then the other. He stood less than an arm's length from her, looking flushed with sunlight and joy and laughter. Behind him the sky was a startling shade of blue, and the day was perfect. She locked gazes with him, took a step closer, near enough so that a deep breath would bring their bodies into contact. And she waited.

A knowing gleam came over Bane's face. He scanned her eyes, her face, and the narrow gap that divided them. "Well, if you are sure about passing on the admiral . . ." He cupped her face in both his hands, drew her closer, and laid a gentle kiss on her mouth.

She wanted to sink into him. The way he cradled her face between his palms was so tender, making her feel cherished. After a moment, he lifted his head and peered down at her.

"I don't want the admiral. I want you," she said simply.

A flicker of unease crossed his face. "You know I'm not a good long-term bet, don't you?"

"I am not sure what that means."

A gust of wind blew a tendril of her hair into her face, and Bane stroked it back. The sensation of his fingers caressing her brow sent shivers through her entire frame. "It means that I think the world of you, but I'm not the sort who will ever settle down and get married."

Lydia smiled. "Bane, it was a kiss. Not a marriage proposal." But the sense of exhilaration that flowed through her made her step closer into the circle of his arms. She could happily stand here until they both grew old and gray.

He cocked an eyebrow at her, rakish eyes still peering intently at her. "You sure about that?"

Her heart raced and nervous laughter threatened to spill out and choke her, but she wouldn't back down now. She affected a casual tone. "I know someone of your shocking good looks must fend off women daily, so I forgive your assumption, but I don't want to marry Admiral Fontaine, and I'm not looking for a marriage proposal from you either." She looked into those blue eyes and felt her knees melt a bit. Hopeless infatuation would make a terrible basis for a marriage, and she would never know if these feelings could grow into something more substantial unless he allowed her to break through the amused tolerance he wore like armor.

She continued. "Think of the upside for you, Bane. It is mortifying for me to be involved with someone so much prettier than myself." Bane's eyes widened in amusement, and, was it possible that he was actually blushing? Yes, there was just the tiniest trace of flush across those beautifully sculpted cheekbones.

"Good heavens, I think I've actually rendered you speechless," she said. Bane still said nothing; he just kept running his fingers across her hairline while his eyes devoured her face. "Can't we just take this one day at a time?" she finally said.

He cupped her face in his hands again, and the way he gazed down at her completely enthralled her. His thumb was gentle as he stroked the corner of her mouth.

"I will probably regret this later," Bane said as he dipped his head and kissed her again. "But for now this feels right," he murmured against the side of her face.

Lydia leaned into him and smiled. At least for now, she had Bane.

He should be taken out and shot at dawn for dallying with Lydia like this, but for once in his life Bane felt like a normal member of the human race. From the time he was six years old he had been an outsider, a loner, but for a few hours this afternoon he had a companion in this world.

He found a pond where he stretched a blanket and brought out a basket lunch. Perhaps he shouldn't feel so guilty. Hadn't Lydia said she had no serious intentions toward him? That meant he was free to indulge in a delightful flirtation and no one was in danger of being hurt. For a few weeks he could let down his guard and enjoy her company. When the time came for him to leave Boston, he would turn off whatever emotion he felt for Lydia and never look back.

He opened the picnic basket, pleased he had been able to find something Greek in her honor. “Some authentic Greek cheese,” he said as he unloaded the basket of its bread, fruit, and a round of cheese.

“I don’t think I’ve ever had Greek cheese,” she confessed. “It sounds a little too exotic for the Laughing Dragon.”

“It seems odd that a person as well traveled as you is so inexperienced,” Bane said. “Never seen a cow, never been in the countryside . . .”

Lydia shrugged. “In case it escaped your notice, I am a *woman*, Bane. There are some limitations on what I am permitted to do in this world.”

He opened his pocketknife and cut off a corner of the cheese. “So tell me what you would do with your life if you were a man.”

Lydia took a little bite, her nose wrinkling at the pungent flavor as she considered the question. “I would like to be a great explorer like Lewis and Clark,” she finally said. “No one has ever been to the North Pole, although Karl tells me the Norwegians are trying.” She gazed into the distance, and Bane knew her dreams were carrying her a thousand miles away. “Just think what it would be like to challenge yourself like that. To keep raising the stakes until you don’t know if your mind and body can handle even another hour of what you are asking of it. I would like the chance to test myself like that.”

This was what he adored about Lydia: a rare optimism and a willingness to reach out with both hands toward any challenge thrown her way. “Why would that be important to you?” he asked.

She paused for a moment. “I suppose I want my life to mean something. I know the admiral appreciates my work. And it is important work, I realize that. But if I were not here to do it, he could hire someone else to fill my position. I want to do something that *no one else can do*.” She paused and her brow furrowed a bit. “Does that make me terribly conceited?”

Although Lydia did not possess a conceited bone in her body, Bane suppressed a grin because he knew her question was serious. "Actually, it makes you rather irresistible in my eyes—but then again, I always hanker after impossible challenges, so perhaps I'm not the best judge."

Lydia tore a piece of bread and offered it to him. "Of course, I have no sense of direction and would surely get lost if I tried to be an explorer, so I should probably choose some other endeavor to make my mark on the world."

Bane reached inside his pocket and retrieved the small flat disk. Without a second thought he pressed it into her hands. "There. Now you have no excuse."

Lydia looked surprised as she opened the cover to reveal a compass. "I want you to always be able to find whatever you are looking for," he said simply. She seemed flattered, if her gorgeous blush was any indication. He'd had an impulsive desire to give her something nice, and his compass was the only thing he had on him. Not the most conventional of gifts, but then again, there was nothing conventional about Lydia Pallas. He closed her hand around the compass. "I want you to have it," he said, looking deeply into her eyes. "Who knows when I'll have to waltz out of your life, and I want you to have something to remember me by."

"Thank you, Bane," she said as she glowed with pleasure. He wondered if this might be the first actual gift Lydia had ever been given. Not a story written in the stars by her father or the peppermint sticks that were handed out to all the orphans on Christmas morning, but an actual, tangible gift from someone who cared about her. The look on Lydia's face as she gazed at the simple compass showed she was as delighted by it as another woman would be by a stash of diamonds.

A shift in the breeze blew a cloud of leaves into the air. Lydia blinked as a fragment of dust must have gotten in her eye. She dabbed at it with her finger, but it was useless. "Bane, there is a handkerchief in my bag. Will you fetch it for me?"

He opened her reticule and handed her the little square of cloth. While she attempted to remove the speck, Bane stared at the contents of her bag. There was almost nothing inside except for a few coins and a little blue bottle. He lifted it out and held it to the light, noting the dark color and syrupy thickness of the liquid.

"Much better. Thank you," she said.

She reached for her reticule, but Bane held the blue bottle in the sunlight. "What is this?" he asked casually.

"Oh, that is my headache medicine. I need it occasionally."

She took it from his hand and replaced it in her bag. She grabbed a handful of grapes and plucked a few free, but the image of that blue bottle was seared in his brain. He forced his tone to remain casual. "What is in it?"

Lydia finished chewing her grape. "I have no idea, but it works. It is the same medicine I always used growing up. Mrs. Winslow's Syrup. They used it in the orphanage."

Lord help me. It was the worst thing she could have said, and his entire body seized with tension. Without conscious thought, he grabbed the bottle from her bag, shot to his feet, and hurled it into the pond with all the force in his body. The bottle landed in the water with a splat, sending a ring of ripples across the pond.

"What are you doing? I paid good money for that!"

"It's poison," he bit out.

"Don't be ridiculous," Lydia said. "It's just a headache tonic. It is made for babies."

He despised listening to people defend the vile tonics, but he reined in his emotions. Lydia might be completely innocent of what made the syrup so wickedly effective, and he watched her carefully. "How often do you take it?"

If her glare was any measure, she was still angry, but she stood up and answered him. “Not often. Sometimes at work I get a pounding headache, and it is soothing.”

“How often?” he demanded. He could tell she did not like his sharp tone, but this was too important to ignore.

“Maybe once a week. Never more than that.”

He studied her expression, the way her eyes did not shift or waver. He could not be sure, but he did not *think* she was lying. A bit of the tension drained away. If Lydia was addicted to opium, she would be taking it far more often.

He drew a ragged breath, but his emotions were still stormy. “I’m sorry I snapped,” he said. “But you need to understand that Mrs. Winslow’s Syrup is one of the *worst* drugs you could put in your body. I have been trying for years to get it banned because it is marketed to teething babies. It’s opium, Lydia. You can’t play around with that.”

Her eyes widened in surprise. “Opium! Are you sure?”

“Dead certain.”

“They gave it to us at the orphanage whenever we felt bad or couldn’t sleep. I’ve never been the worse for it.”

Her words cut him. All over the country, people gave opium to children to lull them into slack-jawed compliance when they were fussy or rambunctious. Orphanages were especially prone to abusing the drug, and the thought of Lydia Pallas, an abandoned child without a friend in the world, lined up to have opium spooned down her throat made him want to smash something.

“Then you dodged a bullet,” he said. “You can’t keep on dosing yourself with this, even if it is only a few times a month. Don’t take it again.”

Little waves still rippled across the surface of the pond where he had flung her bottle. There was no room to argue about this with him. Opium was a corrosive poison that could leach into a person's system and hold her captive before she was ever aware there was a problem.

"All right," she said calmly. "I won't use it ever again." Her face softened and she took a cautious step closer to him, her eyes open and honest. "It is not a problem for me, Bane."

He touched the flawless perfection of her cheek. Lydia was a woman of such unblemished strength and courage it humbled him to even stand in her presence. "I care about you," he said reluctantly. Never in his life had he let a woman get this close to him, and it was a perplexing feeling. He wanted to laugh and indulge her, but more important, he needed to protect her. "I can't look the other way. It could kill you, Lydia."

His arms closed about her and she returned his embrace. The wind swirled around them and it felt like they were the only two people in the world. He pressed the side of his face against her soft hair. In some puzzling way he could not begin to understand, he felt bonded to her, as though he'd known her his entire life, even as she felt new and exciting to him.

He was playing with fire by allowing himself to get close to Lydia, but for once in his life, Bane did not care.

13

On Sunday morning, Bane remained in the church after the other congregants had left. Quiet minutes on his knees helped keep him humble, and it was the position from which he wanted to give thanks for the forgiveness he had been extended. He lowered his head in prayer and asked the same question he had been asking every day for the last ten years. *Lord, how might I undo the damage I have brought into your world? How can I rid the world of the scourge of opium?*

Lydia's image rose in his mind, and he blanched at the thought she might be addicted to opium. From the moment he saw the bottle in her handbag, he could not cease thinking about it. It was odd for someone with only a nodding acquaintance with opium to carry it on her person. The modest amount she claimed to use should have reassured him, except Bane never trusted any opium users to truthfully account for how much they imbibed. Not that he believed Lydia was deliberately lying to him. Opium, especially the version packaged in the charming bottles sold in the pharmacies, was an easy drug for users to become accustomed to without even being aware of it.

Some days he fought his battle in the halls of Congress, some days on the waterfronts where the smugglers flourished. Today, he felt guided to protect a single person. He needed to be certain Lydia would not fall victim to the seductive powers of a drug she had been spoon-fed since she was only a child.

Firm in his resolve, Bane left the church and his footsteps quickened as he strode down the worn cobblestone street. Lydia was a puzzle that fascinated and attracted him like no other woman had. She was an utter contradiction. She had a relentless desire to achieve, and yet she was so rigid in her need for order and security. There was a picture of Lewis and Clark on her desk, yet she had never set foot outside Boston and feared anything that disrupted her routine. Yesterday she told him she wished to test herself to the limits of her physical and mental strength, but unless she was pushed, she would never do it. Dreaming about such things seemed to be enough for her.

As he expected, Lydia was at the counter of the Laughing Dragon having a bowl of clam chowder. "Hello, Lydia," he said as he took the stool next to her. "Still quivering from your encounter with the cow yesterday?"

She looked pleased to see him as she set her spoon down and sent him a heart-stopping smile. "Last night I had the most wonderful dream," she said. "I was sitting at this very counter, and you walked up and did not say a single rude thing to me. I was stunned with amazement."

"And here I am—the answer to your dreams."

The hefty woman who bused tables approached him. "Can I get you something to eat, sir?"

"Your name is Gerta, correct?" The woman flushed a bit, apparently impressed he remembered her name. It would have been impossible to forget it, given how often Bane had heard Big Jim holler Gerta's name. "I'd love a cup of coffee."

When the serving woman placed a mug of the steaming brew before him, he looked up in appreciation. "Gerta, I think this place would grind to a halt if you weren't here to keep it running. I ought to speak to Big Jim about the shoddy wages he pays. You are worth your weight in gold."

Gerta sent him a gap-toothed grin. "Oh, go on with you, young man!" But she was still grinning long after she walked away to wipe tables.

Lydia looked a bit miffed. "Why are you so nice to everyone on the planet besides me? You even flirt with Gerta, and the woman is at least twice your age."

Bane shrugged. "I flirt with Gerta because she makes the best coffee on the Eastern Seaboard. I flirt with you out of sheer pity."

"Careful, Bane . . . if you keep flattering me like that I might fling another marriage proposal at you."

By all that was holy, he adored Lydia. Never had he met a woman who could so easily match him, and it was enchanting. He had an insane desire to crush her in a quick bear hug. Instead, he feigned nonchalance. "Please, no. It would be the third proposal this week. Besides, I came here on a mission. Let me see your reticule," he said abruptly. He did not wait for Lydia to respond; he merely snatched her bag where it lay on the counter. Before she could stop him, he poked inside and began nosing through her belongings. A handkerchief, the compass he gave her yesterday, and a few coins. She had not replaced the bottle of opium.

"And what is it you are looking for this time?"

"Same thing as last time. Just checking up, love."

Lydia rolled her eyes. "I told you I barely use Mrs. Winslow's.

I certainly have not run out and purchased a replacement bottle." Her face softened and she laid her hand against his cheek. "But thank you for caring enough to check up on me."

She tried to mask it, but there was a slight quiver in her voice. Rather than being outraged at the invasion of her privacy, Lydia was touched by his actions. He wondered when had been the last time anyone cared about her welfare or had taken the time to ensure she was out of harm's way. Lydia had nothing to hide; otherwise she would be angry and defensive about the way he nosed through her purse without permission. A burst of relief surged through him. He wanted to sweep her up in a hug and whirl her around in the center of the Laughing Dragon. Instead, he pressed a kiss into her palm. "I also came by to make sure you were being fed properly. You've been looking a bit of a hag lately."

Actually, she looked beautiful, her heavy mass of dark hair lifted up into an elegant twist, emphasizing the coppery glints. He laid a hand across her reticule, his finger tapping against the smooth, round compass beneath the fabric. "Finish your chowder, then let's see if you can use the compass to get us to the Boston Museum of Art. You can show me some of those Greek gods you say I resemble."

"They are all naked."

"And you say I look like them?" He flashed her a wink. "I certainly hope you haven't been spying on me."

The blush that suffused her cheeks was charming, and she was such a good sport that he could not resist the temptation to egg her on. Lydia was smart as a tack, but her real attraction was her sense of humor. When he had found the one tiny chink in her armor—her obsessive need for order—he could not resist fiddling with the items on her desk to see how she would respond. In pure Lydia fashion, she was willing to laugh over her foibles and simply restore everything to order with the minimum amount of fuss.

Five minutes later they were on the street and heading due northeast to get to the museum. He had to show Lydia how to use the compass on city streets, as it was impossible to simply travel in a straight line.

"It's strange; the needle keeps pointing at you," Lydia said as she stared at the wobbly needle.

"My magnetic personality?" He could have explained it was because they were heading north and her concentration on the compass meant he was always a few steps ahead of her, but where was the fun in that? "We need to start heading east here," he said as they approached another corner. Lydia angled the compass to point them in the right direction.

The Boston Museum of Fine Arts was an immense building in the Gothic revival style, but it turned out to be closed on Sundays. Not that Bane cared. He simply wanted to spend time with Lydia. "Let's walk about the grounds," he said. There were a few sculptures scattered around the immaculately landscaped setting, including a dolphin spitting water and a cherub strumming a harp.

As they circled the grounds, he held Lydia's hand, and she made no complaint. This was what normal people did. They courted a fetching girl, looked at sculpture for no other reason than it was pretty. Tomorrow his world would revert back to the next congressional election, the next shipload of cargo entering the Boston harbor. He would need to leave Lydia as soon as he discovered how opium was being smuggled into Boston, but before he left, he wanted to share his gift of faith with her. There was very little else he could give to this glorious woman, but that was one thing he could do for her.

"Last night was a full moon," he said.

She sent him a knowing glance. "I'll bet you are about to ask if I went outside and prayed to the moon."

"Did you?"

"What do you think?" she countered.

"I think the odds are pretty good you stepped outside for a little chat, yes."

Her smile was unabashed and dazzling. "I suppose that is a good way of phrasing it. I don't know if anyone was listening, but it made me feel a little better just thinking that perhaps there was someone or something out there watching over me."

They circled to the side of the museum where a couple of mermaids cavorted in a fountain. His feet crunched against the gravel as they walked, and he thought carefully about his next words. "Lydia, when you were on that boat, living beneath the Mediterranean skies . . . did you ever feel neglected?"

"No." Her answer was automatic. "My parents doted on me. I had everything I really needed."

"You did not have a safe environment. You did not have birthday presents or decent clothing or even the chance to go to school. In fact, aside from a loving family, you really had nothing at all, did you?"

She stopped walking and her mouth hung open. "That's a rather cruel thing to say."

"Bear with me." He held up his hands to placate her. He would never get anywhere if she shoved him away before he could get to the heart of the matter. "Now here you are in Boston. You have a home and a job you love. You have money in the bank, food in your pantry. And yet you are so terribly insecure. You get upset if your ink bottles are out of order. For heaven's sake, ink bottles!"

She raised her chin a notch. "I like things in proper order."

"I know you do. And even if you succeed in purchasing your

apartment and building up a fat nest egg in the bank, you will still want those ink bottles in precise order. I'll bet you have the same meticulous organization in your home as well. What kind of order do you keep your books in?"

"Alphabetized by author."

"And the clothes in your closet?"

"Hanging in the order I wear them. That way I always know which needs to be laundered."

"And you don't think this maniacal need for order is a bit odd? A bit wanting?"

She strolled to a bench beside the mermaid fountain and took a seat, looking up at him. "I'm not the master of the human mind that you appear to be. Tell me what you think it means."

"It means you are looking for security in all the wrong places." He placed a booted foot on the bench beside her and stood leaning over her. "The love your parents showered on you gave you a measure of well-being, but they are gone now. When they died, the moorings of your world were torn out from under you, and you've been seeking them ever since. You *know* there is no goddess of the moon, but you wish there were. Am I right?"

All she did was shrug. He lifted her slim hand into his own. "Lydia, I believe there is a deep, powerful magnet that is pulling you toward the Lord. Your desire to seek out some voice in the universe to speak to is the beginning of faith. *Listen* to that urge. Follow it. Begin living your life the way God would want you to, and I believe the tiny, fragile spark inside will begin to grow."

When she looked up at him, there was cautious humor in her face. "So you aren't going to make fun of me for praying to the moon?"

He kissed the back of her hand. "I am the last person on the face of the earth who could ever throw stones. Just say a prayer for me every now and then. I could use it."

He turned to sit beside her on the bench to watch the setting sun. If he could capture a day and engrave it in his memory for all time, it would be this one. If it were possible, he would give whatever paltry fortune he had in the world to live out the rest of his days with Lydia Pallas by his side. He had always found it easy to compartmentalize his emotions in the past, but a wild, irrational part of his soul was calling out for him to sweep Lydia away, haul her before a minister, and marry her so he could solidify this fragile, glittering bond growing between them.

A bitter smile twisted his lips, for he knew he would be leaving Boston within a matter of days. And then he would turn off these inconvenient feelings and never think of her again.

14

The few, precious hours Lydia spent with Bane each night in the Custom House were becoming the most magical part of her life. Each night she waited for him to meet her at the Laughing Dragon; then they walked the six blocks to the Custom House. Who would have thought reading through stacks of dusty tax registers could be so exciting? But anything done alongside Alexander Banebridge was fascinating to her. He showered her with irreverent taunts, and she flung them back just as quickly. Sometimes they simply pushed the shipping forms to the side and wallowed in the joy of having someone to talk to.

"So why Lewis and Clark?" he asked her. "Why not Abraham Lincoln or Thomas Jefferson? They seem like more traditional people to idolize."

They sat at a large worktable in the tax assessor's office, huddled within the circle of amber light provided by a single kerosene lantern. Lydia pulled another stack of documents onto her lap, idly turning the forms in search of the distinctive stamp of a bill of lading. "I think because they were faced with both a physical and a mental challenge at the same time," she said. "My life seems so small and humble in comparison. Each day Lewis and Clark were confronted with danger and the unknown. They kept plowing forward, pushing their bodies through hunger and disease and exhaustion until they didn't know if they could even last another day. I admire that."

"Would you have gone along with them? If you'd had the opportunity?"

Lydia thought of her cozy apartment, her safe job, and the secure world she had built for herself. "Probably not," she reluctantly admitted. "I like stability too much, but it is fun to daydream about such things."

"Most women daydream of a husband and babies. Adorable little angels who only laugh, never cry."

"Why do you sound so cynical?" she asked. "Don't you want to have children someday?"

"That would require a wife, and I've already told you that will never happen for me." Bane's voice was flat and unemotional as he opened another file and began extracting the bills of lading. It hurt, the way he erected a wall between them so swiftly and completely. The reason she suspected he would never marry hurt even worse.

"Is it because you are already in love with someone?" Lydia asked softly. "Was it Rachel Fontaine?"

Bane froze. "Why do you ask that?"

"You are different when you speak about her. You seem . . . reverent, almost. I rarely see that side of you."

Bane set the file aside and leaned back in his chair. "I was not in love with Rachel. Not in the sense you are referring to."

Lydia was embarrassed at how quickly the tension drained from her shoulders. Bane noticed. "Don't go building any romantic daydreams about me," he warned. His face was serious and his voice was rough with pain. "I think I need to explain exactly why marriage would be completely impossible for me." She could see a muscle throbbing in his jaw and he stared bitterly at the floor beneath his boots. "The Professor's preferred manner of controlling his enemies is not a direct assault—he is too devious for that. He prefers to kidnap or terrorize the people his enemies love. That's how he would try to get to me if I ever married or had children. And Lydia," Bane looked up at her, his eyes intent, "the Professor is perfectly happy to hold on to his hostages for years. I've never let anyone get close to me. I can't risk that, Lydia."

He stood and walked outside the circle of light from the oil lantern, pacing in the darkened corners of the room. "I've never told this to anyone, but I think you need to understand exactly the kind of life I led. I cared deeply about Rachel and I was grateful to her for helping me, but if the Professor had ever learned of my admiration for Rachel, it would have put her in danger. My visits to the admiral could be brushed away as normal business, but if I ever socialized with the family? Attended church alongside them or shared a holiday? The Professor would know I had grown soft, and none of the Fontaines would be safe. I've never allowed myself to grow attached to anyone. I have business associates, but no friends. In earlier years I used to see families in the park and imagine what it would be like to have a family of my own, but it's a ridiculous exercise in torture. I quit doing it a long time ago."

Lydia's heart squeezed at the image his words conjured up. This man lived in *exile*. He was always on the outside, looking at a life he could never touch. She wanted to rush to him, encircle him in her arms, and give him the warmth and affection he had been denying himself, but he had not stopped speaking and she dared not interrupt.

"I don't expect you to be able to understand," he said slowly, "but watching the Fontaine children grow up is the closest thing I will have to a family of my own. I only see them every few months when I am in town on business to see the admiral, but it has been . . ." Bane struggled to find the words. "It has been a great delight to watch those babies grow into toddlers, and then into children. But if the Professor ever learned what that family means to me . . . heaven help them."

Bane's voice was hollow as he looked at her. "And I can never risk your safety either."

Silence stretched between them. She knew the grinding ache of living without the warmth and security of a loving family, and she longed to provide that warmth to Bane. "What if I was willing to take the risk?" she asked.

She could barely discern the outline of his features as he leaned against the wall, his arms folded across his chest. His face was in shadow, but she could sense he was looking directly at her.

"If it were in my power," he said slowly, "I would run away with you to some wild Caribbean island where we could live together in the wilderness. Somewhere we could bask in the sunshine and dance in the rain. We'd eat fish we pulled from the sea and drink wine straight from the bottle."

Lydia leaned forward, a glimmer of excitement beginning to smolder within her chest. Hadn't she always secretly dreamed of doing something bold and daring? With Bane beside her, she would be brave enough to run the risk. "Bane, why can't we? Why can't we just disappear together and never look back?"

A bleak smile touched the corner of his mouth. "Oh, Lydia, you are as innocent as the newborn day," he said. "If I dragged you into the muck of my world, you would always be looking over your shoulder, fearing the next stranger you encountered on the street. I could not bear to watch you grow into a nervous, embittered woman. The Professor's network spans the entire world, and there is *nowhere* we could go where he could not find us."

He pushed away from the wall and began moving toward her. She stood and rushed toward him, feeling his arms close around her. He placed a desperate kiss on the side of her face, then whispered into her ear, so softly she could barely hear the words.

"Lydia, I love you," he whispered. "I've never said those words to another woman, and for the rest of my life, I will be thankful you are in this world. I love your humor and your irreverent, gentle brilliance. I love your courage. I love the way you stand up to me and laugh while you do it. But I can't take you with me. When I leave Boston, you will never see me again."

With an abruptness that startled her, Bane released her and strode back to the table, sitting down and pulling another stack of files toward him. She felt swept up in a whirlwind of emotion, but Bane's face was blank. "We have two more hours to get through all the Italian ship records from last year," he said. "I think we can do it, don't you?"

His voice was light and energetic again. It was as though the achingly beautiful words he had just whispered in her ear had never been spoken.

She lowered herself into the chair, not trusting her legs to support her any longer. "I suppose so," she said weakly.

Bane sat on the edge of the bed in his spartan hotel room, running his fingers along the edge of the photograph of Rachel holding her two children. What would his life have been like had Rachel not intervened and got him aboard that ship heading to Brussels? If he had stayed closer to her, could he have prevented her death?

His shoulders sagged. On the morning of her death, Rachel

Fontaine had been a healthy young woman, but a slip on the ice had broken her wrist. The doctor advised opium to dull her pain while he set the bone. Even if Bane had been right beside her, he would have told her to take it. Just once shouldn't have been a problem.

The doctor administered the opium via injection, but within ten minutes Rachel's lungs began seizing and she could not get enough air. Never having taken so much as a drop of opium before that day, how was she to have known it would affect her that way? Her body had had a profound reaction to the drug. It seized her lungs and made it a battle for her to draw each breath of air as she began to lose the battle against exhaustion. Bane later heard it took her six hours to die. She had been awake throughout the entire ordeal.

He couldn't blame Rachel's death on the opium smugglers, but she was another casualty of a drug that was so freely dispensed and so little understood.

He had never told her what she meant to him.

Back when he knew Rachel, he was still looking over his shoulder every hour, protective of her and determined to stay ten steps ahead of the Professor and his men. He had allowed himself to become soft in Boston. He needed to remember the sense of fear that had kept him alive during those early years on the run.

He folded the photograph in half. It had been careless of him to even carry such a photograph of Rachel and her children. If the Professor had learned of it, he would have known where to strike. Bane would never forget the memory of her face, but that didn't lessen the pain as he held a corner of the photograph to the candle flame and watched as it consumed the paper.

15

On the sixth evening of their work at the Custom House, Bane finally found a solid lead. They were in the office of Inspector Ian McGannon, one of five customs agents who checked incoming cargo and prepared an inventory for tax purposes. At the bottom of McGannon's wastebasket was a single cigar band.

Bane held the band of green-and-gold foil up to the light of the lantern. "It appears Inspector McGannon has expensive taste in cigars," he said to Lydia.

She shrugged. "I don't know anything about cigars."

"I do. *Candemir* are the finest Turkish cigars."

The presence of Turkish cigars in Inspector McGannon's office probably signified nothing, but Bane thought a little peek into the man's desk drawers might not be a bad idea.

The *Candemir* cigar box was in the desk's lower right-hand drawer. The ornate green-and-gold box had an inscription on the top. Bane held it to the lantern and could easily read the carefully printed English letters:

To my dear friend Ian McGannon,
Please enjoy Turkey's finest.

Demir Mehmet

"Lydia, what is 'Demir Mehmet'? Is it a name or a phrase?"

He showed her the inscription. "It is a man's name. Mehmet is a common surname in Turkey."

Bane tapped his fingers across the surface of the box. It wasn't a good idea for a customs official to accept gifts, even inexpensive ones such as a box of cigars, from merchants. Bane opened the lid and poked through the remaining cigars in the box. And then he found what he had spent months looking for taped to the bottom of the box.

It was a list of ships sailing out of the port of Constantinople. And next to each ship was the estimated date of arrival in Boston.

A cold smile curved Bane's mouth. This was precisely the sort of thing a customs inspector would need to know if he was being paid to overlook cargo on specific ships. A quick scan of the dates revealed that four of the ships had already arrived within the past few months. The other six were all due to arrive during the coming year.

"What are you thinking?" Lydia asked. "I don't like that chilling expression on your face."

Bane grabbed a piece of scrap paper from the wastebasket and began making a copy of the list. "I suddenly have a burning desire to check the bills of lading for these four ships," he said. "I suspect a careful examination may point us to the source of the opium that has been streaming into this port for the better part of two years."

Older records were in the basement, where aisle after aisle of filing cabinets stood like megaliths in the darkened interior.

"Where to begin?" Lydia asked.

Bane found the bank of cabinet drawers that held records from the port of Constantinople and began riffling through the files, looking for a ship called the *Black Swan*, which the note indicated should have arrived the last week of July. His mouth twisted in distaste as memories crashed into the forefront of his mind. Over the years he had discovered dozens of ships just like the *Black Swan* quietly smuggling opium ashore and avoiding the staggering taxes the government demanded. Bane found the records for the *Black Swan* and held the lantern high.

The original bill of lading was in Turkish with an English translation appended to the document. A glance at the bottom of the form revealed Ian McGannon's signature. Before the ship could be unloaded, McGannon and the ship's purser would have walked along each aisle of crates in the hold, creating an itemized list of the cargo.

Bane scanned the document, noting the *Black Swan* carried bolts of silk, hand-woven carpets, and barrels of almonds. He handed the Turkish document to Lydia.

"Read the items in the list," he said. "I need an exact word-for-word translation."

"Six barrels of olives, ten barrels of almonds." She had to squint in the dim light and tilted the document toward the lantern. As Lydia read, Bane scanned the English document, noting each item as she read it.

"Four crates of cigars. Fifteen crates of coconuts," Lydia said.

Bane nearly dropped the lantern. *"Coconuts?"*

Lydia double-checked the document. "Yes, right here," she said, pointing to the word.

Bane's eyes narrowed as he scanned the English document. As he suspected, there was no mention of coconuts. Not that he expected to see it.

"Smuggling opium inside the husks of hollowed-out coconuts is one of the easiest ways to transport large quantities. No wonder McGannon did not want the word to appear on the English bill of lading. Especially since Turkey does not impress me as one of the world's foremost coconut exporters. How many crates did you say were in there?"

"Fifteen crates."

Bane's knees nearly went weak. That was thousands of pounds of opium. When opium was transported in coconut husks, it was the refined, dangerous version. And the *Black Swan* was merely one of ten ships on McGannon's list.

Bane's voice grew cold. "Let's find the manifest for the next ship on the list." The trail was white-hot, and Bane was almost certain what he would find. The *Scarletti* arrived in August, and after pulling the documents, he noted the exact same discrepancy in this ship's bill of lading, as well as with the other two ships that had already arrived.

"Each of these documents was signed by Ian McGannon," Bane said. "It is clear to me he was paid to look the other way for ships arriving from Demir Mehmet."

Lydia had a hopeful expression on her face. "If you can prove that McGannon is the source of the smuggling, will that mean you can block the opium coming into Boston? Is this the beginning of the end?"

Her question revealed in stark clarity how green Lydia was in the ways of the opium trade. He closed the file drawer. "No, Lydia. The opium trade is a hydra-headed monster. When we cut off one head, another will grow somewhere else. And when I find out where that is, I will seek it out and kill it there as well."

Lydia's eyes were luminous in the dim light. "This means you will be leaving Boston?" The pain in her voice was unmistakable.

He fought the temptation to draw her within the circle of his arms and comfort her. There was nothing he could do or say that would make this any easier.

"Yes, Lydia. I will take these documents to the authorities in the morning, so there is no need for us to keep coming to the Custom House. I won't have any need for a translator after tonight." He turned away and closed the file drawer so he would not have to see the anguish in her eyes. The slamming of the drawer echoed in the darkness of the room. How foolish he had been to believe he could indulge in a casual flirtation with her and then walk away without feeling like his heart had been torn from his chest.

Bane held her hand as they mounted the staircase leading up to the grand rotunda of the Custom House. A little weak moonlight streamed through the windows, and he knew with painful clarity that he had only a few more minutes with the only woman he had ever loved. He kept walking across the lobby toward the front door, but she refused to follow him.

"I don't want you to go." Lydia's voice was pale and brittle in the darkness.

He did not turn around. He forced his voice to sound calm, but he kept his face averted from her. "I'll get you the two hundred dollars I owe you, but my nearest bank is in Philadelphia, so it may be a week or two before I can get it to you."

A brisk rustle of fabric sounded behind him, and then Lydia tugged at his arm, forcing him to turn and look at her. "I don't care about the money," she said. "I care about you and this awful life you have been leading. Don't shut me out. Don't walk away from what we have."

Lydia's head was high, hopeful determination in her face. How quickly her spirit would dim if she were always on the run beside him, never sleeping more than a few nights in a single location.

He raised his hand to cup the side of her face. "There is no room in my world for orderly ink bottles or safe harbors," he said softly. "Eventually, you would grow to hate being with me."

Her eyes narrowed. "Why don't you just put an end to the Professor? You know where he lives, and if you called the authorities, you could *put a stop* to him."

He could, but he wouldn't. If he snuffed the Professor out, some other drug lord would move in to fill the void, and Bane would have no insight on how to stay one step ahead of him. "It's because I know how the Professor's mind works that I've been so good at predicting his behavior," he said. "I made a vow to do whatever was humanly possible to wreak havoc on the opium trade, and the best way to do that is to allow the Professor to maintain his position."

Now she was angry. "So you are going to sacrifice your entire life to this? Be forever on the run—forever alone—all so you can carry on your one-man crusade."

She was entirely correct. The cost of his crusade never weighed more heavily on him than it did at this very moment, but it could not change the vow he made to himself or to God. The most effective way for him to block the import of smuggled opium was to understand the mind of the man who controlled the operation. He could not abandon that mission.

"I'm sorry I've disappointed you," he said. If he spelled out all the ways he was sorry, he'd be talking until the sun rose. It was time to get out of here and end the agony. Lydia looked wounded and desolate at his words, but standing here wasn't going to make things better, so he opened the door and left the building. The bitter darkness swirled around him as he walked down the icy street.

Lydia's footsteps scurried behind him, and he paused while she caught up to him. Without looking at her and without a word, he proffered his arm for her to take. They walked in silence through the night. This would be the last time he walked beside her, the last time he felt her slim little hand curled around his arm. Lydia was his partner, his match, and she adored him. The knowledge was killing him, but he had an irrational desire to prolong the agony. He slowed his steps as they drew closer to the Laughing Dragon, buying just a few more seconds of her company, a few more seconds of having a companion in the world.

Inevitably they came to the door of the Laughing Dragon. The coach light illuminated the lovely planes of Lydia's face, but her eyes were narrowed in determination. How very Lydia, her refusal to accept defeat. It made him love her all the more.

He pulled her closer, breathed deeply of her clean scent, and pressed his lips against the soft shell of her ear. "Forget you ever knew me," he whispered. "Pretend I never existed. Go back to your world and never look back."

She stiffened in his arms. "I can't do that."

Neither could he. She was branded onto his soul, where her memory would blaze as long as he lived. He extricated himself from her arms, looked down into her beautiful face, and lied.

"I can."

Lydia's mouth compressed into a hard line, and steel flashed in her eyes. "I won't give up on you," she said. "There haven't been very many things in my life that have been worth fighting for, but Bane, you are one of them."

The door banged as she entered the Laughing Dragon, leaving him alone on the street.

Lydia sat at her desk in the Navy Yard office, one eye on an Italian newspaper, and one eye on Willis. It was a few minutes until five o'clock, and Willis was quietly causing quite a commotion. For the last ten minutes he had been holding a hand up before his eyes, alternately wincing and grimacing, although everyone in the office was studiously ignoring him. Lydia had found that Willis usually "suffered in silence" for about twenty minutes. If all three of them ignored him, there was a good bet they would reach the end of the business day before he cracked and shared his sufferings with the world. Lydia, Karl, and Jacob were all earnestly engrossed in the tasks before them, performing heroic work in ignoring Willis's drama, but their efforts were in vain.

Willis could no longer bear the strain. "Could no one block that light shining through the window? The glare of that setting sun . . . it is like ice picks in the eye."

Lydia sprang to her feet. "Perhaps I'll close the blinds," she suggested. She caught Jacob trying to hide his laughter behind a German technical journal as she tilted the venetian blinds across the window in front of Willis. "Is that better, dear?"

Willis still winced. "Now the light is diffused," he said. "That makes it worse, as though it were assaulting me from a thousand directions instead of just one."

Lydia resumed her seat, determined not to let Willis's calamities impact her day. She owed the admiral another eight minutes of scanning the Italian press before she could escape to her own desperate misery of wondering what would happen when she saw Bane again this evening. He had made it quite plain two nights ago she would never see him again, but this morning Lydia learned the admiral had an appointment with Bane after business hours. She intended to be waiting.

She twisted her head to look at Willis, still cringing from the assault of the sun. The man shied away from colorful food, loud sounds, and inappropriate sources of light. Pathetic, but was she much better? Bane did not believe she had the mettle to share his world. He thought her need for order and routine disqualified her for a life alongside him.

When the grandfather clock in the hallway finally struck the five-o'clock hour, Lydia gratefully tucked her newspaper onto the top of the stack she would begin reading tomorrow. She put her pen back into the top left-hand drawer, replaced her Italian dictionary in the correct spot, and straightened the papers stacked on her desk until they were at precise ninety-degree angles with two inches between each set of papers.

"Can I walk you down to the streetcar station?" Karl stood at the office door, already wearing his overcoat, his hat in hand. Everyone else had already left.

"No, thank you," she said. She scrambled for an excuse to linger. "I saw an article in the Russian newspaper about the coronation of a new duke. I'd like to stay and read about it." Karl accepted her answer and left her in the silent office. Her gaze strayed to the etching of Lewis and Clark on her desk. She was nothing compared to those men. Or to Bane. She was more like Willis and his thousand ailments than a person who could boldly tackle the challenges of the world. The headache that had been pounding was getting worse. She opened her drawer and took a tiny sip of Mrs. Winslow's Syrup. Bane had tossed the bottle she kept in her reticule, but she had another in her desk and still another at home. There was no way she would be up for having a painful discussion with Bane if she could not ease the pounding in her head.

It was almost six o'clock when she heard the office door open. She whirled around to see Bane, who looked surprised to see her.

"I had hoped—" He caught himself. "I thought you would be gone for the day." He sounded disappointed she was still here.

"Sometimes I stay late to read an article I am interested in."

"Ah." For the first time since she had known Bane, he seemed to be at a loss for words. "I'm here to see the admiral," he finally said. "He is expecting me."

And with that he strode to the admiral's office, knocked, and let himself in. Not a second glance at Lydia, nor one of his wicked little grins. A look at her desk showed everything in perfect order. How odd that she wished he had at least fiddled a bit with her ink bottles.

His entire demeanor had shifted as he built a wall of ice around himself, but she could not let him shut her out like this. She had finally found an anchor in her storm-tossed world, and letting the demons from Bane's past carry him away from her was not an option.

Bane's meeting with the admiral dragged on. The late autumn sun slipped beneath the horizon, and the evening grew chilly. She tried to pass the time by reading an Albanian newspaper, but her distracted thoughts constantly strayed from the newspaper and wandered to Bane. She should have known he would not be easy. He was a complicated man who hid a vast reservoir of anguish beneath a roguish veneer of charm.

At last the door opened and both Bane and the admiral prepared to leave. "Still here, Miss Pallas?" The admiral was always so excruciatingly proper.

She cleared her throat and held up the Albanian newspaper. "I became engrossed in what I was reading. I won't be much longer."

"Very well." The admiral left the office, and Bane was about to follow.

Lydia shot to her feet, the chair upending behind her. "Bane!"

He paused, his back to her as he held the door. At last he turned. "Yes?"

She was almost speechless. "Are you really just going to walk away?"

He closed the door. The room was silent save for the ticking of the clock on the wall. Bane's expression was pleasantly blank. "I thought I made it clear the other night," he said in a calm voice. "Now that we know who the culprit is, there is no need for us to continue meeting. And I don't have any need for future translations. Goodbye, Lydia."

He turned around to leave again, and she needed to stop him. "You haven't paid me." Her voice lashed out, a desperate attempt to stop him from crossing that threshold.

Lydia grasped the edge of her desk, hoping Bane would make some lighthearted comment about her stingy ways, but he merely extracted his billfold and thumbed through its contents.

"Here is forty dollars," he said, laying the bills on Jacob's desk. Couldn't he even trust himself to cross the room and hand it to her directly? "I will have the remainder delivered to this office after I contact my bank in Philadelphia for the balance. And that should conclude our business, correct?"

"You know that isn't what I'm talking about."

Bane leaned against Jacob's desk, folding his arms across his chest and staring at the floor. "I don't think we need to revisit the reasons I can't afford to allow anyone in my life, do we?"

"I am willing to take the risk." She straightened her shoulders and walked around her desk so she could stand opposite him. He looked so alone, standing there with his arms crossed before him, shutting out the rest of the world. "I know that you come with dangers and problems," she said. "Life with you will never be an easy, blissful thing, but life isn't perfect, and I understand that. I accept that."

All the pain of the world was in his eyes as he dragged them to meet her gaze. "Lydia, *you are perfect*." A sad smile crossed his beautiful face. "You are perfect in every way to me. I would die for you, but I can't drag you down with me. I can't do that to you."

She remembered what he had told her of how fearless he had been when he was a smuggler, how he wielded that fierce courage to accomplish unimaginable feats. Even after becoming a Christian, he had turned the force of that power toward conquering new dragons. But it seemed she had stumbled across the one thing even Bane was too afraid to risk: herself.

"I am willing to take the risk," she said.

"If we were together," Bane said slowly, "you would begin to resent the life I forced you to live. You would grow exhausted and embittered."

"That is not true. I could learn to be stronger."

Bane's smile was sad as he slowly shook his head. "Look at how desperately you crave a home where you can feel safe and surround yourself with your books arranged alphabetically by author. Do you think I have ever had a home, Lydia?" Bane had never mentioned where he lived, and Lydia had never thought to ask.

"There are a series of hotels I use in various cities," he said. "I never stay in the same room twice. I rent a storage room by the wharves where I keep out-of-season clothing, but nothing of value because those rented spaces have been plundered and destroyed twice. I have no books, no collections of photographs or letters or any of the things normal people accumulate to document their lives. I own nothing, because I am always running, and acquiring things would only slow me down and make me vulnerable."

He looked directly at her as he said those words. It was clear that he thought of her as someone who would slow him down and make him vulnerable.

And he was probably correct.

"So this is goodbye, then?" She hated that her voice sounded so thin and vulnerable in the cold, dark office. She wished she could appear nonchalant, as if her heart wasn't shattering into a thousand pieces.

"It has to be."

She nodded, not quite knowing what to do with herself. What was the proper etiquette for when her dreams were collapsing around her? Perhaps it was best not to pretend and simply tell the truth. She looked deeply into his troubled blue eyes.

"There won't ever be another man like you," she said. "For me, you will always be the man I think of as a great, glorious love. I wish I could be more like you. Brave and daring and committed. I expect I will think about you every day for the rest of my life."

It hurt to see Bane's face, normally full of such roguish charm, now drawn and serious. He said nothing as he touched the side of her face, then turned and stepped out of her life forever.

16

The next day began as any other. Willis arrived early to make tea for the office, but by the time Lydia arrived he was pressing cold compresses to his forehead and complaining about the new typeface used by the *Times of London*. "The change in font is playing havoc on my senses," he said. "They ought to have distributed a warning to their readers before springing something like this on us."

Lydia helped herself to a cup of tea, breathing in the familiar, soothing scent. She was numb inside. It was hard to believe this was the exact room where her heart had been shattered just a few hours ago. With the sound of hammers coming from the dry docks and her desk meticulously arranged, everything was precisely as it always was.

Except for the void in her soul that was gaping wide open. She was not quite sure how she would ever regain her momentum.

"Are you all right, Lydia?" Jacob asked, leaning forward in his desk to see her better.

She must have hesitated a bit too long, because he rose and

came to stand beside her. "You look flushed," he said. "Have you been sleeping well?"

Apparently the fact that she spent a sleepless night feeling sick to her stomach was plain on her face. She tried to manage a smile. "I'm okay," she said, but the tremor in her voice gave her away. Karl sprang to his feet and crossed the office in three large steps.

"Is that Bane fellow troubling you again? Should I ask the admiral to keep him away?"

The irony of Karl's question almost prompted a laugh from her. "No, truly, it is all right." She looked at both men standing before her. Karl, with fatherly concern stamped across his Nordic features, and young Jacob, who was always looking out for her. She could not ask for two better companions to share an office. Willis was still holding a compress to his face and moaning softly, no doubt confused as to how Lydia managed to be attracting all the sympathy on a day when his sensibilities had been assaulted by the *Times of London*.

"Please don't worry about me," she said. "This is nothing that a little time won't heal." She did not quite believe that statement, but it was enough to send Karl and Jacob back to their desks.

A moment later the admiral entered the office. Dressed in a dark wool overcoat and full military uniform, he was certainly a handsome man, but this morning he looked unusually distracted, stern even. And he was looking directly at her. Instead of heading to his office as he normally did, he walked to her desk, a somber expression on his face.

"Miss Pallas, I need to speak with you in my office."

She set a technical report down. Never in the four years she'd worked here had he asked to speak with her alone. "Now?"

"Now."

Concern rippled through her. She prayed this had nothing to

do with Bane's insane plan to pair her up with the admiral. Surely he would not have tried to resurrect something along those lines. Or could it be something about his senate campaign? She was an emotional wreck, and the last thing she needed was something else to rock the stability of her world.

She stepped inside the admiral's office and closed the door. Unlike the front office, where they could easily hear the bustle of work in the dry docks, this room was silent except for the ticking of a brass mantel clock. An immense globe graced one corner, but most imposing was the admiral's desk. It was the largest desk she had ever seen, and he was sitting behind it observing her with the stern, uncompromising look he had used earlier.

"Please have a seat, Miss Pallas."

"Thank you, sir." She lowered herself into a leather-covered chair across from his desk and waited.

"Last night I dined with the city's district attorney, and I heard some disturbing information," he said.

"Oh?"

The admiral fiddled with a pen. "Alexander Banebridge dug up evidence of smuggling taking place in the Custom House. It appears he found evidence of a corrupt customs inspector."

"I see," she said hesitantly.

"Word has it that he used a translator to help him with some of the Turkish documents. When he spoke to the district attorney, he did not use any names, but he let slip that the translator was a 'she.' I can only assume he was referring to you." That piercing gaze had her pinned to her chair. She did not know if this was going to earn her condemnation or praise, but his look was unsettling.

"Yes, sir," she said softly.

"Am I correct in assuming you and Banebridge riffled through the offices of various inspectors in search of this information?"

The way he phrased it made it sound pretty bad, but he was entirely accurate in his assessment. "Yes, sir."

The admiral straightened in his chair, replaced the pen in its holder, and looked her directly in the eye. "I'm sorry, Miss Pallas, but your employment here is terminated."

Lydia felt as if she had been shot. She couldn't move, couldn't draw a breath. She could only stare in shock as the admiral continued speaking. "I demand absolute integrity from my employees. Sneaking in and out of offices, even if it was technically legal, is something I will not countenance. Please collect your belongings and leave the office immediately."

She couldn't draw a breath. She was overheated and light-headed, and she was getting dizzy. She fought to pull in some air but could not quite make her lungs respond. Whatever else happened, she needed to escape the admiral's harsh glare. She stood, but everything started spinning and her first step wobbled. Badly.

Admiral Fontaine was at her side in an instant, pushing her back into the chair. He forced her head down to her knees. "Take a breath," he ordered. "Lydia, I said take a breath," he said more firmly.

She obeyed. Oxygen began flooding through her system, and the world regained its kilter. She tried to sit up, but the admiral's hand was still splayed across her back, holding her head down. She stared at the carpet. How stupid she felt, sprawled over in the chair like this.

"I'm all right now," she said. The admiral's hand lifted, and she sat up, still unable to meet his gaze. "I'll just go get my things," she said inanely.

She rose to her feet but was still dizzy, and the admiral took her arm, guiding her out the door of his office. "Jacob, come help Miss Pallas . . . do whatever it is she needs you to do."

She saw Jacob coming toward her. Everything felt like a dream, but she knew with hideous clarity that this was real. The admiral handed her over to Jacob, who walked her back to her desk. After the admiral returned to his office, Lydia looked about the room that had been a second home to her.

"I've been fired," she said blankly.

Karl raced to her side, and even Willis came to her desk. "How is this possible?" Karl asked, astonishment on his face.

"Is he going to let the rest of us go as well?" Willis asked. "Has funding for the research wing been eliminated?"

Lydia shook her head. "None of you has cause for concern. I made a mistake, that's all." She looked at the objects on her desk. Almost all of them belonged to the navy. Two of the pens were hers, as were her framed pictures of Lewis and Clark and the Mediterranean island. She reached for her satchel, but her hands shook too badly to open it.

Jacob laid his hand over hers. "Don't be afraid, Lydia. We will look out for you."

"Yes, of course," Karl said. But Lydia did not miss the look that flew between the two men. They wanted to help, but what could they actually do? Karl's budget was tightly stretched supporting his wife and four children in a tiny apartment. Jacob had even less than she did.

She tugged at the satchel until it opened. "I'll be fine," she said, with more assurance than she felt. "I'm sure I'll be fine." Since she had been fired, there would be no references. Without references, it would be almost impossible to attain professional employment anywhere else.

It did not take her long to put her few belongings into her satchel. She didn't know if she could face saying goodbye to Jacob and Karl and Willis. All she wanted to do was escape as quickly as possible so she could collapse in private.

She closed the Italian dictionary she had been using when the admiral had arrived this morning and put it back in its spot between the Greek and the Russian dictionaries. She tidied her ink bottles one final time when Willis set something on her desk.

"It is a blueberry scone," he said kindly. "I thought perhaps you might like something a little sweet today."

Willis had a voracious sweet tooth, and parting with any of his delicacies qualified as an act of great valor for him. She wrapped the scone in a handkerchief and tucked it in her satchel. "Thank you," she said numbly.

She stood and glanced around the office, trying not to make eye contact with anyone as they stood ringed around her, somber as mourners at any funeral gathering. "Thank you, everyone. You all have been the best office mates anyone could have imagined," she said. It was best to stop before her throat clogged up and she embarrassed herself again.

Just before she reached the office door, a thought froze her in her tracks.

She turned around to face Karl. "I am expecting a letter to arrive here within a week or two. Will you see that it gets delivered to my apartment at the Laughing Dragon?" She would need every dime of the money Bane owed her.

Karl nodded. "Yes, certainly."

Then she turned and closed the door on the best job in the world.

There was only one thought pounding in Lydia's mind as she raced home, clattered up the three flights of stairs, and burst through the door of her apartment. She tossed her satchel on the table, raced to her bedroom, and reached for the delicate blue bottle of headache syrup sitting on her windowsill.

As her shaking fingers pried the cork from the opening, she thought of Bane and her promise she would take no more of Mrs. Winslow's Soothing Syrup. He was so adamant she should abstain from this sort of medicine, but Bane wasn't here, this was the worst day of her life, and she needed something to help her survive the next few minutes. Tension gripped her spine like a vise, racing all the way up her back and into her neck, so debilitating it was hard even to swallow. And she would only take a sip. Besides, why should she keep a promise to a man who had abandoned her and gotten her fired from the only decent job she had ever known?

The syrup was overly sweet, but soon the tension raging in her body would ease. She would not cry. She never cried. Just as she always did when her world was turned upside down, Lydia would muster her forces, make a plan, and get herself out of this mess.

She took another sip. As the strain began to loosen its grip, Lydia's world came into focus. She was an intelligent woman, and Boston was a city swarming with commerce from all over the world. Surely there would be other employers who were in need of her translation skills.

It did not take long for her to learn otherwise.

In the days that followed, she made a list of any establishment that might have need of a translator, including newspapers, publishers, courthouses, shipping offices, even schools. She nearly wore holes in the bottom of her shoes as she walked from office to office. Either there were no positions available or her lack of references stopped the interview in its tracks. Some employers took one look at her and bluntly said they did not hire females.

And adding to her worries was the lack of a letter from Bane. He still owed her over one hundred dollars, and Karl had promised to forward it to her once it arrived. Now that she was out of a job, she needed that money more than ever.

17

The tidewater climate of Virginia was still mild in December. The Professor strolled through Richmond's historic 17th Street Market, scanning the vendors from side to side. The air was laden with the scents of tobacco, dried herbs, and apples. Although he preferred to haunt the antiquarian shops and auction houses of the great cities, the Professor could not afford to overlook the tables set up by tinkers at humble markets such as this. Just last year he had found a fine copy of Jonathan Swift's *Gulliver's Travels* at a tinker's stand. It was easier to acquire his books through auction houses, but those books had already been rescued from the worst danger. The owners of those rare volumes knew their value and would never let them rot among old fishing tackle, but the ignorant people who haunted markets such as these had no appreciation for literature. They were liable to use the pages of a book for kindling or polishing shoes.

He shuddered and moved a little faster. Each week the Professor picked a new city to explore. Mondays through Thursdays, he prowled antique shops, auction houses, and markets such as these.

But come Thursday, he always took the train home to Vermont, where he could live amongst the treasures he had collected.

A stall just ahead had a table dense with old candlesticks and battered picture frames, but his eyes landed on a set of old farming manuals. Ignoring the tinker's invitation to examine some bolts of fabric, the Professor paged through the farming manual. It was around thirty years old and of no great value. He flipped through the volume, savoring the mild, musty smell. A pity. He simply had no room in his home for a book such as this, but it was a shame to leave it here, crammed against a rusty old washtub. He had to accept there were limits to how many books he could save.

He was just about to set the farming manual down when his assistant came rushing forth.

"Professor!" Raymond shouted. Even in the cool air, he looked overheated and fanned himself with a newspaper. "I found mention of something in Boston that will be of interest to you."

The Professor quirked a brow as Raymond opened the newspaper. "It says here that an opium ring has been scuttled in Boston. This has Banebridge's fingerprints all over it," Raymond said. "I think we should send men to Boston immediately. Before his trail gets cold."

The Professor set the farmer's manual down, carefully protecting it from coming into contact with the rusty surface of the washtub. "Get there right away. Find out everywhere he has been, everyone he has seen." All the Professor needed was to find the right person.

And then he'd have Bane at his mercy.

Lydia dreaded returning to the Navy Yard. For the past four years she had felt so safe in the wonderful, busy shipyard, but now it was only a source of humiliation. The worst part would be seeing pity from Karl and the others, but she could not afford to stay away. It had been two weeks since she had been fired, and there was no sign of the letter with the money Bane owed her. She had to either find that letter or find Bane.

Walking past the dry docks was painful. Today, the wonderfully familiar marshy scent of the river, the cry of the gulls, and the rasp of scrapers cleaning barnacles from the ships merely hurt. She didn't belong here anymore. She just needed to get her money and leave the Navy Yard forever.

The moment she stepped through the office door, Karl, Jacob, and Willis all sprang forward to greet her, but sitting at her desk was a young man she had never seen before.

"Lydia!" Jacob said, clasping her hands between his. "It's so good to see you," he said. Karl brushed Jacob aside and gave her a fatherly hug.

"It is good to see you all again," she said. The man standing behind her desk rose to his feet and brushed a swath of thinning black hair from his forehead. There was an awkward pause.

Karl cleared his throat. "Lydia, this is Marco Trivoni. He is the new research assistant for southern Europe."

She wouldn't let the hurt show. She forced a stiff smile to her face and nodded to the man. "Hello, Mr. Trivoni. I hope Jacob's humming isn't driving you crazy."

The poor man looked as uncomfortable as she felt. He laughed a bit. "Not at all. His humming is better than my wife's singing."

"Good," she said.

"Have you found another position yet?" Karl asked.

It was the question she dreaded, but she kept a serene expression on her face. "Not quite yet, but I still have many places to look." Which was not precisely a lie. She was fresh out of options for professional work, but there was plenty of menial labor she had yet to search out.

She met Karl's eyes. "Have there been any deliveries here for me? A letter, perhaps?"

Karl shook his head. "I have been on the lookout, but nothing has arrived."

A strangling sense of disappointment threatened to drive the breath from her body. "Perhaps . . . has Bane been in to see the admiral?"

"I have not seen him since you left," Karl said. "Have you, Jacob?"

Both Jacob and Willis shook their heads.

"I see." She bit her lip as the familiar sensation of anxiety wrapped around her spine. This meant she would have to speak with the admiral to ask how she might get in touch with Bane. She would rather face a firing squad than see Admiral Fontaine again, but there wasn't any help for it. Karl told her the admiral was inspecting an armored frigate on Dry Dock Two.

Lydia thanked Karl and was about to leave the office when Willis stopped her. He pressed a blueberry scone into her hand. "Take this," he said. "The Stolinski Bakery really is the finest in Boston." She remembered the scone he gave her on that awful day she had been terminated. She had eaten it later that evening rather than show her face in public at the Laughing Dragon coffeehouse, but she had been so numb she could not remember a thing about it now.

"I stop by for fresh scones every morning," Willis said, looking at her intently, as though he expected some sort of response.

She inhaled the aroma. "I can see why you do. Thank you again." She turned to leave, but Willis stopped her.

He leaned his head down to whisper in a low voice. "There is a sign in their window that says they are looking for help. I thought perhaps you might find it useful to know."

Lydia froze. She was not too proud to work in a bakery, but it hurt to know her friends saw straight through her façade of well-being. She met his eyes for the briefest of moments, not quite confident she could disguise the naked pain. "Thank you, Willis," she murmured.

The admiral was easy to spot on the deck of the frigate as it lay in the dry dock like a wounded patient. Lydia drew the edges of her cloak tighter around her throat in a vain attempt to keep the December wind from cutting through to her skin. For weeks she had been dreading the unlikely prospect of ever seeing Admiral Fontaine again. Her anxiety twisted even tighter as the inspection concluded and he began walking down the pier toward her. He was preoccupied with something that kept his face closed and shuttered as he strode toward her. Just as he was about to stride past her, she stepped into his path.

"Admiral Fontaine."

He glanced up and his eyes widened in surprise. He gave the faintest dip of his head and cleared his throat. "Miss Pallas. Is there something I can do for you?"

The mild censure in his voice made it apparent her visit was not welcome. A busy wharf was not an ideal location to have such an important conversation, but Lydia doubted the admiral would have accepted a formal appointment with her.

"I apologize for interrupting your day," she began, "but I was hoping you might know how to get in contact with Bane. It is important I speak with him."

The admiral's dark brows lowered in disapproval. "I think the more you curtail your association with Banebridge, the better off you will be. That man has brought you nothing but trouble."

It was true that her life had not turned upside down until Bane had entered it. "Be that as it may," she said, "I have unfinished business with Mr. Banebridge. He has not paid me for some work I did for him, and I am in need of those funds."

If possible, the look on the admiral's face grew even colder. "Would that payment be in regard to overnight employment at the Custom House?"

"Yes."

"Then I am sorry, Miss Pallas. I am not able to assist you in collecting compensation for anything related to an underhanded and immoral activity." He made a move to step around her, but Lydia intercepted him and stopped him in his tracks. Something he said struck her amiss, but it took her a moment to process his comment.

"I can't dispute that it was underhanded," she said, "but I don't think it was immoral." And suddenly that distinction had become quite important to her. "Our motives were good. I am sorry that I lost my job over this, but I think that the country might be a safer place because of it."

Lydia did not know why, but the admiral was scanning her face as if he was seeking the answer to something. The scrutiny caused her to shift in discomfort, but she refused to break eye contact. Finally, he gave up and gestured to one of the vacant iron benches that faced out toward the dry dock. "Please have a seat," he said. "I find myself curious to learn why an entirely sensible lady such as yourself got swept up in this sort of transgression. Banebridge can be relentless when he is pursuing his own particular cause, but I want to know why you went along with him."

She should have thought that was perfectly apparent. "Because there was someone taking bribes in the Custom House."

"What were you saying about making this country a safer place? What did you mean by that?" he probed.

Banishing opium from this country was Bane's mission in life, not hers. But it was not until he told her about the ingredients in Mrs. Winslow's Soothing Syrup that Lydia began to grasp the extent of the problem. In the past two weeks she had relied more heavily than ever on her little blue bottle. Although she certainly did not suffer from an addiction—such a thought was absurd—she could understand the attraction opium had for unsuspecting users.

"Bane told me that opium is slipped into medicine given to teething babies," she said. "The staff at the orphanage where I grew up dispensed that medicine routinely to soothe any number of ailments. They gave it to children who didn't want to take their afternoon nap or were disruptive in the classroom. I don't know if they realized what was in that little bottle of medicine, but I wish I had never been given a drop of it," she said, her voice vibrating with intensity.

She looked the admiral directly in the eyes. "I was never a sickly or troublesome child, and the fact that I was spoon-fed opium by people who were supposed to be caring for me is appalling. So I am *glad* there are men like Alexander Banebridge who are fighting to stop drugging children into docility."

She couldn't be sure, but she thought she saw an infinitesimal softening in the admiral's demeanor. "Do you know of Banebridge's early involvement in the opium trade?" he asked.

"Yes. He told me all of it."

"Then perhaps you can understand why he feels compelled to stamp out the trade," he said. "Banebridge is driven by a need to slay the dragons he set forth in the world. He will stoop to any depths in pursuit of that quest. Even if it means risking the life or well-being of an innocent young lady such as yourself."

"Risking my life? I think that is a slight exaggeration."

The admiral frowned at her. "Slipping in under cover of night in order to plunder the office of a known smuggler? Bane was gambling with your safety, and that is not something a gentleman would ask of any woman, especially not someone he cares for. I hope you are not endowing Bane with some false notion of romantic gallantry, because he will throw you to the lions if it means advancing his cause."

The words had a ring of truth, and they stung. Bane claimed to love her, but not at the price of abandoning his quest. The admiral had not stopped speaking. "I have severed my association with Banebridge," he said. "His goal of reforming the opium laws is commendable, but I refuse to tolerate the underhanded techniques he has been using of late."

"Trying to change the laws will take years," she said. "Decades. Won't it?"

"Probably."

Lydia thought of the children who still lived at the Crakken Orphanage. In all likelihood, several of those children would be lining up this very evening for a dose of Mrs. Winslow's Soothing Syrup to ensure a good night of sleep. By the time the law could be changed to prevent such abuses, those children would have grown into adults and likely have children of their own. Perhaps they would also make regular visits to pharmacies, just as she did, to buy a bottle of the medicine she knew to be so effective.

"I think this issue is too important to wait." She spoke the words quietly, knowing her statement was in direct opposition to everything the admiral believed. "I've read about the abolitionists and what they did before the Civil War," she said cautiously. "They tried to outlaw slavery through legitimate channels, and that crusade lasted more than a hundred years before it was resolved. In the meantime, some of the abolitionists did things that were illegal too. The underground railroad. Waylaying slave ships.

Surely you would not consider those actions immoral, even if they were illegal."

She looked cautiously at the admiral, but there was no softening on his face. "Is this the tactic Banebridge used to convince you to prowl around like a thief in the night?"

"No. I did not even think of this before you spoke of our actions as underhanded and immoral. I will own up to the first, but won't accept the second."

"Then we have reached an impasse," the admiral said. "I can appreciate your point of view, but you must understand that I do not condone it, nor can I support you in any action that breaks the law."

The words hurt, but she refused to be swayed from her objective. "If you know how I can get in touch with Alexander Banebridge, I would truly appreciate it."

"I'm sorry, Miss Pallas. Banebridge has always held his cards very close to the chest, and I have no idea where he is at this time."

She knew the admiral would not lie, which meant her trip here had been pointless. She tried not to let disappointment show on her face as she stood. "Thank you for your time. And although it ended badly, thank you for the opportunity you gave me to work at the Navy Yard. It was truly a privilege."

As she walked along the street bordering the Charles River that housed the dry docks, the rope factory, and the ironworks, Lydia knew she would never see this beloved stretch of land again. It was here she had found confidence in her abilities to support herself and grow into an independent woman. Perhaps more important, the Navy Yard was where she was given the opportunity to contribute to the country that had taken her in and provided shelter to her when she was nothing but a storm-tossed orphan. Now she would need to find a new life for herself, but somehow she could not imagine it would be anywhere nearly as wonderful as this.

18

Despite the dim light of the moon, Lydia did her best to scurry along the poorly lit streets, one eye on the icy cobblestone walkway, the other watching the darkened corners and alleyways to be sure no drunken sailor came lurching toward her. Four o'clock in the morning was no time to be out on the streets, but if she wished to keep her employment at the Stolinski Bakery, she needed to hurry.

Lydia had never given any thought as to how shops had freshly baked bread and warm blueberry scones before the sun even rose. Now she knew it was because a small army of workers braved icy walkways in the middle of the night to fire up ovens, heft cumbersome sacks of flour, knead dough, and stack loaves of bread into delivery wagons. Not that Lydia was permitted to work with the food yet. She did not even qualify as an apprentice baker; her tasks were to feed coal into the ovens, scour the huge metal trays the bread bakers used, and keep the floors clean. By the end of each day, her muscles were screaming for relief, and it was difficult for her to walk the three miles back to the Laughing Dragon.

She breathed a sigh of relief when she rounded the corner and saw the dim lights glowing within the Stolinski Bakery. The little bell above the door tinkled as she entered, and old Mrs. Stolinski looked up from her ledger book.

"You are late again," she said in a voice loud enough for everyone in the bakery to hear.

"I'm sorry, ma'am. The ice on the street made it hard to walk."

"Ice," the old lady muttered as she stared at Lydia. "Nine other employees had ice on their walkways, but they got here on time."

Lydia's gaze darted to the clock above the counter to see it was six minutes past four o'clock. As unpleasant as old Mrs. Stolinski's demeanor was, there was truth to what she said, and Lydia met her eyes without flinching. "I'm sorry I was late and grateful someone was able to get the ovens started." She shrugged out of her cloak and hung it alongside the other employees' wraps. "I promise it won't happen again."

Because Lydia would no longer be living at the Laughing Dragon. Even if it hadn't been too late to buy her apartment, the Laughing Dragon was too far away from her new job and too expensive. She could no longer afford the luxury of living at her treasured apartment, since the bakery paid less than one-third of what she had been earning at the Navy Yard and her expenses had stayed the same.

She had already notified the Brandenbergs she would be leaving the Laughing Dragon, as the deadline had arrived and she hadn't come up with the money to buy her apartment. The contract allotted her two weeks to move out, and she was using that time to find a new place to live.

Just as Lydia had always feared, she was sliding back into the tightening snare of poverty.

Karl's presence beside her was the only thing that prevented Lydia from tossing her satchel down into the snow, collapsing on the cobblestone path, and sobbing like a baby. Karl had taken the morning off from work to help her move, and he shouldn't have to listen to her whine for something that could never be. Besides, she never cried and was not about to start today.

This morning, she had closed the door on her beloved home at the Laughing Dragon for the last time. With the exception of what she carried in her satchel and what Karl lugged on his back, she was losing everything she owned in the world.

"Are you sure about this, Lydia?" Karl asked once again. "I can borrow a wagon if you want to bring more of your things."

She shook her head. She adored Karl, but every time he offered to help salvage her belongings, she felt as if he were ripping a bandage off a fresh wound. "When you see the room I've leased, you will understand," she said. The tiny room came furnished with a bed, a small table, and a trunk to store her clothing. There was no space for anything else. Certainly not enough room for the comfortable upholstered chair where she loved to curl up with a book, or the hand-carved armoire she had bought from a family moving out west. All of it was going to be sold at auction this afternoon. The estate agent told her to expect about forty dollars in proceeds.

The money would be welcome, as there was still no sign of Bane or the funds he owed her.

"Not even enough room for your books?" Karl asked. "I know how much you treasure them. Surely you could find a space. Perhaps under the bed?" He shifted the sack of her clothing a little higher on his back, then grasped her elbow as he helped her cross the street.

It hurt too badly to think of her books. "Everything I really value is right here in my arms," she said blankly. "Do you suppose it is possible to sum up a person's life by what we choose to keep with us? Because I don't think there is anything I truly need other than what I am carrying."

The furniture was gone. The draperies she had sewn by hand were gone. She did not have personal letters or photographs that someone from a normal family would have. She had briefly toyed with the idea of keeping her Lewis and Clark book, but she knew there was no room in her life for foolish daydreams. The knowledge had not stopped a searing ache from ripping through her when she set the book in the box of items to sell. The few treasures she now carried in her arms were precious to her.

"I brought my little picture of the Mediterranean island," Lydia said. "When I see that I can almost smell the salt air and remember Mama's singing as we sorted fish into baskets." She wanted to say more, but thinking of those faraway days caused the lump in her throat to grow and her eyes to mist. The last time she had cried had been her first day of school when she wept tears of joy. Through all the sorrow and chaos of the following years, never once had she broken down and cried. She wouldn't start now.

She kept rambling as they walked, hoping to ease the torrent of sorrow welling inside her. "I brought the miniature model of a navy frigate Willis gave me on my first week of work when he realized my ignorance of any ship besides a fishing boat. No matter how badly it ended, those years at the Navy Yard will always be precious to me," Lydia said. She walked faster as the memories flooded through her.

"And I brought a compass Bane gave me," she said. "I know you don't approve of him, but I think the world of Bane. He gave me that compass because he said I was too much of a sissy to venture into the unknown." She gave a watery gulp of laughter. "He was right. Bane was always right about that sort of thing." Karl was mercifully silent as she walked and rambled on about Bane. "He helped me in ways I've never imagined, and even though it hurts so badly, I'm glad I got to know someone like him. Everyone ought to have a brilliant, glorious rascal in their life just once, right?" She swiped at her eyes, determined that not one tear should fall.

Lydia tightened her arms around her sack. "I brought my copy of the Bible," she continued. "On my eighteenth birthday, the Cracken Orphanage gave me five dollars and a Bible and sent me on my way. I want so badly to believe there is a God out there. I've never been able to make much sense of the Bible, but it means a lot to Bane, so I will begin reading it."

Karl stopped and turned to look down at her, ignoring the pedestrians who had to step around them in the center of the walk. "Bane told you to read the Bible?" he asked, surprise on his Nordic features.

She nodded. "He didn't show that side of himself to many people, but it is there, and it is deep and profound for him. Bane is the most dedicated, valiant man I know," she said. "I want to learn from his example. The loneliness clawing inside me is so terrible, I just need *something*." Tears were threatening to spill, so she drew a ragged breath to get ahold of herself. "I ache inside. I feel pointless. Bane said he was vacant inside before he found God, and I feel vacant too, so I need to keep trying to find God as well. I'll do *anything* to stop this ache inside me."

It hurt to let Karl see her so devastated, so she turned and began walking again. He fell into step beside her. "I used to feel important," Lydia said. "I felt like my job as a translator was helping to make the navy stronger. I thought my parents would be so proud of me, but now all I do is scrape coal residue from the bottom of ovens. I don't know what I am meant to be anymore."

Karl shifted the sack again so he could reach an arm out to wrap around her shoulders. "You are meant to be sad and miserable for a little while. That is the way of a broken heart, Lydia. Come spring, all this will not seem so terrible. I promise you."

She did not believe him, but they had arrived at Bayside Rooming House for Women, and she hurt too much to continue the conversation. She paid the landlady and signed the papers acknowledging that this shabby waterfront tenement was her new home.

Just this once, the landlady gave her permission for a man to help carry her belongings to her room. As they entered the tiny room, a flash of concern showed in Karl's eyes. He noticed the water stain on the ceiling and the threadbare coverlet on the bed, but quickly masked his concern. "This is a fine place, Lydia."

She nodded. "Yes."

He set her satchel down, and just before he left, Karl turned back toward her. "If you are going to read the Bible, don't start at the first page. It is too easy to get bogged down that way. You might start with the book of John, which is a little friendlier to a beginner."

"Thank you, Karl."

After he left, it took her less than five minutes to unpack her paltry belongings. The Mediterranean island picture and the Bible on the bedside table. Her compass she would keep tucked inside her pocket. And when she reached inside her satchel, she withdrew the one item she had not told Karl about.

On the small ledge of the narrow window, Lydia placed her little blue bottle of Mrs. Winslow's Soothing Syrup.

19

One of the advantages of Lydia's job at the bakery was that her workday came to an end at two o'clock in the afternoon. Today, if she hurried, she had just enough time to catch a streetcar to the south side of Boston in order to carry out an errand that had been plaguing her for weeks.

The horse-drawn conveyance clipped slowly through the icy streets, and it took Lydia an hour to arrive at her destination. Her eyes dimmed as she caught sight of the bleak structure that had been her home for nine years. The building was a three-story brick box with tall, narrow windows. The bare limbs of the chestnut trees surrounding the building looked black against the leaden skies.

The familiar scent of old moss and wet slate brought a flood of memories as she walked up the path to the front door. It was not a terrible place to grow up. She was never hungry or beaten, and the Crakken family benefactors insisted on providing a solid education for the children. But despite the orphanage being filled with children whose basic physical needs were met, it was an institution devoid of love, attention, or warmth.

A woman with a face full of freckles opened the door in response to her knock. "I am hoping to see Headmaster Collins," Lydia said.

"Mr. Collins retired years ago. Headmaster Barlow runs Crakken now."

"Very well. May I speak with Mr. Barlow?"

The servant looked apprehensive at the simple request. "If you haven't got an appointment, he is not too keen on visitors." She made to close the door, but Lydia inserted her foot into the doorway.

"Please. I've traveled a long way to be here, and it truly is important." There was something familiar about the woman. Very few people had that shade of carroty red hair, and although it must have been at least a decade, Lydia recognized the trace of a girl she once knew.

"Is that you, Sarah?" Lydia scrambled for the name. "Sarah Longmire? You were here at Crakken when I first arrived. I'm Lydia Pallas."

Sarah scrutinized Lydia, then recognition dawned. "You were the little Greek girl who couldn't speak English!" A smile broke across Sarah's face. "Lord have mercy, now you speak plain as day. Come on in out of the cold."

"How is it you are still here?" Lydia asked as she shrugged out of her cape.

"Well, I got married right after I left, but that didn't go too well. I came back because I didn't know what else to do with myself. I teach the younger students. I don't get paid much, but at least I've got a roof over my head."

Lydia's gaze traveled over the blank plaster walls that had no trace of decoration or any sign that children lived here. It appeared very little had changed at the Crakken Orphanage, but was it possible they had stopped drugging their children into obedience?

"Sarah, when I lived here, it was quite common for the attendants to use Mrs. Winslow's Soothing Syrup. Do you know if they still use it?"

Sarah nodded. "Oh yes. Nothing else settles the children down quite so well."

"I see," Lydia whispered softly. She glanced at the darkening skies outside and knew she needed to speak to someone in authority immediately. She did not have much time if she wished to catch the last car home.

"May I see the headmaster? It truly is important."

Sarah gave a sad smile. "I'll see what I can do, but don't hope for too much there," she said as she disappeared down the hallway. After a few minutes, Sarah returned and Lydia was escorted to the headmaster's office, where she was introduced to a cadaverous man dressed in an ancient frock coat at least two sizes too big for his narrow frame.

"Thank you for seeing me on such short notice," Lydia said as the door closed behind her.

"I generally prefer an appointment," Mr. Barlow said as he stared down the long hook of his nose. "We value tradition here, and a prearranged appointment is the proper etiquette."

"Yes, of course," Lydia murmured. She swallowed hard and tried not to let his piercing black eyes unsettle her. "I lived at Crakken for a number of years and wish to call a medical issue to your attention. I've recently learned that a medication freely dispensed here at Crakken contains a shockingly high dose of opium. The children are given this drug for everything from a scraped knee to a restless spirit. When I lived here there were children who were dosed with it daily."

There was no change on Mr. Barlow's long, thin face. He merely steepled his hands before his chest as he reclined in his chair. "And?" The way he drawled the word gave Lydia the chills.

She cleared her throat. "And as opium is known to be an addictive substance, I believe you must stop using this medicine at once. It is called Mrs. Winslow's Soothing Syrup, and I know that it is still being used here at Crakken."

Mr. Barlow gave a long-suffering sigh. "All our children receive proper medical care, and that includes whatever medicine is deemed necessary by our staff. Mrs. Winslow's Syrup is a highly regarded medication. We have used it for decades, and we value tradition."

"I don't care if it is traditional," Lydia said. "It is a vile drug that could make an addict out of a little child."

Once again, there was no sign her words were getting through to Mr. Barlow. "What do you suggest we do about it?"

"Throw it down the drain! Figure out a new way to soothe restless children. Perhaps a brisk walk in the evening will help expend their energy. Or smaller classrooms. When I was here there were forty children assigned to a single staff member. No wonder it was difficult for them to manage all those children. Surely more staff and a change in exercise regimen would do the children good."

"We value tradition, Miss Pallas. I see no need for exercise that will expose young bodies to the harsh New England climate. Now, if you will forgive me, I must return to my correspondence."

Lydia shot to her feet. "No, I won't forgive you! The only people who can forgive you are the hundreds of children lying drugged behind these stone walls." She was shouting now, but still her words did not penetrate the maddening Mr. Barlow, who slid his spectacles onto his nose and turned his attention back to the letter on his desk.

Bane would never tolerate such a glib dismissal.

His image popped into her head unbidden, and it was easy for her to envisage the way Bane would handle this. He would never fly off the handle as she was doing; he was too clever for that. She forced her shoulders to relax, gathered her thoughts, and smiled into Mr. Barlow's eyes, just as Bane would do.

"I am grateful to Crakken for the excellent education I received here," she said calmly. "I can write well enough to clearly express my opinion, and I will notify the Crakken family of your position on feeding opium to children to make your job easier." She fastened the ties of her cloak. "And if they will not take action, I know there are politicians and ministers who are concerned about the scourge of opium use. Perhaps a public outcry will alert the proper medical authorities to look into the practices here at Crakken."

Even the suggestion of public exposure did not rattle Mr. Barlow, but it made Lydia's heart soar, for this was no idle threat. She had found a cause worth pursuing, something to give her life meaning. Maybe her professional life would never amount to more than scraping coal from the bottom of a stove, but that didn't mean her life would have no purpose.

For the first time in weeks, her battered pride began to mend.

Lydia was stooped over the coal grate beneath one of the enormous bread ovens when Mrs. Stolinski called her name. "Visitor, Lydia." Surprisingly, the woman was much friendlier after the flurry of early morning work. Lydia wiped the coal dust on her apron and walked to the front of the bakery. A smile lit her face when she saw Karl Olavstad standing in front of the counter.

"Come to buy some blueberry scones for Willis?" she teased.

His smile was brief. "I came to deliver this," he said, passing a white envelope across the counter. "Bane came by the office this morning. He said he put a little extra in there on account of it being so late."

"I see," she whispered. She held the crisp envelope between her hands, thinking inanely that Bane had touched this envelope just a few hours ago.

"Look inside," Karl urged. "Is everything there?"

A quick peek revealed a stack of crisp ten-dollar bills. "It is all here," she said. There was also a note, but she did not want to read it with Karl watching her.

"If he had gotten that money to you on time, you would not have been thrown out of your apartment," Karl said in a dark voice.

She shook her head. "I don't have a job that can support that sort of life anymore. I can't blame Bane for that." She closed the flap of the envelope. "Did he say anything else? When he delivered the letter, did he say anything other than about the money?"

"No, Lydia. He didn't."

It had been almost two months since she had seen Bane, and still she thought of him every day. Shouldn't things be getting easier for her by now?

"You don't look good."

Karl's statement hung in the air. Lydia tucked a strand of hair into her bun. "I get up very early in the morning," she said. "I need to be awake by three thirty if I am to get here on time."

"It's more than that," Karl said. "I can't quite put my finger on it. . . ."

She had been feeling terrible lately, and no doubt that was beginning to take its toll on her appearance. In the past, she had always taken a little sip of Mrs. Winslow's syrup to make her feel better. Ever since she had learned what was in it, however, she had tried to cut back, but it was a struggle. Her headaches were frequent, and at night, just after she had begun drifting into sleep, she would jerk awake in the middle of some hideous dream. How odd that these terrible dreams came whenever she was strong enough to refrain from using Mrs. Winslow's. The nightmares were so bad she would usually take a tiny sip of the syrup or she would never get back to sleep. Last night she had not used the drug and had lain awake most of the night as a result. Perhaps that accounted for the hollows she could feel beneath her eyes.

As soon as Karl left, Lydia opened the note from Bane, holding her breath and hoping insanely that perhaps he still wanted to meet her.

He did not. He apologized for the delay in getting her the funds, saying business had taken him to Cuba and weather had delayed his return. He hoped the delay did not cause her difficulty in securing her apartment. He did not even bother to sign the note.

Lydia folded the paper with shaking fingers. Could it have been any more impersonal and remote? If Bane wished to stress just how detached he was from her, this note had done the trick.

The first thing she did upon returning to her boardinghouse was take a large spoonful of Mrs. Winslow's syrup to ease the raging pain in her body and in her soul.

20

February 1892

The sleet hit Bane's face like pinpricks in the frigid evening air. Philadelphia's climate was never pleasant in February, but the wind made it even worse. He lowered his head and pulled the collar of his coat tighter as he hastened to the townhouse near the end of the street. A layer of ice covered the front steps, and he grasped the iron railing on his way to the top. Sleet melded the brass knocker to its base; he had to pry it free before knocking a quick series of raps.

As he waited for an answer, he turned to observe the other townhouses in this respectable neighborhood. Across the street, a bow-fronted window glowed from the light of a cheery fire, and a family gathered on the sofa with a number of children sprawled out on the floor. A little blond girl was opening presents. A birthday? She certainly seemed to be the center of attention as her parents fussed over her. The gaily wrapped box she was ripping into was almost as big as her compact little body.

The door opened behind him. "Banebridge! I'm glad you could make it through this nasty weather." Richard Algood held the door wide. Bane wanted to see what was in the girl's present, but heat was pouring out Algood's door, and he had more important things to concern himself with than what was in a girl's birthday box.

He shook the ice from his coat before hanging it on a rack in the narrow foyer, then followed Richard back to his tiny study at the rear of the house. The moment the door clicked behind him, Bane got down to business.

"How are things looking?"

Richard sighed as he lowered himself into the desk chair. Piles of papers, books, and pharmaceutical journals filled the office. "Unless you can help me pull off a miracle between now and April, my candidacy will go down in flames. There have been no changes."

Bane leaned against the wall of the study. This was his first attempt to initiate reform from inside the pharmaceutical industry. The opportunity had presented itself when he first met Richard Algood, and Bane was quick to act on it. Richard was one of the few pharmacists willing to support restrictions on the sale of opium in pharmacies, and Bane was attempting to get him elected to the presidency of the American Pharmacists Association. It was a fool's quest. The pharmacists had been at the forefront of those blocking any legislation to limit the sale of opium in their shops, but at least Richard's doomed candidacy would force the pharmacists to begin discussing the issue. Bane and Richard were likely to lose the battle, but it would advance Bane's cause in the long run.

Bane folded his arms across his chest. "I have thought of a new angle to attack the problem," he said. "If the pharmacists won't outlaw opium for sale in their shops, would they be willing to limit its use by government agencies? Orphanages, for example. The drug is being abused by orphanage workers trying to make their jobs easier. And workers in the schools too. Surely this is something the pharmacists would be willing to condemn."

Richard straightened. "Funny you should mention that. I just had a letter a few weeks ago from a young woman asking after the same thing. I had never heard of her, but I gather she saw the article I wrote about the dangers of Mrs. Winslow's Syrup and thought I might be able to help. She wrote very eloquently on the abuses of opium in the orphanages."

Richard riffled through the papers mounded on the only other chair in the office until he found the letter and handed it over to Bane.

Bane's breath froze at the sight of the tidy script on the envelope. He would recognize that handwriting anywhere. Forcing his expression to remain blank, he extracted the letter and read Lydia's passionate words. *What mother would give her child an opium pipe in the event of a skinned knee or a common cold?* Lydia went on to fill both sides of the page, describing how the Crakken Orphanage used opium for all manner of ailments. She asserted the innocent-looking serums packaged in attractive bottles were no better than the opium pipes in the illegal dens. Bane's hands trembled as he held the pages that spelled out the subtle horrors of using opium to pacify a restless child.

His brave, passionate Lydia, so earnest and determined to do what was right. He could hear her voice as he read her words.

It had been months since he'd seen Lydia, but he still thought about her every day. When he saw a woman with copper glints in her hair, he thought of Lydia. When he lay awake at night, strategizing his next congressional campaign, he imagined what it would be like to have Lydia beside him, sharing his plans and excitement.

He hoped she didn't still think of him. He hoped she would meet some handsome young man in Boston who would give her a passel of children, while Bane would fade into a distant memory.

It would be easier for him to forget her if he could be certain she was settled and happy.

Richard's voice cut through the haze of his thoughts. "There is nothing I can do about her complaints. That sort of thing is handled by the government, not the industry."

It would take decades to change the law, but an inflammation of public opinion could occur with astonishing speed. And for a privately funded orphanage like Crakken, public opinion mattered.

There were newspapers that would publish this letter. Newspapers like the *New York Times* and the *Christian Crusade* that were powerful forces for shaping public opinion and motivating people to act. And Bane just happened to know the people in charge of the *Christian Crusade*. "Can I have this letter?"

There was very little he could do for Lydia Pallas, but he could make certain her voice was heard.

Jack Fontaine's father told him to hold Lucy's hand so she couldn't get into trouble, which made him feel like a grown-up, even though he was only nine. His father was too busy shaking hands with all the other grown-ups at the fancy party, so Jack had to make sure Lucy didn't get lost in this big museum.

Jack thought it was weird to have a party in a museum, but Papa told him the Boston Museum of Fine Arts sometimes opened at night for special occasions, and this was one of those times. There was violin music and everyone was all dressed up. Papa was wearing his best uniform, the dark blue one with the epaulets on the shoulders and two rows of gold buttons all the way down the front of his jacket.

When they had first come inside the museum, they passed rooms of paintings and tapestries and a whole room filled with statues of naked ladies. His father had pushed him past that room quickly, but Jack had seen them anyway. Now he was stuck upstairs with Lucy in this huge room where the party was.

It used to be that his father was always dragging Jack to go see a new ship or watch the sailors do their training. Now they went to football matches at Harvard and political speeches and fancy events. His father was always shaking hands with people and didn't have much time for him and Lucy anymore.

Jack looked at the weird pictures on the walls that were some sort of new art with splotches of paint everywhere. They were so bad it looked like Lucy could have done them. He wished he could go downstairs to the Egyptian room, where there were sarcophaguses and real mummies inside. Papa didn't want Lucy to see the mummies because he thought she would be scared, but Jack wanted to sneak back for a look.

No one was paying much attention to them, and Jack risked putting his hat back on his head. Papa warned him he had to take it off whenever they were inside a building, but Jack thought it was a stupid rule. He liked the hat Bane had given him, and wearing it made him feel better.

He squatted down beside Lucy. "Let's go downstairs and see the mummies," he whispered. "There are real dead people inside and I want to get a better look." Lucy sent a worried glance at Papa and started sucking her thumb. He pulled it out. "Don't be such a baby," he said. "We can sneak down and be back before anyone notices."

When he stood up to drag Lucy toward the staircase, he bumped into a grown-up. "I'm sorry, sir," Jack said as he adjusted the brim of his hat that had been knocked off-kilter.

"That's a fine hat, young man," the stranger said.

Jack straightened a little with pride. "It is an army slouch hat," Jack said proudly. "Bane bought it for me."

The man leaned a little closer, showing Jack even more attention. "Is this Bane fellow in the army?"

Jack furrowed his brow. "I don't really know. But he brings me presents every time he comes to see us. Last month he brought me a book about the army during the Civil War, and before that he brought real spurs just like they wear in the cavalry."

"What a generous man this Bane fellow is."

Jack nodded. "That's not his real name. My father calls him Banebridge, but we always call him Bane. I've known him ever since I was really little."

The man seemed interested, so Jack took off his hat to show the stranger how the brim of the slouch hat rolled up so the soldiers could march with a rifle and not bump the hat.

Lucy was fidgeting, but Jack kept talking because he liked it when grown-ups listened to him. Except that he missed his chance to sneak down to see the mummies because his father spotted them and started walking across the room toward them.

The stranger must have noticed too. "I'll let you get back to your father now. What a good lad you are. I hope we meet again soon."

Professor Van Bracken watched the trio move to the far side of the room where a soprano was about to perform. A triumphant surge coursed through his body, but he prevented any sign of it from disturbing the polite mask he had perfected over the decades.

For at long last, Professor Edward Van Bracken had found someone Bane truly cared about.

21

Bane was cautious as he approached the Navy Yard. Ever since last autumn's disaster with Lydia, the admiral had wanted nothing to do with him. The blistering contempt in Admiral Fontaine's eyes when he ordered Bane to keep away from the Navy Yard was hard for him to forget, so the urgent telegram begging Bane to return to Boston was a surprise.

Even more unusual, Eric ordered him to report to his private residence rather than his office. Why was Eric at home in the middle of a Tuesday afternoon?

Three armed guards stood at the front of Eric's house. Bane eyed them curiously as he mounted the steps. "Are the British coming?" he jested, but the guards eyed him grimly. One of them escorted him inside while the other two maintained their posts.

The house was strangely silent as the guard escorted him to Eric's private office. Bane opened the door to see Eric standing beside the fireplace.

"Miss me?" Bane asked.

Eric vaulted across the room, and Bane's head snapped back

from the fist that connected with his jaw. "Where is my son?!" Eric demanded. "What have you done with my son?"

Pain shot through Bane's jaw, but he did not defend himself, staring in shock at Eric as he struggled to regain control. Never in twelve years had Bane seen Admiral Fontaine lose his temper in such a fashion.

"My boy is missing," Eric said tersely. "I was told to come to you for answers."

Bane rubbed his jaw, working the muscles and glaring at Eric. "I have no idea what you are talking about."

"Perhaps this will help," Eric said as he threw an envelope at Bane's chest. Bane snatched the creamy paper before it fluttered to the floor. The note inside was short, polite, and ruthless:

Jack Fontaine will be a guest in my home for the foreseeable future. I suggest you contact Alexander Banebridge for the details.

Professor Edward Van Bracken

Bane felt the bottom drop out of his stomach, and he sagged against the doorframe. Rachel's son! After all these years, his worst nightmare was taking shape before his eyes. The Professor had found a weakness in Bane's armor and was moving in for the kill.

Enclosed with the note was a short newspaper clipping. It was about the progress of a bill moving through Congress to curtail the use of opium in medical preparations. The Professor made a small note in the margin:

Tell Bane to put a stop to this. Your son's health depends on it.

"When did he go missing?" Bane asked weakly.

"Two days ago," Eric responded, his voice grim. "The note was delivered the night he disappeared."

Bane handed the note back to Eric, an avalanche of guilt pouring down on him that made it difficult for him to even stand. He closed off the inconvenient emotions and crossed the room to stare out the window, the peaceful sight of gently falling snow a stark contrast to the fear that was roiling inside him.

"Close the door," he said softly. His mind rattled through the options, rejecting them almost before they could fully form. He dreaded telling Eric what had happened to Jack. The odds of getting the boy back were too bleak to even contemplate.

He met Eric's grim eyes. "The man who has your son is Professor Van Bracken, the opium drug lord I told you about all those years ago."

"Why would he go after *my* child?" Eric demanded.

"Somehow he must have learned that your family was important to me," Bane said. "I don't know how, but he figured it out." It didn't really matter how the Professor had learned about Jack Fontaine; all that mattered was figuring out a solution.

"If he wants a ransom, I'll pay it," Eric said.

Bane's voice was bleak. "That's not what he wants."

"Then what?"

The question hung in the air. Bane saw no easy way to soften the blow. "He wants to control me."

Eric's voice was unequivocal. "Then do what he wants." It was not a request, it was an order. He pointed to the newspaper article. "If he wants you to get out of the opium legislation, then get out of it."

"It is not that easy." Bane turned to look out at the snow, unable to bear the anguish his next words were going to cause Eric. "If I do what Van Bracken wants, it will guarantee your son's safety, but it will not gain his release. The Professor is happy to keep hostages for years to ensure good behavior." In most cases, he kept the hostages for a decade or more. In all likelihood, Eric would not see his son again until he was a grown man.

"That is unacceptable," Eric said.

Bane still could not turn around. "I'll get him back. I swear it. If it is the last thing I do on this earth, I will get that boy back to you."

Now that the shock was wearing off, his mind was clicking back into gear. Negotiating with Van Bracken would be impossible. Bribing the Professor's servants was an option, but it also carried the risk of backfiring. He knew Eric wanted his son back immediately, but that wasn't going to happen. It would require weeks or months to study the mansion, observe the servants, and plan a strategy.

"I suspect the Professor is keeping the boy in his mansion in Vermont," he said.

Eric's voice lashed out. "If you know where he is being held, I'm going there with a private army and getting Jack out."

"Don't," Bane said. "The Professor has contingency plans for everything, and your son won't live through that sort of rescue attempt." Bane knew exactly what would happen if anyone ever tried to raid the remote Vermont fortress. Not so much as a bone or a tooth from the hostages would remain. There was an old well that had gone dry decades earlier behind the mansion. The Professor kept canisters of kerosene beside the well, and if Fontaine's army managed to get on the property, they would not be able to save the boy before he was disposed of down that well. There would be no trace of evidence left to support charges against the Professor.

Bane looked at Eric. "The Professor has spies everywhere, and if he gets wind of any rescue plan, he will simply eliminate the evidence. Don't take that risk. Give me the time I need to plan this carefully, and I *will* get Jack out safely."

Jack was probably going to face several months of captivity, and Bane needed to understand the boy's strengths and weaknesses. He spent the next hour asking Eric endless questions about his son. Strengths? The boy was clever. He was mechanically inclined and good with languages. He had a sense of humor he relied on when under pressure. As for weaknesses, Jack's vision was poor and he needed reading glasses, which had been left behind when he was taken. He had no respect for rules and was stubborn to the point of intransigence.

Bane prayed that Jack would rely on his natural sense of humor to help him through the next months, because if there was one thing the Professor despised, it was stubborn little boys.

Bane pulled the cap low over his head, making sure the brim covered his face. With his battered pea coat and heavy boots, he knew he looked like any of the thousands of sailors from the docks along the Boston harbor. He leaned against the grainy brick wall of a hardware store across the street from the bakery where Lydia worked.

Lydia emerged from the bakery at two-o'clock, the end of her shift. She did not glance his way as she walked down the steps, adjusted her cloak, and headed toward home.

She didn't look good. Her face looked ashen and drawn, as though she had not slept for a week. Was it because she was still adjusting to living in a new rooming house? Or it could be the loss of her job at the Navy Yard? When Karl had told him about Lydia's termination, he had been sick for days. He had hoped she would spring back after he left, find some other challenge to sink her teeth into. Instead, she was working herself to the bone in a bakery because he had gotten her fired.

He should be shot for even thinking about drawing Lydia back into this mess. She had suffered enough on his account, and now he was scheming new ways to put her at risk, all because of his own private vendetta against the Professor. He steeled his resolve. He would do what was necessary to rescue Jack Fontaine, and that meant involving Lydia. He pulled the collar of his coat higher and began following her.

The Professor was holding the boy at his Vermont mansion. Bane had bribed a clerk at the market that delivered the weekly supplies to the estate for this information. He scrutinized the lists of supplies the market was sending to the mansion, noting the regular delivery of schoolbooks suitable for young children. The clerk said such schoolbooks had been delivered for a number of years to the estate, which made Bane believe there was at least one other hostage. Last week's list had had a curious item: a special order for a pair of spectacles with frames suitable for a small face. They must be for Jack Fontaine.

Now that he knew where Jack was, it was time to set the rest of his plan in motion. And for that, he needed Lydia.

He thought she would go to her rooming house, but to his surprise, she took a seat on an iron bench at a streetcar station. When the horse-drawn streetcar came to a stop before her, she caught the driver's attention.

"Does this car stop at the public library?" she asked. At the driver's nod, Lydia hopped aboard.

He didn't want to confront her on a public streetcar. Now that he knew where she was going, he would bide his time and wait for the next car.

Lydia was embarrassed at how much she did not know.

She liked to think of herself as a well-educated person, but as she sat in the huge, cavernous reading room of the Boston Public Library, she wrestled with the daunting terminology in the medical textbook before her. It was the only book she had been able to find on opium addiction. She was too mortified to ask the librarian, a grim shadow of a man, if there was a book about opium that was a little easier to understand. What would he think of a young lady asking after such a thing?

But Lydia needed to learn, so she struggled through the dense terminology, seeking insight on the effects of opium dependency and withdrawal. The section on withdrawal mentioned anxiety and insomnia, which Lydia suffered from, but who wouldn't be anxious after losing her job and her home? The book went on to describe nausea, paranoia, and abdominal cramping as other indications of withdrawal. She had none of those symptoms, so that must prove she was not addicted. She was suffering through a difficult period in her life, and headaches and insomnia were perfectly normal at such a time. Nothing to worry about. She straightened her spine and looked up in relief.

And then she saw him.

Sitting two tables away, staring directly at her across the reading room of the Boston Public Library, was Alexander Banebridge.

She saw anguish in every line on his face as he sat motionless, watching her. She did not believe for a second that his presence was a coincidence. It had been months since she had seen him, but now here he was, gazing at her with all the longing of the world in his eyes.

She looked away. A sensible woman would want nothing to do with him. For months she had been staggering through life, feeling like half her soul had been ripped out because he couldn't be bothered to take a chance on her. The temptation to walk away clawed at her. She had finally regained some semblance of a normal life, and now he was back to throw chaos into her path once again.

But if he wanted her back—if he was ready to let her live alongside him and undertake whatever risks or joys came with hitching her life to his—she needed to know.

She closed the medical book, draped her cloak over her arm, and walked over to his table. The room was silent except for the sound of the occasional turning of a page, so she lowered herself into the seat opposite him at the table, leaned forward, and spoke in a discreet whisper. "I should think you have better things to do than stare at me like a besotted teenager. It is embarrassing."

He cocked a brow at her. "You mean because I am so much prettier than you?"

"I never should have told you that."

His smile was a little sad. "Probably not."

Lydia hurt at how easily they slipped back into their old banter. Bane was the only person with her same sense of humor, and it was oddly comforting just to be in his presence again. But it was dangerous as well. Not for the reasons Bane believed, but because Lydia did not know if she could withstand another rejection from him.

"Why are you here?" she whispered, praying he would say that he missed her, that he thought of her every day when he awoke and as he drifted off to sleep at night. That he made a mistake and would do anything to have her back in his life.

"I need a translator."

"Oh, for pity's sake!" she snapped in a full voice. Her words echoed off the high ceilings and marble floors, causing every head in the reading room to swivel toward her. The librarian shot to his feet and leveled her with a warning glare.

Bane leaned forward and spoke softly. "Lydia, I need you."

"No you don't; you need a *translator,*" she said in a fierce whisper. There were more disapproving scowls from the patrons surrounding her, but Lydia had no interest in continuing the conversation. If Bane had asked her to board a ship with him and set sail for the edge of the known universe, she would not have hesitated. The only thing she would deny him was a request to translate a document. She headed to the door, Bane following directly behind her.

A wall of cold air smacked her in the face the moment she stepped onto Boylston Street. She jerked the ties of her cloak together and set off at a brisk march toward the nearest streetcar station.

"Let's go somewhere we can talk," Bane said. "There is a café across the street."

"I can't afford it."

"I'm paying."

She stopped so fast he bumped into her from behind. She glared at him. "That's not what I meant and you know it. I lost *my job* because of you. *My apartment!*"

He blanched at her words. Since Bane was usually so cool, the sight of raw pain clouding his face rattled her composure. It made her want to console him, which was insane. She whirled away and kept striding toward the station. If she spent even another second with Bane, she would be in danger of getting drawn back into the whirlwind. She hastened her steps, darting around schoolchildren and a couple of businessmen blocking most of the sidewalk.

He grabbed her arm, swiveling her to face him. "Hit me."

"What?"

The din of street traffic made her doubt she had heard correctly, but Bane pointed to his jaw. "Go ahead. Back up, take a good healthy swing, and smack me hard, right here. I deserve it and we both know it."

"Don't be asinine."

He didn't back down. "I am responsible for getting you into this mess, and I've felt guilty about it for months. If taking a swing will make you feel better, I want you to do it. Plant me a good one."

Busy pedestrians bumped into her. Lydia felt ridiculous, standing in the middle of a public walkway and arguing with the man who had broken her heart. "I don't want to hit you, Bane. I don't want to speak with you; I don't even want to *look* at you. Just leave me alone."

She set off toward the station, but he followed. "You once told me that you wanted to be like one of the great explorers," he said. "That you wanted to do something important with your life, something that no one has ever done before."

"Foolish dreams of a girl with too much time on her hands." But for a few magical weeks she had felt like his ally in a noble crusade. It was a powerful and thrilling feeling, but now he just wanted to use her. "There are plenty of other people in this city who speak the languages you need. Go hire one of them." She hoped the pain she felt did not show in her voice.

"I think you are the only person who can accomplish this," he said. "The lives of at least two children depend on it, and I know you can help save them." He spoke the words with the utmost sincerity, and despite herself, she was intrigued.

She stopped in the middle of the walk and turned to look at him, scanning his face for deception or guile. What she saw was a man who looked at her with a combination of hope and desperation.

It was maddening, but she still loved him. And she knew down to the marrow in her bones that he loved her back. Last autumn he had pushed her away because he was afraid to let her into his world. Now he was opening the door again, just a tiny crack, but it was enough. If she could wiggle her way inside, make herself indispensable, and let him see she could be brave enough to live in his world, perhaps someday he would allow her to stay. The only way to make that happen was to reach out with both hands and prove to him she was not afraid.

"Let's get lunch," she said.

Unfortunately, Bane's plan made her very afraid.

They sat in the tiny café Bane had mentioned while he explained that the admiral's son had been kidnapped by the Professor, just as Bane had been kidnapped.

"The admiral must be devastated," she said in a shaking whisper. No matter how harshly Admiral Fontaine had treated her, he was a fine man who loved his family. She had only seen his children from a distance, but his devotion to them was unquestionable.

"I know there is at least one other child living at the mansion," Bane said. "The customs inspector at the port of New York lost his son, Dennis, to a kidnapping three years ago, and I believe he is still there."

It sounded like something out of a gothic horror novel. Bane described the mansion as a remote fortress in the northern wilderness of Vermont, near the border of Canada, where the Professor stored his prized collection of rare books.

Bane had a plan for Lydia to infiltrate the mansion. "In January, the Professor bought an extremely rare manuscript, a ninth-century Byzantine Greek copy of some first-century writings, found by archeologists exploring a deserted monastery on the Anatolian Plain. He took it straight to his fortress in Vermont."

Lydia had a sinking sensation in the pit of her stomach. "How does this involve me?"

"Two weeks ago, I learned that the Professor is on the hunt for a translator. He wants someone willing to relocate to Vermont to translate that manuscript."

"Impossible," Lydia said. "Byzantine Greek is very different from the Greek language of today. I am not qualified for the job."

Bane was not dissuaded. "Lydia, I've spoken to a rare book dealer who told me it is not as difficult as classical Greek. He sold me a book that has tables and charts that can help someone who is fluent in modern Greek make sense of ninth-century Byzantine Greek." He set the thin volume on the table before her. "I know you can do it."

Lydia opened the book and flipped to a page of Byzantine Greek text. She might as well have been looking at Chinese for all the sense she could make of it. "It would be a disaster. I can't do it," she said. "I could never pass myself off as some ancient scholar. He would never hire me."

She pushed the book across the table toward Bane, but he slid it right back. "That's where you are wrong." Bane's voice was unequivocal. "The Professor may *think* he is in search of an ancient languages scholar, but he can be easily distracted. Especially by someone who shares his same exuberant appreciation for rare manuscripts. All you need to do is demonstrate some basic ability, then veer the conversation toward the wonders of the rare book world."

Lydia stared at the untouched cup of coffee before her, unable to even contemplate putting anything into her nervous stomach. "I don't know any more about rare books than I do about ancient Greek."

Bane did not miss a beat. "But rare book lore is easier to learn in a hurry. I will work with you and coach you on what you need to know. It won't be difficult to land the job."

He said it with such conviction that it was easy for her to believe him. "And once I am inside the house? What then?"

"Then the real work begins," Bane said. "You locate where the boys are being kept and observe their schedule. They will be closely guarded, so you won't be able to snatch them and run. You probably won't even be able to see or speak with them, so it will take a while for you to gather the information I need. We will devise a method for you to communicate these things to me."

He reached across the table and covered her hand with his. "I won't ever be far away."

And that was enough to persuade Lydia. There were two terrified children out there who needed her. And Bane needed her. She would show Bane she was no trembling flower too afraid to live in his world. If she had any hope of joining her life with Bane's, she needed to prove she was as fearless as he.

She squeezed his hand and locked her gaze with his. "Teach me what I need to know."

22

It was late before Lydia returned to her boardinghouse that night.

"There was a delivery for you this morning," her landlady said as Lydia walked in the door. "I put the package in your room. What a charming young man," the landlady said, a flush blooming across her features.

Lydia blinked. The landlady was usually as cheerful as a hungry bullmastiff, but today her eyes gleamed and her voice was as breathless as an infatuated girl. This must be Bane's doing. When Bane wanted to, he could charm the varnish off the hull of a ship.

Curiosity simmered as Lydia wiggled the key in the lock on her rickety door and pushed the door open. Her dingy room looked as it always did, with the sad coverlet and sparse furnishings, except for a parcel wrapped in brown paper and tied with a string sitting in the middle of her bed.

Bane's handwriting was scrawled across the top of the package:

I couldn't salvage your furniture, but I was able to track this down.

She pulled the string, tossed the paper aside, and saw her cherished book about Lewis and Clark.

The breath left her body in a rush. This book had been sold at the auction last autumn with the rest of her belongings. The faded dust jacket still covered the book, its papery feel comforting as she clutched it to her chest. Bane hadn't needed to do this for her, but she loved that he had. In those difficult years when she worked at the fish cannery after leaving the Crakken Orphanage, this book had been her salvation.

As much as she longed to sink into the pages of her favorite book, the translation manual Bane had given her in the coffee shop must be her only priority. She had but a week to memorize the Byzantine Greek alphabet and grammar.

The text was frightening in its difficulty. Many of the root words looked the same, but the syntax was different. The strange letters and odd diacritical marks made no sense to her. She stared at a single sentence for ten minutes, but could not unlock its meaning without help from the transliteration tables and translation charts.

Alone in her room, without Bane's steady resolve, Lydia felt her confidence drain away. How on earth was she going to learn Byzantine Greek in the space of a few days? The rush of anxiety felt like acid in her stomach. She stood and started pacing the narrow confines of her room, but tension still wriggled along her spine and into her arms, making it hard to stop twisting her hands. She knew this sensation well enough to accept that no amount of pacing or hand-wringing would bring relief.

In the next week she needed to learn not only Byzantine Greek but also the minutiae of the rare manuscript world. She thought it best to fight only one battle at a time, and she could battle Mrs. Winslow after rescuing Jack Fontaine. Lydia uncapped the little blue bottle on her windowsill and took a sip, sighing as relief trickled through her. If ever she had needed courage, it was now.

Bane scrutinized Lydia's face as she studied the antique etching of the Greek island of Seriphos. It dated back to 1790 and was not particularly valuable, but her finger was gentle as she traced the edge of the document that depicted two dragons cavorting in the sea off the coastline of the island. Her lively eyes scanned the whimsical map. "It seems a shame to give such a charming map to Professor Van Bracken. I rather fancy it for myself."

Bane cleared the café table of books and papers as the waitress brought their lunch. For several days he had been meeting with Lydia at the Long Wharf Café to teach her about the world of ancient manuscripts and the quirks of Professor Van Bracken's behavior.

"I'll buy you a dozen just like it once this is over," Bane said. "But the expression of reverence you had when you first held that document . . . work on maintaining that whenever you speak of old manuscripts to him."

He had bought the map for Lydia to bring to her interview as a gift for the Professor. It was unconventional, but he wanted to throw the man a bit off-balance. The inexpensive antique was the perfect way for Lydia to prove she was a kindred spirit. Bane pointed to the water damage that marred one corner of the map. "Tell the Professor your father worked for a map dealer in Greece. Apologize for the shoddy condition of the map, but tell him the story of how you helped your father rescue stacks of maps and rare etchings during a flood. As a reward, the shop owner let you keep any map that was damaged. Van Bracken will love a story like that. It will make him *identify* with the map."

"Identify with a piece of paper? You must be joking," Lydia said.

"Not at all. Professor Van Bracken is on a crusade to rescue rare documents, whether it be from a flood or from crude people who do not value them as much as he does."

There was so much information he needed to pump into Lydia's head, and only two days left to do it. Van Bracken had responded to Lydia's application for the position, and she was going to meet him at the Boston Athenaeum on Thursday morning to discuss the position.

"As other people dote on their children, Van Bracken dotes on his books," Bane said. "You can never show too much curiosity or appreciation for his treasures. At some point in the interview, imply that people who don't love books are ignorant. Stupid. You feel sorry for them, since they lack appreciation for such fine things."

"I would feel a bit snobbish saying that."

Bane shook his head. "Don't think like that; think like Van Bracken. The Greek document he wants translated is over a thousand years old. He does not want his precious manuscript fingered by an ill-bred translator who is only looking to earn a dollar. Prove to him you are a kindred spirit."

He studied her as she sat across from him, idly stirring her cooling cup of coffee. The morning sunlight cast glints off the russet tones of her hair. He teased her about his being the more attractive of the two of them, but truly, there was no sight he loved more than Lydia Pallas. Even the way she held her head on her slender neck was an enchanting combination of grace and undaunted strength.

He wanted to haul her into his arms and never let her go, but it would be unforgivable. Lydia was off-limits to him. It didn't matter that she would gladly rekindle their romantic relationship, as he still could not afford to have a woman like Lydia in his life. Even her company as he tutored her in the arcane world of rare manuscripts was a subtle kind of torture. Everything about her appealed to him. Her humor, her intelligence, even the meticulous way she arranged the cutlery on the table charmed him.

It was time to snap himself out of these thoughts. He rolled up the map and slipped it inside its tube. "Tell me how your study of ancient Greek is going." Anything to get his mind off how much he wanted to run away to a Caribbean island with her.

Lydia pursed her lips. "I hope I never encounter the man who suggested learning Byzantine Greek was not all that difficult," she said. "The transliteration tables are the key to decoding those unfamiliar symbols into modern Greek letters. I've tried to memorize the tables, but it is hopeless. It will take me at least a year to master the language. Without that book, I don't think I'll be able to pull this off. Is there any way I can smuggle the book into the house with me?"

Lydia's possession of that book in the Professor's house was problematic, but if she needed it, there was nothing else to be done. "I'll get you the dust jacket from another book to wrap it in. Try not to flaunt it about, though."

"You can be sure I won't." The tension eased from her face. When she looked at him with her cinnamon-colored eyes, laughter and warmth and love glowing behind them, he was surprised the temperature in the coffeehouse did not burn the building down.

"Quit looking at me like that."

She didn't stop. "Like what?" A little foot nudged his boot. He nudged back.

"None of that either," he said. "Remember, I'm a choirboy, not some reprobate bent on leading you astray." There was nothing he would like more, but one of them needed to be strong, and it looked as if Lydia had no intention of behaving herself.

He drained the last of the coffee in his cup. "Come on. Let's go explore some antique book stores." Maybe it wouldn't be so hard to resist her if he had to focus on steering her back to the study of the intricate world of rare books.

They took a streetcar to Cambridge where they wandered the old colonial streets, darting in and out of shops so Bane could show her the sort of books and manuscripts she needed to learn about. He had already taught her the difference between a folio and an octavo, between an etching and an engraving. Reaching high onto an old wooden shelf in an antiquarian shop, he brought down a fat leather volume.

"Tell me about this book," he said. Flipping open the cover, he pointed to the emblem of an anchor and a leaping dolphin at the bottom of the page. "What is the name of that symbol?"

She glanced at it for only a second. "A colophon. The symbol of the man who printed the volume. The anchor is Aldus Manutius's colophon."

"Excellent." By heaven, he adored this woman. How had she managed to retain all the information he'd been pouring into her? He wanted to tug her into his arms and spread kisses across her face. Instead, he kept peppering her with questions. "And where did Manutius do his work?"

She did not hesitate. "Venice. Sixteenth century."

"Touch the page and tell me what it's made of."

It was made of vellum, but she was resolute in her answer. She stepped so close to him he could smell the clean scent of her soap. "Parchment," she said softly.

He froze. Her mistake shouldn't disappoint him. He had crammed the equivalent of years of study into a single week, but still, these details would be important. He leaned down to whisper in her ear. "Do you want to rethink that?"

"No, Bane. It is parchment." She slid closer and pressed a kiss against his cheek. Bane glanced over the top of her glossy hair, but the elderly shopkeeper was distracted by a woman with two toddlers who had just walked into the shop.

He swallowed hard and took a step back. "Lydia, I need you to dig deep. Remember what we discussed about sixteenth-century bookbinding. What was the strongest, finest material used in the printing industry? What would a printer of Aldus Manutius's caliber use?" His back was to the wall of bookshelves and she had him pinned. "I need you to quit kissing my neck and concentrate here." How was he supposed to be noble when she was so relentless?

She smiled into his eyes. "Bane, I'm tempted to conk you over the head with that book of parchment, which is a general term for any writing surface made of pounded animal skin, but, in this particular case, happens to be *vellum,* which is a subset of parchment. You dullard."

His sides shook with laughter, but he allowed none of it to escape his lips. "Tell me," he said in a calm voice. "Is it the Greek side or the Turkish side that makes you so vexing?"

She winked at him. "It is the American side," she said with a smile. "That's who I am now."

On the morning of her interview, Lydia walked with Bane to the end of a pier that stretched out into the harbor. Gulls cried and swooped around them, the waves slapped against the huge pilings, and their feet clopped over the aged planking as Bane talked. How natural it seemed to be walking alongside him as he spoke about how to navigate the tricky politics within the Professor's household.

"Don't let on that you speak any other language besides Greek," he said. "One never knows when such a skill might prove useful."

She nodded. "I understand."

"The housekeeper, Maria Rokotov, is fanatically loyal to the Professor," he told her. "She is a grim, joyless woman with black hair and piercing eyes that miss nothing. Her son, Boris, is one of the Professor's guards. Then there is Lettie Garfield, the cook. Mrs. Garfield is a grandmotherly type who is basically a decent woman, but she is frightened of the Professor. That fear means she will not hesitate to betray you if necessary."

They reached the end of the pier, and Lydia rested her forearms along the railing as she gazed out across the bay. The harbor was filled with ships coming and going. Her gaze shifted off into the distance, where she could make out half a dozen ships about to disappear into the haze of mist shrouding the horizon.

Bane stood behind her, bracing his hands against the railing on either side of her. "I can't tell you anything about the other servants inside the house, as they are new since I left." His breath was soft against her ear, and she wished she could prolong this minute to last an hour, a day, an entire week. How fleeting her time with Bane was, and if she could not figure out a way to outwit the Professor, they would never have more than these few stolen moments.

The boom of a foghorn sounded and she watched a trawler disappear into the mists on the horizon. She felt inexplicably sad. Alone. She was about to embark on the most dangerous challenge of her life, but all she wanted was reassurance from Bane that he cared for her. With a flick of her wrist she moved her right hand to cover his. "Tell me something nice," she murmured, tracing a pattern on the back of his hand.

She could feel him smiling against the side of her face. "I think you are the bravest woman I have ever known," he said.

If Bane could feel the anxiety clenching her stomach, he would not call her brave. "Not good enough. Tell me something nice about me as a woman."

His lips touched the side of her face, so softly she could barely feel it. "All my life I have been alone. Until I met you—a woman who wants to conquer dragons as badly as I. Now you are the most precious person in the world to me. Lydia, you take my breath away."

Some women might crave compliments on their beauty or kindness, but Bane knew her too well and cut right to the very heart of what she desperately wanted to hear. His words were simple and honest, and she closed her eyes to savor them, knowing they might be the last words of affection she ever heard from Bane.

She reached a hand behind her to cup his jaw as they both looked out into the harbor. "You know I love you, don't you?"

He moved to tighten his arm around her waist. "I know."

And yet tonight she would go home alone, and unless some miracle occurred, she and Bane could never be more than two ships that crossed paths in the night.

23

To Lydia, there was nothing intimidating about Professor Van Bracken's appearance. His posture was ramrod straight and there was a smattering of dark strands amidst his neatly groomed silver hair. A fastidious vandyke beard gave him a dignified air, and tiny lines fanned out from the corners of his eyes when he smiled at Lydia as he guided her into the reading room of Boston's famed Athenaeum. One of the oldest private libraries in the country, it was also the grandest, with vaulted arches, hand-carved ceilings, and huge windows overlooking Beacon Street. The Professor was a member of the private club, which was the only reason Lydia had been permitted inside the hallowed walls. It was still early in the afternoon, so they had the reading room to themselves.

"Thank you for giving me the opportunity to speak with you about your manuscript," she said, proud there was no tremor in her voice as she lowered herself into a chair. Could she really convince this man she was an accomplished scholar of ancient Greek languages?

The Professor's manner was polite but formal. "You have an appreciation of old manuscripts?"

"Oh yes," Lydia said. "I grew up surrounded by them because my father worked for an antique map dealer in Greece. We always had stacks of old maps in our house. In fact . . ." She brought forth the rolled-up engraving Bane had provided for her. "I thought someone with an interest in Greece might appreciate this etching. It is one of many my father gave to me, but it seems a shame for me to hoard them all. I'd much rather give it to someone who can appreciate it."

Lydia feared the gift would be too forward, but Bane had been right in predicting the Professor's reaction. He looked as delighted as a child on Christmas morning as he unrolled the etching. He clasped his hands tightly, making his knuckles crack and pop as he studied the map. "I believe this may be the most thoughtful gesture any business acquaintance has ever offered to me," he said as his dark eyes devoured the document. He appeared fascinated as she recounted Bane's story of how her father had rescued the map from a flood.

"Your father is to be commended," the Professor said. "Any man who would sacrifice his own home to a flood in order to salvage these precious documents from his shop is an extraordinary man. A true hero. Please extend my best wishes to him."

Lydia glanced down. "I'm afraid my father passed away a number of years ago. But yes, I was fortunate that he shared his passion for the rare and wonderful world of old manuscripts with me." She smiled a bit as she let her gaze travel over the hand-tooled leather books that graced the shelves. "It is a balm for my soul to come into a room like this."

"Yes, indeed." The Professor's demeanor had warmed from polite formality into a more genial camaraderie. It was *exactly* as

Bane had predicted. "I understand you have no formal training in ancient Greek, which is understandable given your gender. It is truly a shame an admirable young lady is closed off from such a worthy pursuit. So, how did you acquire your knowledge of ancient Greek?"

Nerves coiled tighter inside her as she braced herself for the most difficult challenge of the interview. "Self-study, for the most part." She tried not to wince when the Professor's eyes widened in astonishment. Lydia rushed to reassure him. "Greek is my native language, so it was not quite the challenge it would be for others." She rattled off a few of the phrases she memorized from the book she had been studying. "By memorizing the transliteration tables and mastering the changes in the diacritical markings, one can gain an understanding of the language." She was immensely oversimplifying things, but the Professor did not seem to realize that, so she kept talking. "From there it merely takes practice. Hours and hours of practice that were always my favorite part of the day. Most of the other children in our village wanted to play games or go swimming in the ocean, but to me, nothing compared to delving into the pages of an old book. And in Greece there were plenty of opportunities to stumble across old literature."

She laughed a bit and remembered the example Bane had told her to use. It went against her nature to roll out a stream of lies, but there were two innocent boys who needed her help, so she tamped the misgivings down. "In truth, I did not mind that none of the other children wanted to study with me," Lydia said. "Somehow, it just didn't seem right for noisy children to be running in, dirty and grubby from the ocean, and putting their hands all over those wonderful pages. My books did not deserve that sort of treatment."

The Professor's eyes glowed. "Exactly! Oh, my dear, I believe I would feel safe trusting you with my manuscript. That codex dates to the ninth century. Can you imagine? For over a thousand years it has been locked away in a monastery vault with no one to read it, no one to admire its beauty and marvel at the hands that immortalized the wisdom of the ages." The Professor rolled her map up and slid it back into the canister. When he looked up, his face was flushed with excitement. "I would like to offer you the position to translate my manuscript."

A combination of relief and fear warred within Lydia. She had pulled it off, gained entry into the Professor's remote, guarded fortress, and was going to give a breath of hope to two kidnapped children. The prospect of what she was about to do terrified her, but Bane was going to be so proud when she told him of her success. She braved a smile and nodded her assent.

"We shall leave for Vermont immediately," the Professor said, rising to his feet and fastening the buttons on his jacket. "The afternoon train leaves at two o'clock, so we must hurry."

Lydia's jaw dropped in disbelief. "But . . . but I need to return to my room and collect my things."

"No time. If we do not catch this afternoon's train, we must wait until next Monday, and that is not acceptable. Not when that manuscript has already been waiting for over a thousand years." He paused long enough to pat her on the arm. "Not to worry. We have plenty of ladies' shops in Burlington where you can select some ready-made clothing. I will gladly pay the fee, as I am the cause of your inconvenience. You may select an entirely new wardrobe. Whatever you need."

What Lydia needed more than anything was the translation book sitting on her bedside table. Without that book, Lydia could not translate so much as a single line of text. And she knew with certainty that none of the shops in Burlington would have anything to help decode Byzantine Greek script.

She grappled about in her mind for an excuse to return to the boardinghouse and retrieve the book. "I have a condition that requires medication," she said. "I can catch the train next Monday and join you, but I cannot leave without my medicine."

The professor wrapped a firm hand around her upper arm and began propelling her toward the door. "We have pharmacists in Burlington as well. We will be there by nightfall, and I will make sure you have everything necessary to begin your work."

The Professor was forceful, but Lydia would not let him pull her. She dug a foot into the thick oriental carpet covering the floor, locked her muscles, and refused to budge.

The Professor stopped and turned to face her. "Lydia . . . may I call you Lydia, since we are going to be working together?"

More afraid than she had been at any time since setting foot in the building, she didn't trust herself to speak and merely nodded.

"Lydia, that Greek manuscript has been neglected for over a thousand years. Those priceless lines of text are waiting to be unlocked, their secrets shown to the world for the first time in over a millennium. Don't you think it has waited long enough to show its secrets to the world?"

She raised her chin a notch. "I should think one more weekend would not make much of a difference to a thousand-year-old document."

A thin smile curved his mouth. "Perhaps not to the document. But I am afraid *I* am unable to endure the strain of waiting another day." He wrapped his hand around her arm, and this time it was like an iron band. "Come along, my dear. We have a train to catch."

Lydia kept her gaze locked on the landscape flying past her as the train carried her north. For hours they had been passing endless miles of dense forest, the trunks of the trees looking black against the snow on the ground. The Professor, seated just a few inches away from her on the bench, was oblivious to her distress as he read a book of essays by Voltaire. From the moment they boarded the train, he had been entirely engrossed in his book, leaving Lydia free to grasp the true extent of her danger.

The absence of her ancient Greek translation book was only part of her problem. Just as bad was the fact she had not worked out a plan to communicate with Bane. They had not yet devised a technique for passing messages to each other. She was going to be stranded with a madman in the middle of nowhere, with no communication to the outside world and no resources at her disposal. And tomorrow morning, the madman was going to present her with a manuscript she had no hope of translating.

Her anxiety caused a headache to pound against her forehead. The jostling of the train ratcheted up her apprehension as she felt herself slipping farther away from Bane with each passing mile. She wished she had her little blue bottle. She knew it was irrational to be obsessed with such a thing at this point, but tension gripped her spine and the ache was becoming painful. There was only one thing that could soothe it.

The moon was high before the train pulled into the Burlington station. The Professor held his hand up to help her descend onto the station deck. It was so much colder in Vermont! The wind pierced her inadequate cloak, which she pulled tighter, hoping to quell the trembling in her hands.

The Professor waved to a man in a nearby carriage. "Simpson! We've arrived," he called out to the waiting man. As the Professor guided her into the carriage, he spoke to the driver. "Take us to the Carlyle Pharmacy," he said. As he pulled the door closed in the carriage, the Professor smiled at her. "I am true to my word, Lydia. Carlyle lives above his shop, and I am certain he would be willing to mix together whatever medication you have need of. Now, tell me what I can have him prepare for you?"

After her fierce insistence this afternoon of her reliance on a drug, she had to give him an answer. She would rather wean herself free of her reliance on the syrup, but the Professor was waiting for an answer.

"Just a bottle of Mrs. Winslow's."

The professor smiled. "If all your requests are so easy, I'm sure we will get along smashingly," he said. When they arrived at the pharmacy, the windows were dark, but the Professor pounded on the door until a sleepy Mr. Carlyle made an appearance. Within a few minutes, Lydia had what she needed, and the Professor assured her he would send a servant to bring a selection of ready-made clothing to the estate on the following day.

"It will take us another two hours by carriage to arrive at my home," the Professor said as she settled back into the richly upholstered seat cushion. Then he did something that set her even further on edge. He pulled all the shades down, cutting off her starlit view of the world. "I hope you don't mind, but I prefer traveling with the windows covered."

This was something Bane had warned her about. The Professor was fanatical about keeping the location of his estate private. Very few people even knew it existed, and he wanted to keep it that way, but her inability to see outside the carriage window was unsettling. Dozens of times the carriage twisted and turned, lurched over bumpy roads, and climbed steeply uphill. Without the ability to see, her mind raced to all sorts of conclusions. Were they traveling along the side of a cliff? Deeper into that impenetrable, awful forest? Were they passing any farms or homesteads at all, or was she truly going to be isolated hundreds of miles from another human being?

She clenched her hands in her skirts and felt the hard, round object in her pocket. Bane's compass! Her hand closed over the small object like a talisman. As much as she longed to take it out and note what direction she was traveling, her instincts told her not to let the Professor know about the compass. The less he knew about her skills, tools, and weaknesses, the better off she would be.

The carriage drew to a halt. "We have arrived," the Professor said.

Lydia's pocket watch told her it was after midnight. "You make this journey each week?" she asked.

The Professor sprang down from the carriage. "I do my book collecting each week from Monday through Thursday. I cannot bring myself to be away from my collections any more than that." He held his hand out to help her to the ground. "Come, let me show you the estate."

The layer of snow reflected the scant moonlight and made it easy for Lydia to see the property. The mansion loomed like a fortress before her, with thick blocks of rough-hewn granite and half a dozen chimney stacks on the gabled roofline. "It looks like an entire army could live inside," Lydia said.

The Professor gave a laugh. "Not quite that many, but I do need space for my collections." Lydia turned her head, noting the trees surrounding the house in all directions. This was not the dense, impenetrable forest she had seen from the train window. These trees had wide spaces between them. Someone had cleared away all the brush and lower branches, making it easy for an observer to see a great distance.

Which was no doubt the Professor's intention. It would be impossible for someone to sneak up to—or escape from—the house without being observed.

The Professor extended his arm to her, and she had no choice but to take it. "Allow me to show you the grounds," he said as they veered away from the house.

"Right now?" It was so cold her breath turned into wisps of white vapor on the air.

"Forgive me, but I must bring up a delicate subject." Her feet crunched through the icy crust atop the snow. "You will be a guest in my home for several weeks. I want you to have free use of the grounds and the house, but I am afraid there must be a few limitations." The Professor cleared his throat. "As an unmarried gentleman, it would look amiss for me to have a young lady living here without benefit of a chaperon. Of course, any untoward speculation is preposterous, but that won't stop the tongues from wagging. So I would prefer that you not show yourself outside the home in daylight hours. I insist upon it, actually."

Lydia's gaze traveled to the line of the horizon. There was nothing but the silent sentinel of maple trees for miles, and this hardly seemed a place where nosy neighbors would be peeking around corners, but she had no choice but to agree. "Of course."

"Night comes early this far north, so you won't be cooped up in the house too long. Please feel free to take exercise anywhere on my estate." He gestured to a black wrought-iron fence in the distance. "The fence marks the edge of my property. The grounds are expansive enough for you to stay within the fence, hmm?"

It was not really a question. She gave a weak nod, feeling more like a prisoner each second.

"Excellent. Now allow me to show you some of the outbuildings." There was a stable, an icehouse, and a large separate structure where the carriage was stored. There was a small cottage near the fence. "A guardhouse," the Professor said. "I have several such cabins with guards stationed throughout the property. I tell you so you might feel more secure. Even as you move about at night, you will never be out of sight from a strong man ready to leap to your assistance."

She wondered how many pairs of eyes were watching her at this very moment. "How reassuring," she murmured, wondering how on earth she was going to escape with two young boys.

24

Bane paced outside the Bayside Rooming House for Women, casting a worried glance down the street. Lydia's appointment with the Professor should have been over by now.

It was possible the Professor had taken her to a café for a cup of tea or perhaps shown her around the Rare Book room at the Athenaeum. Even so, it was past time for her to have returned, and Bane could wait no more.

The matron overseeing the rooming house was pleased to see him, but not pleased enough to allow him access to Lydia's room. Twice he had tried to sweet-talk her into information about Lydia. Had she returned at any point today? Left a message? Twice he had been stonewalled.

It was unlikely there was anything in Lydia's room to indicate where she had gone, but he needed to check it out before hunting elsewhere. He rounded the corner to the alleyway and began peeking inside the windows. Mercifully, most of the people living here were working women who were not yet home at four o'clock in the afternoon. Through the fourth window he had identified Lydia's room by the little island painting propped on the bedside table. He used a blade to slide under the old wooden frame and wedge it up.

Inside, the bedroom was neat as a pin. Lydia's Greek translation book was on the bedside table, placed at an angle precisely ninety degrees to the edge of the tabletop. She had arranged what few possessions she had in precise, immaculate order. How very Lydia. He would have smiled were it not for the panic that was beginning to brew in the pit of his belly.

He had never considered the possibility the Professor would leave directly for Vermont with Lydia in tow. The man had been growing increasingly paranoid over the years, and perhaps he did not trust his newest employee to bring any possessions of her own onto the property.

Bane's gaze strayed to the Greek translation book. *Heaven help her.* Bane felt his knees go weak as the implications crashed through his brain. If she was in the Professor's mansion without that book, she did not have a prayer of translating the manuscript. He sat on the bed, trying to quell his frantic thoughts. His gaze darted around the small room as he rattled through his options.

And landed on a little blue bottle sitting on the ledge of the opposite window.

He glared at the bottle, knowing what it implied, but he had to check. He lifted the cork and sniffed, recognizing the syrupy sweet smell that masked the bitterness of the opium. The bottle was nearly empty.

He replaced the cork, set the bottle down, and covered his face with his hands. Of all the vices to afflict his wonderful, courageous Lydia, it had to be opium.

He wallowed in his grief for all of ninety seconds. Then he sprang to his feet, pocketed the Greek manual, and left the room by the door. He ignored the outraged growls of protest from the matron as he made his way outside the building and headed to the train station. For years Bane had been bribing the clerk at the train station to keep an eye on the Professor, and that connection served him well tonight.

"He was traveling with a woman," the ticket seller confirmed. "I heard the Professor call her Lydia. Never seen her before today."

Bane refused to let panic set in. Instead, he studied the train schedule posted behind the ticket counter. "How close can you get me to Burlington tonight?"

"There is a train leaving for Montreal in half an hour, but it's a freight train." The clerk lowered his voice. "It passes through Burlington, and I suppose you could hop off, if you're willing to ride the rails."

Bane cocked an eyebrow. "But that would be breaking the law," he said casually. He nodded to the clerk. "Thanks for your time," he said as he strode toward the loading deck for the freight trains.

Lydia was chilled to the bone before the Professor finished his tour of the grounds and brought her inside the mansion. The image of an old well surrounded by a brick casement was now branded on her mind. Several large canisters rested beside the well. Bane had told her how the Professor and his men, using that well and the canisters of kerosene, would destroy any evidence of hostages, should authorities ever raid the mansion. It was this risk that prevented Bane from trying to overpower the Professor's guards and seize the children.

The interior of the house was a surprise, a charming mix of elegant antiques with the rustic appeal of New England craftsmanship. Thick oriental carpets covered the floors, and rough-hewn timbers supported the vaulted ceiling in the great room. A cavernous fireplace she could have walked into without fear of bumping her head dominated one wall. Too bad there was no fire burning.

Lydia drew her cloak tighter around her.

"I must apologize for the climate," the Professor said. "I'm certain you understand the destructive force heat is to the delicate pages of old books. I must keep the house chilly to accommodate the collection."

She ran a cold finger along the charming inlay of ivy vines carved into the frame of a tall bookshelf. "I admire your commitment to your books," Lydia said. "A person can always layer on more clothing, but an old book is defenseless."

Judging by the look of approval on his face, it was the right thing to say. "I see you have a deep appreciation for the fragility of those precious antiques." Lydia let her gaze roam across the spines of the books lined up on the shelf. Lovely books, reflecting a wide range of history, literature, and theology.

"All the books in this room are reading copies. Please feel free to borrow anything you see of interest to you." The Professor paused and touched his brow as if he were thinking of something awkward. "Although I am afraid that I must ask you in the future to refrain from making use of this room during the day, so you should retrieve any books you are interested in now."

Lydia turned to look at the man with curiosity. "Please forgive my eccentricities," he continued, "but I must insist you keep to the north wing of the house. I often have visitors in the house, and the presence of a fetching young lady such as yourself could cause no end of damaging speculation."

It was a lie. Bane told her few people ever came to the Vermont estate, and neither did the Professor have neighbors who were liable to speculate on her presence. He was lying to her, and she was beginning to realize why. He needed to keep her away from the boys, who probably had free use of the house during the day. Clearly he intended to keep her isolated in the north wing during the day while the boys were about the house.

The Professor looked over her shoulder. "Now, please allow Mrs. Rokotov to show you the north wing." Lydia was startled to notice a woman had been standing in the corner of the great room, scrutinizing her the entire time. "Mrs. Rokotov is my housekeeper, and her son Boris helps on the grounds. She will show you to your bedroom."

Mrs. Rokotov had thin black hair scraped into a bun at the back of her neck and no expression in her dark eyes. Her face was strong, masculine even, but she moved with the silent grace of a ship slicing through still water as she walked toward them.

"Please follow me, ma'am." Mrs. Rokotov had a low voice, a thick Russian accent apparent.

"Good night, Lydia," the Professor said. "Tomorrow I will show you the manuscript, and you may begin work immediately. I will look forward to seeing your progress at the end of the day."

Mrs. Rokotov proceeded to lead Lydia down a narrow hall where she showed her a washroom and a bedroom. Given the sparseness of the furnishings, the "north wing" was not prized real estate. The bedroom was compact but fully equipped with a bed, a writing desk, a fireplace, and a small chest of drawers.

"I trust you will have everything you need in here," Mrs. Rokotov said.

There were quilts on the bed, but the room was frigid and she had nothing to wear to bed but her shift. "Would it be possible to light a small fire?"

Mrs. Rokotov raised a pencil-thin black brow. "We do not take unnecessary risks with fire in this household," she said. "I can bring you a hot water bottle for your bed."

Lydia nodded. "I would appreciate that."

Mrs. Rokotov made no move to leave the room, but inspected Lydia from the crown of her head down to the hem of her dress that was still wet from slogging through the snow. At last she spoke. "You have no bags? No belongings?"

"I did not have a chance to return to my apartment to pack a case. The Professor said clothing would be provided for me." And she prayed it would be thick, warm, woolen clothing. Lots of it.

Mrs. Rokotov nodded. "A servant will bring you a water bottle and a pair of socks for sleeping. Clothing will arrive tomorrow. Good night."

As soon as the door closed, Lydia collapsed on the bed, sinking into its softness. For the first time since she had met the Professor at noon today, she was alone. She braced her elbows on her knees and cradled her head in her hands. It had been an endless, harrowing day, and tomorrow would be worse. Her reticule was beside her, and inside the bag was a new bottle of Mrs. Winslow's.

She opened her bag and looked at the bottle. Whenever she had bought a bottle of Mrs. Winslow's, the first thing she always did was pour the contents into one of her pretty blue bottles using her tiny funnel. She stared at the image on the bottle. A plump matron played with her laughing, happy baby. She had always found the image disturbing, but even more so now that she knew what made Mrs. Winslow's so effective.

She closed her eyes so she did not have to look at the laughing mother, opened the bottle, and took a small sip. And then another. The real challenge would begin tomorrow.

A sense of foreboding loomed over Lydia as she dragged herself awake.

She raised her head, gazing about the strange room, and then awareness sent her crashing back down against the pillow.

The faint lightening of the darkness indicated sunrise was not far away, but she was in no hurry to rise from bed. The sooner she was out and about, the sooner the Professor would expect to see streams of elegant Greek translations pouring from her pen.

A glint on the bedside table caught her attention. It was Bane's compass. The morning air was frigid as she reached out to snatch the compass and clasp it tightly in her palm as she burrowed beneath the warmth of the blankets. The cold metal soon warmed, and the sturdiness of the compass seemed to provide a link to Bane, almost as if some of his strength flowed into her. Bane would not be cowering under the covers like a foolish girl; he would be calmly plotting a way out of this situation. She needed to think like Bane. How would he handle this?

Bane always analyzed his enemy before he did anything. He scrutinized every strength, foible, or weakness, and used it to predict his opponent's behavior. What did she know about the Professor that might buy her a bit of time before she began translating his manuscript?

And then it came to her. The manuscript was over a thousand years old and the vellum would be fragile and vulnerable. A sweaty palm or a spilled bottle of ink would be a constant danger. Surely a copy must be made. A *working* copy. She could delay the production of a translation by insisting upon making a complete copy of the original text to work from. Depending on how long the manuscript was, it might take her weeks to make a copy of the text.

Fifteen minutes after she awoke, a firm rapping on Lydia's door preceded the entrance of Mrs. Rokotov, who brought an armload of clothing in with her. "These have been collected for your use," she said bluntly. "Breakfast will be available in the servants' kitchen for another fifteen minutes. After that there will be nothing until lunch. The Professor has requested to meet with you at eight o'clock this morning."

Mrs. Rokotov deposited the clothing on top of the bureau and left. Lydia wished Jacob was here so she could make a joke about blunt Slavic manners. Jacob always enjoyed a good laugh, but Mrs. Rokotov's iron face would probably crack if she smiled.

What the clothes lacked in style, they made up for in warmth. The thick flannel underclothes she had on under her dress made the chilly temperature almost bearable. The woolen sweater with leather patches on the elbows looked like a man's sweater, but Lydia did not mind as she rolled up the sleeves. She wrapped a soft cotton scarf around her neck to protect her skin from the rough scratch of the wool sweater, and Lydia thought it looked rather fetching.

The servant's kitchen was empty when she arrived, but there were warm eggs and potatoes, which she gratefully devoured. The room seemed remarkably cozy, as it appeared to be one of the few places where a fire was permitted, and it burned cheerily in the brick-encased hearth. An old farmer's table sat beneath a collection of copper pots and skillets. Lydia's gaze roamed the room, noting all manner of strange equipment and charming hand-thrown pottery crocks. After finishing her breakfast, she prowled among the tools and implements hanging from the mantel.

She had hoped to loiter here a little longer in order to delay her meeting with the Professor, but he arrived in the kitchen while she still held a pair of crudely forged iron tongs before her. She averted her gaze. "Do you know what these are for?"

"Looks like a pair of medieval torture devices, but I have no idea. Ask Mrs. Rokotov. I expect she would know." Which was not exactly the most comforting of thoughts. "Now, let me show you my treasure," he said with a bright tone.

He guided her through a series of hallways, up two staircases, and down a narrow corridor with a barrel-vaulted ceiling and opened a locked chamber door. As she walked, the temperature got even colder. "This is the Priceless Room. It is where I keep the most prized of my treasures. The books you saw in the library downstairs are old, but not priceless. Everything in here most certainly is."

It was an enormous, windowless room. All four sides were covered with elaborate steel vaults bolted to the walls. A single table with two plain chairs sat in the center of the otherwise empty floor. It was a curiously barren room, stark like a prison cell, except that the room was flooded with light. When she looked up, Lydia gasped in surprise. "Is that a *window* in the ceiling?"

"A skylight," the Professor said. "I refuse to permit any flame in the Priceless Room, so there can be no gaslights or lanterns in here. You will need to work by the light from the sky. I won't permit the manuscript to leave this chamber."

He walked to one of the vaults that lined the room and produced a small key to open the lock. "All of the vaults are fireproof, of course," he said as he swung the door open, "but the heat of a flame would be damaging to these most fragile treasures." Another series of locked drawers was inside the vault. Using a separate batch of keys, he opened a drawer and slid out a velvet-lined box.

"Here it is," he said, his voice warm with pride. "A ninth-century codex, recording the wisdom of an anonymous first-century writer whose distinctive prose has been found on three other extant fragments. This is the only complete essay in existence. Is it not magnificent?"

When Lydia saw the size of the manuscript, her heart sank in despair. It was tiny! The codex was the size of a deck of cards. It would take no more than a day or two to make a copy of so small a document.

"Magnificent," she said weakly. Considering its age, it looked to be in remarkably good condition, with creamy vellum pages and clear black letters of impossibly tiny script. Lydia bent closer. Each letter of text was no larger than a grain of rice. There was no illumination or other illustrations, just a dense block of unfamiliar characters.

Professor Van Bracken gestured to a worktable in the center of the room. Stacked on the table were writing tablets, pencils, several pairs of cotton gloves, and a magnifying glass. "I trust you will find everything necessary to begin your work," he said.

"I can't wait to begin," she said faintly.

He pulled on a pair of cotton gloves before lifting the document out of its case. His face was tense as he transported it from the drawer to the table. Once he had placed the document in the center of the worktable, he drew the chair out and gestured to Lydia.

"The document is awaiting your examination."

Lydia lowered herself into the chair, her eyes scrutinizing the unfamiliar characters of the text. It looked a little bit like Greek, but a lot more like gibberish. She hunched over the text, trying in vain to recognize even a few of the characters from her transliteration tables. Seconds later she heard the rasp of paper as the Professor slid a stack of blank pages before her and put a pencil in her hand.

"Please begin, my dear." Her gaze flew to his face. Did he really intend to stand over her while she worked? She did not want to tell him of her plan to make a copy until the last possible moment. If he insisted she work from the original document, she would be caught immediately.

She cleared her throat. "You are blocking the light."

He immediately stepped back. “Of course.” He glanced at the skylight, then at his pocket watch. “It is eight thirty, and I expect you should have usable daylight until five o’clock. Good luck, my dear.”

He closed the door gently, but it sounded like the slamming of a prison door to Lydia.

25

Making a copy of the document proved unexpectedly difficult. The document was made of vellum, a type of sheepskin leather that had been pounded to paper-thin fineness. Over the centuries the vellum had stiffened with age, causing distortion among the characters and making it even more difficult to decipher. Ink clumps and faded patches forced Lydia to guess over several characters.

Nevertheless, the painstaking slowness of the task forced her to deliberate over each letter. As the hours passed, she was able to recall snatches of the transliteration table. She could make an educated guess for about one in five words.

As five o'clock approached, she heard the Professor enter the room. "I have been weak with anticipation all day. I can wait no longer to see what you have begun to translate."

Lydia feigned ignorance. "You expected me to begin translating immediately?" She gave a nervous laugh. "Heavens, I assumed you wanted me to make a copy from the original. It is far too fragile to stand up to the manhandling it would get if I did all my translating directly from the ancient document."

Disappointment marred the professor's face. He moved to stand over her shoulder and inspect the tidy rows Lydia had copied. "The manuscript is so brittle," she hastened to add. "I would never forgive myself if something this precious were to come to harm while I worked on the translation."

His voice simmered with frustration, but he agreed with her. "I'm sorry to seem disappointed, but I will look forward to your translations soon." He nodded to the white cotton gloves she had faithfully worn throughout the day. "I can see you are treating this treasure with the utmost consideration, and I applaud your willingness to take additional steps to secure the safety of my manuscript."

Lydia threw on her cloak and flew out the door the moment she was liberated from the Priceless Room. After eight hours in the windowless room, the walls seemed to be closing in on her with each passing minute, making it difficult to even draw a proper breath of air. Cold air hit her as she left the mansion, but she needed to escape the claustrophobia that had been strangling her ever since she set foot in the house.

She had not taken a drop of Mrs. Winslow's today. Perhaps that accounted for her edginess. She quickened her pace as she walked farther from the house and deeper into the trees that stood like silent sentinels in the twilight. She cast her mind back to the day in the Boston Public Library when she read about the symptoms of opium withdrawal. Aside from agitation and sleeplessness, paranoia had been listed as a side effect. Was that the cause of the anxiety that seemed to ratchet tighter inside her with each passing hour?

She cast a glance at the rapidly darkening sky. She was not supposed to be outside until after sundown, but she would never find traces of those two children if she was confined to a windowless room by day and forbidden to look about the grounds until after sunset. She must take advantage of these few fleeting minutes of remaining light to search for the boys.

If she were a nine-year-old boy, surely the stable would hold the most allure. Hoisting up the hem of her skirts, Lydia headed toward the large building a stone's throw from the house. The snow was a slushy mess near the stable doors, but it was fresh along the sides of the buildings, and there were plenty of markings. She stooped to get a better view. Almost all of the prints appeared to be from large boots, but a few on the corner looked much smaller. A child-sized boot.

Lydia's eyes widened. It was the first solid proof she had found that a child was living in this house. She stepped closer to the small boot print, careful not to disturb any of the precious markings with her own footsteps. A line of the prints led into the undisturbed snow on the side of the stables that backed up to the woods. Lydia crept forward, and a smile broke across her face when she noticed two distinct sets of child-sized prints, one a tiny bit larger than the other. Pushing through brambles and overgrown brush, she followed the prints around the side of the stable, eager to see where the boys had gone.

And then she spotted what they had been up to. The footprints led to an overturned barrel sitting directly below the single window on the back of the stable. The window was too high to look through without the aid of the barrel. Lydia scrambled atop the barrel, careful of the ice crusted along its top. On the window were four small handprints and what looked like a couple of noseprints where curious boys had pressed their faces to the glass.

What had they been looking at? Lydia braced a hand against the rough planking and leaned forward. Through the cloudy window, she could barely make out the outline of horses and some stacks of hay. As her eyes became accustomed to the gloom, she could see a partially finished game of checkers resting on a rickety table. Most boys played checkers, but so could fully grown men. Then her eyes widened in delight when she saw a little red ball and a handful of jacks strewn across a blanket in the corner.

The game of jacks was firmly in the domain of children. This was where the boys sometimes came to play.

Suddenly, a blur of black fur leapt from the shadows of the stables and angry barking filled the air. Two snarling dogs came barreling down the middle of the stable, straight toward her. She reared back and fell off the barrel, collapsing into a mass of scratchy brambles that cushioned her fall. The dogs clawed and scratched on the opposite side of the stable wall. She prayed they had no way to get out or she'd be torn to pieces here on the spot.

Lydia raced to the front of the stable, pushing through the underbrush and shaking with every nerve in her body. The dogs were still sending up the alarm. A beam of light shone across the snow, and Lydia whirled about to see Mrs. Rokotov standing in the doorway of the mansion. The woman's steely eyes inspected her, noting the snow and withered leaves clinging to her cloak.

"What are you doing?" Mrs. Rokotov demanded.

Lydia raised her chin a notch. "I'm taking a walk," she said, proud of the even tone of her voice. "The Professor told me I have free use of the grounds."

Mrs. Rokotov's eyes narrowed. "*After* sunset." The woman's accusatory glare traveled to the stables, where the trapped dogs were still making a racket. "What have you done to stir up Mars and Juno? They do not bark unless someone is prowling where they should not be." Mrs. Rokotov kept her eyes locked on Lydia as she glided down the front steps and moved toward her. "You have broken the rules, and it is my responsibility to ensure order in this household. You are to report to your room immediately and remain there until told otherwise."

Lydia would never find those boys if she was treated like a prisoner. She took a step closer to Mrs. Rokotov. "I am here at Professor Van Bracken's insistence, and from the moment he met me, he has treated me like an honored colleague." Not precisely true, but she needed to be persuasive. "The most important thing in the Professor's world is his rare book collection. That ancient Greek manuscript is more important to him than rules or barking dogs. I am one of the few people on the planet who can translate that document, and I will not allow you to treat me like a misbehaving servant. If you do, I will leave this house immediately and it will be up to you to locate another person who has the ability to translate a rare ninth-century Greek dialect."

The steel quickly drained from the woman's eyes, to be replaced with . . . fear? "You must not leave," Mrs. Rokotov said as she took a step back. "The Professor has very specific needs in relation to his manuscripts. Pardon my manner. I was merely concerned that the sun had not entirely set. I have no qualms about you walking the grounds at this time."

Lydia was still strung too tight to subject herself to the confinement of her room. "Fine," Lydia said, then walked away from the mansion, the barking dogs, and the unsettling gaze of the Professor's most loyal servant.

As she approached the front gate, a young man stepped from the guardhouse. "You must be the new translator," he said with a smile. The man's face was wide and open, and he had a gap between his front teeth.

"Yes, my name is Lydia," she said as she walked up to greet him. "I've been cooped up inside all day and need a walk."

"I'm Lars Hansen. I heard a ruckus up at the house with the dogs. Did they give you any trouble?"

"Other than giving me a heart attack? Not a bit."

Lars smiled. "Well then. You will need to meet the dogs and let them get a good sniff. We let them out every evening to patrol the grounds, so if you want to enjoy a walk at night, it is best to get friendly with them." Lars motioned for Lydia to follow as he walked back to the stable. The moment they drew near the building, the ferocious growling and snapping began again. Lars must have noticed Lydia cringing, because he put his arm around her shoulders as he opened the door.

"Don't be afraid. They won't hurt you if they see you are my friend." Every instinct in her body urged her to flee as two huge black dogs came into view, their aggression barely leashed as Lars commanded them to stay put. He kept his arm around her shoulders. "Friend," Lars said to the dogs. "Lydia is a friend."

It took a while, but the dogs began to calm. "You can pet them, if you like," Lars said.

Lydia would have rather stuck her hand into a vat of acid, but she needed these dogs to be on her side. She braced herself and extended her fingers, letting the two dogs get a sniff and nudge at her skirt. If the wagging of their tails was any indication, she seemed to have passed the test. Lars shooed the dogs away to begin their nightly duty roaming the grounds, and Lydia walked back to the front guardhouse with Lars.

The iron fence loomed before her, a tangible symbol of her entrapment. Despite the spacious grounds, the horrible wrought-iron bars gave her a fresh round of claustrophobia. She wanted to fling the gates wide open and run into the night. And if she was ever going to meet Bane, it would need to be on the other side of those gates where the guard dogs could not go.

She glanced at Lars. "Those bars look narrow enough for me to slip through," she said. "I want to go for a bit of a walk outside them."

Lars looked at her curiously. "There's not much to see out there. Just miles and miles of maple trees."

"No farms? No neighbors?"

"Not for about thirty miles, I'd estimate."

The magnitude of her isolation felt suffocating. "I'd still like a walk," she said. "I have insomnia most nights, and nothing helps so much as a good long walk."

Lars shrugged. "The Professor doesn't like us to step off the grounds, but I can't see that it would hurt, especially if you go late at night after everyone is in bed. It will be our secret, right?"

She kept marching toward the gate and turned sideways to push through the rails. "Yes. Our secret," she said as she turned and walked into the night.

She walked for hours. The moon was bright and a thaw that was setting in made it bearable for her to be out in the cold night air. She looked up. Only a small fragment of the sky was visible to her above the screen of the towering trees, but she was able to see the moon, just a few days shy of being at its fullest. More than anything she wished she could believe Papa's superstitions about the power of wishing on a full moon.

Snow on the ground muffled her steps, and the eerie, unsettling creaking of the trees filled the dank air. Were all forests this loud? She'd never been in the woods before and had no idea trees could make such sounds . . . popping and groaning as they swayed. Almost like they were in pain.

How badly she wanted a sip of Mrs. Winslow's. Within a minute of taking a sip, she would feel the syrup beginning to unravel the tension along her spine. And perhaps she would not be so paranoid as to imagine the trees were in pain.

There was no path she could see through the blanket of snow covering the ground, so she just wandered mindlessly on. In the glow of the moon she noticed buckets hanging off the trunks of the trees. She approached one, noting the steady drip of sap falling into the bucket, landing with a distinct *ping*. Maple sap? She knew people tapped trees for syrup in New England, but had never seen it done. She paid it little mind as she walked through the maple forest, the *ping*ing of the sap now joining the snapping and groaning of the trees.

She closed her hand around the compass in her pocket. Not that she was afraid of getting lost—her trail in the wet snow would guide her home—but she felt closer to Bane by holding the compass. Surely it was just a quirk of fate that it always pointed toward him when he was near.

She glanced at the sky, noting again how close the moon was to being full, and as her fingers curled tighter around the compass, a stunning thought occurred to her.

Bane could always read her thoughts. He knew the way her mind worked and could forecast exactly how she was going to behave before she herself even knew it. She was frustrated to be such an open book where he was concerned, but perhaps this one time it would save her life.

Because if Bane could read her mind, he would know exactly when and where she was going to meet him.

26

Jack Fontaine lined up a row of peas along the top of the mashed potatoes. They had to be straight, or the carrot sticks would not lie properly on top of them.

"Do you think it would work better with another row of mashed potatoes?" Dennis asked.

Jack looked across the dining room table where Dennis sat armed with a whole plate full of vegetables. They had eaten the roast beef and apple pie, but Mrs. Garfield never cared if they did not finish their vegetables. They could usually put those vegetables to good use building miniature forts.

"Another row of mashed potatoes will be good mortar," Jack agreed. He held his breath as Dennis layered more potatoes on the vegetable wall. It couldn't get too high or it would fall over when they began lobbing peas at it from the far side of the table. The goal was to knock it over, but not too quickly.

"Do you think your father loves you?" Dennis asked.

Jack looked up in surprise. "I suppose so," he said, and reached for another pea. He really didn't want to think about his father. It was hard enough living out here in the middle of nowhere without thinking about Papa and Lucy. Sometimes when he thought of them he would start crying, and he was too old to cry.

"It is important that he does," Dennis said. "Bad things might happen if he doesn't love you enough."

Jack was pretty certain his father loved him. At least, he said he did, but Jack wasn't stupid. It was pretty obvious Papa was disappointed because Jack didn't like the sea and didn't want to go into the navy. Every time Jack got on a boat he felt sick to his stomach and he just wanted to get off the boat. And he would never admit it, but the ocean was pretty scary. If he joined the army, he would disappoint Papa, but it was better than nothing.

"I think the more letters you write to your father, the better off you will be," Dennis said. "The Professor says that letters are just as good as real visits. He said that President Adams almost never saw his wife, but they wrote letters to each other all the time and that was just as good."

Jack knew all about writing letters. Dennis had shown him the stack he had received from his father over the last three years. There was also a stack of letters addressed to a boy named Tony, but Tony didn't live here anymore and Dennis wasn't sure what happened to him. When Jack had asked Mrs. Rokotov what had happened to Tony, she had denied there was ever such a boy here.

But Jack knew she was lying. He knew Tony existed because he had seen the letters from Tony's father.

Which made Jack think that what happened to Tony was pretty bad.

He didn't want to think about Tony anymore. He glanced at Dennis and lowered his voice. "I think the Professor has a girlfriend."

Dennis looked up in surprise. "What?"

"I've been spying for the last couple of nights," he said. "I sometimes see her walking around underneath the trees. I've never seen her before."

Dennis looked skeptical. "I've been here for three years, and I've never seen the Professor have a girlfriend. I think he is too old." After a moment he put his fork down. "Is she pretty?"

Jack had to think for a minute about that. "I guess so, but she looks sad. All she does is walk back and forth under the trees, and she twists her hands a lot."

"I wonder if she is a good person or a bad person," Dennis said. Ever since Jack came here almost a month ago, Dennis had been warning him about who was good and who was bad. The cook and a guard named Lars were both good, but almost everyone else was bad.

"What about Mr. Hetley, who delivers from the general store? He's good, isn't he?"

Dennis shrugged. "I don't really know. I'm never allowed out when he comes to make the deliveries. But he seems nice, because anytime I ask for something special, he always sends it right away."

The problem with Dennis was that he was such a rule follower. The last two times Mr. Hetley had made deliveries, Jack had tried to get the man's attention by waving madly from the third-floor room where they were always locked whenever a visitor came to the house. He was never going to get away from this place if he sat around and followed all the rules like Dennis did.

"Come on, let's launch the missiles," Jack said.

Dennis turned the plate so the potato wall was at the correct angle. Both boys went to the far end of the room where they knelt at eye level with the table, lined up a pea, then launched a broadside attack by flicking them with two fingers. The peas did not do much damage, but the wall was no match once they started launching carrot sticks. When the first carrot struck, it carried a chunk of mashed potatoes flying until it smacked against the wall.

The door slammed, and Jack looked up to see Mrs. Rokotov. The woman looked like a scarecrow draped in a black sheath. "What a mess," she said in disgust.

Dennis scrambled to his feet. "We'll clean it up," he said quickly.

The woman's mouth got even thinner. "There is no time. You are to go to the third-floor tower room and remain there until you are summoned. Quick, quick," she said as she snapped her fingers under Jack's nose.

Both boys rushed to obey. Jack knew what this meant. It meant that sometime within the next hour Mr. Hetley would be arriving with his delivery of groceries from the town.

And that meant it was time to put Jack's plan for escape into action.

It wasn't until they were safely locked in the room that he let Dennis in on his plan. "Mr. Hetley will never see us in the window, because it is sunny outside and there is no light in here. What if we start a fire so he could see us?"

"There is nothing to start a fire with," Dennis said.

Jack pulled out a book he had snatched from the professor's study, then grabbed the magnifying glass from Dennis's school supplies. "Yes we do."

Dennis's eyes grew wide with fright. "You can't light a book on fire! The professor will kill us!"

But Jack didn't waste any time. Bright sunlight streamed in through the window and he opened the book. He tilted the magnifying glass at just the right angle, which caused a warm beam of sunlight to strike the page. "Don't worry. I picked one of the really old ones, so he won't mind so much."

"But those are the kind he likes the most!"

Jack looked at the book with skepticism but did not remove the magnifying glass. "Really? It just looks old and ratty to me." Besides, the brittle page was dark with age, which meant it would ignite faster. Who wanted a book this old, anyway?

"I can't believe you are doing this," Dennis muttered. But that was the type of thing a rule-follower like Dennis would say, so Jack did not take his eyes off the glowing beam of light. And it looked as if the plan was going to work perfectly, because a tiny pinprick finally appeared, and then the spot darkened and a wisp of smoke drifted up from the paper.

Jack kept the magnifying glass in place but tossed his eyeglasses to Dennis. "Here, you can help," he said.

He didn't think Dennis would do it, but after a moment the boy angled the eyeglasses and sent another beam of heat toward the tiny pinprick. Jack was frustrated at how long it took for a tiny orange rim to appear around the spot, but when it did, Dennis tossed the eyeglasses down to cup his hands around the tiny flame.

Just as Mr. Hetley's wagon came rounding the bend onto the drive, the flame developed and the brittle pages of the old book curled and blackened as the fire consumed it. A wave of heat came from the book as the other pages fed a rapidly developing flame. Jack grinned as he grasped the cover of the book to protect his hands, then waved the burning pages in front of the window, shouting and calling for Mr. Hetley's attention.

27

Lydia stood at her bedroom window. From this vantage point, she could look west to see the setting sun. Trees prevented her from seeing the exact moment the sun would slip below the horizon, but things darkened quickly once it began to lower.

She needed to escape the prison of this house tonight more than ever. Lydia knew that if she turned her head just a fraction, she would be able to see the bottle of Mrs. Winslow's Soothing Syrup and its deceptively cheerful label. Her nerves were tense. She had slept only in fitful snatches ever since arriving, and she needed the distraction she could find only by walking for miles upon miles in the moonlit forest.

Something bad had happened today. Lydia had been taking her lunch in the servants' kitchen when a big commotion came from somewhere upstairs. She heard Mrs. Rokotov screaming about a fire, and servants were rushing about, filling buckets and bringing wet blankets to smother flames. Lydia raced to the pump to fill a bucket when Boris, the biggest and most ferocious of the guards, grabbed her elbow. "You are to come with me," he said.

Boris pulled her up the stairs, shoved her back into her workroom, and warned her to stay put if she wanted her face to keep looking so pretty. Then he slammed the door shut.

She could hardly sit still while there was a *fire* in the house. Moments after Boris left, Lydia cracked the door open to listen to the ongoing tumult as servants raced up and down stairs, water buckets sloshing and people shouting at one another.

"How dare you," she heard Mrs. Rokotov roar. "You wicked brat. Wicked, wicked, evil brat!" she screamed.

Lydia bit her lip, fearing one of the boys was in danger. She couldn't let that happen. She was supposed to know nothing about the existence of those boys, but if Mrs. Rokotov was going to attack one of them, she could not stand aside and let it happen.

"Lock him up," she heard Mrs. Rokotov order. "Lock him up and destroy that accursed magnifying glass!"

Then Lydia heard something that gave her pause. "The Professor is to know nothing about this," Mrs. Rokotov ordered an unseen servant. "You will all be terminated if the Professor discovers one of his books came to harm while you should have been watching those children for mischief."

Then there was a great deal of discussion. Mrs. Rokotov ordered someone to town to acquire a new rug to replace the damaged. Servants opened all the windows to air out the house and mopped up every drop of water that had been spilled on the three flights of stairs. The Professor was due to return home this evening and no one was to mention the fire.

The moment the sun set, Lydia slipped outside and set off at a brisk pace. She was tense and anxious and wished she had never heard of Mrs. Winslow's Soothing Syrup. She hadn't taken a drop in four days, but it was getting harder to maintain her sanity by the hour.

She nodded to Lars as she approached the gate and slipped through the iron bars to walk among the maple groves. The sound of the sap dripping into the buckets seemed unusually loud tonight. The creaking of the trees was even worse. Was the sap loosening in the trees causing the groaning? Or was she simply imagining things? She felt as if she were not alone, as if she were surrounded by the Professor's spies hidden in the trees.

The disaster today underscored her need to get the boys out of the house. She had eavesdropped enough to surmise that Jack Fontaine had set an old book on fire in an ill-fated attempt to escape. She overheard one of the servants speculating that if it had happened while the Professor was home, he might have snapped and killed the boy.

It had been six days since she had arrived in this house. She had bought herself time by copying the manuscript at a snail's pace but could not delay much longer. She hoped her plan to rendezvous with Bane tomorrow night would work, because if she did not get the translation book tomorrow, the Professor would know her for a fraud.

The plan to deceive the Professor about the fire had worked. He had returned to the house last night and was going about his business as usual, although Lydia knew the servants were still terrified. If the Professor was going to discover the lingering scent of smoke or notice the missing book, it was probably going to be today.

As Lydia and the rest of the staff gathered around the kitchen table for lunch, Mrs. Garfield served bowls of rich Brunswick stew and kept up an artificially bright chatter about preparing for the maple sugaring season. Mrs. Rokotov and her son Boris ate in moody silence, but Lars was a good sport and played along, saying that some of the trees were now big enough to add a second tap.

"I do so love the scent during sugaring season," Mrs. Garfield said. "Why, the whole forest smells like a candy shop!"

Mrs. Rokotov was unimpressed. "Boris, you will be helping Lars tap the trees this year. The Professor will be taking Raymond with him on his trips to Philadelphia and New York this month."

Boris threw down his spoon. "Again? Why am I always stuck in the middle of nowhere while Raymond gets to go everywhere?" His voice carried a trace of a petulant child's, if a three-hundred-pound man could be mistaken for a child. Boris continued to grumble about the unfairness of the tasks, while Mrs. Rokotov remained unmoved. It was only when Boris threatened to take his complaints to the Professor that Mrs. Rokotov stiffened.

"Now that is enough!" Mrs. Rokotov said angrily.

Lydia's eyes widened. Mrs. Rokotov was speaking in *Russian*! Lydia was careful not to lift her head or look at Mrs. Rokotov, remembering Bane's warning not to let on that she knew more than just English and Greek. She knew those who switched languages in front of others did so because they did not want to be understood. Mrs. Rokotov's voice turned hard as she continued speaking in Russian to Boris. "The Professor has been very kind in looking after our well-being. You and I are the only servants he will take with him should he need to flee this house. We are the only ones he fully trusts, and he has prepared everything for such an emergency. A new home to go to. Train schedules. New identities for you and me. All of the documents are ready the moment we need them. You should be grateful you are the one he has selected to accompany him. Not Raymond. Not Lars. You!"

Lydia held her breath. The Professor had a plan for leaving? If he was pulling up stakes and getting ready to set up shop somewhere new, it was *exactly* the sort of thing Bane needed to know. If she could find those documents, Bane would know the location of the Professor's escape house.

Boris's tone was yielding. "All right, all right," he said reluctantly. Then he switched back to English. "I'll quit complaining. But I still think it is unfair I am always stuck out here."

There was an awkward pause. Mrs. Garfield finally filled it by asking Lydia if she would like a nice apple pie for dessert tonight.

"That would be lovely," Lydia said.

"What would be lovely," Mrs. Rokotov snapped, "is for you to finish that translation for the Professor. It is taking you far too long to finish such a small task. The sooner you are out of this house, the better."

The Professor appeared to share Mrs. Rokotov's poor opinion of her progress. When he stopped by that afternoon, his brows lowered in disapproval as he stared at the carefully printed document she had been preparing.

"I had hoped to see progress on the actual text," he said. "A clerk could have prepared a copy in short order. A day or two at most. I see no reason why you have not completed this after almost a week of work."

Lydia stood to face him, hoping the sheer terror running through her veins was not apparent to him. "Some of the ink is cracked, and it has bled onto the vellum in other places. All this makes it very hard to interpret," she said. "Each sentence needs to be analyzed and requires an educated conclusion so errors are not introduced into the copy."

She held her breath, hoping the excuse would hold. The corners of the Professor's mouth turned down, but he gave a brusque nod.

"Very well," he said, skepticism heavy in his tone. "But beginning tomorrow, I am directing you to start the actual translation using the text you have already reproduced. There will be plenty of time to complete the copy once you have made some progress in the translation."

Lydia's heart sank. If Bane did not come to her tonight, she would be out of excuses.

Lydia stared at the first line of the manuscript. There were a grand total of four words she could recognize: *Persia, sea, sky,* and *iron.* If she had the transliteration tables, she could decode this sentence within a few minutes. Without it, all she could do was guess. It had been two hours since the Professor had paid her a visit, and she had been tense with anxiety ever since. She tried to concentrate on decoding the beginning of the manuscript, but her mind kept drifting. What would she do if Bane did not meet her tonight? Maybe taking a bit of Mrs. Winslow's would help focus her mind. She wondered how many miles of forest surrounded the house. Was it really thirty miles, as Lars had said? Even if it wasn't such a distance, she could not run away. She would be abandoning the children, and that was unthinkable. Admiral Fontaine's only son was somewhere in this house, and she could not bear the thought of leaving him to the mercy of the Professor.

A noise on the roof distracted her. Probably just squirrels. Spring was coming on, and wildlife was beginning to stir again. She tried to attack the second sentence of the manuscript, but now the noise on the roof sounded like footsteps. Lydia stood and craned her neck to look up, but could see nothing.

When the smiling faces of two boys filled the skylight, she jumped. They giggled and pulled away from the window.

They couldn't leave! Lydia shot to her feet and clambered onto the table, trying to reach the glass and summon the boys back to her, but her arm was not long enough. Gritting her teeth in frustration, she hopped to the ground and was in the process of lifting the chair onto the surface of the table when the boys appeared again. And this time they were fiddling with the hardware that kept the two frames of the cantilevered window fastened together. They were trying to get in!

Lydia hoisted the chair into place and climbed on top of it. From here she could reach the latch that held the windows closed. With a flick of her wrist she unlatched the hook, and one of the boys pried the window open from the outside.

"Hi! It's cold out here. Can we come in?"

Lydia could not stop the grin that burst across her face. She stepped down from the chair and was about to help them step down, but one of the boys was already dangling from the window frame and the other was not far behind.

She could not believe she had been looking for these boys for a solid week, and yet now they were dropping through a skylight to see her. All three of them were standing on a worktable and staring at each other like idiots.

"Watch for the manuscript!" Lydia gasped. The fragile document was a few inches from one of the boys' feet, but he stepped nimbly around it and sprang onto the floor. Like a real gentleman, he held his hand out and helped Lydia to the ground.

"I'm Jack Fontaine," he said. "Are you the Professor's girlfriend?"

Lydia almost choked. "Heavens, no! I'm merely translating a manuscript." She turned around and helped the other boy to the floor. "You must be Dennis Webster," she said to the other boy.

"How did you know my name?" he asked, his eyes wide with surprise. Jack gaped at her with equal curiosity.

She had little time to waste. "I was sent by Admiral Fontaine to help get you boys out."

Both boys looked stunned, but Lydia kept talking. "I have a friend on the outside who is working on a plan to get you out, but I need to know where you are staying."

"You know the wing that points out toward the west?" Dennis asked.

Lydia nodded.

"There are three chimney stacks on that wing of the house. Our room is on the top floor, the one underneath the double chimney stack."

"Are there any rules you need to obey?" she asked. "Anything you are forbidden to do?"

"We have to be inside the house by nightfall," Dennis said. "We are never allowed in the north wing of the house. And we have to be locked up in the third-floor tower room whenever a visitor comes to the house."

"What about during the day? Are you allowed to move around freely during the day?"

Dennis nodded. "The Professor said we are allowed to go wherever we want, so long as we stay behind the gates. We can go fishing and climb trees. Although I don't suppose he knew that Jack was going to want to prowl around on the roof."

"I've been looking for you for days," Jack said. "I see you walking around at night, and I always wondered where you were during the days. I figured you lived in the north wing, but I've looked in almost all the windows and I couldn't see any trace of you. Today we decided to look down through the skylights, and here you are."

"Here I am," Lydia said, her mind trying to figure out an ongoing means of communication with the boys, as skylight visits would not work for long.

"What about the library off the great room?" Lydia asked. "Are you boys allowed to use the library?"

"During the day," Dennis confirmed. "So long as we don't *burn* anything," he added with a glare at Jack.

Lydia had no interest in playing referee between the boys. "I can use the library in the evenings. We can pass notes to each other through a book." She closed her eyes and tried to think of a volume the Professor was unlikely to use. "There is a set of encyclopedias on the bottom shelf of the library," she said. She had noticed a fine layer of dust across the tops of the books, so they were most likely safe. "Why don't you pick a topic you will remember, and I'll put a note to you there."

"Boston," Jack said. "I'm from Boston and I won't forget it."

"Boston it is," Lydia said. "I'm hoping to meet my friend tonight, and he may have a plan to get you out. I'll put a note inside the encyclopedia by the Boston entry. I'll be checking the same spot in case you need to communicate with me."

"We can do that," Dennis said.

"When are we getting out?" Jack asked. "I'm not waiting three years like Dennis. I want to go home now. Tonight."

If she tried to walk out the gates with the boys, the dogs would alert Lars before they even made it to the gate. Bane had said an escape would take weeks rather than days. She was trying to think of a kind way to tell the boy to be patient when there was a tread upon the stairs in the hall.

"The Professor is coming," she whispered to the boys. Without a moment of hesitation, they both sprang up on the table, but when Dennis hopped on the chair, he was too short to reach the skylight. Lydia scrambled on the table. With strength she did not know she possessed, she picked the boy up by his waist and gave him a boost so he could wrap his hands around the frame of the window. She and Jack both pushed him up and out the window.

"You next, Jack," she whispered. The footsteps were getting closer. She hoisted the boy a few inches, and Dennis helped pull him through. Jack's legs were still dangling from the window when Lydia hopped down from the table, replaced the chair, and took her seat. As Jack's feet disappeared from view, the door to the workroom opened. She had had no time to close the window, and both panes were hanging open into the room.

"Well, my dear. Making progress?" the Professor said as he strolled into the room.

Her fingers shook as she arranged the pages on the table. She slid the beginnings of her pathetic translation under some blank pages. "I'm still polishing off the copy work," she said.

"I see. It's quite drafty in here, isn't it?" And then Lydia's heart sank as his gaze drifted upward and he saw the skylight window hanging wide open. His eyes narrowed and his face went white. "Who gave you permission to open that window?"

Lydia could barely make her mouth move to form the words. "I . . . I . . . did not realize it would be a problem," she stammered. "I thought a bit of fresh air . . ."

"Well, don't think such careless thoughts in the future." The professor's voice lashed out like a whip. "I built this room to protect my precious manuscripts from the elements. I've taken every precaution against flood, fire, or temperature damage of any kind. It entirely defeats the purpose when you open a window like that."

He did not wait for her reply as he hoisted himself onto the table and slammed both panes shut before locking them into place. He still appeared rattled as he descended from the table.

"I'm sure I need not instruct you any further on keeping that window secured at all times. Is that clear, Lydia?"

"Yes, sir."

"Good. Then I will look forward to reading your translations tomorrow. Don't disappoint me a second time," he said in a voice terrible in its coldness.

The sun began setting an hour later, and it became too dim for Lydia to continue work. She left the room, still shaking with anxiety. Unless Bane remembered her comment about always taking a long walk on the night of a full moon, the remainder of her stay at the mansion would be very short. And, without the transliteration book to help her translate, perhaps very dangerous.

Her confidence waning and her nerves spinning out of control, Lydia returned to her room and took a deep draught of Mrs. Winslow's Soothing Syrup.

28

The compass was warm in Lydia's palm as she stepped into the moonlit night, and she prayed Bane's instincts would be strong and he would know how to find her. There was plenty of moonlight, making it easy for her to see the fragile, trembling needle of the compass as it pointed north. She would keep walking until she found Bane. Somehow, she knew he would sense her plan.

She could not afford to believe otherwise.

Lydia set off at a steady pace, her gaze darting between the compass's needle and the thick underbrush beneath her feet. If Bane had figured out her plan, he would be waiting directly north of the house, and she could not afford to stray.

The longer she walked, the more the fear set in. There was no snow on the ground here. In the past she had followed her footprints in the snow back to the house, but that would not be possible tonight. Could she really depend upon the wobbly compass needle to get her back through endless miles of forest? Had she walked a full mile? Two? It was hard to know how close Bane would be willing to get to the house.

It seemed she had been walking for forever, but perhaps that feeling was just from the effort of staring so carefully at the compass while trying not to plow straight into a tree. Scratchy bramble snagged in her skirts and slowed her more. Each time she bent over to tug her skirt free, she had to wait while the needle readjusted to point north.

"Lydia."

The whisper was so soft it barely carried in the cold night air. Her head shot up and there was Bane, a blinding smile of pure joy on his face. He spread his arms wide to welcome her.

The strength drained from her legs, and she sank down onto the damp forest floor. The rush that sent her mind spinning was so strong she feared she was about to faint.

A second later he was beside her, kneeling down as his arms clasped her to his chest. "What is it, Lydia? Are you hurt? Tell me what you need."

"I need *you*." Still clutching her compass, she wrapped her arms around his back and buried her face in his shoulder. She had no strength left as she lay in his arms and let him rock her like a baby. His voice was infinitely tender as he whispered against the side of her face.

"I've got you now. I've got you, Lydia."

"I knew you would find me. I knew you would be here."

She could feel his mouth turn up into a smile against the side of her face. "Of course I came for you. You little Greek pagan. I leave you alone for a week and I catch you praying to the moon."

A watery laugh burst out from deep inside her. "It worked, didn't it?"

"I suppose it did," he said. "And look, I come bearing a gift." From inside his coat, he pulled the slim volume of Byzantine Greek translation.

She ought to stand up and jump for joy, but she felt too wonderful to move, lying in Bane's arms while he smiled down at her with all the love in the world reflecting back at her. She did not break eye contact with him as she took the book. "Only the dullest of men would consider Greek transliteration tables to be a gift."

He winked at her. "Next time I'll bring you a bowl of clam chowder from the Laughing Dragon." He lowered his head and captured her mouth in a kiss so tender she could not help smiling against his lips. At last he pressed his cheek along the side of her face, simply resting there. How wonderful this felt, how soothing. "We need to talk," he said softly.

Why couldn't this moment last forever? She wanted to lie within the shelter of his arms and let him cuddle and tease her until the sun rose. "I know."

He helped her rise and guided her to a fallen log where they both sat, hands clasped tightly together.

"Have you seen the boys?" Bane asked.

She nodded. "They seem to be fine and getting into plenty of mischief. At least Jack is. Dennis wants to follow the rules, but Jack is not long for this world if he keeps it up."

When she explained the incident with the antique book, Bane's eyes grew wide with horror until she told him the Professor knew nothing about it. "The servants are terrified he will find out, so they covered it up, but it is only a matter of time before Jack runs afoul again." She told him about both boys dropping through the skylight to pay her a visit.

"That's good," Bane said. "It means they are not yet completely terrified, which is important if I'm going to get them out."

"When will that be? How long will it take?" She hoped her desperation was not bleeding into her voice, but she didn't know how much longer she could endure living in that icy fortress.

Bane held up a hand to silence her. "I need more information before I can answer that. Tell me who guards the boys."

"The children are allowed to play outdoors, so long as they stay inside the fence. Guards surround the entire property twenty-four hours a day. Dogs too. It is only because Lars is friendly toward me that I am able to slip out of the gates each night. The servants inside the house watch the boys during the day. The worst is the one named Boris, who reminds me of a jackal, always snapping and snarling."

Bane's face was a study in concentration as he listened to her. "Keep talking. What is their schedule? Where do they sleep? Don't overlook anything, no matter how minor it might seem."

Lydia recounted everything she knew about the boys, although she had to confess the Professor had been quite effective in keeping her isolated in the north wing of the mansion. After she revealed every scrap of insight she could provide, she waited while Bane sat motionless as he processed her information. The silence lasted so long Lydia reverted to picking at her nails while Bane thought.

At last he broke the silence. "Does anyone in the household read the local newspaper?"

The question came from nowhere, but Lydia cast her mind about. "I've seen Mrs. Garfield use wadded-up newspapers to start the kindling in the stove. There is a stack of them in the servants' kitchen."

"Start looking through them," Bane said. "In the last month there has been a rabies scare up near St. Albans. It has been widely covered in the newspapers. See if you can find any of those articles and leave them lying about. Better yet, ask Mrs. Garfield if she has heard of any local cases. Tell her you've heard rumors of it being particularly bad this year, and the newspaper stories are confirming it. Suggest you are terrified of rabies."

That would not be difficult. "I *am* terrified of rabies," Lydia said.

She told Bane a ghastly story about one of the girls at the Crakken Orphanage and her terrible death after a bite from a rabid dog.

"Use that," Bane said ruthlessly. "I need you to plant the seed that will help incite panic in the household."

"What are you thinking?"

"I'm not sure yet. But I need an emergency that will require the boys to be brought out of the estate with the full cooperation of the servants. A rabies scare might do the trick." He continued to ponder, tracing tiny circles on the back of her hand. "Start laying the groundwork by putting everyone on alert about the rabies up at St. Albans."

As Lydia realized the danger of the escape plan, a shudder raced through her frame, whether from the cold or from fear, she did not know. Bane pushed himself to his feet and held his hand out to assist her up. "You're cold. I'll meet you at this spot tomorrow night to advance the plan."

Lydia nodded, dreading the prospect of returning to the awful fortress. Bane framed her face with his hands and scanned her face, almost as if he were memorizing her features. How wonderful this felt. How soothing. His thumbs traced the line of her eyebrows as he peered deeply into her eyes.

"You've been drinking opium," he said.

Lydia glanced away. "Why do you say that?"

"Your pupils are tiny. Like pinpricks." Bane did not move a muscle; he just pierced her with a hard blue gaze. "I saw the bottle of Mrs. Winslow's in your room at the boardinghouse. How heavily are you using it?"

Lydia bit her lip. During the most difficult week of her life, she had only slipped twice in her effort to abstain from Mrs. Winslow's, but it was hard to confess even that much. Bane continued to press her. "Back in Boston, you said you used it only about once a week."

She dropped her gaze. "That was a lie," she whispered, hating how thin her voice sounded in the wilderness. "It wasn't until after I tried to cut back that I realized I was taking it most nights." Seeing the pain in his eyes hurt her, so she twisted away from him and walked a few feet deeper into the forest. "I feel so weak. I've been frightened and alone and I know it is pathetic to use it. Now that you are here, and I have the translation book, I'll do better. I know I can." She managed a wobbly smile. "When you are near me, I feel like I can do anything. Climb a mountain, reach for the moon."

Bane's smile was sad. "Follow Lewis and Clark to the Pacific Ocean?"

She nodded. "Even that." It was true. Bane's confidence was contagious, and she always felt like she could see farther, dream bigger when he was near.

He crossed the distance between them and clasped her hands between his. With his face only inches from hers, he peered into her eyes. "I need to know if you are okay," he said slowly. "I can't send you back into that house if you are going to crack. It isn't worth it."

Lydia thought of the two boys grinning down at her from the skylight. She would never abandon them. "I won't crack," she said. "I know what needs to be done, and I'll do it." She did not promise to refrain from using Mrs. Winslow's. She couldn't. But she would endure whatever was necessary until the boys were safely returned to their parents.

The translating progressed quickly now that Lydia had the proper tools. The days she spent copying the text had embedded the characters in her mind, making it easier for her to use the translation book. Within the space of an hour she had the first two paragraphs of text decoded.

After only an hour of translating that morning, the Professor paid her an unannounced visit. The moment she heard his distinctive tread in the hallway, she shoved the Greek translation book beneath a sheaf of blank pages. Should he discover it, the book would prove she was a fraud. The door banged open as she withdrew her hand from the stack of blank pages.

The Professor's imposing frame filled the doorway. "What have you to show me this morning?" he demanded.

Lydia pushed her page of translation toward him. "The writer speculates that the warmth of the sun powers the moon."

Surprise mingled with delight on the Professor's face as he took the page from her, holding the cheap copy paper as though it were a relic of high antiquity. His gaze flew across the page as he devoured the translated lines, his mouth faintly murmuring the words as he read.

It took the Professor only a few seconds to read the passage, but when he finished he was breathing as hard as though he had run a five-mile course. He walked around the table again and again as he read her passages. "Amazing," he breathed. "For a thousand years that document has lain unread, unexamined. And now I am the first person to read these immortal words in over a millennium."

Lydia's eyes widened. *She* had actually read the words first, not that she cared to correct him. The way he kept circling around her and the table made her nervous, and her hand clasped the seat of her chair as she wished he would leave. The way he scrutinized her translation was nerve-wracking, but his next words made her blood freeze.

"You don't know a man called Alexander Banebridge, do you?"

She nearly gasped, and the Professor kept circling her. She forced her voice to remain calm. "Banebridge? I don't think so. Is he one of your groundskeepers?"

The Professor pulled out the only other chair in the room and placed it opposite her. He sat down and studied her from across the expanse of the table, where he might get a view of her translation book. She shifted in her seat and simultaneously pushed some papers to further hide the book.

"No. He is not a groundskeeper," he said with great deliberation. He took a deep breath as if the subject pained him. "I did a little digging when I was in Boston and inquired about your translation work at the Boston Navy Yard." The band about her chest got tighter and tighter. "Very commendable, doing such patriotic work," the Professor continued. "However, it did come to my attention that your former employer, Admiral Fontaine, has a close association with Alexander Banebridge, who was known to be a frequent visitor at the Navy Yard." Lydia fought not to squirm under the Professor's scrutiny as he fastened his gaze on her. "So I will ask you again. Are you acquainted with Alexander Banebridge?"

She would be committing suicide if she admitted it. Lydia pretended to think, then said simply, "There are two thousand people who work at the Navy Yard. I only know a tiny fraction of them. I don't remember meeting a man named Banebridge."

The Professor seemed satisfied. He rose to his feet and placed a hand on her shoulder as he headed to the door. "Very well, Lydia. Please continue with your translations."

Her heart continued to pound for a solid two minutes after the Professor left. Surely he suspected her. Why else would he prowl around the Navy Yard seeking to find an association between her and Bane?

She waited a few minutes for her heartbeat to regain its normal tempo. The Professor's suspicion made her even more anxious to leave this horrible house as quickly as possible, and that meant she needed to start planting the seeds of anxiety about a local outbreak of rabies immediately. Lydia opened the door and checked both sides of the hallway before venturing outside the workroom and down the hall.

Mrs. Garfield looked up in surprise. "You are awfully early for lunch," she said, glancing at the clock hanging above the brick hearth. "I wasn't expecting you for another two hours."

"I know, but I'm famished. Is there anything to eat?"

The cook's face twisted in indecision. "The Professor has rules about when his guests take their meals." Clearly, she was worried about the possible appearance of two little boys Lydia was supposed to know nothing about.

"It is only ten o'clock," she said as she sat on a bench before the weathered farm table. "I'll beat the lunch crowd rush and be out in just a few minutes," she said with a smile.

"I suppose that would be all right," Mrs. Garfield said as she began slicing a loaf of bread. Lydia's gaze darted about the room and landed on the stack of newspapers beside the hearth. She moved beside them and began paging through the stack.

"You must feel so isolated out here in the middle of nowhere," Lydia said, her eyes quickly scanning each page before moving on to the next.

Mrs. Garfield smiled. "I suppose I'm stuck in a kitchen no matter where I'm working," she said. "I once worked at a lumber mill outside of Burlington, where I cooked for sixty men. I felt just as isolated there." Lydia nodded politely while the cook reminisced about her days at the lumber mill, but her entire focus leapt from one headline to the next as she scanned the *Vermont Gazette* in search of any mention of rabies.

And then she spotted it. "Oh my heavens," she gasped, her hand flying to her throat.

Mrs. Garfield dropped her knife. "What is it, dear?"

"Rabies! It says here there is a case of rabies at a farm just outside St. Albans." Lydia scanned the story, then glanced at the date at the top of the newspaper. "Only a week ago! A man and his son were bit by their hunting dog, a dog which later turned out to be rabid. They were rushed to Burlington for treatment, but it is unlikely they will survive."

Lydia did not need to feign her horror. "I knew a girl where I grew up who contracted rabies from a dog bite," she said. "The medical care there was not the best, and they gave her opium to soothe her fever. It was a week before a doctor correctly diagnosed her, and by then it was too late. They took her away before she died."

Mrs. Garfield sank down onto the bench opposite Lydia. "Do you think they could have saved the girl if the doctor had been called earlier?"

Lydia nodded. "I think you have to move really fast, or it is always fatal." She went back to scanning the article. "It says here that a doctor in France, Louis Pasteur, has developed a vaccine for rabies, but it must be administered within a day of the infection. It says the wounds should be treated by cupping." Lydia looked up. "What is cupping?"

The cook looked as confused as she. Lydia looked back to the newspaper. "It says that if treatment is applied immediately, there is a fifty percent chance that the person will not develop a full-blown case of rabies." She folded the pages so the rabies article was on the top. "We must warn Lars and the others who are outdoors about this," Lydia said. And then a sudden inspiration struck. "Perhaps we should keep the dogs confined until the scare is past." If Bane's plan involved getting anywhere close to the property, it would be best if the ferocious dogs would not be a concern.

Mrs. Garfield rose to her feet and continued making Lydia a sandwich. "Leave it right there, and I'll be sure that everyone on the staff sees it. I couldn't live with myself if something like that happened here." She put the sandwich on a plate and pushed it across the table toward Lydia.

"I'll eat this and be out of your way immediately," Lydia said.

The first sign of the approaching train was the vibration of the wooden platform Bane was standing on outside the Burlington train station. The minor vibration intensified until a wall of sound rolled forth as two hundred tons of iron and steel came roaring into the station amidst clouds of steam and smoke. Moments after the steam cleared, the doors opened and Admiral Eric Fontaine stepped onto the platform.

Bane was not surprised Eric was the first man off the train. Since the day his boy had been kidnapped, Eric had been pushing Bane to move faster, work harder, plow further forward. This was how Eric had led his entire life.

It wasn't Bane's style. When handling a scorpion, a person only had one chance to strike. It required carefully examining the landscape, manipulating the conditions, and then absconding with the scorpion's prize before he ever knew what was happening. And that took planning.

Eric extended a hand for Bane to shake, which Bane found a little surprising, given the havoc he had caused in this man's life. "Let's go somewhere we can talk," Bane said. He chose a bench in the middle of a public square. With the barren trees and bleak March climate, there was not another human soul in sight, and it did not take long for Eric to fully grasp the plan and what was required of him.

"The Professor leaves the mansion every Monday night and returns on Thursday. That is our window to get the boys out. The servants are terrified of the Professor, and the only way they will allow the boys to leave is if they fear the hostages are in extreme danger."

Bane told Eric of the doctor's house located thirty miles away from the Professor's mansion. On the outskirts of a rural town, it was the best place to take the boys away from the Professor's henchmen. Bane had already bribed Dr. McKlusky, a struggling young doctor just getting started in the business, to cooperate in the plan. The doctor's house had a single room upstairs where a number of hired guards could aid in rescuing the children from whoever brought them for treatment from a supposed bite from a rabid animal.

"I have a contact inside the mansion who is helping to set the stage by spreading a little preliminary panic about the rabies outbreak in the area. When the boys come running to the house, frightened over getting bitten by a wild raccoon, the odds are good the staff will rush the boys to the doctor for treatment."

"Who is this person you have inside the house?" Eric asked. "Can he be trusted?"

Bane knew there was no use avoiding the question. Eric would eventually find out anyway. "It's Lydia Pallas. The Professor hired her to do some translation work."

The transformation that came over Eric's face would have frightened a lesser man than Bane. "You sent that innocent girl in to do your dirty work?"

The words stung because they were true, and Bane was in the mood to lash back. "You tossed her out on the street without references."

Eric shot to his feet and began pacing around the iron bench, his back rigid and fists clenched. "I can't sit out here on a blasted park bench while a woman is sent in to rescue my son. I need to do more. I need to lead the charge."

"Forget it. Lydia is leading the charge."

Eric whirled around, his eyes flashing with anger. "Lydia is twenty-four years old! She is a *girl*."

Girls like Lydia had been doing warriors' work since biblical times. This job did not call for brute force; it called for intelligence, a will of iron, and a level head. Lydia had all of that, and Eric's implication that she was not equal to the task didn't sit well with Bane.

"Lydia's backbone is pure steel," he said. "We'll put the plan into action in two days, and you'll have your son back soon."

Bane knew all their nerves were stretched near to their breaking point, and if he couldn't get Lydia and the boys out from the house in the next few days, he did not know if they would last another week.

29

In the moonlit night, Lydia pulled her cloak tighter as she trudged toward the iron gate. Lars stepped out of the gatehouse, one hand clutching a rifle and the other holding a lantern high. "Going out for a walk again? Mrs. Garfield says there's rabies about."

Lydia could not afford to undermine that belief, but she also needed to meet Bane. "I've been in a windowless room all day hunched over a manuscript with letters the size of a grain of rice. If you don't get out of my way, I am liable to burst into flame."

Lars blanched. "Um, sure, no problem, Lydia."

Even after she slipped through the gate and into the dense forest surrounding the estate, her nerves were still strung as tight as a drum. She had expected her antsy feeling to subside now that she was on her way to meet Bane. The trees were making the awful low groaning sound that made her feel like they were whispering about her, spying on her. Honestly, if Bane couldn't get her out of here soon, she would be fit for no place but an asylum.

Her hands trembled as she held the compass, making the fragile needle wiggle even more, but the moment she saw Bane's lean figure in the distance, her anxiety drained away. She pocketed the compass and began hastening toward him, but he devoured the space between them with a few long strides and swept her into his arms.

"I missed you," he murmured against her throat. For a few minutes they simply held each other. It felt like his strength was restoring her equilibrium. Always, *always* when she was with Bane it was as if his confidence flowed into her.

Finally, he broke apart from her and told her the escape plan. "Tell the boys to meet me in the icehouse on Tuesday, after breakfast but before lunch. We are going to have to manufacture some wounds on them to make it look as if they tangled with a rabid coon. They'll come running and screaming back to the house. Be there. Insist that they be taken to a doctor immediately. Do your best to go along with them in the wagon. Say you need to treat their injuries during the ride. It would be best if we can get you out at the same time as the children."

"What if they won't let me go with them?"

Bane's mouth thinned. "Do your best, but don't endanger the escape plan by appearing too eager to go." Lydia nodded, and Bane stretched out a hand to stroke the side of her face. "If you can't get out with the children, I will come for you that same night," he said. "Meet me here, and I'll have a horse for you. You need never see this place again."

Bane proceeded to outline the rest of the plan. "Dr. McKlusky will insist the boys be taken into Burlington for treatment, and he'll have some strong men at hand to make sure the Professor's guards can't refuse. We will only arrest the guards if you make it out with the boys. Otherwise, we run the risk of exposing you as the inside spy."

She closed her eyes and leaned against Bane for support. She needed to last just a little bit longer, and then this nightmare would be over. But what exactly would she have to go back to in Boston? She opened her eyes and stepped back to look into Bane's face.

"What will happen then?" she asked.

"When?"

She fought back a sense of panic as she realized what would likely happen once she and the boys were safely whisked away from the mansion. "After the boys are rescued, what will happen to us? Are you going to disappear on me again?"

Anguish clouded his face, and he dropped his gaze. "Nothing will have changed. I won't be able to see you again."

Her knees almost gave way at the statement, but Bane continued speaking. "The Professor will pull up stakes here and simply reemerge somewhere else. If he knows what you mean to me, he would take you and lock you away in some remote location I know nothing about. You would grow old in isolation while he tried to ensure my good behavior. I can't take that risk with you."

She snapped. "Then why don't you just end it? Why do you let him manipulate you like this?"

"How, Lydia? The moment we rescue those boys, the Professor will know what happened, and he'll disappear from Vermont. He will begin again with a new identity in a new location that has already been carefully established. It may be years before I can track him down again."

Bane would not even look her in the eyes, but kept staring stonily into the distance. Her throat felt so constricted she could barely speak. "If you had any idea how much I love you, how strong my feelings are, you would never be able to walk away."

"I do know, Lydia. And that is why I won't have you living that sort of life." A sad smile twisted his lips. "Look at you. There are shadows under your eyes, and your hands are trembling. I know *exactly* what you have been doing to cope with the stress, and it is tearing me apart."

Lydia flinched but raised her chin a notch. "I haven't taken a drop of Mrs. Winslow's since I last saw you."

His angry gaze flicked to her hands. "And you are trembling like a leaf as a result. That is what withdrawal does, Lydia. All over this country there are innocent children who are being spoon-fed Mrs. Winslow's Soothing Syrup because their parents don't know any better. Because of monsters like the Professor. And *I* was responsible for helping him. *I* was responsible for what happened to you in that orphanage and what is *still* happening to you."

Bane closed his eyes, took a steadying breath, and when he looked at her again, his face was blank. "I won't abandon this fight," he said calmly. "From the moment my soul was saved, I knew this was my calling. I knew that I would never be free to lead a normal life. It is my penance for what I have done."

Lydia grabbed his shoulders and shook. "What kind of God would demand a penance like that? I won't give up on you, Bane. I won't give up on the future we can have together."

How could he be so composed when her heart was breaking wide open? He peeled her fingers off of his shoulders and took a step backward. "I need you to put a note to the boys in the book telling them to meet me at the icehouse on Tuesday morning."

His face was expressionless, his tone formal. Bane was pushing her out of his life, shutting her out, and resuming his brusque, businesslike demeanor toward her. She was smart enough to know she would make no progress by attacking his God or his motives. She and Bane were at their best when they were working in tandem toward a common goal. Sooner or later he would realize that.

She unclenched her fists and looked him in the eye. "I'll be ready," she said.

The interior of the icehouse was frigid and uncomfortable, but it was also the safest place for Bane to meet the boys. Protected by a screen of shade trees, it was far enough away from the guardhouses that Bane need not fear discovery. There were no windows in the small stone hut, and it was completely unused at this time of year. Someone had cut blocks of ice months earlier and covered them in sawdust for preservation well into the summer months.

Lars had confined the dogs ever since Lydia raised the alarm about the rabies scare, so Bane had no difficulty slipping into the icehouse in the early hours before sunrise. That was several hours ago, and his fingers were numb with cold. He was bored too, with nothing to do except stare at the case of kitchen forks by his feet as he sat on an overturned bucket beside the door. He hoped the boys were as brave as Lydia made them out to be because the marks he needed to leave on the boys had to look as if they had actually come from a rabid raccoon.

When he heard footsteps, he silently rose to his feet and pressed himself flat against the wall beside the door. The handle jiggled, then the door squeaked open.

"There's nobody here." The young voice was full of despair.

"Are you sure? Let's wait inside." Two boys stepped into the icehouse, their gazes scanning all around the icehouse and into the rafters of the building. Bane stepped out of the shadows, and both boys jumped.

"You're here!" Jack cried out.

"Shh!" Bane warned quietly. "Is anyone else outdoors?"

Jack shook his head. "No one goes out when it is this cold unless they have to."

"Good."

Bane introduced himself to Dennis, who seemed as eager to

escape as Jack. Bane squatted down on his haunches to be eye level with the boys as he went over the plan. He outlined how they should react, who they should run to, and what they should do if the servants were unwilling to take them to the doctor. He had each of them repeat the plan twice before he was satisfied. Bane put a hand on Jack's shoulders.

"Are you sure you are up to this?" he asked. "Tell me honestly, Jack. If you don't think you can do this, I'll find another way."

The lad who was afraid of the ocean and terrified of disappointing his father took on the resolute look of a commander before a battle. "I'm ready," Jack said with a gleam of anticipation in his eyes. Dennis looked equally determined.

Bane nodded. "Then let's get started."

Lydia was working on the translation when a screech pierced the silence. That was her cue.

She flew out the door of the workroom and heard shouts of hysteria coming from downstairs. "Oh my heavens. *Oh my heavens!*" Mrs. Garfield shrieked. Lydia raced with the other servants toward the kitchen and caught sight of the boys as they huddled together on the bench. Both were crying, their faces streaked with tears, and blood smeared on their clothing.

"It was a raccoon," Dennis wailed. "We didn't do *anything* to make it mad, but it came straight at us. I tried to run away but I fell down and it got me." Another wave of sobs came from Dennis, and Lydia's eyes grew wide with concern. Was the boy truly in pain? The wounds looked terrible and the tears were genuine.

Mrs. Garfield sank into a chair, fanning herself. Lars must have heard the commotion, for he had followed the boys into the house. "A raccoon in the middle of the day? That doesn't sound right."

"It *isn't* right," Mrs. Garfield moaned. "There is rabies in the area. Oh, you poor boys. What is to be done?"

Lydia clung to the side of the kitchen door, partially hidden as she watched the scene unfold. Bane's instructions were firm. She was not to intervene unless the servants refused to take the boys to a doctor.

"I don't think there is any cure for rabies," Lars said. "Maybe it was just a crazy coon. It can happen."

Mrs. Garfield shook her head. "No, there is a treatment. Just the other day I saw it in a newspaper. Something about a vaccine." She hoisted herself to her feet and went rummaging through the stack of newspapers beside the hearth. "Oh heavens, please don't let it have been burned already. Where is Lydia? She saw it."

Boris's eyes landed on her. "What are you doing down here? Get back up where you belong."

She stepped into the kitchen. "But . . . those children look like they need help."

Boris looked furious enough to strike her, but she stood her ground. "They are just neighborhood children," he snarled. "Nothing for you to concern yourself with. Now, scat."

He barreled toward her and pushed her backward, but Mrs. Garfield stopped him. "Lydia! What did that newspaper say about the treatment of rabies? These poor boys . . ."

Lydia twisted free of Boris. "There is a vaccine, but the boys need to be treated right away. Within a few hours. Otherwise it will be fatal."

Mrs. Garfield looked frantic, pacing the kitchen and wringing a rag between her hands. "The article said something else about treatment. What was it, Lydia?"

Panic simmered in Mrs. Garfield's eyes, and Lydia turned it up a notch. "It said the only hope is to get to a doctor right away,"

Lydia said. "The odds of surviving are good if treated immediately. There is no reason why these boys can't both be saved, but we must *hurry*."

Lars shifted uncomfortably. "The Professor will kill us all if anything happens to those boys." At his words, one of the serving girls buried her face in her apron and started crying. Boris glared at Lydia. "You and your highfalutin treatments. Get back upstairs where you belong."

He made a move to shove her out of the kitchen, but Lydia sidestepped him. "Those boys need to get to the doctor immediately," she insisted.

"I suppose I can go fetch one," Lars said. "Dr. McKlusky lives a couple hours away. I could probably get him here before sundown."

"That is too late!" Lydia said. "You need to take those boys to him so they can be treated immediately. They will die otherwise, and then we will *all* have to answer to the Professor for why two children died on his property." It was time to ratchet up the pressure. She turned a glare onto Mrs. Garfield, who wilted even further. "What were they doing outside when you knew there was rabies in the area? How could you have been so careless?"

Mrs. Garfield twisted her hands in indecision. "I don't want to be anywhere in this state if harm comes to those boys." The way the color drained from Lars's face made it apparent to Lydia he also feared the Professor's reaction.

Jack lifted his head. "If I die from rabies, my dad is going to be really mad. He's in charge of the whole navy, and he'll make sure all you people get in trouble."

Lars didn't need any prodding from Jack. "I'll take them to Dr. McKlusky for treatment. I'll bring them straight home as soon as they receive the vaccine. We'll bring Boris and a few others to ensure there will be no trouble. The boys can be back in their beds before morning. The Professor need never even know they stepped foot outside this house."

The serving girl lifted her head from her apron, holding her breath while Mrs. Garfield fretted. As kindly as the woman seemed to be at first glance, she was more worried about her own skin than children in danger of dying. Lydia decided she must have no mercy. She stepped closer to Mrs. Garfield and lowered her voice to a whisper so no one else could hear.

"When those boys develop rabies, it will take weeks for them to die. Will you be able to tend to them as they lose their minds and wallow in agony? Knowing that your fear of the Professor allowed the rabies to take root inside their bodies and eat away at their brains? It is not too late to get them to a doctor and give them a fighting chance."

Resolve hardened Mrs. Garfield's features. "Lars, get the wagon out. And fetch Mrs. Rokotov. She will want to go as well."

Triumph surged through Lydia. The plan was working! Those boys were on their way out of this gothic nightmare and would be reunited with their parents soon. She screwed up her courage and looked at Mrs. Garfield. "Should I go with them? I can tend to their wounds on the journey."

Boris grabbed her arm and steered her down the hall. "The only place you're going is upstairs, lady." He propelled her through the hallway and up the stairs, squeezing her arm hard and driving her so fast she stumbled on the steps. As he shoved Lydia into her bedroom, he growled a warning about skinning her alive if she showed her face downstairs before lunchtime.

With the crash of the slammed door still echoing in her ears, Lydia darted to the window, where she had a bird's-eye view as Lars pulled up the wagon. Mrs. Garfield guided the boys outside, fussing over them as she buttoned their coats. Lars sprang down from the buckboard and loaded the boys into the bed of the wagon. Boris was about to get in as well when the black-clad figure of Mrs. Rokotov appeared, her body rigid with anger as she approached the group. She started arguing with Boris, but Lydia could hear nothing from behind her window. She pressed her hands to the cold glass, praying the severe woman would not ruin the boys' chance for freedom.

At last, Mrs. Rokotov seemed to arrive at a decision and hoisted herself onto the front seat. Lydia went weak with relief at the sight. Lars closed the hatch of the wagon with a hearty thump and then vaulted onto the driver's bench beside Mrs. Rokotov. As soon as Boris hopped in the bed of the wagon, Lars snapped the horses into action, carrying the boys away from the prisonlike fortress.

Lydia leaned her forehead against the windowpane, feeling more alone than ever before.

30

As the wagon rolled outside the iron gates, Lydia sprang into action. With the Professor away and the worst of his minions gone, she was free to search the house at will. Mrs. Rokotov had spoken of written plans for the Professor's evacuation, complete with a new house and new identities. This was Lydia's chance to find those plans.

The doctor and the admiral's men were going to insist the boys be taken to the hospital. With the children out of her clutches and free to speak to the authorities, Mrs. Rokotov would realize the Professor was on the verge of being exposed. She would race back to the mansion to set the Professor's escape plan in motion.

Bane had assured Lydia that unless she managed to escape with the boys, the admiral's men were under strict orders to protect her cover. Any attempt to begin arresting the Professor's servants before Lydia was safe could put her at risk of being exposed as a spy and endanger her life.

Unless Lydia could find those papers and foil the Professor's escape. The papers were the key to freeing Bane from the intolerable state of limbo in which he had been living.

Lydia marched directly to the Professor's private study. There was a modest desk, some cabinets, and a bookshelf stuffed to the ceiling with volumes.

She tackled the desk first. The drawers were a disappointment, containing only stationery, writing utensils, and a pouch of tobacco. The cabinets were jammed with files and paperwork. Flipping through the pages, she looked for anything that mentioned an address that could be a new house or train schedules to flee the state. Nothing.

When the setting sun made it too dark to continue, she lit a lamp and felt dwarfed by the thousands of books that lined the walls from floor to ceiling. Slipping the escape plan in the pages of a book would be an excellent way to hide it. Searching each volume would be like examining every blade of grass in a field. Setting the lamp on a table, Lydia began with the bottom shelf.

After two hours, her hands felt grubby and she was growing convinced this was a hopeless quest. Slips of paper occasionally fell from a volume, but they appeared to be innocent: a sales receipt or notes summarizing the book's contents. She couldn't stop searching, but as she shifted the stepladder to attack yet another shelf, despair clouded her spirit. She did not even know what she was looking for, just groping blindly at straws. And after two more hours, she had flipped through every book but found nothing. And Bane would be waiting for her. It was already past midnight and he would be worried if she did not come soon.

Bane chose an ancient sycamore tree with spreading branches that were easy for him to climb and get a better view of the Professor's estate.

Lydia was late. Until now, the plan had been working perfectly. Eric had been reunited with his son, and Dennis's father in New York had been summoned. The Professor's servants appeared to realize they could not prevent the doctor from sending the boys to the hospital, but they gave no indication they suspected Lydia as they fled from the doctor's house. After all, the plan had been cleanly executed and there was no smoking gun pointing to Lydia. None of the servants even knew she had had any contact with the children.

Now all he had to do was get Lydia out of this house and smuggle her to safety. He had tied his horse to a tree less than half a mile from here, as the embankment was too steep for the horse in the dim light. In just a few minutes, he and Lydia would ride away from this fortress and its dark memories.

He would take her to Boston and help her establish a new life. He would get her to a doctor who could help her overcome her opium addiction and stay by her side until the poison was gone from her body.

And then he would walk out of her life. It would be too painful to watch Lydia fall in love with someone else and grow large with another man's child. He knew she would. Lydia was too resilient to wither away as old memories plagued her. She was a fighter that way.

He raised a pair of binoculars to his eyes and finally spotted her scurrying through the trees. Relief flooded through him as he climbed down the branches and ran toward her, sweeping her into his arms and swinging her in a circle. She was here, she was safe. What other woman in the universe could have pulled off such a feat of sheer bravery and bravado?

"My horse is at the top of the embankment. Let's get you out of here."

"I'm not leaving."

He must not have heard her correctly. He grabbed her hand and began tugging her up the embankment, but she dug in her heels.

"I'm not leaving, Bane. I've got a chance to find the evacuation plan that says where the Professor intends to flee."

He pulled back to look down at her face, ice trickling through his veins at what he saw there. Her trembling lips had no color. She was in full-blown withdrawal and it was a dangerous time. "Don't," he said quickly. "Don't do something foolish."

"I have to."

He held her face between his hands. "Lydia! You aren't thinking clearly. You've got the shakes and your skin is gray. Don't think you can walk back into that dungeon and figure out a way to bring the Professor down. It can't be done. Not when you are already half dead."

She grabbed his wrists. "Listen to me! If I can discover the location of where the Professor intends to flee, the authorities can go after him. Just give me time, and I will find it."

Lydia was fighting valiantly, but her voice was weak. She was exhausted, and any fool could see she couldn't last much longer without medical attention. "I can't let you go back in there," he said. "You'll kill yourself."

"Don't you understand?" Her voice held a curious blend of hope and desperation. "If the Professor is dead or in jail, you can have a normal life. *We* can have a normal life. Bane, we are a team. We are stronger together than when we are apart." It was painful for him to see the anticipation brimming in her eyes.

"Lydia, that is just a fantasy."

She grabbed his shoulders and shook. "Bane! Look at what we have accomplished together! Have you ever been closer to bringing Van Bracken down than you are at this very moment?" Anger darkened her face and she shoved him away so hard he had to stumble to keep his balance. "What have you ever really done to hurt that man other than send him some poppies? I want to slay the dragon, make the world safe from his poison, while you merely taunt him!"

Even though the accusation struck home, he had to find a flaw in her logic. He didn't have the strength to turn her around and send her back into that web of danger and deceit. Not when he could have her safely in Boston by sunrise.

"There may not *be* any written evidence of where the Professor intends to flee."

Lydia did not hesitate. "Give me another day. That is all I'm asking, Bane. Give me one more day." She grabbed his hands and kissed them, desperate hope burning in her eyes. "Bane, we are a team. If we can bring the Professor down, there will be no stopping us! We can build a better world where no little children will be lulled to sleep with drugs. We can be free to love each other." She clasped his hands between hers, and his heart nearly broke at the frailty of her grasp, the trembling of her fingers. The effects of withdrawal were eating away at her nervous system, turning her into an anxious, fragile wreck of a woman, but it still did not destroy her hope for the future. How could he not adore a woman who was willing to undergo such an ordeal to chase a dream?

He pulled her into his arms, pained at how thin her body was, how he could feel each of her ribs. He loved this woman with a ferocity that scared him. If ever the Lord created a woman who was perfect for him, he was holding her right now. He could not cast her aside and tell her to continue her life without him. With the Professor moving to a new location, Bane would lose the advantage he'd had when he could track the man. It was time to bring the Professor down once and for all.

"One more day, Lydia. If you can't find those plans quickly, we'll need to find another solution. You can't go on much longer."

Lydia shook her head. "Bane, if you are with me, I feel strong enough to call the moon down from the sky."

He kissed her deeply, wondering how God could have forgiven him enough to bless him with a woman like Lydia Pallas. "Tomorrow night," he murmured against her mouth.

31

For once, Lydia's insomnia served her well as she prowled the house the rest of the night, looking in drawers and beneath the carpets. She checked behind paintings hanging on the walls and ran her hands along the dusty undersides of the furniture. The pain in her head made it difficult for her to function, especially as she approached the Professor's bedroom. It was the next logical place to look, but revulsion skittered along every nerve ending in her body, and the ache in her head swelled even larger at being in this room. A sip of Mrs. Winslow's would wipe out the blinding pain, but she reminded herself only a weak woman would give in to such a vice.

The Professor's bedroom was surprisingly stark. It did not take her long to search the drawers and riffle through the wardrobe. She cringed at even touching his bedding, but she peeled back every cover, squeezed the pillowcases, and pushed her hands deep beneath the mattress. There was nothing.

The servants' wing of the house was the only place left to search. She had avoided it all night, but dawn was less than an hour away and Mrs. Garfield was already up. The others would soon follow. Mrs. Rokotov's room was right in the middle of a wing of sleeping servants, and Lydia would have no excuse if someone caught her ransacking the awful woman's bedroom. After failing to find anything in any of the other rooms, Mrs. Rokotov's room was the only logical place left to look.

Mrs. Garfield's door was open. Lydia held her breath as she passed, praying the cook would not return. She stood silently in the hallway, listening for the stirring of any other servants, but sensed nothing. Reaching a shaky hand out, she twisted the cold knob on Mrs. Rokotov's door, wincing at the tiny squeak the knob made as she slipped inside the room.

The housekeeper's room was as stark as her appearance. Wasting no time, Lydia lifted the mattress and checked beneath the sheets. Squeezed the pillows. Lifted the rug. She opened every drawer and searched the underside of the dresser. She was running out of places to look, but she had to move fast. Anxiety was making her dizzy, but she couldn't afford to waste even a moment of time. She scanned the walls, the ceiling . . . *the fireplace*! Mrs. Rokotov would never break the Professor's rule about fire in the house.

Squatting down, Lydia tucked her head into the opening, the air inside the fireplace as cool and fresh as the rest of the house. This fireplace had not been used in decades. Her fingers rubbed along the grainy bricks of the interior as she reached up high. A surge of triumph flooded her as a packet of papers tumbled down.

With shaking fingers, Lydia opened the pages. There was a deed to a house in California. A train schedule. An inventory of books to be shipped. Her vision blurred as she realized what she held in her hand. These pages were the key to Bane's freedom.

Wasting no more time, Lydia folded the pages and slipped them into her bodice. Just as her fingers touched the cold knob of the door, a commotion echoed up from downstairs.

"Everybody up!" It was Boris's voice, yelling from below. "Everyone out of bed. *Now!*"

People in the rooms on either side of Lydia began stirring. They'd catch her if she didn't get out of Mrs. Rokotov's room this very moment! Twisting the squeaky knob as quietly as possible, she darted into the hallway and scurried down the long corridor, holding her breath as she raced past each servant's door. She made it to the main landing on the second floor in time to turn around and pretend to be emerging from the north wing, just as the others stumbled out of their rooms.

"What's going on?" one of the servant girls asked, clutching a blanket around her. Like the others, her hair was disheveled and she wore nightclothes.

The balcony Lydia stood on overlooked the main entry, and Boris appeared below. "The Professor has been found out," he called upstairs in a booming voice. "We went to Boston last night to warn him not to return. He ordered us back here to box up his books and close up the house. All of you people get dressed and report to the kitchen in three minutes."

Lydia cringed as his gaze landed on her, traveling up and down her fully dressed figure and tidy hair. "You too," he growled. "Get downstairs. Now."

Boris watched through narrowed eyes as she lowered herself gently onto each step, pain bursting in her head with each footfall. She must not faint. The papers were stiff in her bodice and she fought to maintain even breathing so they would not rustle. The moment her foot touched the slate floor, Boris clamped his hand around her arm and hauled her forward. She gasped at the pain that whirled in her head and raced down her spine.

"What are you complaining about?" he barked, the noise making the misery in her head worse. "You are just going to the kitchen for a nice little breakfast."

Mrs. Rokotov waited for her in the kitchen, where Mrs. Garfield was preparing a massive pot of oatmeal.

"You!" Mrs. Rokotov said. "What do you know of Dr. McKlusky?"

Lydia opened her mouth to speak, but no words came. Mrs. Garfield poured a mug of hot tea and slid it across the table to her. "Here you go, dear. There will be oatmeal in a few minutes."

Lydia wrapped her icy fingers around the warm mug, taking a deep sip to buy herself time, then settled down at the table. She could practically smell the anger radiating off Mrs. Rokotov and cleared her throat before answering. "I don't know any Dr. McKlusky," she said. Which was true enough; she had never met the man.

She took another sip of tea to escape the blistering glare of the housekeeper as others began shuffling into the kitchen. It didn't take long for all six guards, four serving girls, and two groundskeepers to assemble.

Boris issued the orders. "Lars will be bringing empty crates inside. All you women begin packing up the books on the ground floor. I'll supervise transportation of the book vaults from the north wing. I want every book in this house packed up by noon. And *you,*" he said, pinning his glare on Lydia. "Get up to your bedroom and stay out of the way."

When she stood, her headache pounded so badly she thought it would explode. She couldn't take this pain any longer. The moment she got to her room she would need a sip of Mrs. Winslow's. She was finding it impossible to keep functioning when her skull felt like it was about to split in two. She held her breath as she walked up the stairs, trying not to jostle the papers in her bodice. In less than a minute she was in her room, holding the cool, smooth bottle of Mrs. Winslow's in her hand. Her fingers shook as she unscrewed the lid and took a deep sip. Even the flavor of the syrup comforted her as it slid down her throat and eased the tension in her head.

She set the bottle back down on the dresser.

Something was wrong. Her hairbrush was slightly angled next to her toothbrush. Neither of them was perfectly aligned with the edge of the table. She never would have left them like that. It did not matter how sleepy or distracted she was, she kept her belongings in meticulous order.

A new round of tremors raced through her, so she badly needed to sit. She made it to the chair in front of the writing desk before her knees gave way. Who had been prowling through her room? Had Boris and Mrs. Rokotov been in here before rousing the servants?

She needed to sit down and think of a plan, and maybe rest for just a few minutes. It would be easier for her to think after she had some sleep. Everything was so scattered and confused. Perhaps she could just put her head down and rest quietly for a few minutes. The writing desk was smooth and cool against the side of her face as she laid her head down. When the teachers at Crakken Orphanage had needed a break, they had told the children to put their heads down on their desks, just as Lydia was doing now. Oddly, the children had always obeyed without complaint.

Her eyes snapped open. It wasn't odd, because those children had been *drugged*. Just as she had been drugged. And it was more than a sip of Mrs. Winslow's. The only thing she'd consumed this morning had been those few sips of tea. Lydia knew what Mrs. Winslow's felt like, and this was different. There must have been something in that tea.

She had to get out of this house. They were already suspicious of her, and as soon as Mrs. Rokotov noticed the missing documents, they would pull the house apart board by board . . . probably beginning in Lydia's room. She had to leave the mansion and get to the spot where Bane would meet her. She had to get out now, while the house was in chaos as servants rushed to pack up the books. She could wait it out in the woods.

She forced herself to her feet, but an avalanche of dizziness drove her back down. Whatever had been in that tea was working its way through her bloodstream and sapping her strength. She couldn't let it. The key to Bane's freedom was in those papers, so she was *going* to make it out of this house. Bracing herself against the wall, she made it out the door and clutched the banister with both hands as she descended the servants' staircase to the ground floor. The racket of hammers and books slamming into crates filled the air as servants swarmed the house like bees in a hive. No one paid attention to anything but the task of packing up the books.

Cold air helped rouse her fading energy as she slipped out the back door. Lydia glanced behind her. No one was watching as she escaped the house.

She wasn't even halfway to the iron gates when she knew she wouldn't make it. The edges of her vision were growing dim and her legs dragged as she walked. She stumbled and went sprawling onto the loamy soil. It took her three tries to get back on her feet.

She needed to hide these papers before she passed out. If anyone found her with them, she was as good as dead.

The icehouse! Surely she could make it that far. Lewis and Clark walked all the way to the Pacific Ocean; she could find a way to walk a hundred yards to the icehouse. She planted one foot in front of the other, her gaze fastened on the small stone building looming closer with each of her steps.

The door of the icehouse was rickety, and the scent of sawdust and stagnant air engulfed her as she stepped inside. Blocks of ice stacked as high as her chest filled the space, and a foot of sawdust topped each tower of ice with more sawdust layered in between each of the blocks. Could she simply slip the papers into the sawdust?

Lydia tried to insert the tip of her finger into the packed sawdust, but the weight of the ice was too heavy. She tried to lift the top cake, but it didn't budge. Wondering how on earth a person removed the ice, she spotted a pair of tongs, a hammer, and a metal file resting against the wall of the building. She breathed a sigh of relief and fitted the file into the sawdust insulation. The finely honed edge slid cleanly into the sawdust, and Lydia was able to wedge open the smallest of cracks. It took some maneuvering on her part, but she finally slid the documents into the layer of sawdust. Then she packed a little loose sawdust into the disturbed area, making the papers invisible.

The exertion helped revive her. She only wobbled a little as she left the icehouse, shaking the sawdust from her clothing. Maybe she could make it out the gate and to the meeting spot with Bane after all. If she could walk to the spot to meet Bane, it would not matter if she fell asleep. All she had to do was keep moving.

"Lydia!" Lars shouted at her from the steps of the mansion. Pretending she didn't hear, she kept heading toward the gate. She had no strength to run, only to steadfastly keep moving forward.

"Lydia, stop." Within a few moments he loped up alongside her. "What are you doing out here?"

"Just taking a little walk."

"You don't look good," he said.

"Watch it with those compliments, or I'll think you are flirting with me," she said. Her energy was fading again, and she was as weak as a kitten.

"Yes, well, it is the truth." He pressed a hand to her forehead.

"Mrs. Rokotov said you weren't feeling well and told you to rest. You really look awful, Lydia."

She tried to laugh. "There you go again."

He put his arm around her waist and turned her in the opposite direction. She was helpless against his strength. "Come on. I'm taking you back to the house. You need to lie down."

She didn't want to go back to the house. If she did, she would fall asleep. She would be defenseless and unconscious, and Bane would never find her.

Lydia tried to pull back, fumbling for any excuse. "I don't want the Professor to catch me napping in the middle of the day."

"The Professor is gone," Lars said. "I heard he won't be coming back ever again, and I need to get you back to the main house right away."

Anything but that. Someone wanted to kill her, but if she blathered about it to Lars, would he believe her? Or perhaps he would tell Mrs. Rokotov what she said, and then they would all know she was trying to get away. "Please, Lars," she said as he pulled her back toward the house. "I don't want to get in trouble."

"Yeah, well, you and me both. I don't have time to look after you today. Too much going on, so don't argue with me." She was no match for the strapping guard. He half tugged, half dragged her behind him on the walk up to the mansion. Never before had the granite building looked so ominous. If she stepped behind the massive front door once more, the odds were good she would never walk out again.

Lars took her to Mrs. Garfield. "Lydia is feeling sick," he said. "I think she needs to be put to bed."

Mrs. Garfield laid a hand on Lydia's forehead. "Oh my, yes. Let's get you another cup of tea and tuck you in." Lydia sagged against Lars but could not drag her gaze away from Mrs. Garfield as she came toward her with the same mug from this morning.

"I'd rather not," she said weakly.

But everything was going dark around the edges. She was floating, or was Lars carrying her? It became too difficult for her to keep her eyes open, and then someone pressed the mug to her lips, forcing tepid liquid down her throat. She tried to spit it out, but Lars's immense, work-roughened palm covered her mouth and prevented it. Then she remembered no more.

32

Bane peered through the barren branches to stare at the mansion, silent and gray in the moonlight. Lydia was more than two hours late.

He'd been a fool to send her inside while she was suffering from withdrawal. The moment he had her back in Boston he would find the world's best doctors to treat her. And then he would make her his wife.

He couldn't walk away from her. Not again. It was time to stop punishing himself for the crimes he had committed more than a decade ago. There were other ways he could atone for those failings, and Lydia would be a worthy ally in his crusade. Lydia brought a warmth and optimism to his world that he had not even known he was missing, and he wanted to give her the same. She already had a deep instinct toward faith that was propelling her toward the Lord, and Bane would walk beside her on every step of that journey until she could fully embrace that faith. Together they would be unstoppable.

Could she have fallen asleep inside the house? The house had been lit up like a Christmas tree far into the midnight hours, and Bane had been able to see people moving about inside. No doubt the Professor was already on the run, but the house had gone dark more than a half hour ago, and still no Lydia. The memory of Lydia's shaky frame and her pinpoint pupils made him certain she was in trouble.

Lydia was in danger and he was the one who had put her there. Now he would get her out.

Bane reached inside his saddlebags and pulled out his revolver. He would probably rouse the house by shooting the guard dogs, so he'd have to move quickly. He squeezed his knees into his horse, spurring the animal on toward the wrought-iron gates encircling the mansion. With less than one hundred yards to the gate, he heard the dogs coming. The two ferocious black dogs came pounding through the snow, growling and snapping, raising their forelegs up against the gate. Bane's horse tried to shy away, but he drove it forward and peered closer at the dogs. A hint of relief trickled through him.

"Juno?" he whispered.

The dog responded. He let out a little yelp, and then the tension between the dog's massive shoulders eased. It had been years since Bane had seen these dogs, but they remembered him.

He dismounted to greet the dogs. "Shh . . ." he whispered soothingly. Both dogs pushed their muzzles through the bars as far as possible, their blunt tails fiercely wagging. Bane approached them with caution, holding his hand out palm first, letting them smell him. "Easy there, Juno. What a good boy, Mars. You remember me, your old friend Bane." Bane had known these dogs since they were puppies, when he had spoiled and coddled them, never knowing when their friendship might become useful. When the dogs let out little yelps, he held his hand close enough for them to lick his fingers.

He tied his horse to a tree, then moved into position to climb the fence. "Behave yourselves," he whispered to the dogs, moving slowly as he wrapped his hands around the spear-point finials on the top of the bars. Despite how gently he lifted himself over the fence and dropped to the ground, the dogs still let out a round of happy grunts as they leapt around him.

"Shh," he tried to soothe them. "Sit," he commanded, hoping someone had trained them in the years since he had been gone.

Miraculously, both dogs sank into the snow, watching him with dark eyes.

No sooner had he set off toward the house than the door of the guardhouse opened. "What's going on out there?"

The man's pale hair glowed in the moonlight. Bane knew it must be Lars, the guard Lydia had told him about. The young man looked freshly woken from sleep, with his overcoat hanging open and a rifle in his hand. The guard went on high alert the moment he spotted Bane.

Bane simply smiled. "Hello there. Are you Lars?" he asked companionably.

"Who are you?"

"I'm Lydia's husband. I've come to surprise her on our anniversary." Bane strolled forward, his hand outstretched.

"Lydia is married?" Lars blurted out. He looked taken aback and a bit flustered.

"Three years as of today," Bane said casually, maintaining eye contact with the guard but intently aware of the rifle hanging at his side. Lars was caught off guard, a bit confused and embarrassed, so Bane kept pushing the matter as he strolled closer. "I always do something to surprise her on our anniversary, and this year I'm hoping to persuade the cook to make her blueberry crepes for breakfast." He was within an arm's length of the man. Before Lars even saw the blow coming, Bane had clobbered him on the side of the head with his pistol. The guard fell unconscious into the snow.

Bane darted inside the guardhouse, looking about for something to bind the guard's wrists. Knowing his time was short, he snatched a bed sheet and tore it into strips. Two minutes later, he had Lars's wrists bound tightly and his mouth stuffed and gagged.

It would hold Lars for a few minutes after he regained consciousness, but Bane needed to move *fast*.

He sprinted up to the mansion, the ominous gray stone looming before him like a bad nightmare. He had never expected to set foot in this fortress again, but he did not break stride as he launched up the front steps, slid around to the side of the house, and identified the easiest window to break. Using the blunt end of his pistol, he tapped against a windowpane until the glass broke and clattered to the ground. He reached inside to unlock the window and lift it open.

He vaulted up the stairs in the north wing, where Lydia said her bedroom was located. It had been years since he had been in this house, but he still remembered which floorboards squeaked and which stairs made noise. He moved quickly down the darkened hallway, forcing his breathing to remain calm and silent. When he found the room, he leaned his forehead against the door, praying Lydia would be safe inside. *Please, please,* he sent up a silent entreaty.

He pushed the door open, silently gliding into the room and staring at the motionless figure on the bed. Holding his breath, he moved forward, the pounding of his heart the only sound he heard in the silence of the room.

It *was* Lydia. Her face was pale as chalk, and she had sunken circles of charcoal around her eyes. He knelt beside her. "Lydia." His fierce whisper cut through the silence. He placed a hand on her shoulder, gently so as not to startle her. He pressed more firmly, but still she made no signs of rousing.

"Lydia, wake up." Even after shaking her more forcefully, she lay in a slack stupor. Bane pressed his fingers to her throat. Her skin was hot and her pulse was thready. He lifted her eyelid and almost fainted at what he saw. This was more than just too much opium.

"What have they done to you?" He realized it would be hopeless to try rousing her. He picked her up, blankets and all, and carried her from the room. Her head rolled back against his arm, and her limp body showed no sign of stirring.

As he reached the bottom of the staircase, the flickering of lantern light down the east hallway was the first sign someone was awake and moving in the house. Bane froze in his tracks. Before he could set Lydia down and reach for his pistol, he recognized the matronly figure of Mrs. Garfield rounding the corner.

She reared back in fright and nearly dropped the lantern when she saw him. "Alexander Banebridge!" she gasped.

"Hello, Mrs. Garfield," he said simply. The old cook had practically raised him, and Bane had always been able to manipulate her so easily during his years at the mansion, but there would be no cajoling her tonight. She was frightened out of her wits, and flattery wasn't the way to handle her at a time like this.

"What are you doing?" she asked, her voice laced with equal parts fear and outrage.

"I am taking Lydia somewhere she can be treated." He took a step forward, and Mrs. Garfield held her lantern higher.

"Don't come any closer," she said. "The Professor will kill me if that woman escapes." The lantern rattled in the old woman's grasp as she tried to stand her ground against Bane.

"Is that what he told you when he ordered you to keep Dennis Webster here for three years?" He took a step forward, careful not to frighten the woman but determined not to let her gather

her wits and summon help. "How many children did you help the Professor hold as hostages, just because you were afraid of him?"

"That is not fair! I did everything I could to make things better for the children who stayed here. You *know* I did my best for those children."

"By baking them pies?"

Mrs. Garfield blanched. "It was more than that!" she said. "I was a shoulder to cry on and someone they could always trust."

"They needed their own mothers' shoulders to cry on, not yours, Mrs. Garfield."

Bane shifted Lydia higher into his arms, her head still slack as it rolled to the side. What had they drugged her with? He needed to get her out of here and into a doctor's care before whatever poison was circulating through her veins could take further root.

He took a step forward, but Mrs. Garfield moved to block his path. "Take her back upstairs, Alex. That girl is not going to leave this house. I won't permit it."

"Think about this rationally," Bane said calmly. "Wouldn't it make sense to fear for your own soul more than the Professor's anger?" If Mrs. Garfield continued to prove difficult, Lars might awaken and get free of his bonds. And then Lydia was as good as dead.

"If you don't turn around and take Lydia upstairs this instant, I am calling for Boris. He will kill you both."

He raised a brow. "And will that make you innocent of our murder? Because you stood to the side while Boris performed the deed? Mrs. Garfield, you stood aside while too many children fell victim to the Professor. Lydia risked her life to save two of those children. Now, I want you to tell me what drug has been given to her."

Mrs. Garfield was becoming more agitated, the lantern wobbling in her hand as she wrestled with indecision. Bane stopped moving forward. Before he escaped this madhouse he needed to know what was wrong with Lydia.

Mrs. Garfield stamped her foot in frustration. "I put a few drops of chloroform in her tea. Just enough to keep her out of trouble."

Bane's eyes widened in horror. A person could die from drinking chloroform. "I'm taking Lydia to a doctor, and I need you to look the other way while I go."

Despite the chill of the night, Mrs. Garfield was sweating and her eyes darted around the room, glancing upstairs where Bane knew the guard named Boris was sleeping. "It is never too late for salvation," Bane said. "You aren't an evil woman; you have only lacked the strength to stand up to the Professor. Be strong enough now to step aside and let us go free."

She moved to block his path. "I can't do it. I just can't."

Bane shifted Lydia in his arms, knowing the next few moments would determine whether they both lived or died. "Mrs. Garfield, turn around and go back to your room. Your soul is more important than your fear of the Professor." He risked a smile, one that was surprisingly genuine. "I have no doubt you will figure a way out of the Professor's web if you choose to walk away. Do something for which you can feel pride rather than shame. I was able to get away from the Professor, and I can help you do so as well."

Bane knew the instant he lost her. Mrs. Garfield closed her eyes and drew a deep lungful of air. "Boris!" she screamed at the top of her lungs. "Come quickly! Boris!"

Bane hoisted Lydia over one shoulder, then kicked the lantern from Mrs. Garfield's hand. It smashed against the wall and the canister split, spewing kerosene that ignited the paneling into a wall of flame.

Bane turned and ran for the front door, Lydia a dead weight over his shoulder. Mrs. Garfield was shrieking behind him, pounding at the flames, but she was no longer his concern. He needed to escape before the entire household awakened.

As he left the house, he shifted Lydia again so he could draw the pistol from his waistband. He walked down the steps to the gravel drive, turned, and took two well-aimed shots at the lanterns that flickered on either side of the front door. More kerosene trickled down the wall, which ignited and fed the trail of orange flame flickering in the night air.

As an eerie glow began to fill the sky, Bane carried Lydia off into the night.

33

Lydia struggled to open her eyes. It would be so much easier to remain curled up underneath a heavy layer of sleep, but she was thirsty and had a headache, and there was something very important she needed to do. When she managed to open her eyelids, it took her a moment to focus in the bright light, but when she did, she could not stifle her gasp.

She was in a *palace*. Yards and yards of silken draperies fell in heavy folds across the bank of windows on the opposite side of the room. The ceiling was dense with carvings in the white plaster, and a chandelier dripping with crystal hung from the center. When she moved a bit, she was surprised at how easily her limbs slipped across the bedding. Silk sheets?

"Hello, Sleeping Beauty."

Lydia jerked her head to the other side of the room and saw Bane rising from a chair. He set a stack of papers on a table and strode toward her bedside, gentle concern burning in his eyes.

"I feel like I am in Versailles," she said, her tongue thick in her mouth.

Bane smiled as he poured her a glass of water from a crystal pitcher on the bedside table. "Close, but not quite. You're in the Fontaine family estate on Cape Grace." He slipped an arm beneath her shoulders and raised her a few inches from the pillow to hold the glass to her mouth. The water was blessedly cool slipping down her throat.

As she lowered herself back onto the silken sheets, she continued to move her gaze, taking in the soft shades of pale blue that decorated the room and the bank of windows overlooking the cold, blustery ocean. Utter bewilderment clouded her mind, and she struggled to remember how she came to be here.

"Cape Grace?" she asked. "Isn't that where all the rich tourists go?"

"Yes, but the town is deserted at this time of year. We thought it would be a good place for you to have some privacy while you recover. Your boardinghouse hardly seemed appropriate."

But how did she get here? And why was Bane looking at her with such caution in his eyes? The way he hovered over her and held his breath made it seem like he feared something was about to shatter or explode at any moment. She must have been hurt somehow because her head felt like it was being squeezed in a vise, but when she pressed a hand to her hair, there were no bandages or signs of a wound. Bane pulled a chair beside the bed and took her hand between his warm palms.

"You were really out of it for a while. We brought you here by train two days ago."

And then the memories came crashing down on her. She had been trapped in that horrible mansion in Vermont. "The Professor! Something was wrong with me and I couldn't function."

Pain filled his eyes. "I know."

"But what happened? I tried to stay awake to meet you, but how did I end up here?"

Bane laid a finger across her lips. "Suffice it to say that there was a fire at the Professor's house, and I was able to get you out in the confusion. You know how obedient the Professor's servants are, and I knew they would be under orders to rescue the books before they came running after us. We made a clean getaway, love."

Despite his reassurance, a sense of urgency was strangling Lydia. There was something very important she needed to remember, but her mind was too scattered to function properly. She had been fighting for something when the drug had taken her down. She had gone outside of the house on a mission. . . .

"The icehouse!" In those final desperate minutes she had hidden a copy of the Professor's plans for a new home in the icehouse. It was the key to finding him and bringing him down forever. "Did the icehouse burn? Did the fire spread there as well?" She had almost *died* to save those papers and could not bear it if they had gone up in flames.

"The icehouse?" Bane still seemed unconcerned. "I can't imagine that it did. The fire wasn't big, just enough to keep the servants occupied while I made my escape. Why the concern over the ice-house?"

"I found the plans for the Professor's escape! I know where he is going."

That got Bane's attention. His head jerked up and his eyes nearly pierced straight through her. "Tell me."

More and more pieces of her memory started clicking together, and she told Bane about the property in California and his plan to ship his books via railroad. She recounted how she had hidden the documents between blocks of ice and covered them with sawdust. Bane stood and paced the room as she talked, his face almost frightening in its intensity.

"We have to go back," Lydia said, rising from the bed. "We have to go back and get those papers before they are discovered."

Bane pushed her back against the pillows. "You aren't going anywhere. You are in no condition to travel. I'll think of another plan to get the documents."

She wanted to argue with him, but perhaps he was right about her being too ill to travel. The throbbing in her head was almost blinding in its ferocity. "My head really hurts," she said, wishing inanely for her little blue bottle.

"I know it does. The doctor warned me you would wake up wishing you could remove your head from your shoulders."

"A doctor has been here?" She clutched the sheet higher, grateful she wore a modest nightgown.

Bane nodded. "There have been a couple. A doctor examined you right after I got you away from the house, and then a specialist came to Cape Grace to see you. He was the one who warned me about the headache."

She felt exposed, naked, knowing so much had been going on around her while she was unconscious. "What kind of specialist?"

"He is a doctor who works with people struggling with opium," Bane said quietly. "Dr. Tilden has been living in the house with us and will continue to do so until you are cured."

Her eyes grew round, and she felt more exposed than ever. "Who all is living here?"

"Admiral Fontaine is here, with both his children. So is his mother. A couple of servants. A cook. And Dr. Tilden."

Lydia wished she could pull the sheets over her head and dissolve. "And all those people think I am an opium addict?" Her voice was hard as she glared at Bane. "You told Admiral Fontaine I use opium?"

"You have nothing to be ashamed of," he said quietly. "Eric is ready to lay the world at your feet because of what you did to save his son. Dr. Tilden has made a great study of opium addiction and will help you rid the poison from your body."

His words did not stop the waves of humiliation that rolled through her. Lydia gathered a fistful of sheets in her hands to stop them from shaking. "Bane, whatever is wrong with me has nothing to do with opium. I went days and days without it when I was in Vermont, and I only used it when the situation was more than any rational person could endure." She locked eyes with Bane, probably the only other person in the entire world who could understand the mind-numbing terror that came from being isolated in that horrible mansion.

"Under normal circumstances I don't *need* opium." Her voice vibrated with anger, and a rim of tears pooled in her eyes. "And you've gone and told all these people I am nothing better than an opium-eater."

She sat up, the agony in her head almost forcing her back down, but she wouldn't let a little pain stop her from something so important. She needed to get dressed and prove to Admiral Fontaine she was a perfectly healthy woman. She had fought *so hard* all those years to earn the admiral's respect, and now Bane had ruined it all. She swung her feet around, and instead of trying to force her back to bed, Bane handed her another glass of water.

"The first thing the doctor said to do is drink plenty of fluids, so let's get started on that right now."

Lydia obliged, not because she was following doctor's orders, but because her thirst was so insatiable she wanted to drink the entire pitcher of water. Bane continued speaking while she drank. "Lydia, you are experiencing all the classic symptoms of opium withdrawal. The thirst, the pain in your head. You have not stopped twisting the sheet since you woke up, and that kind of nervous tension is going to continue for at least a week as the drug is cleared from your system."

Lydia set the glass down, then dropped her head into her hands, curling up in shame. The pain in her head roared to life even at that small motion. The people who owned this house lived like royalty, and she was the fisherman's daughter who grew up on a boat and bathed in the sea.

"I want to get out of here," she said in a thin voice. "I don't want Admiral Fontaine to see me like this, and I don't want to meet all those strangers. Can't you please just help me get back to Boston where I can get better without being humiliated?" Why couldn't she control the wobble in her voice? She was horrified when a tear rolled down her cheek. She swiped it away and hoped Bane did not notice.

The mattress sagged as he sat beside her, folding her hand inside his own. "Lydia, you have never been the weepy sort, but this is another one of the symptoms of withdrawal. Weepiness, sensitivity."

She was so angry she could only speak through clenched teeth. "You told all these people I am an opium addict. That would make *anyone* upset, Bane. I want to go back to Boston. Today."

Bane rose. "Very well. I know you like a good adventure, so if you insist, we can start plotting an escape. This will be fun, slipping out of the Cape Grace castle to run back to your Boston hovel. And look, we still have your compass, so we have that going for us. It will be a bit of a trek, but you are the one who wants to be like Lewis and Clark, so the seventy miles back to Boston would be just a little jaunt. We can camp under the stars and hike along the back roads with nothing guiding us but the compass needle."

For the first time in weeks, Lydia began to feel like herself. She raised her chin a notch. "I know you are making fun of me, but it actually sounds rather appealing."

That seemed to take Bane by surprise. "Really?" The note of hope in his voice was unmistakable.

Anything that would take her mind off the pain in her head and the twitchiness in her limbs would be welcome, but it was more than that. She wanted a sense of purpose in her life, a feeling of worthiness. "The last little adventure you sent me on was the most terrifying thing I've ever experienced. But it was also the most rewarding. I like having a challenge, even if it is frightening."

"Very well, then. I'll take you back to Boston, but you need to prove you are well enough to travel first. How convenient there is a doctor in the house."

The sense of relief was huge. All she had to do was hold it together for a few hours before she could leave with her dignity intact. "And the doctor will tell Admiral Fontaine I am perfectly healthy . . . that I don't have a problem with opium?"

"If that is what he concludes after examining you."

She lifted her chin and forced her hands to stop trembling. "He will."

The smile on Bane's face was cool, poised, skeptical. "Well then, the first thing is to get you up and dressed." Bane flung open the doors of a wardrobe. "Look, clothes that I suspect have been purchased with Miss Lydia Pallas in mind. Stand up, stand up." He pressed a dress made of garnet velvet and trimmed with black satin braiding into Lydia's hands. "No more lollygagging for you. Let's get you dressed and moving about. The doctor stepped into town this morning, but you can come and meet Mrs. Fontaine before he returns."

"Bane, just because I said I like a bit of adventure doesn't mean I'm going to undress in front of you."

Bane winked at her. "Pity. I'll go rejoin the family for a moment. When you are ready, just head down the staircase and turn left. I will be listening for you."

Heaven help me. Bane's mind reeled as he left Lydia's room. The documents he would sell his soul to see were buried in ice and in danger of being ruined.

He strode into another bedroom and hoisted up the sash of a windowpane, leaning outside to test the air. Puddles of melting snow surrounded the house, and rivulets of water dripped from the icicles on the roofline. He ground his teeth in frustration. It was colder in Vermont, and the insulation in the icehouse meant the documents might still be preserved, but not for long.

And despite her denial, Lydia was in the midst of a raging withdrawal from a drug she had been addicted to since childhood. She displayed every symptom Dr. Tilden warned him about: twitchiness, headache, thirst, and weepiness. Soon she would have waves of nausea and days of insomnia.

But he had to get to Vermont. The road leading to the Professor's house was not on any map, and Bane was one of the few people who could find the house. He bowed his head, listening to the patter of melting ice as it dripped from the roof into the puddles below. With each drop he feared for the survival of those documents in the icehouse. He did not have much time.

He would have to convince Lydia to accept help from Dr. Tilden and the Fontaines, and that was going to be a delicate task. There was nothing he could say that would convince her she was sick; it was a conclusion she needed to reach on her own.

34

Lydia fingered the smartly tailored gown she'd put on, feeling like an imposter. Everything in this house spoke of luxury, from the silken bedding to the view of the mighty ocean outside the bedroom window. The heavy brass doorknob was cool in her hand as she twisted it open to enter the hallway. The area outside was as splendid as the bedchamber. The thick rug stretching the length of the hallway absorbed the sound of her footsteps and led her to a staircase curved in an impressive arch as it descended to the main floor.

How annoying that she could not stop her hand from trembling on the banister. It didn't mean anything. Bane said she had been sleeping for two days. Anyone who had nothing to eat or drink for two days would be a little shaky. Surely something to eat would restore her strength.

True to his word, Bane had been listening and greeted her as she turned the corner from the staircase. "We are painting Easter eggs in the kitchen," he said quietly into her ear.

The strength of Bane's hand gave her a jolt of much needed

confidence as he led her toward the kitchen. Her head felt like it would split open with each step, so she tried to glide, moving slowly and cautiously.

The kitchen was lined with cooking ovens and pantry shelves, but in the middle of the floor was a butcher-block work space where Admiral Fontaine and two children were painting eggs. Another woman who looked as starched as Queen Victoria stood beside them.

The moment Lydia stepped into the kitchen, Admiral Fontaine rose from his stool and strode toward her. She had never seen him in anything but a uniform, but today he was wearing a simple white shirt and black trousers. The change in his clothing couldn't account for why he looked so different. It was the expression on his face. Normally he looked so confident, but not today.

He cleared his throat. "Miss Pallas . . ." he said awkwardly, but he grasped her hands between his and gave them a hearty squeeze. And then he stopped talking. He appeared to want to say something more, but his brow furrowed and he swallowed hard. "I am afraid I am at a loss for words."

To her stunned disbelief, he was too choked up to continue speaking with her.

Queen Victoria spared him the embarrassment. The woman wore an exquisite gown of ebony silk embroidered with jet beads, and the upsweep of her gray hair was a masterpiece of engineering. "Welcome to my home," she said smoothly. "I am Victoria Fontaine, and I can't tell you how grateful we are for all you have done for our family." It was as Bane said. This woman did not seem to be looking down on her. A tiny ray of confidence began to build inside Lydia. Perhaps it would not be too difficult to quell Bane's ridiculous concerns about opium addiction.

Before Lydia could respond, Jack sprang off his stool and raced to greet her. "Do you remember me?" he asked. Spatters of paint were on his grinning face, and he was apparently none the worse for his ordeal if his sparkling eyes were any indication.

"Of course I remember you," Lydia said. "How could I forget a boy who climbs on roofs and drops through skylights?"

Apparently, this was high praise, and Jack seemed to grow two inches taller. "We are painting Easter eggs. Do you want to help us?"

Mrs. Fontaine put a hand on her grandson's shoulder. "Miss Pallas must be very hungry. And perhaps she is not quite ready for all this excitement?"

The veiled implication was clear to every adult in the room, but Lydia decided to tackle the issue directly. "Of course I would like to help. I'm afraid Bane may have exaggerated my illness, but I am perfectly healthy. Famished too, if that is breakfast on the counter over there."

Her headache was raging, but food would surely help. Bane strolled to the sideboard and lifted a cover from a warming tray. "The best thing about staying at the Fontaine estate is they feed you like royalty. You've got your choice of scrambled eggs, ham, hash browns, bacon, muffins. And what is this glop?"

"That is good old-fashioned oat porridge," Eric said. "I don't care how humble, it is what they serve aboard ship and what I like for breakfast."

Lydia's stomach started to growl. "I'll have some of everything."

Bane looked at her with caution. "Are you sure? How about some milk and perhaps a little of that glop the admiral likes? It might go easier on your stomach."

She winced at hearing her "stomach" being discussed in polite company but was too hungry to care. "Bane, I'm starving. Have mercy." She started to tremble again, so she lowered herself onto a stool, sinking gently to avoid rousing the monster inside her head. She introduced herself to the little girl named Lucy, and let the child show her how she was adding little gold dots to the eggs they had already painted.

"When I was your age I lived on a boat, and there were no eggs at Easter time, so my papa pulled up oyster shells out of the ocean and told us they would work just as well," Lydia said.

The memory was so vivid she could smell the salt air and hear Papa's booming laughter on the wind. A surge of longing swelled inside her, and Lydia found herself insanely, desperately longing for Papa's unabashed bear hugs and his booming laughter. He must have loved her so much to gather those silly oyster shells for her every year. He had failed in providing a decent home for his family, but his generous heart meant he had never stopped trying. Had she ever told him how much she loved him?

Tears flooded her eyes, and a strangled sob escaped her throat. She struggled to contain herself, but it was hopeless as the ragged sounds ripped from her throat. She clapped a hand over her mouth to stifle the sounds. Drawing a ragged breath, she wiped the tears streaming from her eyes with her hand. She mustn't break down like this in front of the admiral and his family.

"I'm sorry," she managed to say on a shaky breath. "I never cry, but that memory snuck up on me."

Mrs. Fontaine handed her a napkin and Lydia dabbed her eyes, her face heating with embarrassment. Fine impression she was making on everyone. She sniffled and forced herself to smile. "My parents died when I was very young, and sometimes I still get a little emotional."

Bane stood frozen with a plate full of food on the opposite side of the kitchen, watching her through pain-filled eyes. Surely he was thinking her weepiness was another symptom of withdrawal, but it was not. It had been years since she had remembered the way

Papa had collected those oyster shells for her, and it had caught her unawares, that was all.

"I'm starving, and that bacon smells amazing," she said as she pushed herself off the stool. She crossed the room to Bane, and he handed her the plate and a fork.

"Do you want to sit while you eat?" Bane asked. "We can clear a space at the table."

Lydia shook her head. "I'd prefer to stand," she said. It was easier to stand when her legs were this antsy. Even though everything looked wonderful, she had a sudden desire for a nice cup of tea with a big spoonful of Mrs. Winslow's. She forced the thought away and took a small bite of the eggs.

How long had it been since she had had a swallow of Mrs. Winslow's? She paced alongside the ovens to get her mind off the drug and took a bite of ham with some kind of honey glaze. She needed to pretend this was a normal morning. No tremors, no persistent fantasies of a drug she should not be using. She was going to be every bit as ladylike as Mrs. Fontaine.

The little Fontaine girl went back to painting the eggs with new determination. Lydia tried to watch the girl's childish hands place a dollop of the glittering paint on the eggshell, but her stomach was not accepting the food very well. She almost felt like she wanted to throw it all up. She set the plate down and forced herself to breathe deeply, willing her stomach to settle. Bane came to stand beside her.

"I think the milk would have been a better choice," he whispered in her ear.

Anything would have been a better choice. Her entire body was hot, and perspiration prickled across her skin. Her stomach roiled, and she covered her mouth, knowing she didn't have long. Her helpless gaze found Bane's, and he firmly guided her to the oversized kitchen sink. She barely reached it before she lost the battle.

The food came up in two mighty heaves, but then her stomach continued to protest, vomiting up all the water she had drunk. She could sense Bane behind her, shielding her from the humiliating picture she must make. She was still doubled over and retching when a wave of sobs came upon her. Her whole body shook with sobs that sounded like a wounded animal even to her own ears. She wished Papa were here. She was bawling so hard she couldn't even stand; all she could do was cling to the basin like a lifeline. She could hardly even breathe. How humiliating to be bent over a sink in front of these nice people while she vomited and sobbed and shook.

"Come along, Jack," she heard Admiral Fontaine order. "You too, Lucy. We will finish this later." Lydia heard a rustling of fabric and shuffling of feet as the family left the kitchen.

Another wave of shame swamped Lydia as she remained doubled up over the sink. "I think there's something really wrong with me," she whispered.

Through her tears she could feel Bane's hands stroke her back. "I know, darling. Don't worry, I'm going to make sure you get better." His voice was so soothing, with no trace of censure, just the calm reassurance Bane was so good at.

Another wave of nausea overtook her, but she had nothing left to throw up. She clung to the enamel sink as the heaving continued and threatened to tear her in half. The very worst part was the knowledge that Bane was right. She was addicted to opium, and this was her punishment for allowing it to happen.

Bane handed her a damp towel, and she used it to wipe her mouth. He helped her stand, and she looked around the kitchen, assuring herself they were alone. "I am so embarrassed. So ashamed." She had difficulty even forming the words through the shaking of her breath.

Bane smoothed a few tendrils of her hair back from her forehead. "While you were sleeping, I took the liberty of telling Eric and his mother how determined you were to save Jack, even as you battled against your illness. I told them of your history at the orphanage and how you had been spoon-fed that poison from the time you were a child. They know that even after Jack was rescued, you stayed in that madman's house so that you could strike a blow against the Professor. Lydia, they stand in awe of you. *I* stand in awe of you. Who else could have outwitted the Professor and, at the same time, walked through the fires of withdrawal?"

The words soothed her embarrassment, but the shakiness was back in her legs, and pacing was the only thing that seemed to help. Her success in finding the Professor's new base of operations would come to nothing if the documents were ruined before Bane could rescue the pages from the ice. "Those papers are still in the icehouse."

"I know."

"I want you to go get them." There was no shakiness in her voice now, only grim determination. "I don't want you to spend the rest of your life in this ridiculous battle with the Professor. I want him out of your life so you have no more excuses for leaving me. If you walk away from me, I don't want it to be because of that man."

There was a curious mixture of hope and concern on Bane's face as he began speaking. "I want to find those papers and put the Professor in jail for the rest of his life." He folded her hands between his own. "There are very few things in this world of which I am certain, but I know I will love you until my dying day. I want to build a life with you where we can be free to pursue whatever grand adventure your heart desires. But Lydia, I can't be married to a drug addict."

She blanched. His words sliced through her, but she did not

allow herself to look away. She had been lying to herself about her condition for years, but she could never fool Bane. If she wanted Bane in her life, she needed to tackle this problem with no more lies to herself or others. "I will do whatever it takes to get better."

"Will you meet with Dr. Tilden?" he asked gently. "He will be back soon."

She would do anything to escape the misery that was coursing through every vein and nerve ending of her body. "Yes. Yes," she managed to say through trembling lips. "Bane, I'll do whatever it takes." His arms locked around her, and she leaned into his warmth, finding the first comfort she'd had since she had opened her eyes that morning.

Bane watched Lydia's eyes widen in surprise when they went into the spacious library and she met Dr. Tilden. "You went to medical school?" she blurted out.

Bane knew a reaction like Lydia's was typical when people first met Dr. Tilden, but he was confident Dr. Tilden was the best doctor to see Lydia through the difficult days ahead of her.

"I know, I look like I am about twelve years old, but I'm thirty-five, I swear it." The man had a slight frame and light brown hair. "Here, I forgot to put on my glasses. I don't need them, but they are supposed to make me look older." He put the wire-frame spectacles on his face and looked at her hopefully. "Better?"

The glasses didn't help, but Lydia played along anyway. "It's as if I'm looking at my very own grandfather," she said.

Dr. Tilden smiled, and his gap-toothed grin made him look even younger. "I like that you've still got your sense of humor. The next few weeks aren't going to be any fun, so try to hold on to that."

Lydia took a seat at the table, and Bane folded her trembling hand into his own as he sat beside her. He ached with the knowledge of what she was going to endure and would give his right arm to suffer the pain in her place.

"So what am I up against?" Lydia asked.

"It is going to take about two weeks for the poison to clear from your body, but the first week is going to be the worst. Expect massive insomnia. Headaches. You'll also be skittish and overly sensitive about things, maybe even a little paranoid. Have those feelings already started?" he asked.

Lydia let go of Bane's hand, pushed away from the table, and began pacing the room. "All of it." She twisted her hands as she walked to the window and stared out at the bleak, overcast sky. "It hurts to sit still. It hurts to move. I feel like scraping my skin off so I can start over with a different body."

"And paranoia?" the doctor asked.

"When I was in Vermont, I felt like the trees were spying on me." She turned from the window and began pacing the room again, itching the skin on her arms. "Three times since I woke up this morning I have looked out the window and wondered how long it will take me to get to the nearest pharmacy to buy something I know will stop this pain the minute I swallow it."

Bane shot to his feet and grasped her upper arms. "Lydia, I need to be able to trust you. I have to go to Vermont, and you know why. Promise me you won't leave this house."

The doctor looked concerned. "Now is not a good time for you to be away."

Bane kept his gaze locked on Lydia's face. "Promise me, Lydia."

"I want to go with you," she said. "It would keep my mind off things."

Bane looked to the doctor. "Can she travel?"

Dr. Tilden shook his head. "A milk diet will ease the nausea, but it won't cure it. She cannot travel."

The thought of those blocks of ice, melting and smearing the ink on the irreplaceable documents, warred with the sight of Lydia's wistful, pained eyes. "It will take me three days to do what needs to be done. I won't go if it means risking your health. *Can I trust you, Lydia?*"

The damaged, trembling woman standing before him disappeared, and just for a moment Bane was looking into the face of a warrior. There was grim determination in Lydia's eyes, and her iron jaw indicated that she was braced for any battle. "I want you to go, Bane. You can trust me."

The doctor's rules were strict, and Lydia stiffened in mortification as he outlined a plan to ensure she would never be left alone, even for a few minutes. Even worse, the doctor warned that her insomnia would make it impossible for her to sleep for several days, meaning she needed around-the-clock supervision.

She was ashamed to need a baby-sitter. She had had a big argument with Bane about it before he left, yelling that she didn't need watchdogs and any man with an ounce of faith in her would know that. She was a shaking, twitching, nervous wreck, and she didn't want an audience while she suffered through it. Bane calmly informed her he would not leave for Vermont if she did not agree to his plan.

That was the trump card. Bane made her promise to allow Dr. Tilden, Mrs. Fontaine, and the admiral to take shifts baby-sitting her. It made a miserable situation even worse. Instead of being allowed to hole up in the privacy of her room, she had to inconvenience these rich, well-bred people. She was out of place in this house, where every square inch—the hand-painted wallpapers, the plush Oriental carpets, and the crystals dangling from the chandeliers—screamed luxury. She didn't belong here.

It had been a full day since Bane had left. In the formal parlor, Mrs. Fontaine rattled on about her Puritan ancestors while Lydia walked another lap around the room. How many times had she circled this room in the past six hours? A thousand? Two thousand? She longed to escape outside for a good brisk walk, but it had been raining all day, a gusty wind spattering heavy drops against the windows. Was Bane traveling through this awful weather?

The door clicked open. "Mother, I'll take over here," the admiral said. "Perhaps you can help get the children into bed while I sit with Miss Pallas."

This was the moment Lydia had dreaded. She had not been alone with the admiral since that awful day last December. Now here she was, trembling like an opium addict. She turned away and continued pacing so she would not have to look at him. She *was* an opium addict, and everyone in the house knew it.

Mrs. Fontaine sagged in relief. Apparently, six hours of talking about her family had been a strain even for her. "Excellent," Mrs. Fontaine said as she excused herself from the room.

The admiral closed the hand-carved doors of the parlor. He looked as uncomfortable as she felt, standing with rigid posture and a hard jaw. This man could intimidate an angry mob just by glaring down his aquiline nose, but today he looked as uncomfortable as a sinner in a hair shirt. "And how are you feeling this evening, Miss Pallas?"

Like there were termites crawling over every inch of her skin and she needed to jump out a window to escape them. "Fine."

Skepticism tinged his grave face as he glanced around the room. "It looks as though you've worn quite a groove into that carpet."

Lydia's gaze flew to the silk rug. Sure enough, the short silk strands were matted down in the path where she had been walking all day. Her mouth went dry, and her jumpiness got worse. She couldn't do anything right, and now she was destroying the admiral's fancy house with her carelessness. "Oh, my heavens," she said. "I'll pay for the carpet. I have money saved back in Boston."

"Stop talking nonsense. The next time the servants take it outside to beat it clean, the matted areas will straighten right out," he said dismissively.

Her brow wrinkled with skepticism. Was it really that easy to correct the damage? She didn't know the first thing about fancy carpets, and maybe he was just saying that to make her feel better. "Should we check to be sure? If the path won't come out—"

He cut her off. "Do you honestly think I would consider charging you for a stupid scrap of carpet when you risked your life to save my son?" He sounded almost angry. "Do you?"

She turned around and started pacing again, careful to avoid the matted path of crushed silk strands. She hated being in the same room with him. In the past the admiral had been her employer, a man she admired and was proud to work for. Now he was acting like he was beholden to her, and she didn't know how to behave. She weaved in and out of the furniture in the center of the room as she paced in a smaller circle. "I'm sorry if that sounded offensive. I've never been in a fancy house like this before, and I don't know what my manners should be."

The grooves along the side of his mouth deepened as he scowled. "Lydia, your manners are fine. What is more important is the fact that you have the bravery of an entire regiment of marines. I was wrong about you. I put obedience to the rules over the courage it takes to do the right thing, and for that, I am deeply ashamed."

She would rather be dropped into the Black Hole of Calcutta

than continue this conversation. Even thinking about that awful day when she was fired from the Navy Yard caused the lump in her throat to grow. Until yesterday she had not cried in fifteen years, and now she was weepy over the stupidest things, like when Bane laced up her shoes because her hands were too jittery, or when Dr. Tilden told her about his pet mice that died last year. Mice! She was in no shape to discuss anything relating to the Navy Yard.

She beat down her emotions and drew a deep breath. "Admiral Fontaine—"

"Please call me Eric."

She cleared her throat and tried again. "Admiral Fontaine, I would prefer to avoid this discussion, if it is all the same to you."

He looked confused. "But I owe you an apology. I was wrong to be so intolerant, and I should have considered your circumstances before charging ahead and firing you. I can't pretend that it never happened, and I need—"

She cut him off. "Admiral Fontaine, the day you fired me is at the very top of things I want scrubbed out of my memory for as long as I live. Are you *really* going to make me revisit it right now?"

The look of shock on his face made her feel guilty, which was so ridiculous she whirled around so she wouldn't have to face him. Her leg bumped an end table, and a porcelain vase went flying.

Admiral Fontaine caught it a second before it crashed to the floor. He righted the end table and replaced the vase where it belonged. "Let's get you out of this room before you start climbing the walls. Have you ever played billiards?"

Lydia didn't know how to play billiards, but she appreciated how smoothly the admiral changed the topic. Physical activity sounded much better to her than the apology he seemed determined to deliver but that she was not ready to hear.

The game room was on the third floor of the sprawling house.

She didn't realize rich people had entire rooms dedicated to nothing but gaming, but here it was. There was a card table in the corner and a dartboard on the wall, but a billiard table almost as big as the boat Lydia had lived on in the Mediterranean dominated the room. The admiral showed her how to rack the balls and hold the cue, but her trembling hands were clumsy and it took her a while to land a solid strike on the cue ball. After showing her the basics, the admiral racked up the balls and prepared to start a game.

He rubbed a little chalk on the tip of his cue stick and looked at her with caution. "Perhaps you can help me with a problem I'm having at the research wing at the Navy Yard?"

That caught her by surprise. In the four years she had worked at the research wing, everything had functioned like a well-oiled clock. "What sort of problem?"

The admiral leaned over the table and took careful aim, striking the cue ball and sending the rest of the balls scattering across the surface of the table. "Ever since you left, Jacob has been humming 'Oh My Darling, Clementine.' He knows I hate that song. I told him the first week he worked there I hated it and never wanted to hear it again. I never did until the week I fired you. Now he hums it daily."

Lydia blinked. "Jacob always tortured us with his humming. That is nothing new."

The admiral acted as though he hadn't heard her as he fired off another strike at the cue ball. "Once that tune is in my brain, it takes root and repeats itself endlessly. Now, every time I walk through the office doors, Jacob stops whatever he is doing and starts humming that blasted song. He's doing it on purpose. And Willis dumps an unholy amount of sugar into the teapot each morning. He used to only sweeten his own cup of tea because he knows I do not take it sweet. Now I can't even get a decent cup of tea at work.

It is only a matter of time before Karl thinks up a way to make my life a misery, because he is the angriest of them all."

Her lip quivered. She missed her former office mates so badly, and the sweet way they banded together on her behalf made her want to cry. *Again*. She turned away and scratched at her forearms, wondering if plunging into the frigid ocean might ease the nonstop itching. "I'm afraid I can't help you with Jacob's humming. Or the tea Willis brews."

The admiral set his cue down and straightened to look her in the face. "Miss Pallas, it occurs to me that I was overly hasty in my actions last November. If you won't accept my apology, would you at least consider returning to the Navy Yard? I'm sure the research wing would be happy to have your services again. And if it stops the daily rendition of 'Oh My Darling, Clementine,' I would be eternally grateful."

Wasn't this what she had been praying for? She could tell by the hopeful expression on his face that the admiral's offer was genuine, but she remembered the young man with the thinning black hair sitting at her desk the day she visited the office. "You already have another translator for southern Europe."

The admiral leaned over the cue ball and lined up another shot. "I'm sure we can find an alternate position at the Navy Yard for Mr. Trivoni."

With two thousand people employed in the Navy Yard, that was probably true. Lydia paced around the billiard table, trying to pretend her skin didn't feel as if she had been rolling in stinging nettles. She had been happy at the Navy Yard. Would it be possible to turn back the clock and recapture those years? She loved the work and would have the camaraderie with Karl and Jacob once again. She would once again be helping rebuild the American navy into one of the best maritime fleets in the world.

But that was the admiral's dream, not hers. Not anymore.

She looked across the billiard table to see Admiral Fontaine awaiting her answer. "I can't go back," she said. "I want to keep working with Bane to reform the opium laws. Now that I know what a seductive, horrible drug it can be, I want to make sure other people don't slip into the problem I have. I'll do *anything* to save another child from what I am going through."

A hint of humor tugged at the side of the admiral's mouth. "You're not going to help me out with Jacob, then? Get him to quit torturing me with that wretched tune?"

She wanted to laugh, but the tremors were getting worse, so she gritted her teeth as she kept pacing around the billiard table. "Sir, you are on your own."

At two o'clock in the morning, someone roused Dr. Tilden to take over for the admiral. It had been almost two days since Lydia had slept, and she was exhausted.

"What did you do in the Professor's house when you could not sleep?" Dr. Tilden asked her.

"I would go outside and walk. For hours and hours, I would walk through those woods."

"Did it help?"

"A little." Until she had heard the maple trees creaking, and her paranoid imagination told her the trees were whispering about her.

"Then let's head outside." It had stopped raining an hour ago, and Lydia welcomed the chance to get outside. It was a blustery night, and the moment Lydia set foot outside she breathed deeply of the sea wind.

"*That scent,*" she moaned, all the longing in the world in her voice. "How I have missed the smell of the ocean." Lydia set off at a brisk pace through the manicured lawn and toward the craggy outcropping that dropped off toward the ocean. The roar of the waves carried on the night air, and Lydia leaned into the wind. The crashing of the waves against the beach and the soothing rush of the water's retreat were timeless, comforting sounds.

She turned to look at the doctor in the waning light of the crescent moon. "What do other people do to take their minds off things when they are going through this?"

"Some walk. Or try to write down their feelings in a journal. Some pray."

She looked at him in surprise. "Does that work?"

The doctor took an inordinate amount of time before he responded. "I find that prayer works better than any other cure known to medical science. But you must have faith for it to work."

She had been reading the books of the New Testament, just like Karl had told her, but none of those stories seemed to help her battle the fantasies of Mrs. Winslow's Syrup and how good it would feel sliding down her throat.

"Just tell me what to do," she said. "I'm a smart girl. I'll do whatever you tell me until I beat this thing. If I have to walk to California and back, that's what I will do."

Dr. Tilden took a few steps toward a rugged outcropping of granite and sat down. "Lydia, you told me of your efforts to save your apartment, to work for the navy. You studied and learned languages and worked two and sometimes three jobs at a time. All of this is very admirable, but if you try to carry all these burdens on your own, eventually you will exhaust yourself. Neither our bodies nor our minds were built to endure endless rounds of stress without support. If your soul had nothing to lean on in times of struggle, it is little wonder you turned to a crutch such as opium."

Dr. Tilden was not wearing his glasses, and his youthful face was open and gentle as he smiled at her. "Lydia, you are fearfully and wonderfully made. The Lord has designed our bodies and psyches to perform amazing acts of heroism, but we are not machines. Both our bodies and our spirits must be tended and nurtured so they may be strong in times of need. You haven't been so good about that second part. I am here to help show you how."

He held his arm out to her, and they began walking again. "As a doctor, I can explain how your body is ridding itself of toxins, which is shutting down your ability to digest food properly. I can explain how the nerves in your body are in an overly excited state, which is causing your insomnia. All of these things have a scientific explanation and can be treated. But once your body is in good working order, it will require a change in your *spirit* to sustain the cure. You are a woman of awesome talents. It is in your nature to strive and achieve and conquer. I fear that even after your body is cured, if you do not find a source of spiritual support, you may slip back into the use of a crutch to sustain yourself."

All she had ever known was work, but Bane had tried to show her a spiritual side of life. He had made a jest of it . . . but that was his way, always navigating beneath a façade of humor.

She wondered where Bane was at this very moment. How desperately she wanted to please him and prove she was capable of conquering this demon. "Bane should be back in two days. Is it possible I could be through the worst of this business when he returns?"

Dr. Tilden's smile was terribly sad. "My dear, at that point you will be entering the worst phase of it."

35

Less than three days after setting off for Vermont, Bane came careening toward the Fontaine estate, driving his horse hard as his destination came into view. He had the plans. They were in good condition, telling him in crisp black ink *exactly* where the Professor intended to flee and how his organization would take root in a new home a few miles outside of San Francisco. The Professor would first go to the small town of Scranton in Pennsylvania, where his books had been shipped for safekeeping. Once the Professor had been reunited with his precious books, he would lease three railway cars and ride with them out west.

Mrs. Rokotov and her son were supposed to meet the Professor in Scranton, but apparently there was no loyalty among thieves. A little investigation at the train station revealed that although the Rokotovs had sent the Professor's books to Scranton according to plan, rather than joining in his exile, they had fled to New York instead. Bane was betting that when Mrs. Rokotov discovered Lydia had escaped with the evacuation papers, she decided to make a run for it without the Professor, knowing they had all been found out.

Hadn't they covered up Jack's burned book because they feared the Professor? Now that same fear was sending them on the run rather than facing the Professor's rage over what Lydia had accomplished beneath their very noses.

All to the good. Bane was already forming a plan to intercept the Professor and his books in Scranton and deliver him directly into the hands of the law.

He tied his horse to a post and took the steps two at a time as he raced up to the house. He burst through the door and went room to room, looking for someone with whom to share the news.

Eric and Mrs. Fontaine were in the library. "I've got the plans!" he said, his breath coming in short gasps.

Eric rose from his chair. "The documents are still legible?"

"Perfect condition." Excitement surged through his blood. If he was right and the Rokotovs were saving their own skin, the Professor would be left holding the bag in Scranton. With Fontaine's money and connections, they could put the Professor out of commission forever. Then he noticed the exhaustion on Eric's face, and his heart skipped a beat.

"How is Lydia?"

Mrs. Fontaine moved to stand beside Eric, looking equally weary. "Dr. Tilden is with her upstairs. It has been difficult."

The strength drained from Bane's legs, and he sank into a chair. "Tell me."

"I don't think she has slept at all since she woke up four days ago," Eric said. "The cook tried to make things she could tolerate, but nothing stays down. The nausea comes upon her so suddenly that she won't step foot outside the washroom. I hear her crying in there, sometimes for hours. I've tried to offer comfort, but she won't see anyone but Dr. Tilden."

Bane dropped his head into his hands, guilt washing through

him. Mrs. Fontaine put her hand on his shoulder. "Alex, she has been amazing. She has not asked for any drugs and has followed all of Dr. Tilden's orders to the letter. You should be very proud of her."

He should have been here with her. While he was out fighting another battle in his private war against the Professor, Lydia was facing an even deadlier demon. He would not leave her again. As much as he wanted to be the one to drive the stake through the Professor's twisted empire, he had something more important to do here.

He reached inside his jacket and withdrew the fragile pages. "Here," he said as he turned the papers over to Eric. "You deserve to be in on bringing the Professor down. I'll help you devise the plan, but I can't be the one to put it into action."

A gleam lit Eric's pale gray eyes. "I can do it."

Lydia was in agony. The towels strewn across the washroom floor did little to soften the cold tile beneath her bottom. She laid her head against the side of the washtub, her arms dangling limply on the floor. Dr. Tilden had pulled a chair into the room and sat ready to help her whenever the next wave of vomiting wracked her body.

"It is time for another glass of milk," he said softly.

Her belly clenched at the prospect of more milk. Every hour the doctor watched her sip until she had drained the glass. Inevitably, she would vomit most of it back up, but it had to be done. The more milk she could get her body to accept, the stronger she would be to keep fighting the battle.

She took a deep breath. "Okay." It was an effort to lift her aching head from the side of the tub. She twisted on the towels so she could face the doctor and accept another glass of the warmed milk. Her hand shook so badly the liquid threatened to slosh over the side of the glass, but she reached her mouth in time and got it down.

"Excellent," Dr. Tilden said as he took the glass from her. He noted the time in a little journal he was using to track how long she could hold the milk down before it came back up. She laid her head back down against the side of the tub and closed her eyes. It was easier to be in the dark. The doctor had drawn the shade over the single window in the washroom, but some light still leaked through and bounced off the glaring white tile. Nighttime was always the easiest for her.

"Hello, Lydia."

Bane! Her eyes snapped open and she raised her head. He looked awful, terrible. There were shadows carved into his face, and his eyes looked haunted. Her heart plummeted. He must have failed in Vermont.

"The documents?" she asked weakly.

"Perfect condition."

She sat straighter, and for the first time in days a genuine smile filled her face. "Then why do you look so sad?"

He stepped into the washroom and knelt beside her. "Because you are in less than perfect condition, love."

She laid her head back down on the tub. "Oh, Bane. There you go again with all that flattery."

That made him smile, but she knew she looked awful. Her nightgown was stained, her hair straggled down her back, and she could feel the hollows beneath her eyes. How pathetic she must look, sitting on the floor of the washroom. He tucked a strand of hair behind her ear. "I should not have left you."

"Bane, hearing that you have those papers is the first thing that has made me feel good in days."

He pivoted to sit on the floor beside her, holding her hand between his. "How is she doing?" he asked Dr. Tilden.

"As well as can be expected. She has a way to go before she comes out on the other side."

"You probably need a rest. I'll stay with Lydia for a while."

Dr. Tilden nodded gratefully, and he handed his watch and a little notebook over to Bane. "Lydia knows how to keep track of the time. Just note how long she keeps that milk down and give her a glass at the top of every hour."

As the door closed behind the doctor, she leaned against Bane, grateful for the human contact. The doctor had been wonderful, but he could not provide her with the comfort of Bane's arms.

"Now tell me how you are really doing," he said softly.

How could she find the words to describe days of nervous exhaustion and crawling sensations that made her want to scrape the skin from her body? Even her bones itched, but she couldn't get to them, so she tried not to think about it. "Better, now that you are here."

"Eric said he could hear you crying from behind the door."

The breath left her in a rush, and her eyes drifted closed. Would she ever stop embarrassing herself in front of the admiral? "I didn't realize I was that loud." She drew her knees up to rest her forehead against them. She was mortified to have the perfect Fontaines witness her total collapse. "I should have gone back to Boston to do this," she mumbled on a shaky breath.

"Why do you think Boston would have been a better place?"

"Because I would rather be alone than have all these people witness this. You can't imagine how embarrassed I feel." Even Bane's cool, archangel beauty was mildly annoying when she felt like a half-drowned mutt.

His fingers grasped her chin and tilted her face toward him. "Lydia, I love you. *I love you*. Trust me, you stand head and shoulders above the Fontaines. From the time Eric was in the cradle, he was showered with riches and tutors and opportunity. You and I were both thrust out into the world with *nothing*. Lydia, I am in awe of you. I would lay down my life for you. Every day since I found you again I have thanked God you were willing to give me a second chance."

The mention of God made Lydia feel like an even bigger failure. She had been in search of God for months and had gotten nowhere. "I have been praying and reading the Bible and waiting for God to come into my life," she said quietly. "I started reading the Bible at the book of John, just like Karl said, but why hasn't it happened? Why is it so easy for you and others to believe, but I feel like I'm lost at sea, without an anchor and without hope."

Her stomach shifted, but she forced it down. She fought the tears threatening to spill again; this conversation was too important to stop. "I have been looking for a lighthouse, some sort of guidance, but there is nothing. I just keep getting smashed against the rocks and dragged back out to sea again." Her stomach turned again, and she knew there was no more time.

She launched herself to the toilet, and her stomach lurched. Bane was right behind her, holding her hair out of the way as cramps forced her stomach to heave up the milk. Every muscle in her body hurt, and her throat felt as if it had been bathed in acid.

She sat back on her haunches and tried to catch her breath as she clung to the toilet. "It's not that I doubt there is a loving God, I just don't believe He loves *me*."

Bane handed her a glass of water, and she rinsed her mouth, spitting the water back into the toilet. "Finished?" Bane asked.

She waited for another round of cramps, but nothing came. "I think so."

He stepped around her and pulled the chain on the water tank. Lydia wiped her face with the dampened towel Bane handed her, then slid back to her position leaning against the bathtub. She was so exhausted she could barely hold herself up. She would give every dollar she owned to only get a single, blessed hour of sleep.

"Why haven't I found God, Bane? I've read the Bible. I read the part that says if you knock, the door will be opened. If you seek, you shall find. For months I've been looking, but I have not found Him. Why is it so easy for some people, while others flounder in the dark?"

Bane sat opposite her. "If you think God has neglected you, then what am I?"

"A nuisance sent to disrupt my ink bottles?"

Bane shook his head, a mysterious little half-smile on his face. "Lydia, I am your lighthouse. Right now, my purpose in this world is to hold you up and guide you back into port. I won't ever abandon you."

She choked back a bitter laugh. "You said you would never marry a drug addict." The words had hurt when he first said them, and they hurt even more now.

"I won't, but that does not mean that I will give up on you." He sat opposite her and pulled her bare feet onto his lap to rub them with his warm, firm hands. "You are at the beginning of a long process of building a relationship with God. He may not answer according to your timetable. But isn't the thirst you have for God an indication that He is already working in your life? Someone with no belief would not have your curiosity or desire. You may *never* have some earthshaking revelation, but don't be like the person who tears the scab off a wound every morning to see if it has healed. Just keep seeking and trusting. I don't know how long your journey will be, but you are on the right path. Don't give up. Don't stop the quest. Have faith, and *you will find Him*."

A trickle of relief settled over her at his words. For whatever reason, she had not been blessed with a revelation like Bane, or the gift of parents to guide her in faith like the admiral, but that did not mean she had been abandoned. Patience was something she had in great abundance, and if practicing patience would lead her into the Lord's house, she would be patient.

Bane gave her foot a tug. "Why are you worried that I won't marry a drug addict? Don't tell me you are having doubts about your ability to beat this thing."

She rolled her head against the side of the tub to shoot him a heated glare. "Bane, I have doubts about my ability to crawl to that toilet the next time I need it." She ought to be embarrassed, but she had no room left for shame inside her wasted body.

Bane simply smiled at her. "That's why I am here, Lydia."

36

The Professor stood on the loading dock, watching laborers heft crate after crate of his books into the railway car. The contents of those crates were a thousand years in the making. He had sacrificed his life to find, rescue, and preserve them. Many of his books had survived through the dark centuries of the medieval period, the religious wars of the Renaissance, and the slow neglect of the ages. And now, thanks to his meticulous planning, once again his books would be rescued from the danger that threatened to take him down. This was merely one more wrinkle in a thousand-year battle to rescue these priceless artifacts from a world that did not deserve them.

"That is the last of them, sir," a sweaty laborer said as he crossed the train station platform for payment.

"Very good," he said as he paid the laborer, his eyes scanning the platform. Mrs. Rokotov and that fool Boris should have been here by now. There was no excuse for their tardiness in meeting him, and he would waste no more time worrying about them. He was already several days behind schedule. It had taken longer than he expected to arrange to lease the railway cars for his books.

In total, he had three railway cars full of books, and within the hour they would be speeding to their new home in northern California, where the cool climate was ideal to protect his treasures. He took one last, lingering look at the railway cars before heading toward the passenger car at the front of the train. It bothered him to be several car lengths away from his books, but he did not want to call attention to himself by insisting on a particular order of the railway cars.

He boarded the passenger car, turning sideways to move through the crowd of workingmen and day laborers who filled the compartment. He kept his face carefully neutral, despite the tawdry, rough-cut look of most of the passengers. What could one expect when you rode a train from a town like Scranton? There appeared to be only one gentleman, seated directly in front of him, whose tailored jacket indicated he was a man of substance. The rest were common workmen.

No matter. The train pulled out of the station, and the Professor retrieved *The Last of the Mohicans* from his jacket. The novel was pure pulp, but worthwhile nevertheless. He was somewhat like the lead character, the last of a proud and dying breed. The train was several miles outside of Scranton when the gentleman in front of him turned around.

"Professor Van Bracken?"

He stiffened. He had hoped to leave that name behind forever, but he would maintain a calm and professional demeanor until he could distance himself from this man. He looked up. "Yes?"

The dark-haired man smiled. "I am pleased to finally meet you. I am Admiral Fontaine, the man whose son you kidnapped last month."

The man's voice was so conversational, it took a moment for the Professor's frozen mind to process the words, but he recovered quickly. "I'm sure I don't know what you are talking about."

Admiral Fontaine stood and put his hands on his hips, allowing his tailored coat to fall back and reveal the pearl-handled revolver on his hip. "Yes, you do. Allow me to introduce my companion, Mr. James Lockwood." The bull of a man next to Fontaine stood and turned around. "Mr. Lockwood is the lead field agent of the Secret Service Agency. Perhaps you have heard of them? They investigate fraud against the U.S. government, including tax evasion."

These men were going to seize his books. His treasure was in danger. The Professor shot from his seat and was about to bolt toward the door when all the men in the railway car stood up in unison.

"Actually, every man in this car is working for the agency, so there is nowhere for you to run." Cold contempt dripped from every word Fontaine spoke. The door was blocked, the windows bolted shut. He was surrounded on all sides by crass, muscular men.

"I won't let you seize my books." He would kill himself first.

"They are already taken. The railcars were disengaged before we left Scranton."

His heart skittered in a rapid tempo. He was dizzy and short of breath as he sank back onto the bench. "You can't do this," he gasped. "Those books belong to the ages."

"I rather think they will belong to the Library of Congress when all is said and done," Fontaine said. "You have run up quite a tax bill, so I think donating those books to the government might be a good start."

If there was any mercy in the world, he would be struck dead here and now. He would give his entire fortune if he could order his heart to stop beating or his brain to shut down. His books would be unpacked by filthy hands, looked at and fingered by masses of nasty, crude people who would use a public library. But there was no mercy, only a ham-fisted man who forced him back into his bench. *The Last of the Mohicans* fell to the dirty floor of the railway car as an agent jerked his wrists forward and slapped handcuffs on him.

His world was over.

37

Ten days into Lydia's treatment, she was finally able to snatch a few restless hours of sleep per day, which gave Bane time to step outside and see the Fontaines off on their journey back to Boston. The carriage was packed and ready for departure outside the admiral's grand estate, but Eric's face was grim as he headed toward Bane. "Make sure Lydia takes this," he said, holding out an envelope.

Bane flicked a speck of lint from his coat. "I can't *make* Lydia accept it," he said casually. "You aren't exactly her favorite person."

The admiral pressed his lips together in a hard line. He cut short whatever he was about to say as another servant trudged across the gravel drive, carrying a lunch basket to the carriage. The children and Eric's mother were already aboard, waiting for Eric to join them.

Eric lowered his voice so the servant would not hear. "Get Lydia to take this, or I'm cramming it down your scrawny throat."

Bane gave the admiral his most pleasant smile. "Try."

Lydia had more important things to worry about than listening to an apology from Eric, who was still champing at the bit to win her forgiveness before he went back on the warpath. From the moment the Professor had been clapped into chains, Eric had launched a mission to search out and destroy the rest of the servants who had participated in holding his boy hostage. Eric had been there when the local militia unit had raided the Professor's mansion, only to find it vacant and abandoned. Like rats fleeing a sinking ship, the Professor's guards and servants had vanished into the countryside well before the militia arrived.

They would probably never be punished. America was a vast country, and it would be easy for them to disappear into the coal fields, the prairies, or the burgeoning cities out west. . . . But Bane didn't envy them trying to escape Admiral Fontaine's wrath. The man had unlimited resources and a relentless determination to seek justice.

Some of that determination was evident to Bane now as Eric took a step closer, jerked Bane's hand out, and slapped the envelope in it. "Don't be an annoying tick, Bane. If you can get Lydia to accept this, I'll consider letting you back on my senate campaign."

Bane tucked the envelope into his breast pocket. "Lydia and I think along the same lines, so naturally her judgment is perfect. You can be sure she will see the wisdom of your offer."

It might be a little trickier than he made it sound to get Lydia to accept the admiral's offering, but Bane knew Eric's offer was in her best interests. If it also got him back onto the admiral's campaign, so much the better.

Three weeks into her treatment, Lydia experienced her first full night of sleep. When she awoke, the muscles in her body were calm, restored. Her mind was clear as she listened for the soothing sound of the waves breaking on the shore. Turning to glance at the clock, a faint smile curved her mouth as she realized this was what seven blissful hours of sleep felt like. She lay in bed, savoring the sensation of absolute contentment.

Thank you, she whispered into the morning air.

Whom was she speaking to? She could not put a name to it, but power was flowing through her, flooding her with a sense of well-being.

A copy of the Bible on the bedside table caught her gaze, and she was inexplicably drawn to it. Lydia pushed herself into an upright position, wanting the weight of the heavy Bible on her lap. Karl's advice about starting with the book of John had not worked out so well, so she simply opened the book to a random spot and landed on a passage from Song of Songs:

> *Rise up, my love, my fair one, and come away*
> *For lo, the winter is past, the rain is over and gone;*
> *The flowers appear on the earth; the time of the singing of birds is come.*

Lydia's breath caught in her throat. Could she have asked for a more fitting passage at this exact moment? She had survived the deepest winter of her life, and after a brutal freeze, her body and soul were beginning to emerge into the warmth of spring. She wanted to read more, but her eyes brimmed with tears, for it was no coincidence she had opened the book to this passage. When she stopped struggling so hard to understand God and had simply flipped open the Bible at random, she had come upon the passage that gave her a profound sense of comfort.

It was no coincidence. *She knew.* A loving God had just sent her a message when she was finally open to hearing His words. She was no longer a storm-tossed orphan without a home, no longer adrift in a world without an anchor. Bowing her head, she savored the odd combination of peace and hope mingling within her spirit. Part of her wanted to remain motionless in bed to solidify this feeling in her memory for all time, and another wanted to dash outside to run in the surf and laugh at the sky.

She pulled on a satin dressing robe and looked out the window at the spectacular view. Along the shore, the grasses were turning green and the world was ready to shake free of hibernation. And somewhere above that mighty ocean, a loving God had just whispered a message of comfort into her ear.

Today was a new beginning. She would read and study and seek out other people of faith to hear their stories as well. There was so much to learn! She had not felt this joyful eagerness to learn since her first day of school more than fifteen years ago. She did not know what her future held, but she was ready to embrace the challenge.

When she joined Bane in the parlor later in the morning, she showed him the passage from Song of Songs. He did not seem to be the least bit surprised at her opening the Bible to that particular page. "When you learn to spot the signs, you will see evidence of the Lord's work in many places throughout your life," he said simply.

"I feel like I have so much to look forward to. So many things to consider in a new light." She turned to look at Bane. "I need to thank you for being my lighthouse. You did not turn away from me when you knew I lacked faith. And you stood by me even when you learned about my horrible problem with Mrs. Winslow's."

Bane's smile was rueful. "I am the last person who could ever have the right to throw stones." And when she looked at his rakish smile, she knew he was absolutely correct. They were two imperfect people who had weathered the storms of life and had battle scars to show for it.

She settled deeper into the cushions and let her gaze scan over the richness of the room. Never in her life had she seen such splendor and wealth in one location, but it held no allure to her. She wanted to drink out of a pottery mug instead of a porcelain teacup. She wanted to sleep on cotton instead of silk. "I'm ready to go home," she told Bane. "I miss my old life at the Boston harbor. I want to listen to the peddlers selling oranges in the morning and watch the fishermen haul in their catch at the end of the day. I want a hearty cup of clam chowder at a dockside coffeehouse."

Bane strolled toward her until he stood at the opposite end of the deeply upholstered sofa. "I wonder if you will change your mind when you see this note." He reached inside his jacket and extracted a small square envelope that he held aloft between two fingers.

"What is it?" she asked. Bane's sober demeanor made Lydia suddenly fearful of what the scrap of paper contained. Bane continued to scrutinize her through intense eyes, and she shifted in discomfort.

"It is possible I forgot to mention one tiny detail about rescuing Jack," he said slowly. "When the admiral's son was first kidnapped, he issued a sizeable reward for anyone who helped to get the boy back. As it happens, that person was you." He handed the envelope to Lydia.

The envelope was a thick, creamy paper, and her fingers trembled as she opened the flap to extract a check. It took her brain a while to process what she was seeing. *"Ten thousand dollars?"* She counted out the zeros at the end of the number, but she had read it correctly the first time. She stared at the check, barely able to grasp what that amount of money meant. "I didn't do it for a reward," she said numbly.

"I know," Bane said. "We *all* know that you went into that house with no knowledge of the reward Eric posted, which is another reason you are so impressive in his eyes." He sank down onto the sofa beside her. "Now, before you start arguing about accepting this money, you should know that the admiral intends to hound you until you accept it. He's still miffed you won't take your old job back, and he's looking for any way to soothe his guilty conscience. You'll be doing him a favor by accepting the money."

She stared blankly at the check. "I've probably been fired from my job at the bakery by now."

"No doubt." He nudged her with his elbow. "If I can persuade you to take the reward money, he'll let me back onto his election campaign. He'll flounder without me, and besides, I could use another senator in my back pocket."

"You are *so* arrogant." She fought back a grin as she folded the check and slipped it back into the envelope. "But I'll take the money. I have no desire to return to howling poverty."

"Do you still want to go back to Boston?"

She rested her head against his shoulder, her mind reeling with the implications of sudden wealth. She could go anywhere in the world. She could dress in silk and never work another day in her life.

But her soul longed for Boston. With Bane. Perhaps she could even buy her old apartment at the Laughing Dragon, which was the only home for which her heart truly longed. "I want to go home, and that means Boston," she said with a confident smile. "Would it be possible to leave today?"

Bane smiled. "Let's get you fed, and I'll make arrangements to get us to the train station."

It was the cook's day off, but Lydia's appetite had returned with a vengeance, and she had a craving for macaroni with cheese. Bane insisted they were up to the challenge. From her work at the bakery, Lydia knew how to fire up the stove, but she had never been trusted with handling the food. Bane had even less experience, but plenty of confidence.

"After all, we have a recipe book and all the proper ingredients," he had said. "How hard can it be?"

An hour later, the formerly pristine kitchen was strewn with milk spatters and bread crumbs. Lydia sat at the worktable and stared at the sad results of their labors. "How can macaroni be both burned *and* undercooked?" she asked as she stared at the scorched crust of cheese that covered the crunchy pasta.

Bane lounged against the wall of the kitchen, completely useless, as he had been all morning. "I don't know, but the sight of you with flour on your face while you pout at that mess is quite charming. Well worth the trouble we went through."

"What trouble? I did all the work, the only thing you did was read the instructions. You must have read them wrong."

"My reading skills are perfect," he said. "You bear full responsibility for that catastrophe." He pushed away from the wall and sauntered toward her, amusement twinkling in his eyes as he brushed flour dust off her nose, then leaned over to kiss her. "It is going to take a brave man to marry you, Lydia Pallas."

He tossed the words off in an offhanded tone, but Bane never said anything he had not carefully thought out. Lydia's eyes widened as she pulled back to stare at him, looking for a trace of mockery, but his smile was warm and his eyes were full of pride.

"Are *you* the brave man, Bane?"

"Indeed I am. And I can think of no higher privilege than sharing my life with you." He reached inside his pocket and set a simple gold band on the counter. "Are you up for it?"

The smile that lit her face was so broad it almost hurt. "So you don't think I am addicted to opium anymore?"

Bane shook his head. "I think you have conquered that particular battle. Now that the Professor is safely locked away, I can settle down anywhere in the world, but the only place that holds any attraction for me is right beside you. There are more battles to fight, more laws to be passed. I would like to work toward those goals with a wife by my side. And I'm afraid no one but you will do."

Lydia's heart raced so fast she could hardly sit still. For so many lonely months she had longed for a normal life with Bane, and now here he was, offering himself to her with joy on his face.

She must not let him get the upper hand. It would be a terrible way to start a marriage. "Why would I marry a man so much prettier than I? It would be a daily humiliation."

The warmth in Bane's eyes did not flicker. He kissed the back of her hand and winked at her. "Think of all the embarrassment I will suffer marrying someone who is wealthier than I. People will say I married you for your fortune and that you married me for my looks. It is a dilemma."

She could not stop grinning at him. "I suppose we should get married just so we can make each other miserable."

She expected him to meet her with a typically irreverent quip, but Bane's next words made her heart turn over. "Lydia, I want us to be married because you are the other half of my soul," he said simply. "I never felt complete until I joined forces with you. Now I can't imagine a life without you in it."

She supposed she ought to say something equally reverent, but the lump in her throat prevented her from speech. Bane understood, and she smiled as his arms closed around her.

Epilogue

Six Months Later

The evening was cool and clear as the carriage rolled down the street, rocking gently as it bumped over the cobblestones. "I don't have much of an appetite," Lydia said to Bane, whose face was outlined by the bright moonlight streaming through the carriage window. How could she have an appetite when she was so nervous?

As always, Bane could sense her anxiety. "You'll do fine, Mrs. Banebridge," he said with confidence. Lydia could still barely believe she was married to this astounding man, but she had the gold band on her finger to prove it. "Last night you met three senators, two chief justices, and the Secretary of the Treasury, and you dazzled them all. Tonight will be child's play in comparison."

The glittering event last night had been at the Library of Congress to celebrate the largest donation in the library's history. The books and manuscripts from Professor Van Bracken's house were on display at the impressive gala attended by the most prominent members of Washington high society. The Professor had mounted a futile legal battle from his cell on a remote island prison off the coast of Florida. He claimed he purchased the books lawfully and the government had no right to seize them. Legally, he was correct, but the government had estimated that the Professor owed thousands of dollars in uncollected taxes for two decades of smuggling opium. Since he could not pay that debt, the government had legitimately seized his assets to serve the public good.

Lydia was glad the books were no longer locked away in a secluded fortress where only one insane man had access to them. She implored Bane to keep her role in apprehending the Professor quiet, wishing only to forget about those horrible days in the mansion. Bane had honored her request for anonymity from the public, but everyone closely associated with the case was aware of what she had done.

Which was the cause for this evening's dinner. "Just a small, intimate gathering," Bane assured her, but could anything be small and intimate at the White House? The First Lady had heard of Lydia's role in acquiring the treasure trove of rare books and wanted to welcome her to Washington.

Lydia sat a little straighter and adjusted her skirts. This was the world she had signed up for when she had joined her life with Alexander Banebridge's. Two months after they had married, Bane had pulled some strings to get her essay about the abuse of opium in orphanages published in a national journal. The public exposure shamed the Crakken family into taking action against its continued use in their orphanage. The incident was Lydia's first success in attacking the scourge of drug abuse, and she was eager to continue fighting the battle wherever it led. Most of the time she and Bane lived very modestly, having moved back into her apartment on the top floor of the Laughing Dragon. They traveled from city to city to promote legislation and groom the right sort of political candidates to run for office, but Lydia always loved coming home to Boston.

The carriage rolled to a stop and Bane sprang out to assist her. She grasped her taffeta skirt to the side so she would not trip on her descent. Who would have thought the shoeless girl from the *Ugly Kate* would ever wear taffeta? Lydia had three fancy dresses to wear to special events such as these, but most days she dressed simply in modest cotton dresses that would befit a fisherman's daughter.

As she walked through the front door of the White House, she paused to glance up at the full moon. "Can you believe it, Papa?" she whispered.

Bane heard her comment and squeezed her hand. She still talked to the full moon, only now she was certain someone was listening. First thing each morning and last thing before she fell asleep at night, Lydia uttered a simple prayer to God, giving thanks for the gift of Bane and a wonderful new purpose in life.

Historical Note

Although Admiral Fontaine and his team of translators are entirely fictional, the Office of Naval Intelligence (ONI) was real. Despite the dramatic advances in naval technology in the second half of the nineteenth century, the U.S. government believed the Atlantic Ocean was a permanent buffer against naval threats and lost interest in developing the navy. The government invested the majority of military funding in westward expansion by funding the army and allowing the navy to slip into decline.

Established in 1882, the ONI's early activities were entirely aboveboard. Naval attachés were sent on observation tours to the ports of Europe, where they gathered shipbuilding intelligence. They asked for and were given copies of blueprints. They interviewed industrial engineers. They took photographs of ports and weaponry. When asked for comparable information about the American navy, the naval attachés were authorized to provide it. This was a time of peace throughout most of Europe and America, and such activities were not regarded with suspicion. The naval attachés scooped up technical manuals, product catalogs, newspapers, and engineering journals, sending them all home to be translated at the ONI.

As for Mrs. Winslow's Soothing Syrup, it was first marketed

in 1849 as a remedy for teething babies and restless children. No mention was made on its label about the healthy dose of opium it contained, and Mrs. Winslow's was wildly popular in Europe and America. Advertisements touted "It soothes the child, softens the gums, allays all pain . . . the little cherub awakes bright as a button." By the late nineteenth century, Mrs. Winslow's Soothing Syrup was listed as the cause of widespread drug addiction and began appearing on children's death certificates.

Agitation for reform of such medicines gathered momentum in the 1890s, but was met with fierce resistance from politicians, pharmacists, and newspapers, who relied on advertising from drug companies. It was the slow and steady drumbeat of doctors, reformers, and a few brave politicians who ultimately enacted state laws limiting opiates in medicine. In 1906, the Pure Food and Drug Act outlawed "poisonous patent medicines" on a national level. Although opium could still be sold over the counter, the law forbade the sale of preparations unless the ingredients were listed on the label. After Mrs. Winslow's Soothing Syrup was forced to list opium on its label, the company was met with public outrage. Mrs. Winslow's eventually eliminated opiates from their medicine in 1915. No longer an effective medicine, the company went out of business in the United States but still sold the syrup in England until 1930.

Discussion Questions

1. At the beginning of the book, Lydia is attracted to Admiral Fontaine, but she never pursues him because she thinks he is above her. Have you ever felt this way in a relationship? Is it possible to develop a healthy relationship when there are stark differences in class, upbringing, and educational backgrounds?
2. Lydia's parents loved her, but were they *good* parents? Love is a requirement for any good parent, but what other qualities are necessary to provide a child with a strong foundation?
3. Opium was a legal drug in the nineteenth century; it did not carry the stigma it does today. Does the legal status of a drug change the way people perceive the dangers of use? Is there less shame in becoming addicted to a legal drug rather than an illegal one?
4. Lydia and Bane bend the law when they slip inside the Custom House to look for the opium smuggler. What is the difference between things that are illegal and immoral? Are there ever times when a Christian should ignore a law in order to work toward a higher purpose?

5. Bane's childhood in the Professor's mansion taught him the safest way to live was through cool detachment from emotion. Lydia's obsessive need for order is a reaction to her early years of instability. Do you have any quirks that are echoes of something that happened in your childhood?
6. Despite her terrible childhood, Lydia is an optimistic person. Psychologists credit a sense of resilience to people who are able to maintain optimistic attitudes through times of trauma. On the flip side, many people are pessimistic despite a slew of good fortune. Is it possible to change this orientation, or is it simply the way we are wired?
7. Lydia never actually forgives the admiral for his harsh treatment of her. As a Christian, is she obligated to do so?
8. Bane manipulates people like the admiral, the granite mine owner, and even Lydia in order to advance his crusade against opium. Is it ever ethically acceptable to manipulate people for a higher cause? Do you predict his manipulative ways will continue in the future?

Curious about Bane's earlier years?

The Lady of Bolton Hill features Bane's life of crime with the Professor and how he breaks away when he encounters a lovely minister's daughter he has been ordered to kidnap.

Clara Endicott has made a name for herself as a journalist in nineteenth-century Baltimore, but she still remembers the young man—a poor factory worker—she adored as a child. When Daniel Tremain grows up to become an industry giant, Clara encounters him once again. Despite his astonishing corporate victories, Daniel cannot forget the woman he idolized from the time he was an adolescent. As their rekindled love begins to flare, a scheming young villain named Alexander Banebridge threatens to ruin them both. Can Clara unravel the mystery in time to save the only man she has ever loved?

More Adventure and Romance From Elizabeth Camden

To learn more about Elizabeth and her books, visit elizabethcamden.com.

Caught on opposing sides of their families' fierce legal battle, will Libby and Michael risk everything for the truth—and love?

The Rose of Winslow Street

When a female journalist comes face-to-face with her childhood sweetheart after years apart, her career—and life—are in danger. Can they face a painful reckoning before it's too late?

The Lady of Bolton Hill

If you enjoyed *Against the Tide*, you may also like…

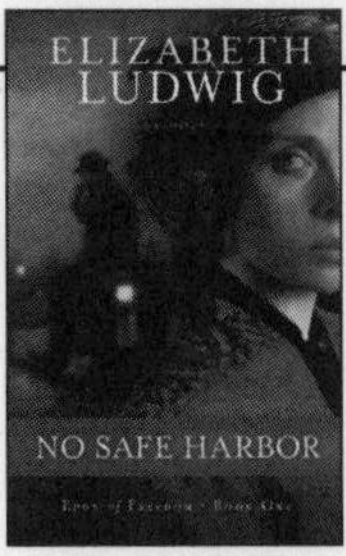

Desperate to locate her brother, Cara travels to America, where she is thrust into a web of danger. Her questions may bring her closer to her brother, but they also put her at the mercy of dangerous revolutionaries—including a man she's grown to love.

No Safe Harbor by Elizabeth Ludwig
Edge of Freedom #1
elizabethludwig.com

Masquerading as a governess, Lady Sumner is on a mission to find the man who ran off with her fortune and reclaim what's rightfully hers. But when all her plans fall by the wayside, will Eliza find that God has a better plan in mind?

A Change of Fortune by Jen Turano
jenturano.com

When Lily Young sets out to find her lost sister amidst the dangerous lumber camps of Harrison, Michigan, she will challenge everything boss-man Connell McCormick thought he knew about life—and love.

Unending Devotion by Jody Hedlund
jodyhedlund.com

BETHANYHOUSE

Stay up-to-date on your favorite books and authors with our *free* e-newsletters. Sign up today at bethanyhouse.com.

Find us on Facebook.

Free, exclusive resources for your book group! bethanyhouse.com/AnOpenBook

anopenbook